D0065298

CROWN
OF
OBLIVION

Also by Julie Eshbaugh
Ivory and Bone
Obsidian and Stars

CROWN
OF
OBLIVION

JULIE ESHBAUGH

HarperTeen is an imprint of HarperCollins Publishers.

Library of Congress Cataloging-in-Publication Data

Names: Eshbaugh, Julie, author.
Title: Crown of oblivion / Julie Eshbaugh.
Description: First edition. | New York, NY : HarperTeen, an
   imprint of HarperCollinsPublishers, [2019] | Summary: "A
   teenage girl, indentured to the royal class, must risk her life and
   compete in a cutthroat race in order to win her freedom"—
   Provided by publisher. | Summary: Astrid, indentured to the royal
   class and long-time surrogate for Princess Renya's punishments,
   impetuously decides to risk her life and compete in a cutthroat
   race in order to win her family's freedom.
Identifiers: LCCN 2019021108 | ISBN 978-0-06-239931-1
   (hardback)
Subjects: | CYAC: Indentured servants—Fiction. | Magic—
   Fiction. | Social classes—Fiction. | Contests—Fiction. | Fantasy.
Classification: LCC PZ7.1.E84 Cro 2019 | DDC [Fic]—dc23
LC record available at https://lccn.loc.gov/2019021108

Typography by Erin Fitzsimmons
19 20 21 22 23   PC/LSCH   10 9 8 7 6 5 4 3 2
❖
First Edition

For Dylan. You will always be my happy thought.

PROLOGUE

Four years ago

Lightning flashes. For a moment, the nighttime world beyond this dormitory window is as bright as if it were noon. The green hedge that hems in the yard appears, and beyond it, the gray palace wall. Then just as quickly everything's black again, and I count under my breath.

One . . .

Two . . .

Three . . .

Four . . .

Five . . . Thunder rolls across the roof.

Five. The storm is almost here.

Another flash, but this time, there's something else out there. Between the hedge and the wall. A boy. I forget to count. It was just a glimpse, but I thought it could be my brother Jayden.

Then the thunder, so close my bones rattle, and then

another flash, and the boy is gone. A tree branch scratches at the outside of the glass. *Not him, not him, not him,* I whisper to myself.

By the time the rain starts, I'm sure it wasn't Jayden, or anyone else. Something, but not a boy. A deer maybe. It doesn't matter. The rain is coming down so hard now I can't see out, even with the lightning, and this game I'm playing with myself is done. The rain roars against the slate roof, loud enough to wake the other girls, so I hurry back to my cot and pull the covers halfway over my face before anyone can catch a glimpse of me out of bed.

But being quick is not enough. A few of the girls are already awake. Behind me, Lily whispers something to the girl in the cot beside her. I tell myself she's talking about something else. But then Dina murmurs under her breath, "Did you see her scars?"

It's nothing, I tell myself. *Let it go.* But all I want to do is sit up and scream at them to mind their own business. I don't need their pity.

"Knock it off, you two." It's the voice of Mrs. Whittaker, and now it's so much worse. I wish she hadn't heard, but the storm is loud enough to wake most of the twenty girls in the room. I'm sure they're all listening now. "If Astrid weren't under that whip, don't you realize one of you might be? It's not just the princess she's sparing, but every one of you."

No one says a word after that.

Could she be right? I suppose if I weren't the princess's surrogate, one of these other girls would be, so maybe what she says is true. Maybe I'm not just suffering in Renya's place, but in theirs, too. Though I don't know if I want to think about that. I don't want to resent all these girls in the same way I already resent Renya.

The siren interrupts my thoughts.

It's so loud, it drowns out even the rain and wakes any of the girls who were still sleeping. Everyone sits up. Embeds flash in the dark like red fireflies. Whispers pass from cot to cot. Everyone is wondering who the siren is for, who's been discovered missing. Lightning flashes again, and I remember the boy I thought I'd seen through the window. I pull the sheet off and sit up, and just at that moment a figure appears in the doorway with a light in her hands. The light points down, but even in the dark, the mix of authority and anxiety I feel flowing from her tells me it's Renya. I wonder how much she heard.

She flips on the overhead light.

"Princess!" cries Mrs. Whittaker, and I can tell she's wondering, too.

"I'm sorry to disturb you all, Mrs. Whittaker," Renya says, though it's clear from her tone she's not sorry at all. "I need to speak with Astrid right away." She sounds like a schoolteacher speaking to a roomful of children, but I know her too well. There's a shiver when she says my name. There's more than a little fear in her.

"Of course!" Mrs. Whittaker's voice is the chirp of an anxious bird.

Renya is in a hurry. She grabs me by the arm and pulls me out through the door.

"Slow down," I say. I don't ask why she's come to drag me from my bed in the middle of the night. I think of the siren and the boy outside in the rain, and I decide I don't want to know. "You're going to pull my arm off."

But Princess Renya doesn't slow, and it isn't until we're descending the back steps that she speaks to me at all. Here, tucked inside layers of the palace's stone walls, the thunder's just a muted murmur. The light Renya holds bounces off the smooth plaster walls of the narrow stairway, so that, wrapped in her white dressing gown, her auburn waves tossed across her shoulders, Renya's silhouette suggests an angel or a ghost. I feel all too human beside her in my thin nightgown, my slipperless feet cold against the tiles. "It's Jayden," she whispers, and I know what she's about to say, but I don't want to hear it. I want to go back to my cot in the dormitory. "He wasn't in his bed tonight. The siren is for Jayden."

"I saw him," I say, wishing I could just stay quiet, wishing I could keep it a secret and somehow make it not true. "Just before the storm. He was running toward the palace wall. I saw him through the dormitory window."

Renya pulls me into a dark corner at the bottom of the second set of stairs and shuts off her light. It smells like mold down here, but that's not the reason my stomach is sick. "They're going to be looking for you," Renya says. Her fingers are digging into my arm. "Sir Arnaud will want you to help him find Jayden. He'll want to use you to form a bridge."

She's talking about a Pontium bridge, strong magic. Magic that could be used to track my brother through his connection to me.

"So what are we doing? Hiding?"

"We're going to find him first." Renya drags me into a room at the end of the corridor. It's windowless and pitch-black, but I don't have to see to know where I am. This is the room with the whipping post. A room I know too well. Every cell in my body seems to flinch, as if even the darkness that fills this room could hurt me. "If I bridge to him, you can warn him. Convince him to come back before they drag him back."

I shake my head, though in this thick darkness, Renya can't see me. "I'll try," I say. I want to tell her he's so stubborn I doubt he'll listen to me, but she knows Jayden well enough to know. Still, the words are on my lips when I flip the switch and the overhead bulb throws light across the walls.

We both gasp, and my hand flies to my mouth. The whipping post stands in the center of the room. The sight of it never fails to make me sick, but that's not what just punched me in the gut. I expected it. It's always here. But I hadn't expected to see wet blood splattered across the back wall, dark and red and angry.

Jayden's blood. It must be. It's not mine—Renya's been on good behavior, and I haven't received lashes in weeks—so it can only be Jayden's. Like me, he's a surrogate. I suffer for Renya's wrongs, and my brother suffers for the wrongs of Prince Lars.

Something must have happened. Whatever Lars did, it must've been serious and it must've been tonight. Jayden and I walked back together from Papa's tiny apartment just a few hours ago. He'd been happy and whole, teasing me about the storm. Now he's out there in it, rain washing the blood down his back.

I spin to face Renya. "Are you sure you can?"

"Do you doubt me?" I think she'd smile if she weren't standing in a room splattered with my brother's blood.

"Of course not," I say.

Parents and children, siblings, lovers—all those bound by Pontium energy—can be connected by a Pontium bridge, but the bridge is only as strong as the practitioner's magic. I might not know a lot about Enchanted magic, but I know more than most Outsiders do, and I've never seen anyone with Pontium as strong as Renya's.

The slashes of red seem to pulse against the bright white walls, and I can't wait for the bridge to take me out of here.

Renya stands in the center of the room with her eyes closed and her hands upraised. I'll never get used to the sound. If the power that moves the highest clouds across the sky had a sound, this metallic hum would be it.

It's not long before the light changes. The white walls, the red stains, the bare bulb hanging by a wire overhead all dim as the room is washed white, bleached by a blinding light. By the time the sound fades to a reedy tone, a window of sorts opens in front of me.

And there he is.

My older brother, Jayden, crouches on his knees in front of an open cupboard, packing a knapsack with food, which honestly makes me quite angry, because I know our father can't possibly have enough to spare. He's been sick—so sick he's in danger of losing his indenture at the foundry—but he would give any of his children his last piece of bread if they asked for it. I can't see anyone but Jayden, but I hear my seven-year-old brother, Marlon, singing a song.

Well, one line of a song, over and over. Marlon repeats a lot. The staff at the Outsider clinic call it a *vocal tic*. It gets worse when he's stressed, or sometimes when he's happy.

Right now I'd guess he's excited his big brother is home in the middle of the night. He's too little to know what happens to an indentured Outsider who is caught running away.

Jayden's black hair is plastered to his forehead with rain, but he whips it out of his face and looks up when he notices the change in the light. His eyes meet mine, and though he tries to hide his true reaction, he can't fool me. I see his shoulders flinch and the rapid blinks before his eyes narrow.

"Renya," he says. "I was expecting you. Who's there with you, besides my sister?"

"It's just me," I say. "For now. But they'll find us soon enough, and when they do, they'll find you, too. There's no hiding from Pontium, Jayden. You know that. And if Renya can reach you through me, then Sir Arnaud, the prince, the king . . . all of them will be able to reach you through me, too."

"Thanks for the warning," he says, "but even Pontium has a limit, and I plan to stay out of its range."

I suppose I should feel encouraged by the thought of Jayden running so far away that Pontium can't reach him, but I just feel hollow, imagining my brother that far from me. Hollow, imagining the space in my heart that Jayden currently occupies, empty. I feel like I can see that space, like a bare bulb hangs inside it like the bare bulb above my head right now, and if I would let myself look at it, it would terrify me, just like the empty space my mother used to occupy terrifies me.

"Tell him to come back," says Renya, her voice thin and wispy, as though she's far behind me, like the Pontium bridge is a long tunnel of energy and she hasn't come all the way through.

"Please come back," I say.

"Astrid, you know that's silly. You know there's no turning around for me now."

He's crouching beside the table where I sat with him at dinner tonight. There used to be five of us at that table when our mother was still alive. Starting tomorrow, there will never be more than three.

Jayden must hear something outside. His eyes widen as his body goes still. He reminds me of a feral cat, and at this moment, I know he won't come back. Worse, I know he shouldn't.

Maybe Renya thinks there's hope in begging him to return, but really, what kind of hope is there? His previous life is over. I realize that now. If they catch him, he's dead. Quickly, if he's lucky. Slowly, if he's not. The princess may believe she could convince them to be lenient, but she's almost certainly wrong. That's not a precedent they can afford to set.

I watch him as he closes up his knapsack, still crouching on the kitchen floor. The dim red pulse of his embed peeks out above the neckline of his tunic, like a heartbeat. I can hear our father, just outside the circle of the bridge, telling little Marlon to go hug his brother goodbye. After all this time I'd expect the bridge to shrink, but somehow Renya expands it, so that the circle engulfs my father in his chair with my younger brother on his lap.

"Astrid!" Marlon, so innocently ignorant, laughs with glee, and the sound cracks my heart like it's made of glass. He reaches for me, but pouts when he can't quite feel my hand.

Here in the palace I hear voices at my back, just beyond the closed door. It swings open and bangs against the wall, and Sir Arnaud is suddenly breathing on my hair, peering over my shoulder at Jayden as he climbs to his feet. Prince Lars is right on his heels. He tumbles through the door and groans when his eyes land on Jayden.

"Perfect," Arnaud says. "You've already formed the bridge." He looks into my face, and somehow he smiles at what he sees there. "Don't look so surprised," he says. "You should've known I'd find you, Astrid. My skills with Cientia may be nowhere near as strong as the princess's skills with Pontium, but I was able to track your fear from three floors above."

I refuse to cry, especially not here in front of Arnaud,

who I'm quite certain held the whip as this insane amount of my brother's blood was flung across these walls. Or in front of Prince Lars, either. One word slips through the prince's lips—my brother's name, as if it were a prayer. The rest of us stand as still and silent as the whipping post.

But Marlon, still grasping at the Pontium shadow of my hand, has something to say. "Look, Jayden!" He needs a haircut. His straight black hair, so much like Jayden's, hangs in his eyes. With one movement, he swipes it away and points to Lars. "Your friend."

"No," says Jayden. "He's not my friend. Not anymore."

Marlon says something else. *"Weeooo, weeooo, weeooo."* He's mimicking a siren he hears. The Enchanted Authority must already be searching the streets of the camp.

Right beside my ear, Arnaud is switching on his comm. He tips the camera end toward Jayden, broadcasting an image of his face. "This is a general call to all units of the Authority," he says. "The runaway has been located by Pontium bridge. He is inside a residence in Camp Hope. . . ." Arnaud turns the comm toward me and swipes it once in front of the embed that flashes red at the base of my throat. My family's address appears on his screen and he reads it out loud. "Three Front Street. Unit twenty-seven." He has the nerve to look me in the eye again. For a moment, there is a tiny fragment of compassion in his gaze, but his mouth is set in a hard, merciless line. "As always, deadly force is authorized if the runaway cannot be apprehended alive."

Shouts can be heard from beyond the boundaries of the Pontium bridge. Guards are already hammering on my father's front door. Renya's bridge shifts and focuses, and my eyes lock on my father—so frail I had to help him to the dinner table tonight—as he struggles to get to his feet. Marlon tugs at his hands, playfully trying to help him from the chair. Something splinters loudly, and men's voices fill the room. Marlon begins to wail.

"Where is the boy?!" It's one of the King's Knights, pulling Marlon off his feet by his belt.

"Hey!" I shout. "He's only a child!"

Marlon's legs pump the air like they're treading the sea. The Knight screams into his face, "Where is the runaway?!"

"Where is the runaway?!" Marlon repeats. I cringe, afraid the Knight will slap him for this perceived insolence, but he only drops him and shoves him out of sight.

The Knight, a big man drenched through with rain, turns and faces Arnaud. I notice for the first time that the bridge has been steadily shrinking. Now it's no wider than the shoulders of this man. I can't remember when it last showed Jayden.

"Make a thorough search!" Arnaud shouts. Water drips from the Knight's scarlet-lined cape, collecting into a puddle at his feet. "He was just there. I saw him with my own eyes."

Authority guards push into the apartment, the first Knight moves out of view, and my father's chair is knocked into the frame, spilling him to the floor. Marlon stumbles toward him, his forehead bloody. "Papa!" he cries, struggling to help him up. But Papa stays down. His only reply is a ragged cough.

"Extend the bridge!" Sir Arnaud demands, as I drop to my knees and reach for my father, but of course I can't touch him.

All at once the Pontium bridge collapses. Marlon, my father, the Authority guards, and the Knight—they are all gone.

The room goes silent. My ears are ringing. Sir Arnaud shouts at Renya to reopen the bridge, but she shakes her head. She is ashen and breathing hard. "Out of strength," she says.

Arnaud is not a large man. I've always thought of him as dignified and fine, like a sculpture of a man come to life. This may be the first time I've seen his hair—wavy and quite thick for a man old enough to be my own father—so disheveled and out of place. His eyes blaze, but then he runs a hand across his mouth and sets his jaw. "This is not personal," he says to me. He doesn't know my secret, that I have Cientia myself. That I knew at the moment Jayden slipped away and bested him, it became quite personal to him indeed.

"We know where he is, and he won't be able to outrun us," he says, but I know he's not as sure as he sounds, and that fills me with hope. "We'll get him."

The echoes of his boots recede as he follows Lars along the corridor. Still on my knees, I cover my face with my hands.

"Not if he's fast enough," Renya whispers.

"Run, Jayden," I say into my cupped palms. I know I should be quiet, but I can't help but scream, "Run!"

ONE

I t is decided I will wear red.

What I wear is of little importance to me, but apparently it is of great importance to Princess Renya and Sir Millicent, because they have spent the better part of the morning pulling dresses from Renya's closet and holding them up under my chin. It's tedious and annoying, but I keep telling myself that I can endure all this and more, because eventually they will settle on a dress, and that dress is what I will be wearing tonight when Renya finally fulfills a long-overdue promise to help my father.

But Renya and Millicent aren't thinking about my father or how tonight will change his life. Their minds are on the fresh scabs on my back, wondering which dress would best conceal the blood if those scabs were to open up at the Apple Carnival.

I've pulled on and tugged off at least a dozen of Renya's dresses, my wounds stinging as they stick to the bandages meant to keep my blood from Renya's clothes. My hair crackles with static as the fifth red dress in a row is whisked off over my head. I ran out of patience three dresses ago, and I don't try to hide it when Renya hands me red-dress-number-six. I watch Sir Millicent and the princess through the silky fabric as I tug it on over my head. Both girls furrow their brows.

But then I push my arms into the sleeves and the dress drops onto my shoulders and the skirt falls into place. Renya's eyes warm. She is a girl with no hard edges, from her wavy hair to her flouncy skirts. So different from Sir Millicent, whose shoulders are always as straight as a curtain rod. She is so much like her father, Sir Arnaud. Her fake smile is not nearly as convincing as Renya's.

"What?" I say, tired of pretending I don't notice.

"Nothing," Millicent says, her eyes hovering on my hair.

I shrug, glance at Renya, and steel myself to try on red-dress-number-seven.

But Renya wags her finger at me when I move to pull this dress off. "No, no . . . That's it. I think that's it."

I turn to Millicent. Not that I care about her opinion of me, but I know she has one. Her eyes have finally left my hair and found the dress, and she nods. "Once she's been tidied up a bit, I think she'll look . . . nice," she says, running the palm of her left hand across her own perfectly smooth, dark brown hair. It's pinned up, as usual, in a high tight bun. I don't think I've ever seen Millicent's hair down. For all I know, it's long enough to reach the floor.

"Millicent, *love*," Renya says, in the way she does when she's about to ask you to do something she thinks you won't want to do. "Would you mind going and checking on the departure plans?"

"We're all leaving at six," Millicent says. "It's the same every year."

"Would you be a dear and check anyway? I just want to be sure. You understand, right?"

Millicent's face shows she understands she is being dismissed. For a moment, her gaze lingers on me, and I can sense her resentment the way a sheep can sense the coming rain. "Of course, Princess," she says, as she pulls the door closed behind her.

"Sit down in front of the mirror," Renya says as soon as we're alone. "I'll see if there's anything I can do to make your hair look nice."

I drop into the chair and try not to feel insulted. Renya takes a couple of swipes at my jumble of hair and mists it with some sort of spray. Like the hair of all indentured Outsiders, it's required to be kept short, to expose my two blinking embeds. In Renya's mirror, under the silky fabric of the red dress, the one at the base of my throat is barely noticeable. But not the one in the back. I can see its blinking reflection in the window behind us.

Watching Renya hover over me in the mirror, I can't help but notice how much we resemble each other—we both have wavy hair, both have brown eyes. Except I look strained and exhausted, and she looks bright and alive. Plus I have embeds. But really, if not for those few things, we could be sisters.

Renya sets down the brush—I think she's satisfied, but it's possible she's given up—and opens the top drawer of her vanity. She lifts out a small scroll tied with a blue ribbon. "Would you like to see the royal order?" she asks.

"Is that it?" When I see it in her hands, my stomach flutters like it's full of hummingbirds. Renya slides off the ribbon and unrolls the paper. Like all royal orders, it's written by hand in a flourish of black calligraphy on faintly rose-colored paper. My eyes devour the words:

> *Be it known to all citizens of Lanoria that the holder of this order, the indentured Outsider Oscar Jael, is granted the right and privilege to seek and receive treatment for any and all of his personal medical needs, present and future, at the Citizens Hospital of the King's City.*

Below this one sentence, in curling black ink, Renya's father, King Marchant, has placed his signature and seal.

Renya has finally come through for me. Just a few hours more. Then my father will be on his way to the Citizens

Hospital with this order in his hands, and I won't have to be fearful anymore.

"My mother's been dead since I was seven years old," I say to the princess as I slide across the smooth rear seat of her motorized carriage right at six o'clock. "But this evening, you've said no more to me than she has." It's true, and it's odd, because Renya is almost never sullen. On the night of the carnival, of all nights, I'd expect her to be buzzing with anticipation and gossip, but she's as quiet as the dead.

She gathers her skirt up and pulls in her feet, and the porter shuts the carriage door behind her. "Sorry," Renya says. "It's just something my father said to me at tea."

Whatever was said, it's filled her head and sealed her lips. Thoughts light in her eyes, but she doesn't share a single one.

The carriage lurches forward. We are just passing through the palace gate, and I can see all the way down the hill to the shoreline. With the sun setting and the rooftops glowing gold, the city reminds me of a living heart, the roadways reaching into the countryside like arteries.

I fidget in my seat, smoothing the skirt of the borrowed red dress and checking and rechecking the small purse I carry, which holds nothing but the royal order. Beyond the city, the edge of the bay is marked by twinkling lights, except for the smudgy shadow of the wall that surrounds Camp Hope. I visited Marlon and Papa there just this morning, to make sure they fully understood where they needed to be at the Apple Carnival, so that the princess could hand Papa the order while drawing as little attention to it as possible. *I don't need fancy citizen doctors,* my father had grunted. *If royal orders are so easy to come by, get one for yourself, or one you can use to help Marlon.*

Don't worry about me, Marlon had said, repeating words he'd heard Papa say a million times. But I'd seen the anxious look in my brother's eyes. So often he seems blissfully unaware, but Marlon knows what it means to be an indentured Outsider. He knows what lies ahead of him.

At the door, I'd tried to cheer Marlon up with a riddle. He's a master at puzzles of all sorts. *What feeds bees, people, worms, and fires, in that order?*

An apple tree, he'd said. *Too easy.*

I'd stood there shaking my head. *See you both tonight.*

See you both tonight, he'd repeated, and closed the door behind me.

The carriage is already halfway down the hill, and still Renya hasn't spoken. "So what is it, then?" I say when I can't stand it anymore.

"He warned me to be on my best behavior tonight." For a moment I don't understand. The king always warns Renya to behave. But then she adds, "They're expecting members of the OLA to be at the carnival. The Enchanted Authority is on high alert."

OLA stands for Outsider Liberation Army, and their name tells you everything you need to know about them. They provoke complex feelings in me. Of course I want liberation, but their violent methods sometimes cause Outsiders more harm than good. "If the OLA disrupts the carnival," I say, "you may not get the chance to give my father the order tonight. He'd have to wait—"

"I suppose."

But that's not what's churning up Renya's mood. The princess has a history with the OLA that is personal and dark, and now, I understand why she's so sullen and withdrawn.

If it had ended differently, it would have been as romantic as a fairy tale. A fairy tale about a princess, a boy from the OLA, and a secret romance. But the romance was discovered, and instead of happily ever after, it ended with the worst beating of my surrogacy. I could have died—*would* have died—if it hadn't stopped right when it did.

It took a week in the infirmary before they were sure I'd survive. It's something we never talk about, and we're not going to start tonight.

Before the silence between us can become any more uncomfortable, the carriage comes to a stop, and the door beside Renya is pulled open. We are in the center of the city in Queen Rosamond Square, at the edge of the Apple Carnival.

Everything is decorated with flowers—vendors' stalls and carnival games and clusters of tables under bright red awnings where food will be served. Garlands of poppies and apple blossoms are wound around every pole. Chains of daisies crisscross overhead, back and forth above the footpaths. And intermixed with it all are a thousand twinkle lights, flickering to life in every corner of the square.

Not far away, someone is playing a lilting tune on a tin whistle, and I can't help but relax. The threat of the Outsider Liberation Army upsetting my plan to get this order into my father's hands seems more remote now than it did in the carriage with sulky Renya.

But then I notice Prince Lars stepping from his carriage just ahead of us, and of course Kit, his surrogate, is with him, and I doubt there are enough twinkle lights and tin whistles in all of the King's City to keep me in a good mood if they are going to be around all evening. To be honest, I hate the sight of them. They are both brutal and cruel, and have done enough to hurt me over the years for me to never forgive them. I turn my head quickly so as not to let them catch my eye.

A breeze drifts over us, carrying the warm scent of apples baking. Renya grabs me by the hand and tugs me toward the carnival gate.

"Princess!" It's the voice of Sir Arnaud, climbing out of the king's carriage behind us. In front of us, a line of

Enchanted Authority guards move together to block the princess's way. "You know better. Please adhere to protocol!"

Enchanted Authority guards are always around to protect the royal family, and on a night like this one, with rumors circulating about the OLA, I'm not surprised to see so many. But Renya's not happy. In her eyes, the guards are here to enforce Sir Arnaud's restrictions on her, or maybe to protect her from her own inclinations. Renya spins on her heels, and I can see the angry child inside her—the angry child who has never really gone away even as she's grown up. I can tell by the sour expression on Sir Arnaud's face that he can see it too. But then his daughter, Sir Millicent, steps forward and sets a hand on Renya's arm, and she calms a bit.

We've grown up together—Renya, Millicent, and I. Tonight is the first time since she joined the King's Knights that I've seen Millicent in her black-and-red dress uniform. It has a strange effect. She looks like she's aged years since I saw her this morning.

"Well, Princess," calls Arnaud from behind us, "we have thirty minutes until the opening of race registration. You seem to be leading the way, so where to?"

It's funny how a person's words can seem so accommodating while their tone is anything but. Good thing Renya doesn't care. She presses forward, her eyes bright and hot under the flashing lights. The air smells of cider as we linger to watch two flute dancers skipping in circles. I'm trying to figure how they keep from falling down, and then one does. I offer a hand but then we're moving on, and I lose the dancer's grip as I'm jostled by a few of the biggest Authority guards. The cider smell fades, but I pick up the scent of apple cake again. At a poppy-strewn booth, Renya takes up a handful of darts, but throws only one at the spinning target before passing the rest to Prince Lars. She's restless. "May I?" she asks the attendant at the darts game, scooping up a few loose poppies.

"Of course!" The attendant is an old man—a citizen Outsider—with white hair that sticks to the sweat of his neck. I notice the scar where his embed was removed when he satisfied his indenture. I shouldn't be surprised—an indenture is supposed to be only twenty-one years, so in theory, many people should satisfy them. But taskmasters are allowed to add time to indentures for so many reasons, it seems like they get longer instead of shorter. He smiles with slightly gray teeth, and I feel his pride bubble over.

Renya tugs two hairpins from her head. With one she pins a poppy into her own hair, and with the other she pins one into mine. She grins, and I scold myself for my nerves. Nothing will go wrong.

"Do you see the pendant around this old citizen's neck?" Renya whispers into my ear as she leans close, pretending to check the pinned flower in my hair. "See the entwined circles? That's the secret symbol of the Third Way. It's subtle enough to escape the Authority's notice, but another underground member would recognize it."

"Are you sure?" I say, following her as she drifts down the aisle. The Third Way was an experimental settlement, where Enchanteds and Outsiders lived as equals. "I thought that was outlawed years ago."

"It *was* outlawed," Renya says. "But people break laws every day."

At every stall, shouting to be heard over the music and the voices of the crowd, Renya asks where she might find a silver honeypot. Each vendor points her in a different direction, and each gives her a sample of their own wares, which she accepts cheerfully and passes off to me, so that my arms are soon awkwardly overfull. I'm in danger of dropping something by accident, or maybe even on purpose. We still haven't found a silver honeypot when Sir Millicent presses up behind us. "They're about to open registration for the Race of Oblivion. It's time to head to the stage," she shouts.

One of the guards steers us between two stalls and shines a light on a set of wooden steps. When we get to the top, I discover we've climbed to a platform that overlooks the central hub of the carnival on two sides. One faces the parade route, the other an ancient stone building known as the Queen's Temple. It's said to be the oldest temple in Lanoria, dating back to the days when the first Enchanteds arrived, pioneers from a dying homeland, searching for a new world.

They found Lanoria, and claimed it. By the time the rest of their people came—refugees from that very same homeland—they were calling themselves the Enchanted, and dubbed the newcomers Outsiders.

Looking at that ancient temple, accessible only to Enchanteds, I think of the story my father told me, of how the Outsiders had no choice but to submit to the system of indenture, since the homeland they'd all come from could no longer support life, and the Enchanteds declared that resources were too scarce to share without restriction. The only scarce resource in Lanoria is power, he'd said.

"The parade will come straight down that avenue," Renya says, pulling me from my thoughts. She points to the street that passes directly beneath us. "We'll have the best view from up here." Somewhere along the way, she scooped up more hairpins. One by one, she pins at least half a dozen poppies across the crown of my head.

I can't keep my eyes from the crowd. Authority guards are holding the masses back from the parade route behind metal barriers, but people still jostle for the best view along the railing. Soon the royal family will come down from the stage to briefly greet a short line of carefully vetted Enchanteds and even a few Outsiders in a controlled demonstration of how accessible they are to their subjects. Normally I wouldn't pay any attention at all, but today my brother and father will be in that line. Renya will meet them and shake their hands, and she will discreetly hand my father the royal order giving him access to the Citizens Hospital.

I'm panicking until I spot them in the crowd, right along the barricade where they belong. They're both dressed up, so much I didn't know them. My father is coughing into his elbow, but Marlon waves at me. "There they are," I say under my breath. I know better than to make a big scene. Renya does not look down, but gently turns my head back to face her and fastens a final poppy in my hair.

Beside us, a microphone squeals to life. Prince Lars clears his throat. He is introducing the annual Race of Oblivion, but I can't hear him. I'm too distracted by the thought of my father walking into a real hospital and receiving treatment from a real doctor. Getting treatment that he's needed for so long—treatment that will rid him of that cough and make him strong again.

Someone in the crowd lets out a whoop, and I jump back, startled. "People are stepping up to volunteer for the race," Renya whispers. "Their bravery—or foolishness—is being acknowledged." I nod. Far out in the crowd a circle has been roped off, and a knobby old man in a judge's robe stands holding an open book. As volunteers step into the circle, each adds their name to a page in the back, and I wonder how many people who've signed their names on the preceding pages are dead.

For the winner, the Race of Oblivion means citizenship,

but there's only one winner each year. For many of the other contestants, the race means death. It's cruel, really. Stripped of all their personal memories, racers wake with amnesia somewhere outside the city walls, with nothing more than a short list of instructions and a map to the first clue. If I think my life as a surrogate is a life without mercy, I know it's nothing compared to what happens in the race.

I watch a woman enter the circle and sign her name. She's a big, sturdy woman with a pretty face. A man waits for her outside the rope, holding the hand of a toddler. When she lifts the pen after signing, the man in the robe raises a small knife to the base of her throat. With a motion so quick I barely notice it, he slices the skin over the woman's embed and pulls it out. Blood coats his fingertips. I groan, and Renya bends toward my ear again. "It's gory, isn't it? And pointless. They still keep their second embed until the race starts."

"It's ceremonial," whispers a voice behind me. It's Sir Millicent. The red-lined cape of her uniform brushes my shoulder as she leans closer. "It represents the racer's loss of identity." My hand goes to my own embed at the base of my throat. The woman is already back beside her husband, lifting her little girl. "If she wins, her whole family receives citizenship," Millicent adds. "She must be doing it for the child."

I watch the volunteers file up in turn, maybe two dozen

in all. There are only a few entrants left in line when a bell in the tower of the Queen's Temple tolls eight times.

Eight o'clock. It's finally here. Renya gives my hand a small squeeze. "And now the parade!" calls Lars over the loudspeaker. "I'd like to invite the parade master, Sir Augustine, to strike up the first band and send them on their way down the avenue. In the meantime, as we await their arrival, my family would like to take a few minutes to greet some of you."

In the distance, maybe a few blocks away, the first notes of the frenzied melody of a jig start up, all fiddle, tin whistle, and drum. Renya turns and whispers into my ear, "This is it."

I hand her the small purse I've been holding with the royal order inside, and she tucks it under her arm. I'm suddenly as unsteady as a drunk. Everything speeds up and my vision narrows, like I'm watching the proceedings through the wrong end of a telescope. Renya gives my hand another squeeze before stepping away from me and following King Marchant and Prince Lars down a set of steps to the street. The crowd waves from behind the barricades. A woman with a camera runs ahead of them, a flashbulb going off over and over like a strobe.

It's happening. My father will soon shake Renya's hand and receive the royal order. It's just moments away.

The king is moving along the line of people, letting each

one bow or curtsy and give their names. People in the crowd behind are standing on tiptoe and craning their necks to try to see what's happening at the railing. Only a bent citizen Outsider woman and a young Enchanted boy separate King Marchant from my father and brother, who stand like two dignitaries. Marlon keeps a hand under Papa's elbow. I'm certain that's all the assistance our father will allow. He is a proud man.

Heat fills my chest. My head expands, as if it might pull me up and carry me over the crowd like a balloon. I wonder what will happen next. Will Papa be able to see a doctor at the Citizens Hospital tonight?

Sir Arnaud is suddenly beside me. "That's your father, is it not?" he asks me. "The person to whom the princess will be giving the royal order the king signed this morning?"

"Yes," I say, all at once remembering the one time Sir Arnaud saw both my father and Marlon—on the night Jayden ran away, when he saw them through the Pontium bridge. Right before Jayden slipped past his men and beyond his reach.

I turn my gaze back to my father. His eyes are locked on my face. He is smiling. I wish my mother were alive to see Papa this happy.

Then he coughs.

At first, it's a small cough, nothing. But that cough is followed by a hack, and then another, becoming loud and deep and as raspy as a growl. The King's Knights who stand like a partition behind the group at the railing all move back, as if Papa might infect them. Anger ignites in me, but my father ignores the Knights. His eyes are on the king, who is stepping widely around him. Lars follows, not even offering a hand to my brother. I wonder if he recognizes them from that night.

It doesn't matter. Renya is next. I'm watching her without blinking as she takes the purse from under her arm and lifts out the royal order. It's in his hand! But then he's coughing again, grasping at the railing, and Renya backs away.

I watch helplessly as my father sways, buckles, and drops to his knees behind the metal fencing.

My breath catches in my throat and my hands fly up, as if I might pull my father to his feet from here. The music grows louder; the band that leads the parade is getting closer. Another cough tears the air, and Marlon tugs something from his pocket. He hands it to Papa. It's a cloth handkerchief, bright and white and clean.

I've never known my little brother to carry one, and it occurs to me that this was something that he thought of as he prepared for this day. Perhaps he decided to carry a handkerchief like a proper gentleman. Or perhaps, I think, he brought it in the event our father collapsed in a coughing fit as he greeted the princess.

The white handkerchief is balled up in my father's hand,

held to his lips. The cough comes heavy and wet, and then, mercifully, it stops.

My father's hand drops to his side, but he doesn't get up. He raises his eyes to mine. His lips curl into a strange, apologetic smile. His eyelids flicker, he sags forward, and his body drops heavily against the barricade.

The handkerchief rolls from his hand, stained crimson with blood.

Marlon falls to his knees and leans low over Papa's slumped body for what feels like a long time. I wait for my father's cough to return, but there's nothing but an odd murmur. Across the railing from them, the royal family is whispering among themselves.

Then Marlon lifts his face. His lips move, but I can't hear him. It doesn't matter, I know what he said. As I rush down the stairs to the ground and to Papa's side, I hear the words repeated, passed from one member of the royal family to the next.

"He's dead."

TWO

By the time I come up beside Renya, my father is flat on the ground, the royal order lying wrinkled on the pavement beside him. I reach through the metal railing of the barricade, grasp his hand, and pull it to my cheek. It's still warm. "I'm so sorry, Papa," I whisper into his palm. "I'm so sorry I was too late."

If anyone can hear me, I'm sure I sound contrite, but the truth is, I'm angry. How long have I been begging the princess to do whatever needed to be done to get my father access to proper medical treatment? My father may be owed an apology, but not from me.

Beside me, Marlon coughs. He's not sick, of course—it's just his vocal tic—but his impression of our father's horrid hack has been honed to perfection by years of practice. The King's Knights behind Marlon take another step back. I bite my lip and draw in a deep breath to keep from screaming.

Marlon coughs again. He's scared, and he's telling me so.

I force myself to release my father's hand. My legs feel like pudding, but I struggle to my feet. "Renya," I whisper into the princess's ear. I feel her flinch. Her eyes dart from side to side. She feels the gaze of the crowd. I do too. My Cientia prickles with the revulsion rolling off them.

Two emergency workers—both Outsiders—have appeared. Wearing medical masks over their noses and mouths, they drag my father's body away from me and slide him onto a stretcher. Neither of them looks at me, but they glare at Marlon.

I hate them.

"He's not sick!" I say, pulling Marlon up to his feet beside me. "It's just a tic—no worse than a *habit*." I swing back around to face the royal family, but only Renya remains. The king and Lars are already fleeing back up the stairs to the stage.

But Sir Arnaud has come down to the street. He's heading toward me, holding his cape across his lower face. He sweeps Renya behind him, as if Marlon and I are toxic. "Astrid," Arnaud says. "Listen to me. Your brother needs to be examined. Let us help him."

Someone touches my shoulder. My head jerks around and behind me, on Marlon's side of the barricade, I find a group of Authority guards, all wearing masks like the Outsider emergency workers. Hands close around Marlon's upper arms, and his grip tightens on my hand. His eyes go wide. Although he's big for a boy of eleven, his face looks suddenly like it did when he was little. I haven't seen this much fear in his eyes since the night Jayden ran away. Sir Arnaud never got Jayden, but now he's got Marlon.

My brother's wrestled away from me, and I lose my grip on his hand. "Wait!" I scream, but there's no waiting. The guards close around him, and he's shuffled away like a criminal. I want to fight them. I want to knock them to the ground and pull Marlon back to me, but the barricade blocks my way and they're already disappearing into the crowd.

"Renya, do something, please," I say, but Sir Arnaud stands between the two of us, as if he's protecting her.

She shakes her head, the smallest of movements. "It's too late now, love," she says. "It's too late."

"The parade is almost here," Arnaud barks, stepping toward the stage and waving us toward him. He's right. I can see the first band a block away. It's so loud I can hardly hear his voice over the music. "Princess, you'll need to move to safety," he calls. He crosses to the steps leading up, and Renya follows, but she stops in the middle of the street when I don't move.

"Astrid," she says, holding out her hand. I shuffle up beside her. My head is swimming. "I'm so sorry about your father," she says, and I know she's trying to say the right thing, but it only makes me angrier.

"Are you?" I snap. "What was he to you?"

Her mouth works. A puff of breath escapes before she pins her lips closed between her teeth. Her eyes harden. "What was he? He was the father of my *friend*." She draws out the last word, ending it with a hard *d*. It feels like an accusation. "Don't forget how hard I worked to get that royal order for him."

"Oh yes," I say. "That was quite an effort. Quite a sacrifice on your part—"

"Astrid," she says. Her hands have wrapped around my wrists. I notice that my own are balled into fists. Would I have struck her? Did her Cientia feel it coming? "You have a right to be angry and you have a right to feel wronged, but I worked hard to convince the king to sign that royal order. I may not have known *your* father, but you also don't truly know *mine*, so save your condemnation for someone else."

Her eyes burn, bright and scalding. There's a taste in the air like gunpowder—steam and sulfur—and I know my Cientia is noticing Renya's indignation. I don't know if convincing her father to sign that order was difficult or not, but she did it. She helped me. That's more than anyone else did. "I'm lost," I say. "I don't know where they took my father's body. I don't know where they took Marlon." Hot tears spill onto my cheeks, which only makes me angrier.

"I don't know either, but I'll find out," she says. She glances up the avenue. The band leading the parade is just a half a block away. "But right now we need to go back to the platform."

I let her lead me by the hand. It isn't until we're climbing the steps that I notice all the flashbulbs going off, and I hope they are mostly pointed at the parade and not at us, though I doubt it.

Back on the platform, King Marchant stands center stage, looking down on the parade. The wind is gusting, and his white hair is blowing back in a way that makes him look far less dignified. Prince Lars is on his right with Kit behind him, and then Sir Arnaud. The prince is turned away from the railing, glancing back at us. He looks a great deal like Renya, only in place of her auburn hair, his is almost blond. His eyes are cold. He's handsome in that way a vampire might be handsome.

Below us, the parade draws a torrent of sound from the crowd. People are all calling out, but not in unison . . . not even the same words. Some are shouting *Hail the harvest!* while others seem to simply be yelling *Apples!* Renya takes her place on her father's left, and I stand behind her. Between carts overflowing with red and green apples, military officers pass by on horseback, accompanied by children on bicycles. My eyes can't fix on any one thing. A gust of wind catches one of the flowers pinned in my hair and it breaks free. Renya's hand shoots out, trying to catch it. She misses, but when she watches it float away, her gaze lingers on her father and Sir Arnaud.

When she turns back to face me, she smirks like a child who's found a way around the grown-ups' rules. "What are you planning?" I ask, knowing whatever it is, it almost certainly will put me at risk of a beating.

Before she can answer, though, a voice calls out, and it's not *Hail the harvest* or *Apples* or anything like that. It's a scream in pain. I look down directly below us on the street, where a wagon is passing by in the parade.

To call it an applecart would be like calling the palace a barn. This is a massive wagon, loaded down with bushels of silver-skinned apples, decorated with so many flowers it looks like someone died. I'm so distracted by the pageantry of it, I almost forget what called my attention, but then I hear it again.

A scream.

It's coming from the front of the cart. A half dozen Outsiders are strapped into harnesses, men and women, some old enough to be my grandparents. An Enchanted taskmaster walks behind them, a wide-brimmed hat on her head. There are no horses or mules—these Outsiders are pulling this enormous cart. They're slump-shouldered, their bodies leaning hard against the load. All of them are suffering, so much so I can't tell who screamed. But then I hear it again, and I notice an old woman, harnessed near the front, who buckles to her knees.

I can't help but think of Papa, down on his knees. I wish I could run down the steps to help this woman, but I know it would be futile. Horses could pull these carts, and they'd do a better job of it. But that wouldn't remind Outsiders what we're worth: the strength of our backs. Our resilience. Our ability to survive the hardest struggles, to be hurt, fall down, and still, to get back up again. It's the role of Outsiders in Lanoria, and even when there's a parade, the Enchanteds make sure we don't forget.

A line of Authority guards on horseback moves up beside the cart and blocks my view. The wagon rolls on—the woman must have gotten up—and if she's still screaming, I can't hear her voice anymore.

When I turn my attention back to the princess, I notice she's backed me up to the steps we came up earlier that lead down to the hidden space between the stalls. She presses her hand into mine. I realize what she has in mind, and my heart rattles with panic. She says, "I can see by the look on your face you think this is a mistake."

"I do."

"Hear me out. There are medics stationed just one block away. I saw their white tent from the railing. You want to know where they took your father and brother, don't you? Then that's where we need to ask."

"Renya, if we get caught—"

"Don't be silly; we won't get caught." She wraps a shawl

over her head and shoulders. It's one that a vendor foisted on her, red with silver trim. It does help hide her hair and face, but still, this scheme of hers is dangerous. "I never found a silver honeypot. If anyone asks, we went out looking for one."

It's pointless to resist her—she's going to do what she wants anyway, and she *is* trying to help me—so I let her lead me down the steps and into the crowd. With so many people, everyone's invisible, even the princess, as long as she keeps her head down, and she drags me behind her as she cuts a winding course along the parade route.

Once we're inside the white medical tent Renya is immediately recognized. The Outsiders bombard her with bows and curtsies, and the Enchanted taskmaster makes a bit of a fool of himself trying to address her, blurting out nonsense like *Your Loveliness* and *Your Enchanted Highness*.

"*Your Royal Highness* will do," I say. Renya eats it up with a spoon.

But she knows how to get what she wants. She's both calming him down and buttering him up. Pulling him aside, she speaks low, as if to take him into her confidence, so I step back out to the street and watch the spectacle: Enchanteds popping sweets into their mouths and pinning flowers in each other's hair, while Outsiders scurry to serve them or struggle under unbelievably heavy loads. The sounds of the carnival—music and shouting and the feet of dancers pounding on the stones—blur together into one deafening roar. I wish I could lose myself in the festivities, find a silver honeypot and be happy with it. But now that my father is dead, every inequity I see at the carnival strikes me like a slap. My Cientia picks up so many emotions in the crowd—the sour heat of desperation and the heavy darkness of pain, swirling with the light citrus sting of raucous joy. Inside me, my grief ripens into rage.

Someone tugs hard on my hand, and I spin around, ready to snap, but it's Renya, her eyes fiery. "That taskmaster was more than happy to help me," she says. "Your father was taken to the Citizens Hospital." I swallow hard. The irony of this is so cruel, my eyesight momentarily blurs with tears, but I blink them away. "He was declared dead when he arrived. I'm so sorry, Astrid. He's in the hospital morgue."

My head jerks up and down in a frantic nod. "And Marlon? Did the taskmaster know anything—"

"He could only guess, but he thought they probably took him to the Outsider clinic at the gates of Camp Hope."

"That was my guess, too." I suck in a deep gulp of night air, close my eyes, and let it out, just to be sure the tears are no longer threatening. "We should go back."

"Sure," she says. Then she pulls something from behind her back and lifts it to my eyes. It's a silver apple cut in half, top to bottom, with the middle scooped out and replaced with a spoonful of warm honey.

"A silver honeypot," I say, taking it from her hand. "Where did you find it?"

Renya's lips quirk into a small smile, but whatever her answer, it's drowned out by a loud noise—not one sound, but a series of sounds—the *rat-tat-tat* of fireworks, but way too close. The blasts send everybody scattering, and Renya is carried away by a surge of the crowd that pushes her one way and me another.

The honeypot slips through my fingers, and someone in the anonymous crowd presses a piece of paper against my palm in its place. It's a leaflet emblazoned with the words *Outsider Liberation Army.* Suddenly I realize that the explosions may not have been an accident.

Just as I begin to get my feet steady under me, another blast goes off overhead, and a brand-new wave of people comes running down the street, falling against me and pushing me back. I'm flung against a set of doors and swept through, along with two Enchanted women with tear-soaked faces. One of them drags a little boy by the hand. Flower garlands are strung around his neck. The doors close behind us.

After a long moment, the boy begins to wail. I leave these three and climb a set of stairs to the second floor, hoping to get a clear view of what's happening outside, or even to catch a glimpse of the princess. But everything outside has gone dark. Electricity must've been cut to the strings of lights. I'm just heading back down the stairs, when someone calls through an open doorway behind me.

"Looking to put your name in for the race?"

I really don't want to rejoin the two Enchanted women and the crying boy, so I peer into the dimly lit room and see a white-haired man standing behind a counter. "Then you've found the right place." Above his head a wooden sign hangs from brass hooks: *Race Administration.* "You got here just in time. I was closing up when the explosions rang out." He taps an open book in front of him with a pen. "Hooligans, that's what they are. The OLA won't get any respect from me." I can't help but step closer. The man is thin and bumpy, like he's made of driftwood. I'm convinced I saw him earlier, outside. "The OLA wants to disrupt the Race of Oblivion, and do you know why? Because if they can't have citizenship, nobody can have it."

I recognize him now. "You're the man in the robe. You held the book the racers signed."

"Of course I did. I'm the senior registrar. It's my duty and honor to welcome the brave Outsiders who enter the Race of Oblivion." There's an air of suspicion about him; he thinks I'm up to something. He waves me closer and holds out a pen. "A minute later, and I would have been gone. You are here to enter the race, are you not?"

I catch the scent of anise—the scent of a secret. He's hiding something from me. Not that I'm surprised—most people have secrets—but when I sense a secret in a man who's trying to cajole me into entering a race that starts with amnesia and usually ends with death, with nothing but a desperate sprint across the continent in between, my defenses understandably go up.

"Why would you think I'd enter that terrible race?"

"*Why?* To win! Why would anyone enter?"

I do my best to lay the heaviest stare I can conjure right on his face, letting him know I am not easily swindled. "You can save your sales pitch for someone so desperate they're foolish," I say. "If you think that's me, *you're* the one being foolish." I want to add something more—there's some truism my father always pulled out when he thought he was being set up—but the words escape me.

I wish he were here.

"Ah, all right then," he says. He closes the heavy book with a thud—the book the racers signed—and slides it into a drawer beneath the countertop. "I had you wrong." The enthusiastic lilt is gone from his voice. I must have been right about him trying to entice me into entering, because he's dropped that act entirely. He pulls a key on a long chain from his pocket. "I just thought . . . after what happened before the parade . . ."

"Before the parade?" He gives me a sorrowful smile, and I know what secret he's keeping. "You saw my father die, didn't you?"

"I did. Right at the princess's feet. When I saw you walk in here, I thought—"

"You thought I was signing up to spite the princess."

His eyes widen. I flinch, hoping I haven't made my Cientia too obvious. "You read people very well," he says. "Something like that could give you an advantage in the race."

Could that be true? I've never asked myself what my Cientia could do for me in the Race of Oblivion before.

"Oh well. Too loyal to the princess, I suppose. Or maybe you don't believe you could win."

He's wrong. Loyalty wouldn't stop me from entering. But he's right that I've never considered the Race of Oblivion something I could win. Yet he thinks otherwise. My Cientia makes me sure of it.

But does it make me sure I could win the race?

I watch him slide the key into the drawer's lock and turn it. "Wait!" I say.

There's a rumble from the floor below. More carnival goers have found their way inside the building. My eyes go to the banner above the registrar's head. It reads: *All the Privileges of Citizenship*, and beneath that *For the Winner and Their Family*.

"The winner *and* their family . . . including all their siblings?"

He finally meets my gaze. "Of course."

The commotion downstairs becomes louder. A man's

voice shouts, "Astrid Jael!" My heart beats like a drum. "We are seeking the Outsider Astrid Jael on behalf of Princess Renya."

"I'm here!" I call out. Then quietly, to the man in front of me, "Put that book back on the counter."

I think of Marlon, the fear in his eyes as they wrestled him away from me. How I'd wanted to fight to keep him. The registrar unlocks the drawer and pulls out the book. Feet thunder up the steps behind me. I think of Jayden, so far away. I could find him and bring him home.

The registrar holds out the pen. I glance up at the banner once more. *All the Privileges of Citizenship.*

I'm scrawling my signature into the book when the Enchanted Authority guards come up behind me. Renya is with them, her face bright red with heat and fear.

And with the swift flick of a blade, the driftwood man slices the skin over the embed at the base of my throat. "Congratulations!" he calls out, plucking it from my chest and holding it, bloody and blinking, in his open hand. "Welcome to the Race of Oblivion!"

THREE

S ince the day I signed up to race, everywhere I go, I feel the breath of Death on the back of my neck. But tonight is the first I hear its footsteps.

I notice them just as a thick cloud rolls across the sky, snuffing out the moonlight as abruptly as switching off a lamp. The night was dim before but now it's truly dark, and not with the soft, velvety sort of darkness that fills a house when the doors are all locked. This is the sort of darkness that sends a shiver across your skin, even though the air is still warm.

I pause at the next corner, and I curse myself when I can't help but glance over my shoulder. The streetlights throw meager halos of light. Whoever is following doesn't mean to be seen.

Now I wish I'd never turned. What did I hope to see? A citizen of this quiet block, conscientiously sweeping her stoop after dark? It's late, later than honest people walk the streets to do honest business. But if the footsteps belonged to a thief, wouldn't he have made his move by now? Which leaves only one possibility. I feel Death's breath once more against the skin of my neck, even if I know it's just the warm breeze, and I realize it won't matter if I hurry or if I drag.

If it's them, there's nothing I can do to escape.

I slide my hand between the silky folds of my skirt—the remnant of a once-fine tablecloth that caught too many spills—and close my fingers around the key in my pocket. As the moon slips out from behind its cover, the castle gate materializes in the distance, the black iron glowing silver. I'm almost there.

But then I hear my name behind me . . . *Astrid*. The voice is both soft and sharp, and it cuts right through me like a velvet knife.

I know the voice before I turn, and I can tell she is agitated and excited about all the wrong things.

"What are you doing here?" I glare at Princess Renya, intending to bore holes into her with my stare, but she doesn't even flinch. "If you're found outside the palace wall at this time of night, I may never recover from the lashing." I spin back around to pour my full attention into opening the lock. "How did you end up behind me?"

"I came looking for you—"

"I said I'd be back by curfew, and there's still an hour to

go," I say, trying to keep the fury out of my voice.

"It couldn't wait. I had to find you before somebody else did—"

"Shh!" I pause, listening for guards patrolling beyond the wall. There's only the weak breeze and the flutter of a solitary bat. "Just wait until I get us both inside—"

"No. We can't. *You* can't." I feel the tension rise from Renya's skin like mist rising from a lake. She leans so close her lips brush my ear. "They came for you."

I pull back. "All right then."

"You're scared."

"I'm not," I lie. Maybe to myself more than to her. "Even when I heard your footfalls on the pavement tonight, I thought it might be them. I'm ready."

"You say that only because you haven't seen them. I have."

I turn my attention back to the gate—this conversation is futile, I won't be turned from my path—but my hand shakes so much, Renya nudges me aside and takes the key. As she does I feel her fear, cold and dark as the ocean. Of course, this close, I know she feels the same in me, though I can't help but hope that mine isn't so deep and lush.

"I'm glad you're scared. You should be," she says, pocketing the key somewhere in the layers of pale blue gauze that make up her dress.

"What are you . . . ?" I huff out a sigh. We're so close

to safety, but she keeps pushing it away. "Keys work better when they're not in pockets—"

"We're not going inside until I've talked you out of this," she says, before stalking off into the dark. I have no choice but to follow her, and she knows it.

I might appreciate the princess's lack of respect for authority if it didn't affect me so directly. If the stories of her many rebellions weren't written in the scars on my back. But they are, and my resentment of her grows a little deeper every time she refuses to conform.

She takes a narrow path along the base of the palace wall, to a place where a wild stretch of land slopes downhill, overlooking the city. It would be a gorgeous view if I weren't so sick to my stomach. I hear her feet as she shuffles off the flagstones and onto the grass. "Renya?" I breathe. "Please stop." When I finally catch up to her, she's seated under an olive tree, the moonlight glowing in her auburn waves, which tonight are wild and messy. She smiles up at me, a sly, apologetic smile. I don't return it.

"Do you think this is helping me? I need to go back. *You* need to go back," I say. "Do you want me whipped on the night they take me?"

"I don't want you to go at all! I've *seen* them, Astrid. Their long cloaks. Their hooded faces. The syringes in their hands."

She doesn't have to name them. I know she's talking

about the Asps, the men and women who administer the drug to the contestants in the Race of Oblivion. The drug that will knock me out. The drug that will rob me of my identity by erasing all my personal memories. Since I signed up to race, too many people have made a point of telling me how terrifying the Asps are, but Renya's description goes a bit too far. "Syringes in their hands? Really? I find it hard to believe they walk around carrying them—"

"Stop making light of this!"

I'm about to plead with Renya again to lower her voice, but she catches herself. Casting a glance at the palace wall, she drops her voice to a whisper. "Do you even know why their faces are hooded?"

"Renya—"

"To protect their identities! Because when you come back to yourself—when you finally remember who you are and realize what's been done to you—they could be the first on your list of targets for revenge."

If I live to seek revenge, I think to myself. Fortunately, Renya can read my moods but not my thoughts. "I won't need revenge," I say instead, "because I intend to win."

Renya climbs to her feet. "I know you think you can win because you have Cientia—"

"Renya, please. *Please* be quiet!"

"I can feel your confidence. How sure you are of yourself," she says, but I don't like the way she says it. Like she doesn't share my confidence.

"It's not just the Cientia. You know I'm a strong fighter—"

"I know you've been my sparring partner at Hearts and Hands—"

"I've been your sparring partner who *beats you* at Hearts and Hands." Enchanteds are mad about Hearts and Hands, because it's an intense test of fighting skills and magic. Renya and I practice behind closed doors, of course, and she's gotten good, but I'm better. "I don't just have Cientia. I have Cientia *honed for battle*. I've had the best training, thanks to you."

Renya's hands roll in her pockets. I hear the key jangle at the end of its chain. "You know," she says, "since you entered, everyone's been begging me to talk you out of it." I consider this. I want to ask who *everyone* is, but I let her talk. "I've heard stories. . . ."

"What kinds of stories?" I hate myself for asking, instead of grabbing her arm and dragging her back to the gate. But I can't help myself.

"I heard that a few years ago, a racer died of heatstroke a mile from a remote desert checkpoint. The contestants who came after her read the solution to a riddle she'd written on her palm before stepping over her body and leaving her for the buzzards." She pauses, checking my face for the appropriate level of horror. I'm trying to keep my expression neutral, but if she's reading my feelings, she knows she's rattling me. "The following year, a contestant froze to death one night in the Wilds. The next racer to come along broke his fingers to steal the solution to a puzzle scrawled on a scrap of paper crumpled in his fist."

I roll my eyes, but the truth is, I've heard these stories, too. They keep me awake at night.

"Then last year," she continues, "only two racers survived to cross the finish line. The first received full satisfaction of his indenture and citizenship for his whole family. The second, only an hour behind, went home with three additional years of indenture—the penalty for losing. Of course, he still had his life, which is more than the other contestants had at the end."

"You can't know those stories are true," I say, though I'm feeling a lot less confident than I was before she started talking.

"Look," Renya says, her voice low. "What if . . ." She hesitates, and my heart flutters, anticipating what she might propose. "What if I could convince them to change your indenture? Make it so you're no longer my surrogate."

She bites her lip, waiting for my reply. This is something she's never offered. Something I doubt she can give. But she's desperate. And I'm tempted.

It's true that I have not had an easy life as her surrogate. We've been together a long time—I came to live here in the palace when I was only seven years old, when my mother died and her indenture to the royal family was left unpaid. Renya and I were the same age, and she needed a surrogate, and my family had a debt to pay. Since then, I've seldom been far from Renya's side, and what might look like forced companionship from the outside feels like real friendship from the inside. Which is both good and bad. As her surrogate, I am valued only to the extent my pain causes Renya pain. The more she cares for me, the more she can be manipulated through my pain. So in a way, her affection for me is a curse.

But as hard as my indenture has been, I'm not entering the race to escape it.

"You know this isn't about you," I say. "You know it's all for Marlon. If I win—*when* I win—we'll both become citizens. Even *Jayden* will become a citizen! He could come home. He and I could find jobs and a little place where the three of us could live." My father's too-small apartment with its too-small windows comes to mind, and I wish I could just go back there—just go *home*—but someone else lives there now. After Papa died, the Authority sent Marlon to a dirty hovel they pass off as an orphanage. The palace stables are cleaner. He's stuck there until he's assigned an indenture. I visit him almost every day, and every day is bleaker than the day before. When he first got there, I thought he'd start mimicking more and more. But something worse happened.

He stopped mimicking. He stopped talking at all.

I never thought I'd look forward to the race starting, and I guess I still don't, but I look forward to it ending.

"I know I can win, Renya. I'm *sure* that I can. For Marlon and Jayden, for me—for *you*, too. We could truly be friends if I were a citizen." I mention our friendship because it's the only thing I can think of that could make my entering the race somehow about her. Since her fear is more for herself than for me, maybe the anticipation of our reunion will convince her that letting me go is a better bet for her than trying to force me to stay.

Not that she could force me. Every Outsider is entitled to enter. She knows that as well as anyone. I'm going.

"If you really want to be a friend to me," I say, "then look after Marlon if . . ."

"If you die a horrible death?"

"Renya, please. Just promise me, if something happens, you'll see to it he gets a decent indenture. Maybe something here at the palace, tending to the horses, or even the dogs. He'd like that. But please," I say. "For my sake, come inside with me now."

Renya takes a step back and almost tumbles. I reach out my hand and catch the gauzy fabric of her sleeve just in time. At first I think she's upset at what I said, but then her eyes widen, locked on something beyond my shoulder.

"Are you—"

My words cut off as a wave of fear so thick, so cold, and so dark crashes over me, I feel like I could drown in it. Like I'm a tiny raft and Renya's fear is a tidal wave.

Then I feel the prickle of something else. A flood of despair, as if darkness itself were an emotion.

I don't want to turn. It's almost solid—I feel my back pressing against a wall of pain—but I know I can't just stand here like this either. I'm ready. *I'm ready.* I told Renya I was prepared to face them and I am.

I turn and see what Renya sees, what frightened her so much it drove her through the palace gates in search of me. Three figures stand slightly uphill from us, draped in long black robes, their faces concealed by hoods. They seem to hover rather than stand, like personifications of Death itself. I can't even tell if they are men or women—it doesn't matter. They are just what they are.

Asps.

My stomach rises and falls like the sea in a storm, but I won't acknowledge it. Not my roiling stomach or my careering heart. I wouldn't let Renya see fear in me, and I won't let the Asps see it either.

It's then that I realize how greatly I misjudged Renya. How could I have assumed that her fears were only for herself and not for me? But it's too late to let her help me now. Too late to do anything to save myself.

So instead, I bite my lips between my teeth to hold them

still, and remind myself what courage really is. Not the lack of fear, but action in the face of fear. And not selfish action, either, but action taken in love. Like sneaking outside the palace wall in order to warn a friend. Or willingly entering the Race of Oblivion to save your brothers from lives of misery.

The Asps each take a step toward me, and I realize another way I misjudged Renya. I had been wrong to assume she was exaggerating.

Just as she'd said, in their gloved hands, each of them holds a syringe.

FOUR

My eyes catch on the hand of the Asp closest to me, and I notice the liquid in the vial, a cool blue color. I think of that blue mixing with the red of my blood, as a figure emerges from behind the tallest Asp.

It's Sir Arnaud, with a pleasant smile on his lips and a hard warning in his eyes. His uniform as commander of the King's Knights makes him appear just as intimidating, yet far more elegant, than the Asps. Who would dare argue with a man in a bloodred cape with a sword at his hip? Just behind him his daughter, Sir Millicent, appears.

"This is a gorgeous spot from which to view the city," Arnaud says, as if we're all out here to have a picnic and we've been waiting for him to spread a blanket on the ground. I know him well enough to understand that this act he's putting on is for my benefit. His position allows him the constant choice between cruelty and mercy, and at this moment, he has chosen to be merciful to me. He could easily send me to the whipping post immediately—he sees Renya right in front of him—but he instead takes a moment to admire the view and comfort me with a smile.

It's lucky for me. I may still find myself under the whip tonight, but for now it looks like I may avoid it.

"Princess Renya and Astrid," he continues. "How are you this evening?"

"We are well," Renya replies. Her eyes scan the hooded faces of the Asps. We are anything but well, and everyone present knows it.

"I came looking for you both to explain that Astrid was needed in the infirmary, but I see our visitors have found her."

The infirmary . . . that makes sense. I've been wondering where they would do it. The infirmary is downstairs on the first cellar level, away from the residential rooms but still above the cold storage, and worse, of the deeper levels.

Renya heaves a sigh so heavy her shoulders shrug. Her eyes shift from my face to Arnaud's before she steps around us, heading straight up the path toward the gate, leading our unlikely procession inside the palace wall.

"Don't let the Asps scare you; they're harmless," Arnaud whispers to me as we step through the double doors held open by two Outsider footmen, who turn their faces rather than look at me. The Asps file in behind us. They are far less otherworldly up close, where I can hear them sniffle and cough. Still, they're harmless the way being buried alive is harmless. The fact I'm still breathing doesn't mean I'm safe.

Inside the grand entranceway of the palace—a room with curved alabaster walls and an impossibly high ceiling—we find Prince Lars. He wears a midnight-blue riding jacket and a scowl. "Finally," he says, and my stomach clenches at the anger in his voice. "Do you not realize, Princess Renya, that all of Lanoria cannot stop to accommodate your whims?"

But Renya, as if to prove that all of Lanoria can and will accommodate her, ignores him and leads the way to the narrow flight of stairs that descend to the infirmary. Behind us, Arnaud's boots slam heavily on the marble floor, and I wonder if his mercy toward me has run out.

The tidy rooms that make up the infirmary block are all dark tonight but one—the very last room at the end of the hall. A sliver of light bleeds from under the closed door.

Sweeping past Renya and me, the Asps lead us into a small cell of bright white walls surrounding a solitary cot. "This room is not the last thing anyone wants to see," I say. "Is it meant to serve as a preview of the white silk lining of my casket?"

"Astrid!" Sir Arnaud snaps. "This is not a time for jokes!"

Renya steps to my side as I stretch out on the cot. "That's sweet that you think you'll be buried in a casket," she says.

She gives me a very sad smile, and I wish I hadn't tried to kid with her at all.

The Asps gather around, and the dread I've been shoving away comes rushing back, bursting out of Renya, too, so I can't tell where her feelings end and mine start. I notice the wrist and ankle restraints on the sides of the cot as four other Outsiders file in, including Kit, Prince Lars's surrogate. He wears a very fine high-collared shirt—a recent castoff from Lars—and his arms are crossed in front of his chest.

Of course he volunteered to help.

We might both be surrogates, but Kit and I are far from friends. He has always hated me, and there's no lack of palace gossip as to the reason why. Some say it's because Kit was beaten the day he arrived, as Lars's punishment for having helped my brother Jayden escape. There's no evidence that Lars actually helped, of course, but Kit was punished anyway.

Whatever Kit's reasons, he hates me, and he's made that more than clear. And the treatment I've received from him over the years has made me hate him back.

Renya flicks a glance at him when he steps to my side. "That's all right," she says, positioning herself between Kit and me. "I'll handle her restraints."

"Princess." This one word spit through the commander's teeth carries an entire lecture on the appropriate actions of royalty. Renya narrows her eyes and tosses a glare over her shoulder, but she yields her place by my wrist to Kit.

Each of the Outsiders slides one of my limbs into a restraint and holds me down, and I wonder if I'm expected to thrash when I receive the drug. I hope not. For some reason—I'm not sure why—I can't stand the thought of losing my dignity. It's one thing to fall into Oblivion, it's another to flail into it. Though I'm focusing on the wrong concerns, I'm sure.

Once Kit has tightened the restraint on my right wrist, an Asp approaches and wraps a tourniquet around my upper arm. Kit leans over and whispers into my ear. "Good luck," he says, though I'm not sure if he's being sincere or sarcastic.

I feel my veins swell. A different Asp has come to inspect the crook of my elbow. Renya appears at my left side. She's nudged one of the Outsiders, a stooped man who works in the gardens, from his place. I suppose Arnaud knows he won't win, because he doesn't shoo her away this time.

Renya touches the base of my throat with cold fingertips, tracing the still-pink scar that marks where my embed used to be. "It's healing well, considering that man took no care in making the cut."

Seriously, the fact she can spare some concern for the prospect of a scar on my chest when I'm about to enter a deadly race boggles my mind. "What about the other one?" I say. "The embed in the back?"

"It will come out once you're asleep," says Arnaud, and I cringe at this. I hate the thought of being handled and moved about, like I'm nothing but a rag doll.

A pinprick and then a burn . . . The Asp beside me pushes down on the first plunger, and my eyes press shut. What little I know about the drugs I've gleaned from rumors. Three drugs are given, one by each Asp. The first is just a tranquilizer. I already feel its effects, my muscles melting into the cot like wax on a hot rock.

The second brings Oblivion.

The third brings deep sleep.

A second pinprick, but I hardly notice the pain. The second Asp steps back, the empty syringe in his hand, Oblivion already coursing through me.

My lungs expand. The room brightens. The whiteness yields to colors that throb at the edges of my vision. I hear music, like wind chimes, and it occurs to me that I am hallucinating. My breath fills my lungs and I feel the oxygen it carries to my every cell. It's icy cold, and yet it heats me. I open my mouth and a laugh breaks in my throat. My eyes find Renya's, and I see fear in her. "Don't be afraid," I say. "I feel wonderful."

"No pain?" she asks.

"No pain," I answer. I stare into her brown eyes, and I feel awash in love for her. I know it's the drug—I know this unbounded well-being will pass—but right now I feel invincible. I can hardly wait to wake up in the race. I feel like I could run across the continent tonight and be at the finish line by morning. Like I will never tire again.

This must be the purpose of the restraints. My arms and legs strain against them, testing their strength to contain me. I'm surprised they do.

The third pinprick comes, and before the needle is out of my arm, the world begins to blur at the corners. A mist rises from the floor as Renya watches my face. "She's slipping away," she says. I want to tell her I'm still wide-awake, but my mouth doesn't work. I let my eyes fall closed for a moment. When I open them, I'm alone. The door to the corridor is closed.

I want to say Renya's name, to call her back to my side, but my body won't respond. The restraints feel like heavy weights. The music is still there, the colors still pulse, but it's fading. The door opens. Only my eyes slide to the person who steps through. My head is too heavy to turn.

In the doorway stands the king, draped in a navy-blue robe. He walks in, alone. This must be a dream, another hallucination from the drug. His beard glows the same bright white as the walls, like snow clinging to cheeks so pale, they're almost transparent.

"I wanted to see you before you left us, Astrid," he says. "I can see in your eyes—your wide-open pupils—that you are feeling the effects of the drug. I hope you are comfortable."

I try to smile, to tell him how good I feel, but the third drug has trapped me as if I've been turned to stone.

"I know all about this drug, Oblivion. Maybe too much," he says. "I've come to depend upon it. Not total Oblivion, of course, but enough. Enough to feel like a great man." He steps toward me and lays a hand on mine. He's warm. Could it be that the king is actually here? "I've come looking for the Asps. I need them to make me comfortable, even at the expense of their own comfort. It terrifies them, to share the drug with me. But it's only small doses, the smallest that will do the job. To make me feel like the great man I know I no longer am.

"But I will be great again soon, Astrid." He smiles. "Do you know why I've told you my secret? Because I know yours." His voice drops to a whisper. "I know you have Cientia."

My heart races. The king is not really here. I'm sure of that. As he stands over me, his beard catches fire, and when he speaks again, his breath is like a wind that fans the flames. "Don't be afraid," he says, the fire racing up to his hair. "I won't tell anyone, though I doubt I'm the only one who knows. It's become quite obvious, I'm afraid."

As the king speaks, flames spread to the walls; they flicker across the ceiling. I wish I could scream. *It's all in your mind*, I tell myself. *None of it's real.* "I'm going to make changes," the king continues. "I know the Outsiders are suffering—your own family is suffering—but all that will soon change. I will be the great leader Oblivion makes me believe myself to be." His smile widens, and beams of light shine through the gaps between his teeth. "I'll leave you now, but first, one more secret. I'm sure you must be curious to know why you have Cientia, when all other Outsiders do not. Well, I know why, and before you go, I want to tell you."

The door opens. A figure enters. My Oblivion-poisoned eyes try to make sense of what they see. At first it's an Asp, then a bear, then my father. Then someone I know—a face so familiar—but I can't place it. Something is clasped in the figure's raised hand. . . . A syringe? A knife? Then the hand comes down, and the body of the king slumps to the floor.

Fire has spread to every part of the room. Everything burns except the figure that bends over the fallen king.

As I stare, I feel myself slipping away. The flames burn less bright. The roar in my ears fades. The figure in the center of the room approaches and leans close, whispering into my ear.

"It doesn't matter what you saw here." I try to place the voice, but it's muffled and indistinct. "In a few minutes, you will have forgotten this. You will have forgotten everything. And before any of it comes back to you, you will be dead."

FIVE

I wake to pain.

The sound of the whip tugs at my mind just before the pain of the lash returns, splitting me in two.

I want to scream, but all I can do is groan. As I slump forward, my gaze goes to my bare knees, grinding into a dirty stone floor. A floor I don't recognize, in a room I don't know. Sweat runs from my forehead, burning my eyes. I wear nothing but thin underclothes—white splattered red. My wrists, bound above my head, burn as they strain against rope.

Where am I? What could I have done to deserve this?

The crack of the whip returns, followed by searing pain. My mind searches for answers, clutches at thoughts, but each lash drives them away and plunges me back into a dark pit of pain. I hear my voice again, but this time it's only a gasp. I want to let go—to let the pain pull me under and hold me there—but a stubborn strength won't let me give in. I try to raise my head to see the face of the one who holds the whip, but my eyes swim with tears and the person's features smear.

Then a voice cuts through the pain. A girl screams, "Stop! You've hurt her enough!"

"*I've* hurt her?" A boy's voice, calm and measured. "Put the blame where it belongs, sister."

I try to identify the voices, grasping for something to latch onto to slow my mind in its race toward madness, but then another lash sends every thought scattering, until the voices go silent, and mercifully, darkness crashes down.

I wake again, pulling myself up from deep sleep, this time roused by a rhythm I can't quite make sense of. For a moment I'm half alert and half still dreaming, and I have the feeling of standing on the deck of a boat, letting the dream slide below the surface, watching it disappear into the depths. That's how it feels at least, and I understand why when I open my eyes to find myself draped across a rock surrounded by the sea. Each wave that crashes against the rock mists my body with spray that is soft everywhere but on my back. There, each successive splash stabs like a dagger.

Over and over, fists of water pound the base of the rock before retreating. I have no idea how I got here, or even where I am. I feel the echo of the lost dream, and I'm convinced it was a dream about home, but now that I'm fully awake, I can't think of where home is.

I steady myself and look around. I'm stranded on the point of a jetty. In front of me, a wide beach of black sand stretches in both directions, but the path across the rocks is submerged beneath the waves. The sun is directly overhead, and a shimmering haze of heat rises from the distant sand, like a curtain hanging up instead of down.

I watch the waves. As I do, I try to think of home, and when that's not there, I try to think of the face of just one member of my family, but nothing comes. Making it easy on myself, I try to think of my own name, but even that's gone, maybe dropped into the sea with my dream.

Each wave brings pain, so I breathe in and out in time with the waves, to make the pain more tolerable. A shadow grows behind me, stretching out toward the sea.

I may not know my own name, but I know misery, and this is it.

I try to concentrate on all the things I do know, to distract myself from all the things I suddenly don't. I know that the landmass in front of me must be Lanoria, because that's the name of the only landmass I can think of.

So if this is the coast of Lanoria, it must be the east coast, because the sun is moving toward the land.

Other things I know: The tide is going out. In time, the rocks of the jetty will be exposed and I will be able to walk to the beach. I don't recognize the white dress I'm wearing, but it's so drenched by sea spray I can see through it, and I recognize the underclothes I wore as I was lashed.

The whipping. The voices—a girl and a boy. That memory of my life before I woke stands alone, a single scrap of paper in an empty drawer.

When the tide goes out, I wade to the empty stretch of sand. The jagged rocks claw at the skin of my bare feet, but compared to the pain in my back, it's nothing. There's a small measure of comfort in the fact that my one personal memory assures me that I can be strong in the face of pain.

On the beach, I find a knobby black rock that's almost big enough to be called a boulder, sitting in the middle of the sand as if it's been dropped from the sky. Pinned beneath it, a ragged piece of cloth flaps in the wind.

A map.

My hands tear at the sand around the map, and the sand tears back, wedging under my nails and digging into tiny cuts on my skin. It doesn't slow me. My thirst has my full attention now, and all my thoughts turn toward the hope that this map will show a freshwater source.

But when it finally comes free, it's nothing more than a few simple markings in black ink on white canvas—a straight line leading to a tower, and a small *x* that I can only guess marks the place I'm standing. No circle representing a pond or lake, no farmhouse or village or stream. A star hovers in the space above the tower, a building shown as a rectangle around hash marks that might represent a ladder or stairway. That's it.

Flipping the cloth over, I find a few lines of text:

You are a contestant in the Race of Oblivion.
Win the race and you and your family receive citizenship.
Finish but fail to win, and your indenture will be extended by
  a minimum of three years.
Drop out, and your indenture will be extended by a minimum
  of seven years.
Your first clue is:
Come to the lighthouse, Astrid.
Climb to the window outside.
Your next destination will be written on the wall, at the place
  where light doesn't pass through glass.

My mind is racing like a runaway train, and it's veering toward panic. I breathe in through my nose and out through my mouth, and challenge myself to find just five things I can see and understand: the land I'm standing on is Lanoria, the water at my back is the Emilia Ocean, the two people standing down the beach from me hold fishing poles, the shadows circling my feet are cast by gulls, and the cloth in my hands contains a clue.

A clue in the Race of Oblivion, which is something else I

understand. And now I get it—the reason I can't remember my name or where my home is. Because I'm in a race that starts with the purge of personal memories.

I wish this knowledge were comforting, but it's anything but. I'd be more comforted to know I lost my memory in just about any other way, to be honest. At least then, my lost memory would be my biggest problem. If I entered this race, then the worst is all ahead of me.

I flip back to the line drawing on the other side of the cloth. The tower . . . it must be the lighthouse in the clue. It's terrifying, the thought that I have no choice but to pursue this clue to this unknown lighthouse, when all I want to do is find a drink of water and go home.

"I'm not staring just to stare," a man shouts. It's one of the two fishers, standing near the water not far away. "It's definitely her. That's why I'm looking."

"You're looking because she's a girl in a damp dress that's clinging to her." It's the other fisher, who I can only guess is the first one's wife. She's big and broad and so is the man, and they are both red-faced from the wind. Just like the gulls, they sound like they're arguing. "Don't try to fool me," she says.

They are both staring now. I can't help but wonder if they have water, and what *It's definitely her* might mean, so I start toward them.

"Look. Here she comes," says the man. "You can't deny

that's her. So sad about her father."

"Excuse me!" I don't get too close, mostly because they are staring at me like I'm something to be feared. "Do you know me?"

"We don't *know you*, so much as know *of* you," calls back the man. The surf is loud and the wind breaks up his words, but I catch enough to understand. "A lot of people are talking about you. On account of what happened at the Apple Carnival."

"What happened at the Apple Carnival?"

At this, the woman hooks his arm and draws him back from me. "She's in the race," she says, tapping the base of her throat. "There's nothing where her embed should be."

My hand moves to my throat, and my fingers trace a fresh scar. "Where are your embeds?" I ask. "Are you in the race, too?"

"We're citizens!" the woman calls back. "Satisfied our indentures years ago. Now move along. We can't risk getting caught helping a racer."

"Why not?" I've moved closer and they've stopped moving back, and I'm close enough now to see the jug of water in the sand by their packs. "What could happen if you help a racer?"

"What could happen?" She laughs, but it's an exaggerated laugh, to show how stupid my question is. "She wants to know what could happen. Only a huge fine and maybe a little jail time for giving aid to a racer. That's all!"

"It's got to be on account of her father dropping dead like that. It's got to be," says the man, and the hairs stand up on my arms. "That's got to be what pushed her into the race."

"My father? What happened?"

"Move along!" shouts the woman, and a wave of something dark, with a bite like cold wind, hits me in the face.

"It's just that I'm thirsty," I call back, swallowing my pride because that's what you do when your throat is burning and your mouth's gone as dry as the sand.

"Move along, I said!" she calls again, lifting the jug and holding it behind her. The man shakes his head and turns back to his fishing rod, but the woman never lifts her gaze from me until I'm south of them, and even then, when I throw a look back, she's still watching me go.

By the time the lighthouse finally comes into view, my thoughts keep switching between grief for a father I don't remember and doubts that the fishers truly recognized me at all. My thirst doubles and then triples, so much that my legs drag, but when I see the lighthouse, I have to force myself not to sprint.

As I come closer, I spot something so odd I think dehydration must be playing tricks on my eyes. A boy climbs the exterior of the lighthouse, looking a lot like a four-legged spider against the whitewashed bricks. He's working his way up by finding toeholds in the places where the mortar between the bricks has crumbled away, or where the surface of the wall is uneven and little ledges jut out here and there. He does not make it look easy. He hovers about halfway between the top and the bottom of the tower, outside a solitary window framed by black shutters.

I peer down at the map until my sun-weary eyes manage to focus on the words again. *Climb to the window outside.* Until now, I hadn't realized those words were meant to be taken so literally. I squint up at the boy again, wondering what I might offer him to reveal the next clue to me.

If I could offer the boy water, wouldn't he be willing to share with me whatever clue he's found? I know *I* would bargain for water right now.

I circle the base of the tower, but there's nothing. No tap, not even a puddle. A short distance inland, a line of cornstalks grows higher than my eyes, obscuring the road and everything else beyond it. Arching over this sea of green, irrigation pipes spray a fine mist into the air, but it all soaks into the soil. Not a trickle runs out from beneath the stalks.

A road sign stands beside a driveway that cuts through the corn. One arrow points toward me: *Chertsey Light.* The other arrow points away: *Pope's Lake, 8 miles.*

So there's a lake, but eight miles is a long walk.

I turn my attention back to the boy overhead. He's pulling himself onto a windowsill that stretches beneath the window and its black shutters. Once he's sitting, he tugs something out of his pants pocket—his map. He flips it over to read the clue, and I turn mine in my hands and read it again, too.

Your next destination will be written on the wall, at the place where light doesn't pass through glass.

The boy looks up at the wall, then swivels on the ledge and looks north. His hair is so long on top of his head that sandy brown curls fall into his face, but he brushes them away as he shades his eyes with his right hand, grasps the ledge with his left, and peers into the distance. His shoulders are broad and his legs are long. Like mine, his feet are bare. I watch him, staying out of sight, wondering if I could make it to the window—at least six stories off the ground—without falling.

As I watch, he slides off the ledge and starts his descent, using all his strength and size to hold on, and I know I don't have the skill to climb that wall on my own. A deal is my only hope.

So I rehearse my speech as he eases himself down the wall. *I can offer you my help. We would have an advantage if we worked as a team.* Maybe he doesn't understand the clue. Maybe it's unclear. If he's willing to tell me what it says, I could help him decipher it.

He wears tan work pants and a dark tunic. As he gets closer, I begin to doubt he will accept my offer. Up close,

I can see the strength in him that allowed him to make the climb. He's got strength in the way of a person who's worked hard for it. When he turns to look for his next toe-hold, loose curls hang in front of his face, giving him the appearance of someone who can do the impossible with his eyes closed. Nothing about him says *needy* or *desperate*. His face is as composed as the surface of a quiet lake. He doesn't even appear to be thirsty.

I keep my eyes on him, and when his body is dangling from a height of about five feet, he lets go and drops to the sand, falling hard onto his back.

He never makes it onto his feet.

SIX

As soon as the boy hits the ground, three figures, a woman and two men, spring out from the deep shadow that stretches behind the lighthouse. I hadn't even known they were there, but they're on him in an instant. The men kneel on his shoulders to hold him down as the woman— her feet wrapped in thick-soled boots that are terrible for this heat but great for causing pain—stomps on his hand.

His head flips back and he bares his teeth at her like a horse, thrashing so hard that sand kicks up around him. The woman's brows tug together in her ruddy face, and she plants her other foot on his chest. He goes still, but I'd be surprised if he's given up.

"That was an impressive climb," she says. Her voice is a growl. It's the voice of a big woman, or of a small woman who's lived a hard life. And she's not a big woman. "What did you find marked on the wall outside the window?

Tell us, and we won't break your hand." He remains silent except for a second hard thrash against the ground. There's no real chance he'll throw the men off—they're both built like concrete pylons—but the woman slams the toe of her boot into his ribs all the same. "It would be very difficult to win the Race of Oblivion with a broken right hand. Or even worse, without an eye." She bends over him, brushes the pile of unruly hair from his forehead, and one of her two companions smashes a fist into his left eye socket.

The boy spits in his face.

The man's fist jerks back as he recoils, and he wipes his face with the back of his hand. I feel the anger rise in him, and in my mind's eye, I see his intention to rear back and lunge for the boy's throat.

As his weight shifts off balance, I know this is my chance to put the boy in my debt. I have to run, but I manage to reach the man in time to seize him around the neck. He bucks as hard as a mule, but he was mid-lunge when I grabbed him, so his balance is lost. His eyes are full of shock when they meet mine before his leg buckles and he crumples to the ground, his head almost knocking against the boy's.

The woman tips toward me, and when she does I feel her surprise at the fact I've entered into the fight. I can practically smell the astonishment on her, a little like the scent of singed hair, or a rotten egg. I see her hands flying up to my face, but before she can touch me I throw my arms up and block her. The bottom of my dirty foot finds the center of her chest, leaving a sooty smudge on her tan tunic as she reels backward.

By now the boy is struggling up from the ground. Both men have backed away, but their eyes stay on me. "Cientia," the first man mutters. He's a redhead, his eyes rimmed with ginger lashes, and he suddenly looks quite childlike, his eyes popping wildly. I can still see the smear of spittle on his cheek.

Of course this is ridiculous, but if he wants to believe a few lucky moves were guided by Enchanted magic, that's fine with me. It would matter only if he were right, and he can't be. His gaze runs over me as if he's trying to search out where the magic is hidden, and then his feet pedal backward before he turns and flees into the forest of corn.

I watch him run hard after his two partners, knowing I've found my bargaining chip.

The spider boy is on his feet, and from up close, he looks a lot less like a spider. He's all angles—knees, elbows, shoulders—all the way up to his cheekbones. The only things softening the edges are the curls on top of his head that drape over his angled eyebrows. He brushes off his clothes, peering under his pushed-up sleeves at his elbows. They're scraped, but it's nothing too bad. He clenches and unclenches the hand the woman stomped on. "I guess I owe you my thanks," he says. For a moment I think he will extend his hand, but if he's contemplating it, he decides against it.

"You're welcome," I chime, taking a step closer as he takes one away. "You would've done the same."

"No," he says. He shakes his head. His eyes touch mine, and I see there's a second soft thing about him besides his curls. His eyes are soft—a pale shade of hazel under dark lashes that curl like his hair. For a second I feel pinned by his gaze and I almost look away, but before I can, he drops his eyes to the ground. "No, I wouldn't have." With that, he turns and limps away, toward the narrow lane that cuts through the corn and out to the road.

"Wait!" I say, hurrying after him. He keeps walking, forcing me to talk while matching his strides. "Didn't I just save you? They were going to break your hand. Gouge out an eye, even. I think we need to discuss repayment. You owe me—"

"You helped me out of your own free will," says the boy, whirling on me. He pulls himself up to his full height and turns those soft hazel eyes hard. I wonder if he's trying to intimidate me.

It doesn't matter; I won't have it. I might be smaller than him, but I am not insignificant.

What I did for him is not insignificant.

His eyes search me, as if he's assessing me. If he is, I must come up lacking. "We're both racers. I don't owe you my assistance and I don't owe you my trust. I did owe you my thanks, and I gave it to you. Now I'm going. I won't even wish you good luck, because I certainly wouldn't mean it." His voice is matter-of-fact. If it held even the smallest bit of irony, I'd probably think he was joking. How can he walk away after what I did for him?

"There's only one prize," he continues. "Only one person wins. Look out for yourself. If you have an instinct to sacrifice for someone else, you better fight that instinct, or you'll be the first to die."

He shuffles away—either the attack or the drop from the lighthouse wall has left him hurting—and my rage burns in my chest. I feel the same anger flowing back toward me from him. "I wish I knew your name," I call at his back. "I may have forgotten everything else, but I want to remember your name. A name I will curse until I win the Crown of Oblivion."

To my surprise, he spins and rushes back to me. "It's Darius," he says, his face still possessed of that lake-water calm I saw earlier.

"What?"

"My name. It's Darius. Pronounce it properly when you curse me."

Before I can respond, he strides away. I watch his bare feet on the pavement, wondering how far he'll get without shoes. I wonder how far I will get, too.

"Wait," I call, just as he reaches the place where a curve in the road will hide him from my view. I want to let him go—I feel like a groveler calling to him one more time— but I have to ask. "How do you know your name?"

"It's on the map," he calls back, without even looking over his shoulder.

I find my map where it fell when I came to Darius's defense, and there it is.

Come to the lighthouse, Astrid.

How did I miss that detail? I guess I assumed that line of the clue was a quote from a book or a poem, not a direct reference to me. "Astrid," I say out loud, but it sounds no more familiar to my ears than *Darius*.

Alone, my roiling rage begins to quiet. I circle the base of the building, scanning the exterior for a way up. Though I tried the door as soon as I arrived at the lighthouse, I try it again. Still locked.

He did it, I tell myself. *Darius made the climb. If he can do it, you can do it, too.*

I look up and notice what might be a handhold—a small, irregularly shaped brick that protrudes from the wall a foot above my head. I reach for it. I find a tiny ledge jutting out about two feet off the ground, and I wedge my toes onto that. My hand trembles and my heart pounds, but I pull myself up. I reach up with my left hand and find the next uneven brick that will give me something to grab onto.

My muscles resist, but I climb. My shoulders tighten, my feet cramp, and when I look down, my stomach coils into a knot. But I climb.

With each inch gained, I keep my promise and curse his name. I curse him for not helping me. I curse him for leaving a debt unpaid. But more than anything, I curse him for his warning. *You'll be the first to die.*

I reject his warning, and I will prove him wrong. He'll see. I won't be the first to die, and I won't be the last. I'll win the Crown of Oblivion, and with every step along the way, I will curse Darius's name.

SEVEN

My whole body shakes with exhaustion when I finally stretch up and take hold of the ledge beneath the window. I'm almost there, but in this moment, the *almost* counts for quite a bit. Wind gusts up along the wall and ripples along my dress, but I manage to keep moving upward, until I find myself on my hands and knees on the narrow sill.

I remain there for a long time, waiting for my heart to calm down, until I realize that the fear is getting worse instead of better. When I finally find the will to move, I drop into a sitting position and hang my legs over the side.

Once I'm steadied, I let myself look down at the ground. A small crowd—maybe five or six people—gathers below, watching me. Racers, lying in wait for me to bring them the clue.

I'll need to get past them when I head back down, but I can't worry about that now. One thing at a time.

My eyes skim along the horizon, and I see where the lane Darius took joins up with a road, but I don't see Darius. Instead, I see rows and rows of corn. The landscape is nearly flat, but the ground is broken into a patchwork of fields, all of which would be barren land if it weren't for the long arms of silver pipe stretching over them, throwing wide arcs of water into the air.

The corn hides Darius from view, along with any other racers who might be approaching from whatever places they awoke from the drug. I glance up and down the beach, but except for the crowd at my feet, I see no one.

Out on the sea behind me, a boat floats like a toy in a tub. At first I think it's a fishing boat, but then I realize it's somebody's yacht. Somebody is out on the water having fun while racers are risking their lives for the Crown of Oblivion.

What could have made me risk *my* life? What in my forgotten past provoked me to choose this? *You'll know when you win*, I tell myself, but I can't win until I convince myself to turn enough to look over my shoulder at the wall. Gripping the ledge on either side of my thighs again, I take a deep breath. I want to wait until I feel ready to move, but if I'm honest, I know that moment will never come, so I force myself to twist in place and look behind me.

I turn enough to see that a candle burns on a table inside.

Outside, five letters are written in a column to the left of the window in pale gray paint.

The shutter on the left is stuck halfway between open and closed, sticking out at a ninety-degree angle to the brick wall. I try pushing on it, but it won't budge. The hinges must be frozen with rust.

The letter *P* is painted at the top of the window, on the wall above the shutter. Below the *P* is an *O*. At the top of the shutter is another *P*, and below it, also on the shutter, is an *E*. On the wall just below the shutter is an *S*.

P

O

P

E

S

Popes? As I look out at the level fields of corn, the word seems meaningless. I remember Darius looking north, his hand shading his eyes from the sun, but when I look north I see nothing but green stalks. Corn, corn, and more corn. But Darius is taller than I am. He'd see farther from a sitting position.

My legs betray me with their shaking as I pull them up beside me and shift onto my knees. Without letting myself think about what I'm doing, I get to my feet and straighten until I'm standing on the window ledge. My hands brace against the walls on either side, and I let my back touch the pane of glass.

Now I can see beyond the corn in every direction.

The compact roofs of a few houses stick up along the road, and beyond them, I spot a white farmhouse with a silo and two barns. Beside the farm, a broad field of bright red flowers blooms. The air bends in the hazy heat, making the field of flowers look like a puddle of blood. North of the farm, a village sprouts up. I can see a clock tower rising above sharply pitched rooftops and narrow streets.

Even farther up the road, I spot a lake. It's the northernmost landmark I can see. I remember the signpost at the base of the lighthouse: *Pope's Lake, 8 miles.*

P O P E S. The next checkpoint is eight miles away.

But first I have to get to the ground, and the obvious option isn't much of an option at all. When I look down, I don't see the upturned faces of racers gathered beneath the window; I see open jaws waiting to devour me. As much as I fear climbing down the wall, I fear reaching the ground more.

I turn back to the window. The candle on the table illuminates a small room. I wonder who lit the candle and what they would do if I kicked in the glass to get inside.

I'm still wondering when a sound startles me and draws my attention away from the candle, out to the fields of corn. A shout, followed by a scream. A scream of a person in pain.

Nothing else sounds like that.

Then again . . . a shout followed by a scream.

Then again. And again.

Something in the screams reminds me of the pain of the whip on my back in the only memory I have. With each scream, the memory plays like a recording. You'd think a person with only one memory would want to hold on to it, but you'd be wrong.

For some reason, despite the bleeding gashes on my own back, the screams shock me. The sounds on the breeze sicken me the way the sight of my own blood might. My stomach squirms like a sack of snakes. Still, I listen. The only sound missing is the crack of the whip. I can only assume it's carried away on the wind.

I surprise myself when I sit back down without much fear. The need to escape the screams is more motivating than I would've believed. Reaching behind my back, I grip the edge of the window and try to raise the glass, and I'm surprised when it slides up an inch or two. I'd assumed it would be locked. Peering over my shoulder into the room, I'm nudging the window up an inch at a time when a breeze gusts under the sash and blows out the candle's flame.

With the inner room darkened, the sun reflects off the glass, turning it as opaque and reflective as a mirror. A girl looks out at me, a pair of dark eyes under thick black bangs, and I realize the girl is me. It's unnerving to see my own face and not know it. But the shock fades quickly when I notice the letters *P* and *E*—the two letters painted on the shutter—in the reflection beside my face. So now those letters are doubled:

P

O

P P

E E

S

Where light doesn't pass through glass. That's part of the clue. And light doesn't pass through glass where it reflects.

What I'd believed to be *POPES* is actually *POPPEES*.

But what does *poppees* mean?

Facing north, I picture what lies beyond the corn that blocks my view again. The farm, and the field of flowers. Bright red flowers in full bloom.

Poppies.

I don't want to go to Pope's Lake. I want to head to the farm.

Staring at the reflected letters, I consider my options to hide the clue. I could break the glass. Or, if I can climb inside and find a match, I can relight the candle.

I look down. The small crowd at the foot of the tower still looks up, and above them, a racer is climbing. A woman, with wind-burned cheeks, dark brown hair, wide eyes, and an even wider smile. "Hello there!" she calls. Her voice is light, almost a laugh. For her, the climb seems even more effortless than it was for Darius. "Stay right there, now," she says. She has a long thin neck and long thin fingers, and she finds each new handhold faster than the last. "Stay right there, because I'm coming for you," she says. Her mouth is open in a broad grin, like she's laughing without sound.

Watching her rise, coming closer and closer, I grip onto the ledge with both hands. There is very little space on this windowsill. We will not both fit here, side by side. She sees that.

I twist in place and look into the small room again. I need to get in there, but before I can pull my legs up, those long thin fingers wrap around my ankle.

"Ready to switch places?" she asks.

When I turn back to look, for a fleeting moment, her eyes are full of triumph. But then I give my leg a hard shake, just once.

The fingers of her left hand, still gripping the wall, wiggle loose. A flash of bare truth passes over her face. Her grin goes slack as her mouth falls open.

Then I shake my leg once more, and she lets go of my leg.

Her hand swipes at the wall, reaching for a handhold. But her feet are already loosening from their perch. She's there a moment, almost hovering in midair.

And then she's gone.

Instinct seals my eyes shut and turns my head away before she hits the ground. Below me, a man screams. Keeping my gaze steady on the sill, I raise the window, swivel my legs into the room behind me, and drop onto the floor.

I shiver. The room is cool and feels soaked in the sea. The wooden table is swollen and warped, and the air smells like sea spray and mildew and a hint of smoke. I shove the window all the way open so it can't reflect the letters for the next racer who makes the climb, and just as I do, a blast of wind hits me from behind.

Not from the window. From the opposite side of the room, where a narrow corkscrew stair is visible through an open doorway.

A floorboard creaks, and a cold gust pelts me again, but now I know it's not wind. It's fear that acts like wind, chilling my skin and raising up goose bumps. Not my own fear either, but someone else's—whoever is waiting on the stairs. I take two slow steps, my shadow crossing the threshold to the stairwell ahead of me. As it does, a girl jumps into the room with so much force she knocks me to the floor.

She has surprise on her side, but that's all. Small and underfed, she's no more than a waif. I lift her off me like I might lift a wiggling dog. Pinning her to the floor is no trouble at all. She overflows with fear, so much that it chills the room.

Still, she fights hard, squirming and kicking and flailing

a long time before she finally lies still. I slide away from her slowly, half expecting her to start fighting again as soon as I let go, but she remains sprawled on the floor where I held her down.

"So I guess you want the clue," I say.

"I don't need your stupid clue." The words fly out of her mouth, coated in a thick accent from the rural north. "I already read the letters myself, early this morning." She sits up, running her hands through pale blond hair. "I was the first one here—"

"How did you get through the locked door?"

"It wasn't locked when I got here. I came through the door and locked it behind me."

We sit on the floor facing each other, and I watch her glaring at me. She can't be more than sixteen years old. She looks like a magpie, with shifting, wide-open eyes set over a sharp beak of a nose. And just like a magpie, she's small but quick, and maybe a little bit dangerous.

"So if you have the clue, why are you still here?" I ask. "This is a race." I think about Darius's words. *There's only one prize. Only one person wins.* "Shouldn't you have been on your way to the next clue a long time ago?"

"I knew I'd never get past that mob waiting outside. Unlike you, I can't fight like an Enchanted." Her magpie eyes dart to the window and back to my face. "I watched you save that other racer. So do you have it?"

"Have what?"

"That magic? Do you have Cientia?"

I hesitate. *Could I?* It shouldn't be possible. Every Outsider is inoculated against the Three Unities at birth. And I may not remember my life, but I'm in this race, so I know I'm an Outsider. "I can tell you're afraid. But I don't think it would take Cientia to know that. So I don't know."

"Fine, keep your secrets," the girl drawls, pronouncing the word like *sacreds*. "But I have *water*. . . ." She pauses to let it sink in. I try not to react, but I know I fail. If I ever possessed any subtlety, it got left outside on the window ledge. "And I'm willing to share it with you if you'll get me out of here."

Water. Just the thought of it makes my throat burn. "I'll have to see the water before I do anything for you. I won't let you trick me."

"No problem at all."

She scoots toward the doorway to the stairwell and returns with a canteen in her hands. A drip seeps out of the closed spout and splashes onto the stone floor.

"I'll help you," I say, "but you need to give me a drink right now."

I expect her to argue, but she hands the canteen to me without hesitating. The water slides down my throat, cool and fresh. "Thank you," I say, then immediately regret it. I don't owe her any thanks, because we've made a bargain.

"Where did you get it?"

"I stole it from the house next to the place where I woke up. I think the Enchanted woman inside saw me take it, but she let me get away with it."

We each take one more slug from the canteen and climb to our feet. My eyes sweep from the girl's straw-colored hair to her dirty pants, and I try to imagine an Enchanted woman looking the other way as she stole this canteen. She does look pitiful, if you don't meet her razor-sharp eyes. "What's your name?" I ask when we get to the bottom of the stairs.

"Jane," says the girl.

"All right, Jane. Let's go."

ƐIGHT

The door is thick and heavy, and its hinges groan loud enough to announce us to everyone outside. There are six racers crowded together—three men and three women—and all of them are looking up at the window when we emerge. My first instinct is to run, but before we can, they've boxed us in.

One of the men—a boy really, sixteen or seventeen, with arms the size of tree trunks—locks his gaze on Jane, and I realize it was a mistake to bring her out with me. He grabs her by the upper arms and flings her to the sandy ground, but before he can raise his foot to kick her, I'm between the two of them, ready to catch him by the ankle. He flies backward, his head connecting with the white brick wall.

"Stay down!" I manage to bark at Jane, but I never even glimpse her because I'm spinning into a kick. It lands solidly on one of the two women coming up behind me, but the impact stings my foot and makes me fear I've snapped my ankle. But I get lucky—she grabs onto the other woman as she goes down and takes her with her.

I'm set, ready for the next one to come at me, but the third—a pretty woman with the build of a man—signals to the others to stay back.

"She's got magic. Can't you see? She knows what you're going to do. . . ."

She's still speaking but I don't hear her, because the boy with the huge arms is coming at me from behind. I turn just in time to dodge his fist as it swings toward my face. Ducking under his arm, I grab Jane, drag her to her feet, and push her in front of me. "Let's go," I say, shoving her up the lane toward the road. She keeps looking back, but I won't let her stop.

"What was that?" I hear from over my shoulder. A ripple of confusion stirs the air, filling my ears with a sound like crashing waves. Maybe it is the waves. Maybe the tide's come up. But Jane and I are moving fast, and before long we are at the intersection with the road, and I feel nothing but the scalding pavement under my feet and Jane's constant undercurrent of fear.

The corn casts shade at the edge of the road, so we walk where the surface is cooler. Jane walks backward a distance ahead from me, her magpie eyes locked on me like I'm something she doesn't trust. "What am I feeling now?" she asks when she sees me glaring back. "What am I about to do?"

"Walk up this road," I answer, rolling my eyes. "Not really a question that requires magic to answer."

Her mouth quirks into a momentary smile, but the look of suspicion and hunger in her eyes doesn't change.

"The house where you stole the water this morning . . . Do you think we would find food there?" I ask. Dust from the road cakes my feet as we walk. The sun heats the backs of my legs. I can't remember if my skin tans or burns.

My lack of memories made me scared at first, but now it just makes me angry. I keep turning toward my memories, the way a person might glance down at their wrist before remembering a favorite watch has been stolen. Each time I notice them missing, I get a little angrier.

"I'm sure the old lady has food. You planning to steal some?" Jane traces her eyes over my upper back. "You're bleeding pretty good," she says. I felt my scabs open during the fight. "Maybe she has some medicine you could steal from her, too."

"I thought you said she looked the other way when you stole the water," I say. Just the mention of it makes me thirsty. "If she was willing to let you take the water, do you think she would be willing to give us something to eat and help me with these wounds?"

Jane's whole body clenches like a fist, her shoulders rising up to her ears. Whether I am using Cientia or not, it's obvious to me she's growing more frightened with every question I ask. "I'd never expect to get help from an Enchanted," she says.

"But you said she—"

"The house isn't far. We can figure out what to do when we get there." The fear keeps rolling out of Jane like it's pouring from an open tap, so I decide not to talk about it anymore. I decide not to talk about anything, so we walk in silence.

After a few minutes, Jane looks over at me and hands me the canteen without me having to ask. When I pass it back to her, I try to tamp down the feeling that I'm taking advantage of her. I know she thinks she has the clue figured out, and maybe she does. Maybe she saw the word *POP-PEES* and lit the candle as a way of hiding the reflection and changing the word to *POPES*. This road leads to both the farm and the lake, so for now, I won't worry about what level of help and trust I owe her.

For a long time all I see ahead is row after row of corn, so that despite my hunger, I decide I will never eat corn again. But then finally I notice a gap in the green on the left-hand side of the road—a driveway marked by a stone pillar about shoulder high, beside a dried-up patch of lawn. The words

Heaven's View are engraved into a sign mounted to the pillar, a title that could be true only if your idea of heaven involved unlimited supplies of corn. "That's the place," Jane says. "It's a little house off by itself. The woman is old and it looks like she lives alone."

"You woke up behind that house?"

"*Yay*-ah," Jane drawls. "My map was under an old truck tire in an unplanted field. The first thing I did was spit out a mouthful of dirt."

The house is set back from the road at the end of a narrow drive. It's small but neatly kept, with flowers growing in window boxes that drip like they were just watered. I grab Jane's wrist to stop her. Behind the house there's a packed-dirt courtyard overrun by about a dozen chickens, and behind that a small barn. Walking through the barn door is an Outsider farmhand. I can see the blink of his embed from here. He carries a metal bucket with a creaky handle to the back door of the house.

Jane and I slide out of sight just inside the stalks of corn. A cool mist sprays across my feet from the irrigation system—so soothing after walking so far on the hot pavement—but it's not enough to drain the tension from my body. Not with this man just feet away. I'm not sure if he'd chase us off or what else he might do if he saw us, and since we're carrying a canteen that was stolen from this house, I'd rather not find out.

The back door is slightly ajar, and he calls out from the doorway a name I can't quite hear. My eyes sweep the property while he waits for an answer. I notice the dusty field with its truck tire beside the barn, and I imagine Jane coming to her senses here. It's certainly a step up from a rock in the middle of the sea.

The farmhand calls out again, waits another moment, but then gives up, setting the bucket of milk inside the partly opened door. When he's safely out of sight, Jane and I creep up to the house, leaving a trail of wet footprints. "Maybe we should just go in and take what we need before the woman comes back," Jane says. The inside of the house smells like onions and bread. Jane slips through the door and disappears.

After a moment in the hot sun shooing away flies drawn to the milk, I follow her in.

I don't find Jane, but I find a woman facedown on the kitchen floor, a butcher knife sticking out of her back. Dried blood stains the ties of her white apron a dark red. Squatting down beside her, I touch her shoulder, but it's obvious she's dead. Her chest is still. Flies crawl on her face and on the doughy skin of her arms.

"Jane," I call out, but I feel a blast of fearful wind behind me, just like I felt in the lighthouse. And just like in the lighthouse, she bursts through the doorway and charges at me, this time with a kitchen knife raised above her shoulder.

Before I can get up she's waving the knife at my throat, and all I can do is drop onto the floor beside the dead woman and roll out of her reach. I'm shivering and sweating all at the same time, unable to process what's happening, so I let my instincts take over and kick at Jane's scrawny legs. She grabs at a high-backed kitchen chair as she loses her balance, and it topples down with her.

She drops the knife on her way to the floor, and before she can find where it lands, I snatch it up. "What are you doing?"

"You felt me coming," she says, and her lips twist into a smirk. "I think you do have that Enchanted magic. Maybe your daddy was Enchanted. Did your whore mother sell herself to some taskmaster?"

"Shut up!" I snap. But something inside me squirms. Because I'm standing over her with a knife in my hand, instead of lying on the floor with it in my back.

I can't understand it. I can't explain it. But I can no longer deny I'm using Cientia.

Unlike at the lighthouse, Jane lies still once she's down, maybe because this time a knife is pointing at her face. "You *killed* this woman. You said she looked the other way—"

"I lied, and you believed me. You're the most gullible girl I've ever met. You need my help, and it looks like I could use yours. Now put down the knife and let me up."

"I'm not *that* gullible," I say.

"You need my help—"

"You're afraid."

"Not of you, I'm not."

"You are. You've been planning to kill me all along, but you've been afraid, because you knew if you failed, I'd kill you. But you were wrong. I'm a racer, not a *murderer*—"

"That's why you need me—"

"Shut up!"

I sweep my gaze around the room, searching for something to bind Jane with. I bite my lip and try to keep from shaking. How did I get here? A minute ago I was on the road, worried about the sun and what I owed Jane. Now I'm trying to tie her up to keep her from killing me.

My eyes land on the dead woman's bloodstained apron ties. Certainly an appropriate choice as far as irony goes, and since I don't spot anything else that would do the job, apron ties it is.

"Turn over," I say. When Jane's response is nothing but a glare, I lean down close to her face with the knife until she turns away, then flip her by the shoulders so she's facedown, setting a knee in the middle of her back. I have to stretch to reach the knotted ties and cut them free with the tip of the blade. It slices right through the fabric. "This is a very sharp knife," I say. "If you'd only moved a little quicker, I'd be dead for sure."

The house is hot and the dead woman is starting to stink

a little. My head swims like there's not enough air. I try not to think about the woman's blood covering the apron strings as I use one to tie Jane's hands behind her back. The second one, even more brittle and stiff than the first, I use to tie her ankles together.

"You need me," Jane says. "You can't abandon me here."

I don't answer. Instead I take a black canvas shoulder bag from the counter and stuff it with food that will keep— some nuts and crackers, an apple, plus what's left of the fresh loaf of bread I smelled from the door. I hate to take it from a dead woman, but I also know I need it much more than she does now. In a drawer I find a tube of something called Healing Helper that claims to *soothe and defend against infection in cuts, scrapes, and burns.* When the bag is full, I'm ready to go.

"You can't leave me," Jane seethes. Her magpie eyes stare up at me but I look away.

"I can do whatever I want," I say.

"What if no one finds me? I could starve to death."

As angry as I am, I know I can't leave her here. Not to keep her from starving to death, either. That farmhand we saw would find her eventually. But I need to be sure she's arrested so she can't continue in the race.

Her hands still tied behind her back, I untie Jane's ankles. "The blade is an inch from your ear," I say, yanking her up to her feet. It's a tricky balance—the knife in one hand and

Jane's upper arm in the other—but I lead her past the bucket of milk, through the open back door, and across the courtyard. The barn is dim and heavy with the smell of damp hay, and inside we find the dead woman's cow and a milking stool. On a shelf I spot a folded newspaper, and a pen next to a half-filled-in wager sheet for a Hearts and Hands tournament. I grab the pen and drop it into my bag. Glancing at the newspaper, I notice the page on top is filled with lonely-hearts ads—*Man seeks woman for conversation and maybe more.* A full-color ad with a picture of a pretty girl fills the bottom-right corner. *Poppee's Dance Hall, Village of Hedge,* it says. *Where the Ladies Are Always Friendly.*

Poppees . . . the clue! It's not a reference to flowers at all. It's a dance hall! I remember the town I saw from the lighthouse, just beyond the farm. Could that be the Village of Hedge? I silently thank the lonely farmhand for holding on to this paper. "I hope you find love," I mutter under my breath. Jane throws a glance at me but keeps her mouth shut.

Once the cow is untied, I shove a leg of the stool into Jane's hands. The cow is on the small side with a spotted brown coat, and she eyes me suspiciously, but she follows when I tug on the rope at the end of her halter.

Dragging Jane alongside me, we make awkward progress as I lead the cow to the middle of the road in front of the house. A breeze ripples through the tall corn all around us, but the sun still bakes down. Using the cow's long lead of rope, I tie her to Jane and then push Jane down onto the stool, snaking the end of the rope through the legs and knotting it under the seat. "When someone eventually comes by, they'll stop," I say. "The bloody apron ties should lead them to the woman you killed." I almost wish her luck, but then I remember what Darius said about not wishing someone luck if you don't mean it.

I turn up the road toward the village, my feet already burning. As I walk away, Jane calls to me, her voice full of panic. "Don't leave me. You need me. I'll die in this sun."

"You'll be found before you die," I call back.

"I could still be a good partner." Her voice rises as I walk away. The road bends, and when I look back, she's hidden from view by the green wall of corn, but she still shouts to me, "I can help you. Who will put that salve on your back?"

I don't know who will put the salve on my back, and I don't care. I will not be accepting help from any other racers.

The road bends farther, and the sound of Jane's voice fades behind me. Another sound drowns it out—the electric hum of the engine of an approaching vehicle. I hide myself behind the first row of cornstalks and watch it pass.

It's a truck. The bed is too high for me to see into, but I assume from its large size and the mud on its tires that it's carrying goods from the farm. As it goes by, I spot two young men hanging on to the side. Their hands on the truck's rail and their feet on the sideboard, they stay out of sight of the driver, who most likely has no idea they are there. They are simply stealing a ride.

As I watch them, a realization dawns on me. The thing I need most—the thing that could mean the difference between winning and losing the Crown of Oblivion—is transportation.

After the truck passes, I run along behind. I don't want to be seen, but I can't stay away. I know the driver is about to discover a cow in the middle of the road and, tied to that cow, a girl.

NINE

The truck is beyond my view when its screeching brakes tell me it's come to a sudden stop. Running up behind, I slide into the cornfield across the street from the dead woman's house to stay out of sight, and push my way between two rows. The ground is wet, and cool mud oozes between my toes. As I come alongside the truck, both boys hanging from the side drop to the road and run straight into the corn, passing right by me. One, about eighteen years old with old eyes in a young face, slows and gives my bloody back a long look. He's an Outsider but not a racer—he's still got his embeds. He's just running. Maybe running away. His mouth works like he's about to ask me a question, but then his companion calls from deeper in the cornfield, and he turns and follows without saying a word.

Back in the road, the farmer driving the truck—an Enchanted man with gray hair cut very close to his block-shaped head—shouts at Jane through the open window, blares the horn, and finally opens his door and steps out. While he's out of the truck, I take advantage of the chance to sneak up to the tailgate and peek inside the bed. Outsiders sit with their backs against the cab and sides, their hands tied in front of them. Their faces are dirty and their clothes are stained with sweat.

If I hadn't already accepted that I have Cientia, there'd be no denying it now. I thought the fear that radiated from Jane was strong, but it's no match for the storm of emotions rising from the back of this truck. It's not fear—it's something more fixed than fear. Fear is about the unknown. There's more of an inevitability to the feelings that wash over me now—more like dread of something terrible that is coming and can't be stopped.

No one reacts to me except a broad-shouldered woman wedged into the corner. I don't realize she's a woman at all at first. Her hair has been shaved off, and a scar splits her left cheek and drags the corner of her mouth down into a scowl, so at first glance, she not only looks like a man, she looks like a cruel man. But when her eyes land on me and her brows go up, she transforms into someone's mother. She twists in her seat to look over her shoulder in the direction of the farmer. When she turns back to face me again, she shakes her head hard. *Don't*, she mouths. She lifts her bound wrists as if to show me what my fate might be if I got caught, though I have no idea what she means. What horror could cause the dark dread flooding me from her and the others? Beside her, a thin old man shakes his head at me too, but most of the others keep their eyes lowered as if they don't see me. One boy mouths *Stop it* to the woman who is trying to warn me.

I should leave. I don't want to put anyone in danger. But when my gaze falls on something sticking out from under a dark green tarp in the center of the open truck bed, my palms mist with sweat. It's a motorbike tire. I'm not sure how I know, but I recognize it immediately. I know it's a motorbike, and I know I can drive it.

The farmer is standing over Jane in the road. For a moment I worry that she's talked her way out of this and he's going to let her go. But then he turns toward the house, and with only a quick glance back at the truck, he drags Jane toward the driveway, the stool bouncing against the backs of her legs and the cow trailing behind.

I take my chance. I climb into the truck and pull off the tarp.

Just as I'd hoped, I find a motorbike lying on its side. But my exhilaration is cut off by another discovery. Under the tarp, huddled beside the motorbike, sits Darius.

His hazel eyes meet my gaze, and I feel like a child who has just seen a magic trick for the first time. Darius is as unexpected as a white rabbit pulled from a hat. He flinches in surprise, then rises up on one knee and peers through the windows of the truck cab at the road ahead before turning to look back toward the farm. "Are you going to be taking that tarp?" he asks. "Because it was serving a purpose where it was."

"You can have it," I say, dropping the crumpled tarp beside him. "But I'll be taking this bike."

Right beside the bike is a wide plank of wood, and it's not hard to figure out it's there to be used as a ramp. As I slide it to the open gate and let one end tip down to the road, I can't help but wonder what Darius is doing hiding away on a truck heading south. Did he already find the clue at Poppee's Dance Hall? Could he already be making his way to the third checkpoint? It certainly wouldn't do me any good to ask him, and I know I can't worry about Darius, or even these unfortunate Outsiders, right now. Instead, I grab the bike by the handlebars, pull it upright, and wheel it down the ramp to the ground. Darius watches me. "You know how to handle that?" he asks.

"Don't worry about me," I say.

"I'm not."

I don't give myself time to try to read Darius's feelings, though there's a scent like the air right after the rain, and I know that's the smell of regret. Regret or rain, and it hasn't rained. But it could be from anybody—not necessarily Darius—and I don't have time to let it matter. I allow myself one brief glance over my shoulder to be sure the driver isn't returning from the house yet, when the Outsider woman who tried to warn me away catches my eye.

I wish I could ask her if the village in the distance is Hedge, but I don't dare bring it up in front of Darius. My gaze lingers on her scar. I'm wondering how she got it, when she smiles and mouths, *Good luck.* I can't help but return her smile. I know she means it.

With Darius watching me, I climb onto the bike. It's sized for a man, but it's only a little big for me. It takes some extra effort to hold it up, but I know I'll be fine once I'm moving. I turn the key, crank the pedal to engage the battery, and press the ignition. The engine hums, and I shift into gear and take off toward the village without so much as a glance at Darius.

For a while, I notice nothing but the changing crops— corn, beans, something else I don't recognize—and the long silver arms that spray bucket after bucket of water onto the ground. I'm fairly certain I've never worked on a farm, because nothing is familiar.

Not like this bike. Riding this bike feels right. It's the first thing to feel right since I woke up on that rock.

I spare a quick glance over my shoulder, just to be sure no one's following. Nothing but the dark ribbon of road stretches behind me. The sun is dipping a bit toward the west, and I watch the shadow of me and the bike, one dark shape like we're one creature. The engine heats my legs and feet, but at least there's a cool wind against my skin as long as I'm moving.

I slow the bike as I pass the farm. I want to give the field of poppies a long look, to be sure I'm not missing anything. As the engine quiets, a series of staccato sounds pierce the air, and wariness inflates like a balloon in my chest. I recognize the sounds. They're identical to the screams I heard from the lighthouse.

When the rows of corn finally run out, my view opens up to a field planted with low-growing crops. Nine Outsiders are bent over, filling baskets, their embeds blinking under their shirts. The tenth—a woman and the only Enchanted—stands straight, her hands twitching by her sides. The taskmaster.

Her face reminds me of a potato, lumpy and splotchy, shaded by the wide brim of her straw taskmaster hat. She aims her hands at the back of a bent picker and grunts out a breath. The Outsider drops to his knees and coils into a ball, shrieking.

A burst of panic prompts me to stop. I've got to help this man. But before I can even climb off the bike he's straightening, brushing the back of his hand over his forehead. He sucks in a few quick breaths and then returns to picking, without even a backward glance, and I realize, *This is something he's used to.* The potato-faced taskmaster turns her attention to the next Outsider bent over a basket.

No whips. Of course there are no whips. A whipped worker can become sick. Their wounds can become infected. Projectura—the third of the Three Unities, along with Cientia and Pontium—leaves no wounds behind. Not on the outside, at least.

I must have suffered before I entered this race. I'm an indentured Outsider, and I volunteered for the Race of Oblivion, and from what I've seen of the race so far, you'd have to be crazy or desperate to do that, and I don't think I'm crazy. Did I suffer like this, or did someone I love? I think of the woman with the scar in the truck, how she reminded me of a mother. Could my own mother be suffering like these Outsiders? Is that why I'm racing?

The taskmaster lifts her head in my direction. Her eyes lock on my face, and my heart pounds like a piston. I've lingered here too long. I let out the throttle, pick up speed, and fly away.

TƐN

It isn't long before there's heavy traffic on the road, so I know I'm getting close to the village. The corn is so high, it's hard to see what's ahead, but then I round a bend and pass a slow-moving truck, and all at once the sharply slanting rooftops of the village are right in front of me. It looks out of place, like it sprang up from the farmland out of nothing. I pass through a gate under a sign that reads *Village of Hedge* and turn down a narrow cobblestone lane that's flanked by high gray walls. The streets are so narrow and the buildings so tall that they block the sun, and afternoon all at once becomes evening.

Not knowing where I'm going, I turn right at some corners and left at others, wherever I can get through, between pushcarts and bicycles and an occasional horse-drawn cart. The streets are so slender, people move in single file, like ducks. Gas lamps burn in shop windows, and light pours from open shop doorways. I scan unfamiliar face after unfamiliar face, until my gaze snags on a face I recognize: the ginger-haired man who attacked Darius at the base of the lighthouse. The one Darius spit on. In front of him walks a boy with straight black hair, droopy shoulders, and bare feet. Another racer. Having seen them, I make it my business not to be seen, but this young boy—he can't be older than fifteen—stops in the middle of the intersection and blocks my way. His expression is too senseless for me to believe he is hindering me on purpose, but it doesn't matter. I don't have time to waste. I gun the engine and swerve around him, cutting things a little too close. He jumps back into his red-haired companion, and when I throw a quick glance over my shoulder, I glimpse the redhead making a vulgar gesture at my back.

This corner of the village is darker and quieter, the streets illuminated by neon lights. I turn down a block lined with men standing alone, their heads lowered, their faces in shadow, their shoulders braced against the buildings as if they are holding them up. When I bring the bike to a stop, many of them look up. A few appear to be young. None appear to be happy. Every door on the block is closed, and muffled music seeps out into the street. It might be early afternoon, but on this block, it's night. If there's a dance hall in this town, this feels like the right neighborhood.

Leaning the bike out of the way, I pocket the key and

decide I have no choice but to approach someone. I don't have time to waste.

"I'm looking for a place called Poppee's," I say to the nearest man, trying to sound self-assured and failing at it. He is not much older than I am, and he smiles. I'm not sure if this is good or bad.

"End of the block," he says, his eyes moving up to my head and down to my feet before returning to my face again. "You might want to wash some of the dirt off before you go in there, though."

I bristle at this comment, but I nod my thanks and leave him to watch me walk away. Right before the corner, I come to a building with lights shining behind closed drapes on the upper floors. I feel as vulnerable and out of place as a fox wandering into a gathering of hounds. I may not know where home is, but I know it's not here. I can feel it in my bones.

The doorway is set back from the street and tucked under a balcony, and between me and the doorway stand four men. No embeds, so Enchanteds or citizen Outsiders. They look up at me as if I have just interrupted their conversation, though no one was speaking. "Poppee's Dance Hall? Is this it?" Not one of them responds; they just stare. I wish this dress weren't so dirty, and that there were a little more of it. They all step back and watch me as I pass between them and pull hard on the heavy door.

I enter a room that would be pitch-dark if not for the giant red neon flowers that cover every wall. Poppies. The ceiling is low and painted black, and the room smells like sawdust and beer. Directly in front of me is a podium, and leaning against it is a woman with jet-black hair, a long neck, and a black dress that flows all the way to the floor. She is striking, but she commands my attention for only a moment, because in the back of the room a band kicks in, and they are loud. Every note is hot and cool at the same time, overlapping into something sensual and erratic, matching my erratic pulse. It's a reel—the kind of tune that's played fast but still works if you want to dance slow. I can barely keep from swaying to it.

A voice shouts over the music. It's the woman at the podium in front of me, waving her hand in my face. From up close, I can see that she is much too old to have hair so black. "Here to work?" she asks, her mouth close to my ear.

I'm not sure what to say, since I'm afraid that anything other than *yes* will get me thrown out. "I'm waiting for someone," I say. The door opens behind me and a flock of women pushes in from outside, carrying with them a cloud of laughter and perfume. The girls are all Outsiders, their embeds flashing, but the few men who have already arrived are all Enchanteds. They watch the girls from the edges of the dance floor with such predatory glares, I can only imagine the hands that are hidden in their pockets have claws in place of fingers.

Something procedural is happening at the podium—I think the girls are signing in—and with my head down but my eyes up, I slip by and find a dark corner where I can get my bearings. They're playing a waltz now—all guitar, fiddle, tin whistle, and mandolin—and it almost seems familiar. The bandleader calls out its name: "Down a Lonesome Road."

From the shadows behind my back comes a voice, and it's got all the friendliness of a broken bottle. "Racers aren't allowed to go anywhere they want to, you know."

I spin around and plant my hands on my hips. The man in front of me sways on his feet, emboldened by whatever he's been drinking. "Dirty dress, no shoes. You are a racer, aren't you?" When I don't answer, he answers for me. "Of course you are, because you're a germy little urchin who believes that all of Lanoria should be disrupted so a bunch of selfish Outsiders can fight over a shortcut to citizenship."

His tunic is open at the neck, and I can see his scar. He's a citizen Outsider. "I don't mean any disrespect," I say.

The room is filling up quickly. A hand falls on my shoulder, and I almost jump out of my skin. When I whirl around, the face of an Enchanted man is too close to my own face for comfort. He has a thin mustache and a patch of beard on his chin, and something about him makes him seem even dirtier than I am. Without thinking, I shove his hand off my shoulder.

"Didn't mean to startle you, doll," he says, and his smile is bright but not warm. His eyes are skittish. He's tall and wiry, but he slouches, so his arms hang in front of him instead of at his side. He reminds me of a willow tree. He's with another man who's practically leaning on him. "Just wanted to see if you needed me to tell this guy to shove along."

"I can tell people to shove along just fine on my own, thank you."

His friend, also an Enchanted, is less jumpy. He leans forward and whispers into my ear, "If you don't turn down your mouth a bit, you're going to be tossed out of here before we even get to dance." I step back to take him in. He's built as if he were made from wooden blocks, square and sturdy, and his eyes are a little heavy. I notice how clean and white his tunic is when he slips out of his jacket and hands it to me. "And put this on. Your back is a bloody mess."

This is an accurate statement, so I accept the jacket and shrug it on. "So let's go then," he says. "Dance floor's behind you."

"I . . ."

"Let me guess. You don't actually work here. Good.

Then the dance will be free." When I don't move, he adds, "You *are* looking for a clue or something, aren't you? Well, the dance floor has a better view of the room than this dark corner. And if I step on your foot, don't squawk. You don't want anyone noticing you're not wearing shoes."

The next thing I know I'm in the middle of the dance floor, holding his hand. He sets his other hand on my hip. I try to read him, but there are so many intentions swirling around me, I can only hope the more sinister ones aren't his.

I set my hand on his shoulder and we begin to shuffle in a slow circle. I don't look at his face, but that doesn't stop him from speaking low into my ear. "You might not be able to tell," he says, "but many of the people in here know who you are."

Now I can't help but look at him, and he smiles at the obvious jolt he's caused me. We keep turning, and I try to search the room. Maybe I was wrong, and I'm not far from home after all. Maybe someone here knows my father and can tell me if it's true that he died.

The dance floor is getting crowded, and people are pressing in around us. I keep catching people staring at me, just before they avert their eyes. "What I mean is," my partner continues, "people here know you from the papers and the news network. You gained a bit of notoriety from an incident that happened before the race, and then a bit more when people found out you had entered." He slides his hand into his pants pocket and pulls out his comm. Tipping it up so I can see the screen, he watches my reaction when I notice it's a picture of me, sitting on the ledge outside the lighthouse window.

"Who took this?"

"Someone who thinks people will be interested in your story."

I stiffen. "And why would that be?"

"Lots of reasons. Like I said, there was an incident before the race that made people take notice of you. I can't tell you what it was because I'm not going to get accused of helping a racer. But I will tell you this." He lowers his voice and breathes into my ear. "Some people who have seen you fight are saying you might have an advantage over the other racers. An advantage no Outsider should have . . ."

My heart pounds. "Why would anyone say that—"

"*Why?* Kid, you know why. Just like when you got into those fights, you knew where the next punch was heading."

"But I don't have—"

"Don't bother lying to me. You're not the only one with Cientia, all right?" He tightens his arm around my waist, pulling me in a little closer. "I'm not trying to scare you," he says, and his lips are so close to my ear, his breath warms my skin. "I'm trying to help you stay out of trouble. Stop making your Cientia so obvious, or you'll never get through the race without the Authority tracking you down and taking you in. It's only an advantage if you don't get caught."

The song ends, and he steps back from me, looking down at his comm. From through the crowd his willow tree friend appears, his skittish eyes roving all over my body before he says, "I think it's my turn to dance."

I'm not sure I want to go on dancing, though, so I shove my hands into the pockets of the borrowed jacket. Something slips between the fingers of my left hand, something soft wrapped in plastic. I have an idea what it might be, and if I'm right, then I shouldn't pull it out and look at it in front of all these people.

The willow man grabs my waist—the next song, another waltz, is starting—and my hand twitches inside the pocket, itching to slap him across the face, but I stifle the urge. I need to be here to search for the clue, so I place my own hands as lightly as possible on his shoulders. "Come on, now," he says, and I realize I'm so distracted, I'm barely moving, just shifting my weight from foot to foot. "Make this a proper dance, or I'm going to turn you in. I think the Authority would love to hear about a racer with Cientia."

I flinch at this threat, and he laughs.

The music picks up speed, but the dancers all around us keep the same steady pace, some of them hardly moving, so that their dance is little more than an embrace. Men's faces flush red from the heat, and women's dresses stick to their backs. Maybe it's the circles, but I'm starting to feel ill. I'm wondering how I can break away so I can properly search for the clue when my dance partner's hands slide down my back, not even slowing at my waist before they are somewhere they do not belong.

I plant both hands on his chest and shove.

He stumbles backward, bumping into several couples. Men turn and glare, and a few of them shout. I feel outrage churning through the crowd. If it weren't so packed in here, he would've ended up on the floor.

"You know, actions have consequences." This is what he says to me—this is what *he* says to *me*—as if the person who just shoved him for putting his hands on her doesn't understand the consequences of actions. If I weren't so sure I'd be flung out of here and never get to look for the clue, I'd teach him something about the consequences of actions, with a kick to the groin that he'd never forget.

I jab my hands back into the pockets of this jacket and notice that the ring of people standing around me are all staring. A few of them—mostly Enchanted men—raise their comms and snap my picture. My dance partner, his eyes hardened to little brown beads, steps toward me. It almost appears that he's coming back to dance, but my Cientia tells me that's not his intention. I'm wondering how a brawl in this dance hall might affect my chances of winning the race, when someone pushes through the crowd and comes up beside me, placing a hand in the middle of the willow man's chest.

I'm shocked to see it's Darius.

"She's not worth it," he says, loud enough for me and anyone else who's listening to hear him. "This place is full of girls prettier than her." His eyes sweep from my head to my feet. "Cleaner, at the very least." He slips what looks like a folded bill into the man's hand. "Why don't you go find one and ask her to dance?"

The man looks down at the bill and grunts. But he walks away.

Darius turns, and for the first time since I met him this morning, his lips quirk into a smile.

"Well, now that that's taken care of," he says, "would you like to dance?"

ELEVEN

You've got to be kidding me," I say, digging my hands deep into the pockets of this jacket, as if to emphasize my point. But Darius doesn't seem to get it. "I've got better things to do at the moment," I snap.

He tries to answer, but the band drowns him out, and there's something happening near the door that's causing a commotion. Darius glances back over his shoulder, and we both see the cause at the same time: a few officers of the Enchanted Authority are talking to the woman at the podium. I feel a ripple of anxiety flow through the crowd. Even the Enchanteds in here would rather avoid the Authority. My hand goes to the plastic baggie in the left pocket of this jacket. The guards at the door, and the stir they're causing among the patrons here, suggest my suspicion that it contains contraband might be correct.

But I don't care about that. All I care about is what the

blocky Enchanted man said. *Stop making your Cientia so obvious, or you'll never get through the race without the Authority tracking you down and taking you in.*

The entire dance floor seems to shift toward the back, away from the front door. People turn and stare at us. Do they suspect these officers are looking for me? I wish I could run out of here—just run home—but without my memories, I'm as good as homeless. "All right," I say, stepping closer to Darius. "I'm taking you up on your invitation to dance. But only because I need to keep a low profile. And just until those officers are gone."

Darius grins. With so many eyes on us, his composure is impressive. His right hand floats up from his side, just enough to lightly touch my waist. His left hand enfolds my right. Despite the black dust from the road that I can feel on his skin, there's something nice about how solid his hand feels. I swallow.

I can't help but wonder if I have a boy in my life, and if he provokes me the way Darius is provoking me right now. In this way that makes me want to look at him, but also makes looking at him impossible.

"I probably should know your name if we're going to dance," Darius says. His mouth is very close to my ear. "Have you figured it out yet?"

I don't like his smug tone. "It's Astrid."

"Well, *Astrid*," he says, tasting my name as if it were a

piece of chocolate in his mouth, which I *also* don't like, "it looks like those Enchanted Authority guards are heading out, but I just located two other people of interest in this room." He turns me around in another circle, and I see what he's talking about. Two racers loiter near the front of the bandstand—the small woman with the big boots who stomped on Darius's hand at the lighthouse, and the boy with the tree-trunk arms who jumped me and Jane. I try to hide the stress I feel at their sudden appearance, but he notices because he says, "Don't worry. They're no closer to finding the clue than you are."

"What's that supposed to mean?" I begin to question how I could've forgotten for a moment how I feel about Darius—my commitment to cursing his name. "For all you know, I already have the clue and I'm just waiting for the right moment to slip out of here."

"What's keeping you?"

"*You*, for one thing. It isn't my intention to be followed."

"You have to be going somewhere before you can be followed." I shoot him a dirty look, which only seems to please him. "Look, I didn't come in here to harass you, or to follow you to the next checkpoint. I came in here to offer you a deal."

The music changes and the crowd around us thins and then swells again, as people find new partners. Someone stumbles and stomps on my toe, but I don't even turn. The band takes up a waltz again, and Darius and I sway in time. The bandleader calls out the name of the tune: "Down a Lonesome Road." They played this one earlier. "What kind of *deal*?" I ask, and I do my best to hide my interest. I don't think I fool him.

"I need to take back my earlier warning not to help anyone." I manage a sidelong glance at his face. His brows are tense, pulled together over his hazel eyes. The playful smile is gone. "I have decided to help you, and that's the reason I came and found you here. But . . . I also won't lie to you and tell you that I changed my mind because I knew I was in your debt. I'm making an exception out of necessity, because you have transportation and I need it. We'll both need it, at least in order to reach the next clue. So I'm willing to tell you what only I know."

"You have the next clue—"

"Yes—"

"And no one else does?"

"Not yet."

"And you're willing to share it with me because I have the bike?"

I see in his tight expression that this isn't easy for him. "Yes."

"How do you know that no one else knows the clue?"

"Because once I figured it out, I made sure it stayed hidden."

I pull away from him. "So I'm in this dance hall risking arrest, looking for a clue that can't be found?"

"I understand your anger," Darius starts.

"You don't understand anything about me," I snap. "Just tell me the clue."

There's a long silence between us. I notice a woman standing in the corner, pointing a fancy camera at my face. I turn my head. Darius says, "If I tell you the real clue before you agree to team up with me, I give up all my leverage." I can't help but wonder if, in his life before the race, he had reason to negotiate bargains. He seems to be experienced in maintaining the upper hand. "Once you have the clue, what motivation do you have left to help me?"

"Maybe the debt I would owe you for helping *me*? Not all people would leave someone who helped them with nothing in return. Wait. I take that back. You didn't leave me with *nothing*. You left me with a warning. A warning not to help *anyone*."

"I made a mistake. But I want to point out . . ." His eyes move to my face, and when his gaze meets mine, I turn my head away. He isn't giving me enough room to breathe. "You didn't exactly help me out of *goodness*, you helped me to set up an exchange. I'm just asking for that same thing now."

He's in need. I have the bike, so I have the upper hand, and he doesn't like it. Even if I didn't have Cientia, I'd still be able to feel that. And I'll be honest—it doesn't feel bad. "How did you even get here? I left you in the back of a truck heading south—"

"The driver picked up a girl in the road. He turned around and came right back to Hedge. Dropped her off at the police station."

A laugh ripples out of me before I can stifle it. Darius shushes me and I nod. I don't want to attract any more attention. But it feels good knowing that little spotted cow helped me get Jane out of the race and turn Darius around, all at the same time.

Still, Darius knows where the next clue is, or so he claims, and if he's telling the truth, no one else does. "All right," I say. "Tell me where we should be going. Tell me, and I promise we'll go there together. But remember this: the bike is mine. I am the driver and you are the passenger."

"So we have a deal?" A tug at the corner of his mouth almost becomes a smile.

I nearly smile back, but I catch myself. "Just tell me," I say.

He glances around and drops his voice. "I got to this dance hall before they even opened for the day—the band was inside, practicing, and the door was propped open to the street. The bandleader was calling out songs: 'Down a Lonesome Road' and 'To the Girl Next Door.' They rehearsed those two songs over and over—they were quite rusty at them at first—but the leader kept telling them to take it from the top. 'We've got to play both these songs a lot today,' he told them."

"It's the clue."

He nods. "It took me a while to find out what it means. I walked next door to the billiards hall and asked around."

"And?"

"And I found out that, if you are good at darts, you can win a wad of mackels. And if you're willing to pay a few of those mackels to the right person, you can find out that *The Girl Next Door* is the name of a roadhouse, far to the south."

"*Down a lonesome road*," I say.

"Correct. Spend a few more mackels, and you can even convince a person to draw you a map." Discreetly, he reaches into the pocket of his pants with his right hand and produces a folded paper napkin with marking on it.

I can't help but imagine this scene: Darius, dirty and scraped, nonetheless charming a bunch of drunk, dart-playing Enchanteds. I wonder if they were female, but I don't ask.

"So how did you hide the clue?" I ask.

"I came back in here and paid the bandleader not to play 'To the Girl Next Door' anymore today."

"You *what*?" I pull my hand from his grip and shove his other hand off my hip.

"Hold on! He wouldn't go for it. He said he'd get in

trouble, but he agreed to give me a head start. And that was a while ago."

"All right," I say, but I scowl at him. I promised to take him with me, but I didn't promise to like him. "I guess we're heading south."

We turn toward the door, shouldering past a few dancers who seem to have grown roots into the floor, but just before we reach the raven-haired woman at the podium, we both stop. At least a half dozen Authority guards are heading in. The one in the front hands the woman some kind of official document. I make out a single word across the top: *Warrant.* My stomach sinks. I'm not sure what's about to happen, but I know it's not going to be good.

"Where do you think you're going with that jacket?" a voice growls into my ear.

I spin to find the first Enchanted man I danced with, the one who looks like he was built from blocks. He's been drinking, I guess, because the blocks are caving in.

His sleepy, bloodshot gaze drifts to the officers beyond Darius's shoulder, and his eyes wake up fast. He takes a step backward.

The band abruptly stops.

Darius presses on my back from behind. "They're coming in," he says. Everyone around us shifts; every neck cranes to see what's happening.

The blocky Enchanted man, who a moment ago was demanding the return of his jacket, no longer seems to care about it. I stay with him as he snakes deeper into the crowd. He never slows. I spot his friend in the corner where I met them, just at the same moment he does. He turns and shoves me away. "You can keep the jacket. I don't want it," he says. A bright light flashes across a few faces in the crowd. One of the guards is sweeping a battery light back and forth. "Just stop following me."

"I'll stop following you," I say, "if you'll show us the back door."

TWELVE

Without comment, we are swept through a door in a dark corner that leads to a cramped back room. The first thing I notice is the smell. There's something sweet, almost syrupy, lingering in the air, like someone just melted brown sugar in a pan. At first glance the space looks like some sort of workshop, but I can't tell for certain because it's full of men packing stuff up and carrying it out the back door with a sense of urgency I can only imagine was brought on by the presence of the Authority guards.

I catch a glimpse of something that looks like an electronic scale, and a few large plastic bags. Some appear to be full of ground coffee, some full of flour. A few of the men carting the equipment away shoot grubby looks at the Enchanted man who brought us in, but one of them slows and gives me a half smile. He rests the heavy cardboard box he is carrying on one hip. "Revelry or Oblivion?"

"Excuse me?"

He tugs two small baggies—one filled with black powder and one filled with white—from a breast pocket in his tunic, and a light flicks on in my mind. The bags I'd seen were not full of coffee and flour, but street versions of the drugs Revelry and Oblivion. "Are you looking to remember, or to forget?"

"They're not looking for anything. They're looking to leave," snaps the blocky Enchanted man, and the tension in the room suddenly jumps. Not that I care. All I care about is the door on the opposite side of this room, the one that keeps opening and closing as they shuttle out their equipment. It opens, and I can see the alley out back, lit with the yellow light of gas lamps, and then it closes, and someone blocks my way. It's a woman—a really big woman—who places the palm of a huge hand in the center of my chest. "What do you think this is, a turnpike? Get her out of here," she says. She reaches for the knob of the door we've just stepped through, but our escort moves to stop her.

"They're *racers*," he says. "They're just going out the back door."

The big woman whirls around, and I can tell a confrontation is coming, but before she even opens her mouth, I've dashed across the room and slipped out into the alley. The door slams closed behind Darius.

I think we're free and clear until light bleeds into the

alley from behind us. Someone's followed us out. The door bangs shut, and someone grabs my shoulder from behind. "Not so fast. I've decided I'll take that jacket back after all."

"Of course," I say, shrugging my bag from my shoulder and sliding the jacket off. "Thanks for the loan." I drape it over his arm. He is quite drunk. He looks at it as if he's forgotten why he wanted it.

I've made it around the corner and back to the bike before I dare open my left hand. "What's that?" asks Darius. The clear plastic baggie, no bigger than my palm, stuffed with a bright white powder, is visible for only a moment before I clamp my hand closed over it.

"It's mine, that's what it is," I say, dropping it into my bag's inside pocket when I take out the key to the bike. "Mind your own business."

I don't wait for Darius to tell me which way we are headed. As soon as he's climbed on behind me, I take off.

It takes me a few wrong turns, but we find the village gate, and my body actually feels lighter as I leave the shadow-filled Village of Hedge and return to daylight. We're back on the farm road, and I'm forced to ask Darius which way I should turn. He's tugged the folded napkin from his pocket and he's staring at the hand-drawn map. "Turn south," he says into my ear. His chest is pressed tight against my back, but his hands grip the seat, rather than me. I appreciate the discretion, though I can still feel his heart beating against my spine. "Follow this road until you come to a crossroads, then turn right. That's the King's Inland Highway. We stay on that road for a very long time."

"I thought you said we were headed south?"

"We are. Inland and south."

So without another question, I slide the bike into gear and take off. We fly down the corridor of corn, and before long, with that puddle of blood I know to be a field of poppies just coming into view, we come to the crossroads. I remember the potato-faced taskmaster and I think I hear a scream far away, but I know the bike's too loud and it's only in my head. A faded signpost points west, engraved with the words *The King's Inland Highway*. It's a fancy name for nothing more than a second corridor of corn, but I lean the bike right and leave the farm road behind.

The landscape is nothing if not familiar. Over the sea of corn, a network of silver arms pumps bucket after bucket of water into the air, and I spot rainbow after rainbow hanging in the mist as if they are caught in sticky spider-webs. We ride on, the road bends south, and we move beyond the reach of the silver arms, until the corn ends and the flat fields on either side of the road give way to rolling stretches of twisted brambles. Darius never says a word, but sometimes he points at something interesting, like a truck way out on the horizon, kicking up a grimy cloud behind it. Sometimes I feel his chest rise and fall against my back, and it's a strange comfort.

We drive into the late afternoon, our shadow lengthening beside us, until we come to a place where nothing grows on either side of the road at all. The ground breathes out puffs of dust as we pass. High overhead, birds fly in a thick flock. They must know where there's water somewhere. Down here on the ground, as far as the eye can see, everything is dry.

The asphalt becomes gravel, and the gravel becomes dirt.

I check the battery gauge. The last charging station was miles back near the last of the cornfields, and the needle is floating around an eighth of a charge. We could probably go one more hour before I started to truly panic that the battery might drain before we saw another station.

"The person who drew the map for you," I call over my shoulder. "Could they have been trying to send you to your death?"

"I beat her boyfriend at darts. That's where I got the mackels to buy the map."

So yes, I think. Definitely could have been hoping to send Darius down a long road that led to nothing. "There's a half-full canteen in my bag," I say, and I wonder if we'd be able to push the bike back to that last charging station before nightfall.

I shoot a quick glance over my shoulder, hoping to get an idea of the distance we've come, and I'm surprised to see a vehicle close behind us. It's a little four-seat motorized carriage—more a cart than a carriage, really—with a driver and three passengers. "They've been back there for a while," Darius calls into my ear. "They might be following us."

I want to ask Darius if he has an idea who it might be, but there's no point in trying to have a discussion while the wind is robbing half of our words. So I decide to pull over. If they are following us, we'll soon know.

The bike isn't idling for more than a moment when the little cart pulls to a stop alongside us. It's all open, just a frame without roof or doors, so I know in a moment that two of the passengers are racers, the same two racers we saw in the dance hall. The boy with the tree-trunk arms glares at me, while the woman looks away. Her hair, the color of muddy water, stands straight up from her forehead from the wind.

I recognize the driver as the woman who was trying to take my picture with a fancy camera in Poppee's Dance Hall. No embed, no scar. She was born an Enchanted. She unfolds long legs from under the wheel and climbs out of the carriage. Her camera hangs around her neck. Before I can raise my hands to cover my face, she's snapping my picture.

"Will you stop that!" I say. She lowers the camera, peering over it at me with a quizzical gaze, like I'm a monkey in a zoo who just started screeching. I really don't care if I've hurt her feelings, all I care is that she stops. Her companion—an intensely upright young Enchanted man with an expression far too eager for me to trust—steps out of the passenger seat and strides over like he's about to try to sell us something. Instead he asks, "Why did you stop?"

"You should see it as a favor we're doing you," Darius says. He peers out from under a tightly furrowed brow, and if Darius's looks could be called rugged, they're all the more so in comparison to this elegant man-boy. Darius's voice is low and there's something implied in his tone. Not truly a threat, but a warning. "There are strict rules against lending help to racers." He shoots a look at the backseat of the carriage. The two racers sit watching us, like dutiful children waiting for their parents to return. "The penalties are harsh if you get caught. So really, we're protecting you from your own worst impulses."

"You've got us all wrong," says the man, and if his expression is overeager, it's nothing compared to his voice. "This isn't about our *worst* impulses, it's about our best. We're concerned with the public's right to information. Most Enchanteds have no idea about the horrors of the race. We want to translate the struggles of the racers into words that will come alive on the printed page." My face must be dressed in the blank stare of the truly confused, because he adds, "We're *journalists*." When I still don't know how to respond, he adds, "We're documenting the race."

I shake my head, just the smallest of movements. "Why—"

"*Why* would we take on such a difficult task? *Why* would we risk failure, when failure could result in such dire consequences?"

Listening to him, you'd think *they* were running in the Race of Oblivion. I don't say this, though. Instead I say, "*Why* would anyone want to read that?"

I've forgotten about the long-legged photographer. She sneaks up on the opposite side of me and says my name. "Astrid!" My head turns toward her and her shutter clicks a dozen times.

I want to grab her camera and kick it across this dusty road, but I think better of it. I hold my arms tight to my sides and ask, "How do you know my name?"

"Lots of people know your name, because of what happened at this year's Apple Carnival. I realize you can't remember, but I assumed someone would've told you by now. You were so tragic. That's why everyone's rooting for you. That's why we need to share your story."

"*What* story?" I ask. I remember the words of the fisher I came across on the beach. *It's got to be on account of her father dropping dead like that.*

"It happened at the Apple Carnival," says the man-boy. "The royal family was greeting a few people from the crowd before the parade. The princess was speaking to your father when he collapsed. You tried to help him, but it was too late. Your father died right at your feet."

He keeps talking, but his voice fades to background noise as I repeat these words in my head: *Your father died right at your feet. . . .*

Your father died.

Just like the fisher said.

"I mean, what could be more tragic?" He asks this looking right at me, as if this is a question I could somehow answer.

"Don't be ridiculous," the woman says. "What happened next, with her brother, made it far worse."

She's lowered her camera, so I finally feel safe looking at her. She has the confidence of a woman who is just beyond her girlhood. She wears a white tunic tucked into a short blue skirt, both of which are far too crisp for this heat. Her hair is carefully styled and as short as an Outsider's, and her brown eyes are so wide set, I almost have to shift my focus back and forth to look at them both at once. She possesses an effortless beauty that, for some reason, I associate with money. "Here, I took this one on that day."

She holds out the camera so I can see its small display on the back. It shows an image of a girl. She wears a red dress, and she's leaning over a man who's flat on the ground beside a metal barricade. "Is this me?"

The woman nods. She looks so stricken, I think she

might cry. I feel overwhelmed, looking at this image of a stranger, in perhaps the darkest moment of her life. A stranger, who is me. Darius is looking at the picture, too. I don't have to wonder what he's feeling. Shock radiates out of him. "It doesn't even look like you," he says. He's right, but I know it's me. Maybe not the version of me standing here now, but some version of me.

"And that's your father," she adds, quite unnecessarily. I stare at the face of the man on the ground, and though my mind has no memory of him, my heart does. My chest grows tight, like an invisible band is wrapped around my ribs. I have to pull my eyes away from the image to draw a deep breath.

"What happened with my brother?" I ask. I'm not sure why. I dread the answer, but like with my father, something in my heart clicks into place at the thought of him, even without my memories. "You said what happened with my brother made it even more tragic."

While I wasn't paying attention, the young man retrieved a notebook from the carriage. He's furiously making notes. Like the woman, he is far crisper than this heat should allow, and he radiates a quality only Enchanteds have. The best word I can think of to describe it is *vitality*.

Behind him, the boy with the tree-trunk arms is climbing out of the carriage.

"You tried to help your brother," says the girl. She's

scrolling through images on the camera screen. "But the Authority dragged him away."

"And that's why people are rooting for me?" I ask. But they are both too absorbed—the man in his notes and the woman in her photos—to answer. So instead I say, "Could you show me a photo of my brother?"

The photographer looks up, but it's Tree-Trunk Boy who answers. "Hey now," he says. I had expected a voice as thick as his arms, but it's thin and boyish. "You're giving her too much help—"

"How exactly?" I start, throwing him my most fearsome expression, in hopes of reminding him who bested him in the fight at the lighthouse. "Remember, they were giving you a ride, following us. *That's* help. In what way is it a help to learn about my dead father?"

"I'm more concerned with your not-so-dead brother," the boy sneers. "If you see his picture, couldn't you maybe find him and ask *him* for help?"

I try to work this out in my mind—how I might find my brother with nothing but his face to go on—but I can't ignore the uptick in tension. From beside me, Darius takes a step closer as the woman racer starts to climb out to join us. Her hair still stands up from her weathered face, and she's rubbing her palms on her pants. I wonder if we're destined for another brawl, right here on the King's Inland Highway, and if I'll be able to take the advice of my blocky dance partner and not make it too obvious that I have Cientia.

I have no doubt these journalists would put that in their story, maybe even make it the headline.

"No. No no *no*. Her brother could never help her." The young man wags his pen back and forth, to emphasize his point. "Never," he says again.

My insides churn and my heart races, like I'm riding downhill in a carriage with no brakes. There's no way to stop without crashing. So I brace myself—I'm ready for the crash—but I have to wait for this pen-wagging boy to get around to crashing it. He can see how I'm waiting for it, and he seems quite pleased. "That's the *tragic* detail," he continues. "That's the *poignant* detail that makes Astrid's story so particularly compelling to our readers."

"*What's* the poignant detail?" I'm practically shouting. "Why could my brother never help me?"

I know what he's about to say. He's about to say, *Because your brother is dead.* I'm braced for it. I'm ready.

But I'm wrong. He says the only thing that could possibly be worse.

He says that my brother is in the race.

THIRTEEN

The wind blows hot and dry, raking over my skin like claws. I hadn't noticed, but I notice now. I notice the way I'm standing with my hands in tight fists, my shoulders tense and raised, my breath coming in big gulps. I watch myself like I'm standing outside myself, and to be honest, I look pretty pathetic. But that stops now. I'm sick of being toyed with.

"So my brother, who you say was dragged away by the Authority—"

"Yes. After your father died." This from the boy scribbling in his notebook, but pausing long enough to hold up a finger, like a schoolteacher correcting a child's error. "First your father died. *Then* the Authority dragged your brother away—"

"I got that part!" My eyes drill into him as if to dare him to raise that finger again. "Now you're telling me that *same* brother is in this profane manipulation we're calling a race?"

"Correct," he says.

And then the woman takes my picture.

"Give that to me!" I scream. This time I really will kick her camera across the road, or better yet, run it over with the bike. Her neck is bent at a weird angle because I'm tearing at the camera strap, and she's shrieking, which gives me more satisfaction than it should give a good person.

But I'm not trying to be a good person. I'm trying to win a race, and this woman and her long legs and her fancy camera are getting in my way.

A hand wraps around my forearm and pulls me back. A voice comes from behind me. "Stop messing with her." It's Darius, and he's not talking to me, but to the woman with the camera. I let him pull my hand away. "You've had your fun."

Her wide-set eyes fill with surprise. "I was only . . ." She doesn't finish. Instead, she takes Darius's picture.

The wind blows its claws across my skin again, and I feel something in Darius that's about to erupt. It's the same rage that's boiling up in me. But then a weird cry comes from over by the carriage, one that could come only from an animal, and we all turn. I'm sure that an injured bird has just dropped from the sky.

But it's not an injured bird. It's the female racer. She's

made herself small, crouching over those big shoes that stomped on Darius's hand. The sound comes again, like a dying gull. It makes me queasy.

"Memory sickness," mutters the photographer, and her camera has forgotten me and Darius and is now trained on the woman as she drops over and squirms on the pavement. The man-boy flips his hair from his eyes and opens his notebook to a fresh page. They both crowd the woman so that she's blocked from my view, and I'm thankful.

"Let's go," I say to Darius, my voice low. His eyes are wide, but he gives a short nod. Without another word, we creep to the bike and take off.

I'm shaken, and judging by the look on Darius's face back there, he is, too. I know he's probably thinking of the grotesque noise coming from that racer, and whatever memory sickness is, but I'm full to the top with the thought of some brother of mine in this awful race. I try to imagine someone I love making that climb to the window of the lighthouse, and I feel even more ill than I felt going up that wall myself. I would worry about crashing this bike, if there were anything but blowing dust to crash it into.

The gauge shows the charge is almost spent. I pull to the side of the road and cut the engine.

"Is it dead?" Darius asks. His voice is flat and even, but I can sense he's scared.

"It will be soon."

The sun is gone, obscured by airborne dust. I know I need to figure out if we're closer to the roadhouse or to that last charging station, but all I can think about is whether my brother could survive this long trip south without a motorbike.

While I'm sitting here thinking, a few vehicles come out of the dark cloud behind us and disappear into the even darker one ahead: a large truck, a motorized carriage, a horse-drawn cart, even a motorbike with a sidecar. So *yes*, maybe my brother could make it without a bike, if he found someone willing to give him a ride.

But is he even heading in the right direction? Or is he at Pope's Lake? Or waiting for the bandleader at Poppee's Dance Hall to call out the name of a song Darius paid him not to play?

I would love to tell Darius our deal is off, but first I have a question. "The winner of the Race of Oblivion . . . they get citizenship for their whole family, right? So why would my brother enter the race if I did?"

"They're lying to you," Darius says.

I really don't want to look at him—just the thought of him paying off that bandleader makes me want to slap his face—but this statement can't be ignored. "Who is?"

"Those two back there. *Mr. and Mrs. Arrogance.*"

"You mean the journalists?"

"Yes."

"You think they were lying?"

"People like *that*," he says. He's practically spitting the words, his eyes burning, but then he reins himself in. He goes as still as a cloudless sky, but inside he's a storm. My Cientia senses it. I really must learn to hide my emotions as well as he does. "They're selling something. A story. A photograph. The bigger the drama, the more it sells."

This is something I hadn't considered. "So you think they made up the part about my brother being in the race?"

"Maybe. Or the part about your father—"

"We saw the picture."

"We saw a picture of a girl that looks something like you, bent over a man lying on the ground. That doesn't prove that what they said about the picture is true."

This kind of throws me. It's both a great relief and terrifying, because I don't know what's true, and I'm afraid to hope. How could I dare believe that maybe my father is alive, maybe my brother is not in this horrible race, only to learn again that those things are true?

Sometimes it's safer not to hope.

"We might have enough charge to reach the roadhouse," I say. "We definitely don't have enough charge to go back."

"Then we keep going," Darius says.

The wind is so full of dirt now, I can hear bits of sand spraying against the metal body of the bike. A carriage appears out of the dust, and at first, I worry it's the journalists again, but it's a tiny two-seater with a young woman at the wheel. Her blond hair is pulled back into a no-nonsense ponytail, and she scowls at us. From here, I can't tell if she's an Enchanted or a citizen Outsider, since I can see her only from the chin up, but my Cientia, like her expression, tells me she's conflicted.

"Need help?" she calls. "Is there someone I can contact for you?" She holds up a comm, but I shake my head.

"Battery's nearly dead," I say. "Do you know how far the roadhouse is?"

"The Girl Next Door? Too far to walk. Especially with the weather threatening." She opens her door and puts one foot out. There's fear in her. "Look, I can see you're racers, but . . ." She glances back the way she came, shading her eyes with her hand, but visibility is horrible. "I'll take you as far as the roadhouse. I can only manage one, with the room I have. So, sir, I'm sorry, but she'll need to find a way to come back to get you."

Definitely a citizen Outsider. No Enchanted would refer to a racer as *sir*.

I must stand staring at her a bit too long, because she raises her voice. "Look, there's a storm coming. Tornadoes. When the wind pulls the sand from the ground like this, it's a sign. They might hit, they might not, but I don't want to read about two dead racers in the paper tomorrow, knowing I could've helped."

Storm coming. Something about those words makes the

hairs on my arms stand up. "Astrid, take the ride," Darius growls into my ear.

"And give *you* the bike? What if the charge lasts and it makes it all the way to the roadhouse? You'll just claim I gave it up and it's yours—"

"That wasn't even on my mind, and with a storm threatening, and an offer of a ride, it shouldn't be on your mind either—"

"So you're saying you wouldn't keep the bike if it made it—"

"I didn't say *that*."

A rumble rolls across the sky from back toward Hedge, and we all look up. But still, I don't move. The woman closes the carriage door. "If you're not coming—"

"She's coming," Darius says. He folds his arms across his chest and takes a step back from me. "Astrid, go."

"Promise me you won't keep the bike if it makes it there."

"Promise *you*? I should be making *you* promise *me* to come back for me if it *doesn't* make it."

I hesitate. "I'll promise if you'll promise."

Darius shakes his head. "Whatever your life was before this race, it's made you tough."

"Is that a compliment?"

"It is."

"Well, save it. I'm looking for a promise, not a compliment."

Thunder rolls down from the north again. The woman calls from her carriage, "Are you coming or not?"

"One second!" I call over my shoulder to her. I open my bag and pull out the canteen.

"Here's my promise," says Darius. "You take the ride, and I'll bring the bike. If it makes it, it's still yours. But if it doesn't make it, you need to promise to come back for me somehow."

"All right. I promise," I say. I hand him the canteen and he takes a drink.

"Then let me keep this for now," he says. "That way I'll know you really mean to come back for me."

"Thanks for the trust," I say. I take a long drink from the canteen, but I put it back in his hands before I stomp off to the passenger side of the carriage and climb in. I look out the window at him, though I'm not sure what I'm hoping for. A wave goodbye? He's already straddling the bike, and then the carriage pulls away. But before we're even a half a mile down the road Darius speeds past, disappearing into the dust.

This little carriage doesn't have much power, and the ride to the roadhouse drags on and on. My driver doesn't seem to recognize me, and I'm relieved. She talks about her dog, telling me some long-winded story of how it once saved her life, but I don't hear a word. Instead, I run through a million scenarios in my mind.

Darius tampered with the gauge, and the bike wasn't even low on charge.

The roadhouse was never the checkpoint at all, but he led me here to ditch me and take the bike.

I even have a conspiracy theory: *he's doubled back to meet up with the journalists and the other racers, and they are all long gone, drinking from my canteen and laughing at me as they go.*

But then my driver points at something ahead. "There it is, on the left," she says.

A sign swings on a hinge above the road, and behind it, a low brick building—probably originally red but soot black now—squats against the dust. Beside the building, I spot a row of charging pods.

As we come closer, I manage to make out the lettering on the sign through the grit the wind lifts from the road. *The Girl Next Door.*

She pulls the carriage to a stop beside the bike, which is parked near the front door. Darius stands next to it, tossing and catching the key, waiting for me.

FOURTEEN

My first thought when we walk through the door of the roadhouse is how difficult it will be to find the clue in here, it's so dark. I can't make out a single feature in the room except the scattered pulsing red lights of embers, so I know there are Outsiders in here, if I know nothing else. And a band, because I can hear the music.

This band could not be more different from the band at the dance hall. They sound neither hot nor cool, but warm. The darkness in this room wraps around me, and it makes me homesick, even though I can't remember home. I want to remember, and I try to let one familiar thing float to the top of the dark lake in my mind's eye, but then a barwoman calls out, "What can I get you?" and I'm reminded again of the one thing I know: I'm a racer.

I stiffen. Behind me, Darius says into my ear, "Answer the woman."

"Money isn't one of the things I have going for me," I say under my breath.

Darius leans forward and speaks over my shoulder. "Two corn vodkas, please." She responds with a crisp nod, but she doesn't move. The blood seeping through the shoulders of my dress has caught her attention.

Dirty, blood-soaked dress. Tangled, dust-caked hair. I must be a sight. Her mouth tenses at the corners, and I think she's about to tell me I'll need to leave—maybe tell us both we need to leave since we don't even have shoes—but instead she asks my name.

My heart hiccups in my chest. "Who's asking?" I say, sweeping the room with my gaze. "Are there Authority guards here?"

"No," she says with a quiet laugh, as if the question is silly. "And *I'm* the one asking." Her smile is warm, but not enough to put me at ease. I take in her floral tunic, her clean, strawberry blond hair, the delicate outlines of three tiny stars tattooed in black ink across her left cheekbone. She leans toward me, the craning of her neck distorting the scar at the base of her throat where an embed once was—a scar that declares that she's a citizen Outsider. She asks her next question in a conspiratorial tone. "Are you Astrid?"

I nod.

"I've seen your picture. People are talking about you." Then, when she sees me flinch, she adds, "Just people, not

Authority guards. Not yet, at least."

A young Enchanted woman, with bloodred hair piled up on her head and a look of disdain on her face, steps up to the bar. The barwoman cuts off the conversation and turns to wait on her.

"I'll take the key to the bike now," I say, and even in this dim light, I can see Darius roll his eyes.

"Fine." He drops the key into my hand.

"And the canteen," I add.

"Just you remember," he murmurs as he hands me the canteen, "you stole this water. You stole that bike. They do *not* belong to you. I could've thrown you off the bike and taken it from you at any time."

"So why didn't you?"

He pauses before answering. "Sometimes it's more effective to work as a team."

"Careful," I say, smirking. "There's only one winner." I try to force a laugh, but I can't, not even as I throw Darius's words back in his face. After all, it's true that only one person wins, and there's no guarantee it will be one of us.

I glance around, torn between the need to find the clue and the need to do it without Darius finding it, too. My eyes land on a trio—two men and a woman—in the corner. Like us, their embeds have been cut out. Also like us, they're dirty from head to foot. "Do you recognize them?" Darius asks.

"Two of them, I do," I say. "The woman . . . I remember

her from the lighthouse." My eyes shift to the two males, and my mouth goes dry. Inside my chest, there's a buzzing instead of a beating, like there's a knot of frantic bees where my heart should be. "The ginger-haired man you should know yourself—he was one of the trio who jumped you," I say. My eyes work over the other man—a boy, really, maybe fifteen or sixteen years old. This is the boy who blocked my way in the middle of the street in Hedge. "I don't know the third one—the boy. He's a stranger."

This is all I say. But this is not all I'm thinking.

What I'm thinking is: *Could it be true that my brother is in the race? And if it is true, could one of those two boys be my brother?*

If I believe the picture of the wavy-haired girl on the photographer's camera is me, then the ginger-haired racer is a paler version of me.

So. Possibly my brother.

The other boy reminds me of a cornered animal—black-haired and slump-shouldered, his eyes never leave the door. I can't quite decide if he's cowering or if he's ready to bolt. Maybe he can't decide, either. "The boy seems nervous," I say. "Maybe the other two threatened him—forced him to take them this far."

The barwoman returns. "See if these fit," she says, handing a pair of thong sandals to Darius. He slides them onto his dirty feet. His heels hang over the edge of the soles a bit, but they'll do.

"Thank you." Darius meets her gaze. "It's a relief not to be asked to leave."

"We get racers in here every year. I'm not supposed to help, but what's a pair of shoes some drunk left behind, right?" Darius smiles at her and she smiles back, the line of stars on her cheekbone pulling up toward her ear. It's dark in here, but I think she blushes.

This provokes me a bit, and I can't help but study Darius's face like it's something I need to solve. It'd be dishonest to say he's not attractive. The truth is he's quite attractive, but I'm surprised the barwoman can tell through all the dirt and bruises. He's certainly a mess. I stare at a ridge of dried blood right beneath his bruised right eye, until I notice he sees me staring. He looks like he's waiting for me to say something.

I just say, "You should wash your face."

"Let me get you that corn vodka," the bartender says. "If you want to clean up, there are restrooms near the door. I'll take Astrid with me to find some shoes that will fit her."

She leads me through a cluster of tables where people sit watching the band, stopping at a doorway in the rear wall to pull out a key. From here I can see into a small side room where another stage overlooks rows of empty chairs. There's a furnace in the corner in need of cleaning. Grime coats the walls. At least a dozen Enchanteds are lined up at the door. "There's a tournament tonight," says a figure beside me. It's a white-haired Enchanted man, with his tunic too tight for his rain barrel body. "You're a racer, right? Well, make sure you stay out of the way. It'll get quite rowdy in here before long."

"Hearts and Hands," the barwoman adds, filling in the blanks she must see on my face. "It's a sport."

"That much I remember," I say.

"Of course you remember," the man snaps. "Oblivion may cause amnesia, but it leaves you with memories of your culture and your people, right? So of course you remember Hearts and Hands! It's tradition!"

"It's bloody," the barwoman adds.

"Ah, but the blood isn't what it's all about," says the rain barrel. "It's about the fighter who feels the jab before it's thrown. Who ducks before his opponent's foot leaves the mat." He leans close to me. He's very drunk. "*Magic* is what it's about."

I take a step back. Has he heard rumors that I fight like I have Cientia? Is that why he's talking to me about Hearts and Hands? And if he's heard it, has the Authority heard it, too? I tell myself I'm overreacting, that he's just making conversation, but I can't help but look around, making sure Authority guards aren't in here looking for me.

Just at that moment, the black-haired boy from the trio of racers wanders by, searching for the clue, I'm sure. Nerves flutter in the pit of my stomach, and not just because I need to find the clue before he does. I can't stop myself from grabbing his arm when he steps near. He springs back like a startled rabbit. "Are you all right?" I ask, voice low.

His eyes narrow. "Are you all right?"

"What?" I can only guess this is sarcasm—throwing my words back in my face like this—and it hits me like a slap. I have to ball my hands into fists at my sides to keep from actually slapping him back. I never should've said anything, but he looked so much like a victim. Looks can be deceiving, clearly, and now I've made a fool of myself by showing concern. "Those people you are traveling with are violent," I growl, furious at both him and myself. "You be careful."

"You be careful," he says.

The urge to slap him returns, but thankfully, the bartender has just unlocked the door and she's ushering me through. We climb a short set of stairs and step into a small bedroom, and I'm able to shrug off my anger at the smart-mouthed boy. "This is my place," she says.

"You live here?"

"I do."

The room is small but lovely. I'm not sure what it is about the brightly lit space, the flouncy curtains, and the neatly made bed, but tears come to my eyes. Could it be the simple fact that a room like this seems like a luxury beyond my imagination, after just one day in the Race of Oblivion? No matter what the cause of my reaction, I tamp it down, swiping at my eyes before I really make a fool of myself.

"What do I have that would fit you?" She opens a small closet door, revealing a handful of dresses on hangers.

"I couldn't. I can't—"

"Please. I want you to wear one. I saw your back. . . ."

I drop my gaze to the floor. I can't look at the pretty dresses or the face of the girl who's kind enough to offer one to me. "They're your own possessions. I couldn't—"

The barwoman sets a hand to my chin and lifts my face. I pull away. I don't like strangers touching me, even generous ones. "I'm sorry. I don't know what you're saying if you don't look at me. I'm deaf. I can only understand you if I read your lips."

"I don't understand," I say, but what I really mean is, *That can't be true.* She's heard everything I've said, all this time. But then I replay all our interactions in my head, and I realize I've looked her in the eye every time I spoke until now. "How?"

"It's not easy," she says. "Except for drink orders and other common questions I get, it can be quite difficult to read a stranger's speech. Fortunately, you don't speak too fast, which helps."

"I'm glad," I say, "But what I meant was, how did you become deaf?"

"Oh," she says, smiling and shaking her head at the misunderstanding. "Battery factory. Indentured there since I was twelve. They used an auditory form of Projectura to control us—a sound that caused all kinds of pain to our ears. Over time, my hearing went away, but so did the power of the Projectura against me. Until one day, I could no longer hear at all. And they could no longer control me. That was the end of my time at that battery factory." Her eyes flick over my face. "Don't feel sorry for me," she says, and I close my mouth. I stop trying to find words. "I was lucky. The manager here, Emmeline, needed some help."

"I thought *you* were the manager," I say, wincing when I feel the way my mouth exaggerates the shapes of the words.

"No, I'm just Mary," she says. "But Emmeline's been very good to me—she paid off my indenture. We grew up together. My mother was indentured to her mother." She turns around and pulls a pale gray dress from the closet. "How about you wash up, and then you can try this one?"

"I don't have time—"

"You do if you hurry. Bathroom's through there."

I'm so miserable in this filthy dress, I can't refuse. The wounds I opened up fighting at the lighthouse have started to throb, and I can't help but worry about infection. While I do a quick wash of my hair and face in the tiny sink, Mary runs a towel under warm water in the tub. The mirror steams up. She presses the damp towel against the back of my dress until the fabric peels away from my skin without ripping open the wounds.

Once I've pulled on the gray dress, Mary wipes the steam from the mirror with her sleeve so I can see my reflection. A stranger looks back at me. I look more like the girl in the photo now, with skin that glows and hair that's almost glossy. But when Mary combs my bangs out of my eyes and adds a silver clip to hold them in place, I shake my head.

"It's beautiful, but I can't accept it—"

"Take it." Mary stands behind me, looking at both our reflections in the mirror. She reaches over me and straightens the clip with her fingers. "It's not expensive, but it makes you look like a million mackels. We've both suffered, right?" She touches my back lightly through the dress, then points to her own ear. "We're in the same family. You must take it."

After Mary finds me a pair of flat black sandals that are a little big on me but fit better when we adjust the straps, she leads me back downstairs.

I see Darius before he sees me. He has finished his corn vodka and is watching the band. But then the light pouring through the open door catches his attention and he turns in my direction.

I try to read his expression, but it hardly changes. A rapid flutter of his eyelids, a hard swallow. If he has an opinion of the change in me, he doesn't let it show. At least not on his face.

But when I walk to his side, his emotions wash over me

like a sudden hard rain. His gaze moves to the dress, then back to my face, but I might not suspect a thing if I didn't have Cientia. But I do, and it gives him away. His reaction is cool and moist, clinging to him like dewdrops on a leaf.

Desire.

FIFTEEN

As I walk up beside Darius, feeling like a clean coin in a filthy pocket, I curse the heat that's flooding up my neck, and I remind myself he doesn't have Cientia. He hands me my corn vodka, and I am so happy to have a reason to look away from him.

It's as clear as water, but the smell hits me before the taste, reminding me not to gulp it. The first sip burns my throat, forcing a cough and a wince before I can set it back on the bar. When I look up, both Darius and Mary are grinning at me. "What were you expecting, lemonade?" Darius asks. Mary reaches for the glass, but I pick it up again.

"I like it," I say, and Darius actually laughs out loud.

"You don't act like you like it," he says.

"Well, you don't act like you like me."

"Who says I do?" He raises an eyebrow at me, but I turn away, scanning the room for anything that might suggest a clue, and downing the rest of my drink to make a point.

The place is filling up, and the line at the door of the back room is getting long. I don't like the crowd. The more people to see around, the harder it will be to find the clue. "There's a Hearts and Hands tournament happening soon—"

"I heard," I say. The other three racers are still at their table. They couldn't have found the clue yet, either.

So maybe it's in that back room.

The roadhouse's front door keeps swinging open and closed, brightening the room with intermittent light. When the back room finally opens for seating, Darius and I move to the doorway, where, standing, we manage a view of both the stage and the main barroom. "Excuse me, *miss*," someone says as an elbow digs into my ribs. It's an Enchanted woman pushing in from behind me, with a voice like the bottom of an ashtray.

People stand six deep behind the chairs, and closer to the stage Enchanteds jostle and shove for the best view. They are loud—some seem to have arrived drunk—so I pull my feet back to protect my toes and return to studying the menu for any hint of the clue. Mary comes over and asks us if we'd like to place another order. While she has our attention, she nods toward the bar. There, occupying the same two barstools where Darius and I sat, are the big-voiced woman and the tree-trunk boy, along with their escorts, the journalists. Mr. and Mrs. Arrogance, as Darius called them. "Another came in behind them, but separately," Mary says, a little too loudly.

Darius nods at a fair-haired woman leaning on a stool in the corner. "Know her?" he asks me.

I shake my head, but she's a racer. Filthy from head to toe, with a fresh scar where her embed should be. She's anxious—her small dark eyes never stop moving.

The only other thing worth noting is that she is wearing a coat. I notice this because, though it's far too hot for one right now, a cold night is coming. I hope I don't come to envy her that coat.

Darius leans forward and says something right into my ear, but I don't hear it. It's buried under the shouts of the crowd that turn both our heads around. The first two fighters are making their way to the stage.

The first is a bruiser of a man—not tall but as wide as a bull, with a bald head covered in tattoos of silver and gold ink. His eyes sweep the front of the crowd and a hush falls over them at the sight of him. Something like fear—no, not fear . . . *respect*—washes from the front rows and flows to the back. Murmured whispers replace the shouts.

When his opponent enters, his appearance prompts a few gasps but even more groans. He is a foot taller than the first contestant and stripped from the waist up; his muscles appear to be straining against his skin, as if it shrunk in the bath and can no longer contain him. Every vein in his arms and chest bulges, and even from my spot against the door I can see a heartbeat pounding in his neck, beneath a curtain of wavy black hair. The first man seems as diminished as a mouse in the presence of a snake.

A woman climbs onto the stage—a girl really, no older than I am—dressed in a bright green leotard, with bare feet and a face painted silver like the moon. Her lips are bright pink and her eyes are ringed in black. She stands between the two men, holding each at arm's length. The room falls silent, every eye strains forward, and she counts down: *Five . . . four . . . three . . .* When she gets to *one*, she leaps into the air and flips backward, artfully removing herself from danger and drawing scattered applause.

The big man lunges forward almost immediately, but his opponent is already moving, so quickly he's dodged him before the big man takes a step. The smaller man's Cientia anticipated that lunge. I anticipated it, too, and now I feel the big man's intention again—I see his foot leaving the stage's wooden planks, feel the swish of his hair as he turns to throw a roundhouse kick. I brace myself as if I were the first man, waiting for the blow to come. My hands fly up to cover my own face. *Block*, I whisper into my balled fists. But even though I feel it coming, the first man doesn't, and the kick lands squarely against his jaw.

Blood flies from his mouth, splattering the front row of

spectators. A roar goes up like the growl of a wild animal. The sound repeats, repeats, repeats again, until I recognize the word they are all calling out: *more*.

The moves don't slow. The big man tries a second kick, this time blocked. A jab by the smaller man to the big man's chin sends him wobbling. A second blow sends teeth clattering against the back wall, followed by a spray of red. A high kick to the side of his head knocks him to the floorboards.

The big man gets back to his feet, sways as if drunk, and tumbles from the stage into the gap in front of the first row of seats. Everyone is on their feet and I can't see him as he falls, but a sickening crack announces his head's collision with the stone floor.

He stays down. The green-clad harlequin bounces onto the stage to raise the hand of the first man as the crowd erupts in chaos. Some cheer, some call out for a chance to fight the winner, and a handful hurry toward the door, maybe hoping to cash in their bets, or perhaps to avoid the bookmaker altogether.

As the crowd churns, I watch the young harlequin regain their attention with a bright white towel. I'm angry with myself, because I'm so sucked in by the spectacle, I'm worried I'm missing something crucial to the clue. I vow to drag my attention away, but she runs her towel across the back wall, cleaning away blood and a layer of grime. When she shows it to the crowd again, black with a few flecks of red, they hiss in reply. A woman in the audience climbs onto a chair and shouts, "More blood!" before the chair collapses and she disappears behind the broad backs of the men. The harlequin nods and bows, applauding the audience in return.

Then she somersaults from the stage, and I stare at the suddenly clean back wall, noticing a carved wooden sign that had been too smeared with soot to be seen before. At one end, something like a train depot is engraved, beside what appear to be tracks. A line connects it to an engraving of a squat little box of a building—the roadhouse. The line continues, running along the length of the sign to an engraving of the lighthouse on the far right.

Over each building, a star is engraved.

A star I've seen before.

I've seen it on the map to the lighthouse, the one I found when I woke up. The map is tucked inside my bag, which rests on the floor against my ankle.

But Darius's map is already open in his hands. And there it is. "The star above the lighthouse," I whisper. He nods. It's identical to the stars that mark the buildings on the sign behind the stage.

Glancing over his shoulder, he folds the map and slides it back into his pocket. "That's it, right? The lighthouse . . . the roadhouse. Whatever that third building is—that's our next checkpoint."

The band is still going, but like most of the people in here, they've gotten louder and slower as the afternoon turned into evening. We find Mary behind the bar. The two racers with Mr. and Mrs. Arrogance aren't far away, but I don't need to ask my question out loud. Instead I mouth it to Mary, knowing she can read my lips.

The sign above the stage in the back room. What's the building on the opposite end from the lighthouse?

She leans in so we can hear her over the music. "The outpost. It's at the start of the cross-desert railroad. The roadhouse is the center point between the lighthouse and the outpost. That's why everyone stops here when they're traveling."

I can't help but reach around Mary's shoulders and pull her into an awkward hug, then immediately regret it. If another racer is watching, they might wonder what I'm grateful for. Maybe they'll assume it's the clean clothes and not the clue. In any event, Darius and I can't leave just yet. We can't make it obvious the clue is in the back room.

Darius pulls the wad of money from his pocket and peels off another fifty-mackel note. "Astrid has a canteen in her bag, and it would mean the world to us if you could fill it with water from the tap without anyone noticing."

Mary nods, and I hand her the bag.

"So our deal," I whisper to Darius once she's gone, "was to share the bike this far."

"You can't ditch me here," he says. But the anxiety in his voice makes it clear he knows that I certainly can. "We both found that clue at the same time—"

"What does that have to do with anything? We both found the clue, and now we're both free to travel to the outpost—"

"And the dead battery? How are you going to pay to use the charging pods?"

I hadn't considered this, and the realization that I again need to depend on Darius, especially after making it clear that I was ready to move on without him, forces my teeth together in a tight clench. But it's not a concession, I tell myself. It's simply a new bargain. "So you'll pay to charge the bike, and that will get you a ride as far as the outpost," I say. I want the terms to be clear, so he doesn't expect any more than I'm willing to give.

When Mary comes back with my bag, it looks the same but it's heavier.

"We'll have two more corn vodkas." Darius smiles and slides the fifty-mackel bill across the bar to her. "And you can keep the change."

I feel the shimmer of shock in Mary. "You should keep your money—"

"We have enough," he says. "And we don't want to be in anyone's debt." He glances sideways at me, so quick I almost wonder if I imagined it.

Mary tucks the bill into the pocket of her black apron.

Neither of us drinks our vodka. We just wait. When the crowd in the back room is in full swing again, I notice three of the racers in the room—the woman who stomped on Darius's hand, tree-trunk boy, and the woman who came in alone—move to the doorway, drawn to the chaos.

Perhaps it's their intention to watch the matches. Perhaps it's their intention to search for the clue. It doesn't matter. We're out of time, and Darius and I need to leave.

Darius leans over the bar toward Mary. "Who do we pay to use the charging pods?" he asks.

"They're dead," she answers, and my heart drops into my stomach. "The charging truck is late—it should've been here yesterday. He may be here tomorrow. . . ."

I shake my head.

"Too late," Darius says. All at once I feel anxiety spike in him. He takes a swig from his corn vodka and leaves.

"Thank you," I say. I touch the hair clip and she nods at me, but then I turn and hurry to the door. I don't know what Darius is planning, and I suddenly fear that I'm the one who's going to be ditched.

In the lot, I find Darius tugging on a battery from another bike—one with a sidecar attached. "The charge is almost full," he says. "They must've stopped at that last station—"

Before he can finish, a man comes out the front door, first walking, then running when he realizes what Darius is doing. It's the ginger-haired racer who punched him in the eye, the one Darius spit on. His face goes red like a fuse ready to blow. He grabs Darius by the shirt with both hands, throwing him into the road so hard, Darius sprawls across the ground.

I missed it. The sense of his intention . . . I hadn't felt him coming. Maybe because he came from inside. Maybe because Darius's anxiety was overwhelming me.

But that first move is the only one I miss.

While he waits for Darius to get to his feet, I grab him by both arms from behind. I catch him off guard, but he's much bigger and stronger than I am, and he shakes me loose with little effort. He turns, towering over me. "The little magician," he says.

I see Darius behind him, running back to the bike to get the battery. I keep the guy occupied, dodging and ducking while I watch Darius pull the battery free. I land one strong kick to the racer's chest, and it slows him. I land a second one, and it almost knocks him down. Darius struggles a bit to connect the battery to our bike, and I don't know if it's because I'm distracted, but I lose some of my speed, and the ginger-haired racer lands a blow to the side of my head.

I stagger back, almost tripping over my own feet. My vision goes black just for a moment, but it's a moment too long. He follows up with a second swing to the same spot, and my legs crumple under me. My palms and knees scrape raw when I hit the ground.

The bike pulls up beside me, but before I can get to my feet, the ginger-haired racer climbs on behind Darius. I'm still struggling to get up when the bike takes off, disappearing into the dust that obscures the road.

SIXTEEN

I may have worried I was being played when Darius passed me on the road on the bike earlier, but it's nothing compared to how I feel now. Did they conspire to steal the bike from me? How did Darius know that this time, the ginger-haired racer would beat me? I'm still standing on the road outside the Girl Next Door, wondering where I'm going to get a ride, when I hear an engine coming toward me through the dust. I think I recognize its sound, but visibility is so poor, he's almost right in front of me before I know for certain it's Darius, returning on the bike alone.

"Get on," he says. "While I'm still in the mood to share the bike."

I'm not sure if he truly believes the bike belongs to him now, or if he just thinks he's funny. Either way, he's wrong, but I'm not about to argue with him about it. I climb on and Darius speeds away. We don't get far before we pass the other racer along the side of the road, but we're going too fast for me to see the look on his face, which is a shame.

We fly into the darkening night, the air losing the heat of day, the wind chilling me as it ripples over the clean gray dress. An occasional vehicle passes, mostly trucks headed inland like us, so big and dark I can't see who's inside. It isn't long before the sun sets completely, and we seem to be the only travelers left on the road. I begin to hope that we've passed the halfway point between the roadhouse and the outpost.

Before I can ask Darius what he thinks, the bike stalls. We coast to a silent stop.

Darius turns. It's so dark, his hazel eyes are a flat gray. "Battery's dead," he says. "That's as far as the bike goes."

I climb off the back and walk in a slow circle. The wind is blowing hard, rippling my dress like a flag and carrying waves of black sand across the road. Well, what I think is the road. With the headlight dead, it's hard to tell. A sickle moon is just clearing the horizon, and the little bit of light it gives reveals a nightmare landscape. In every direction, emptiness stretches. As far as the eye can see.

We don't say much to each other. We just start walking. I know we won't survive long out here if the temperature keeps falling, and I'm sure Darius knows it, too, so what's there to say?

It's hard to know how long we walk, but I watch the

moon rise high over gray ground. Sand fills the spaces between the straps of Mary's sandals as I trudge forward, and it rubs my feet raw. My skin, numbed long ago by the cold wind, begins to burn at the tips of my fingers, toes, and nose.

"I'm tired," I say. "Maybe we should sit down and rest, try to huddle together to keep warm."

"If we sit down now," Darius says, "I doubt we will ever get up again. We'll die before the sun comes up—"

"And you think shuffling forward into the wind is going to keep us alive?"

"I think walking is going to get us to the outpost."

"Not at this rate," I snap. I decide to run, in part to warm up and in part to leave him behind, but my body won't cooperate. I stumble forward, my legs as heavy as if they were knee-deep in syrup. When I slow to a walk again, I haven't gotten more than a few yards ahead of Darius. I stop and let him catch up, and thankfully, he lets the whole thing go without comment.

After a long stretch of silence between us, Darius grabs my arm. He points to a spot in the road, and I see her too—a woman sitting on the ground. She sits perfectly still, facing away from us, her outline barely visible in the thin moonlight.

"Hey, are you all right?" Darius hurries ahead of me, but I know why she doesn't reply. I feel nothing from her—no fear, no startle, no relief when Darius lays a hand on her shoulder.

He doesn't look at me when I catch up. "She's dead."

The woman is an Outsider. Her eyes are closed but her mouth is open, as if she fell asleep in the midst of saying something.

"She's a racer," I say. "The one who came into the road-house alone." I recognize her by the coat she's wearing. I worried I would envy it. Turns out I do. "She must've been in one of the trucks that passed us earlier."

"Maybe she was a stowaway and got caught—"

"But if that's right, she froze to death pretty quick. She couldn't have been out here any longer than we have—"

"No, but look at her," Darius says. "She's old . . . too old to be a racer. Someone's grandmother, maybe. I bet she had a bad heart. . . ."

He's right. What I'd taken for fair hair under the lights at the roadhouse, I see now is gray.

I'm glad Darius doesn't say anything more. I feel tears coming. I'm holding them back, but I swear if he says one more word about this old lady's heart they will pour down my face, and I don't want them to freeze on my cheeks.

She looks more asleep than dead. I picture her sitting down right in the middle of the road when she got too weak and too tired to keep going. Sitting down to wait for someone to come along and help her. Her mouth is open just enough to reveal a crooked tooth that juts into her bottom lip. I imagine she hated that tooth. I wonder if it showed when she smiled. "Someone must've passed her. But no one stopped."

"Too big a risk to help a racer, I guess."

I remember the Outsider farmworkers in the back of the truck. The way some tried to help me, while others tried to warn them not to. "Would you have helped her?" I ask.

Darius still doesn't look up or speak, but he nods.

My thoughts turn a sharp corner and alight on the small baggie of Oblivion tucked into the pocket of my bag. It would be so nice to take it out and hold it in the palm of my hand, bright white and clean. It would glow silver in this moonlight, I bet. *If I snorted a bit of that Oblivion now, what would I lose?* I wouldn't remember Darius. I wouldn't remember how we got here. I wouldn't remember Mary or the motorbike or anything that happened at the roadhouse. *And what would I gain?* A feeling of well-being. A feeling of strength. The belief—however fleeting—that I would live to see tomorrow.

And I could forget this woman, sitting dead in the road.

"I'm taking her coat," I say.

I don't know what I expect from Darius—if I expect condemnation or maybe a fight to have the coat himself—but instead, he helps me remove it from her body. I'm glad to have the help, because touching her is enough to fill my mouth with the taste of hot bile. She's as cold as ice but not yet stiff. She couldn't have been sitting here dead for very long. When we jostle her, her head snaps backward and her mouth falls open. Her tongue is dry and pale.

As cold as I am, I have to turn away from her before I can slide my arms into the coat. My hands burrow deep into the pockets and I immediately feel some tiny measure of warmth. It gives me a twinge of guilt, since Darius saw her first, so I say, "I'll warm up a bit, and then you can take a turn with the coat later."

Darius doesn't respond. Probably thinking we won't have a *later* to worry about.

I button the coat all the way up to my throat and shrug the straps of my bag onto my shoulders. Darius drags the dead woman's body to the base of the dunes beside the road. I'm not sure why but I don't ask. The wind shifts direction. A gust comes from our right, carrying a blast of sand across the dunes, and something else.

Boredom. Restlessness. And some other feeling. Something I can't place because it's being carried from too far away. But it's there. At least for a moment, until it's scattered with the blowing sand. Even inside the coat a sudden chill makes my body shudder, not from the cold but from the haunted feeling of other people where there shouldn't be anyone around.

I stop walking and turn in place. "I *felt* something."

"What kind of something?" Darius says, but it comes out like *Wha kind ov sussing*.

My heart skips. "Are you all right?"

"I'm fine," he says, scrubbing his face with his hands. "*What kind of something*," he repeats, and this time he pronounces it slowly and deliberately, the way I spoke when I learned that Mary was reading my lips.

"The kind of something I feel when people are around."

Darius's head finally snaps up. His eyes are as wide as a bullfrog's. "What do you mean?"

I swallow. I may know I have Cientia, but I've never said it out loud. "You remember what those racers said about me, when I fought them off at the lighthouse?"

"That you can use Enchanted magic?"

I nod.

"Are you saying they were *right*?"

I bite my lip and nod again.

"But how . . ." Darius holds my eyes with his. I feel confusion in him, but then he looks away and shakes his head. "Never mind. You can tell me later." He looks around. "Where did this feeling of people come from?"

I point over the ridges of sand that fence us in on the right, and Darius starts out, leaving the road behind him and climbing up and over the uneven drifts. The wind pummels him, the sand shifts under his feet, and he struggles with every step. Still, he presses forward, until he turns and sees me with my feet still planted on the road. "What?"

"I'm *scared*, that's what. You think it's smart to leave the road—the only place we at least have a tiny hope of being found—and walk straight into the dark across empty sand?"

"If you really felt people, there must be shelter. Or a vehicle."

I can't see his expression in the dark, but I can feel his trust: a small vibration, like a heartbeat. His trust terrifies me. I don't know if I deserve it. At the Hearts and Hands match, I felt so sure of the strength of my Cientia, but now all that I feel is fear.

But then the wind gusts again, and it's there—the boredom, the restlessness, and the third emotion I couldn't get before: resentment. "I just felt it again," I say, "stronger this time."

Without another word—why waste the strength?—I catch up to Darius. Together, we trek out over the ridges of sand, putting the road behind us.

Farther and farther behind us.

We walk so long without seeing anything, I become convinced I've got it wrong. The emotions still wash over me in sporadic waves, but the endless, unbroken sand is hard to argue with. There is nothing out here. At the crest of every ridge, the view ahead reveals a broader stretch of the Black Desert. What if the wind is blowing in circles? What if the people I feel are actually behind us?

But then we climb yet another ridge—it might be the tenth or it might be the thousandth—and in the distant sky a blinking light glows red. An electrical tower. And at its base, lights glow in the windows of a guardhouse.

If we could run, we would run. As we are, we stumble toward the small building as if it were a palace. The lamplight in the windows glows a golden yellow. If heat were visible, this is what it would look like.

It takes all my effort not to storm right through the front door, but I know we wouldn't be welcome. Instead, we duck down so we can't be seen by anyone looking out, and we approach from the side of the building where a hulking sandcrawler is parked. The sides of the truck are so broad and high, they block the blowing sand. While I crouch beside the huge belt, Darius tries the driver's door. It opens, and without a word we both climb into the cab.

It's not heated, but just getting out of the wind is unbelievably good.

Darius searches for the keys. When he fails to find them I push up against him. "We can share the coat," I say, and his arms slide under it while we both huddle behind the steering wheel. I'm tucked up tight under his chin. His teeth chatter so hard I feel like a jackhammer is trying to break through my skull. "Are you all right?"

He's silent, but I notice his head bounce against mine as he nods. I notice his arms around me. I notice his breath in my hair. I notice the fear pouring off him, as cold as his hands on my waist, even through the fabric of Mary's dress. I notice so many things that I notice nothing.

"I'll be all right," he says finally. "Warming up is almost worse than staying cold. Like there's ice cracking inside my bones."

At first Darius gives off nothing but cold fear, but as his shivering slows, I notice a bit of hope, subtle in the air around us, like the scent of tea leaves steeping in hot water. It's so inviting, I almost dare to hope too. "This truck won't be enough to save us," I say. I look down at my toes, wondering if they'll be black by morning. Wondering if I'll be alive in the morning to see them. "Not unless it's running. We've got to get the keys." When he doesn't say anything to that, I add, "Three. There're three people inside. I think it's three, at least."

"Probably guards," Darius says. "This is a guardhouse, right? They're here to keep this tower secure."

I pull back from Darius. I need room to think. "What if the tower suddenly became *insecure*? Would the guards leave the station to investigate?"

"You're thinking about sabotage—"

"Just enough to draw them out."

Darius nods, grunts, "All right," and turns away to rummage through a metal box of tools in the backseat.

I stare through the film of dust that coats the windshield,

thinking about how hard it will be to step back out into the cold to save ourselves. It's so much easier to pretend you're safe than to admit you're not and keep fighting.

Darius pulls a heavy wrench from the backseat. "This could do some damage," he says.

Then we're back out in the wind, climbing a ladder that leads straight up through the center of the tower toward the stars. The sky is cloudless, covered in a blanket of stars so thick it reminds me of snow. I barely noticed the stars until now, I've been so focused on what's been happening on the ground. Even now, I can't really appreciate the stars, so beautiful against the blue-black sky, they make me want to live to see them another night. A growing part of me wishes I could stop striving for life and lie down and die, so the beauty of the stars only stokes my anger, to be honest.

Stars are for people safe enough to enjoy them.

I force myself to stop thinking about stars and concentrate on the climb. In the light, it would be perilous. In the dark, it should be impossible. The steps are no more than narrow rungs, and the wind gusts so hard I worry it could blow me right off the ladder.

The higher we climb, the sicker I feel.

About every ten feet, we pass a platform. Each one is the same as the last—a flat, empty square of metal so thin it hums in the wind. When we reach the tenth platform, about a hundred feet up, we finally find something different. A box built into the frame of the tower, with a panel of lights blinking in its metal door.

Letting go of the ladder, even to crawl onto a wider platform, does not come easy. My fingers are frozen, and if I wasn't convinced I'd freeze to death if I stayed on the ladder, I doubt I would ever slide out onto the floor.

Darius shames me. Stepping from the ladder with the big wrench tucked under his arm, he strides to the flashing panel while I cower on the floor. I remember his spiderlike climb up the lighthouse. "Don't you have any respect for heights?"

"Everyone's got their strengths," he says, as he slams the wrench against the panel and the lights flicker, then return to their rhythmic flashing. He swings it again, this time bringing it down against the latch, and the door to the metal box pops open.

I get only a glimpse of the noodle soup of wires inside. Darius doesn't hesitate. He clamps the wrench onto the wires and, tugging hard, rips them free.

Sparks crackle in the dark, and Darius falls toward me, landing hard on his back at my feet. His breath heaves out but then his eyes flip open, shining in the moonlight as he stares up at me from the floor. For a moment, he smiles. I think he's going to laugh. But instead he curls onto his side and presses his palms to his temples. Instead of a laugh, a weird sound ripples through his lips, like the cry of a dying bird.

The blinking light at the top of the tower has gone dark. The lights in the station are out.

It worked.

"Can you move?" I speak right into Darius's ear. This plan depends on speed, and we are quickly running out of time. I shake Darius and put my lips against his ear again. "Can you climb down with me?"

But Darius lies as still as a dead man, and on the ground, the door to the guardhouse swings open.

SEVENTEEN

A silhouette steps out of the guardhouse and into the night, sweeping a handheld light across the ground. The light turns upward, illuminating the path of the ladder through the center of the tower. I pull Darius to me and huddle away from the edges of the platform, knowing we must be visible but still hoping we're not.

I don't dare breathe.

But then the light moves away; the space around us goes dark again. The beam bounces off the ground and then the wall of the guardhouse. Then the door. Then it lights up the windows from the inside.

I draw a deep breath that bursts back out of me in a loud huff. "Darius!" I say, probably louder than I should, but it does no good. He doesn't reply. He only clutches his head, his eyes squeezed shut, as if there's a painful sound that only he can hear. A choked cry leaks from his lips, and it's hideous.

I remember the female racer with the journalists, the way she'd made such a similar sound. And I remember what they'd called it. *Memory sickness.*

Shouts spill out when the guardhouse door bangs open again. Anger and annoyance rise up from the ground as the first man stomps back out and approaches the tower.

Again, light filters up from below. The ladder vibrates in time with the guard's steps. He's climbing.

From my knees, I lean into the opening in the floor and look down the ladder. I have a clear view to the top of the man's head. At first I think he's wearing a helmet, but then I realize he's bald, his bare skin a shiny dome. His battery light traces a wide arc back and forth—he's tucked it, bulb up, into the waistband of his pants as he climbs hand over hand, hand over hand. He's so close, the light hurts my eyes each time it sweeps by.

How could I have thought this was a good plan? How could I have made such a brilliant mistake? But Darius had thought it was a good plan, too, hadn't he? We'd hardly discussed it. Back then, huddled in the sandcrawler and looking into the warm house, it seemed unimaginable that the guards would leave it so quickly to come out into this vicious cold, before we could even climb down.

The movement of the light makes the tower feel like

a swinging pendulum. The guard's boots ring against the rungs. I feel like I'm inside a ticking clock.

I'm out of time.

I have only one idea. I've known I would try it eventually, but even so, my stomach flips like a fish for fear of what will happen if this fails. But I didn't remember I had Cientia, so maybe this is something else I've forgotten. My only other option is to fight, and fighting this high up would almost certainly be the last thing I ever did.

I stretch my arms toward the man's lowered head. Press my palms out as if to hold him back. My eyes squeeze shut and I concentrate on pushing my anger and my fear out through my open hands.

Nothing happens. Nothing at all. If I thought Darius could see me, I'd be mortified by how stupid that attempt at Projectura must have looked.

My heart thumps in my chest as I try to remember the potato-faced taskmaster and how she used Projectura against the farmworkers. She held out her hand, and she let out a grunt.

She *breathed* out a grunt.

The guard is so close now. I raise my arms again, squeeze my eyes shut again, but before I can breathe, the man on the ladder is yelling and my lids fly open.

"Vandals!" he calls out, with the self-satisfaction of a child with the right answer. "Well, you're in trouble now."

He's rising again, the light swings and blinds me again, and my eyes press shut. My hands go up, and they're shaking so hard you'd think I was waving.

This time, it's different.

This time, something ignites behind my lids, a match flaming to life. But before it flares up, it's out, extinguished by a rush of air that flows out of me and down.

It's not the match, I realize, but the breath that blows it out. That's where the power lies.

A short cry flies up from below, and my eyes snap open. The guard shakes his head like a dog shaking off the rain. Like he's been rattled. Like he's been kicked in the head by a foot he can't see.

His head shakes, but his hands return to the ladder, and he's climbing again. He is getting so close, I can hear him cussing me out under his breath. My instincts tell me to get to my feet and prepare to fight, but I force myself to stay on my knees. I push my arms out one more time, press my eyes closed one more time, and the breath rushes from me again.

There is a loud, high shriek.

I open my eyes to see him fall. The back of his head slams into the platform right below him. His elbows hit the next one. Each collision slows his fall, but none of them stop him. He drops past the lowest platform and lands in a heap on the ground, his legs pulled up, his arms protecting his head. At first he lies still, and I wonder if he's out. But then he's on his knees, then on his feet. The light traces his path as he limps back to the door, swings it open, and slams it shut behind him.

Right now, I can't be gentle with Darius, but I can apologize later if we make it out of here. I shake him, and when he doesn't respond, I shake him *hard*. So hard his head bounces off the metal floor. With a gasp, he opens his eyes.

"Can you climb down?" I ask. "It's now or never." He stares at me like he's playing my words back in his head. By the expression on his face, I think maybe he doesn't remember where we are. "Darius," I say, "we have to go *now*."

Just as I'm about to shake him again, he surprises me. He sits up and looks down at the ground, as if looking for the guard. Then he slides his feet through the hole and starts climbing down.

Halfway to the ground, the door opens again.

I freeze on the ladder, and luckily for both of us, Darius freezes too.

The man in the doorway calls back into the guardhouse. "You can wait for them to come down if you like. I'm going up there to *throw* them down." But then the open door is buffeted by the icy wind, and he must reconsider, because he steps back inside, yanking the door shut behind him. It slams, and the whole building rattles on its frame.

Darius reaches the bottom of the ladder and drops to the ground. I'm right behind him.

The door flies open again. The wind catches it and pulls it from the hand of the man standing in the doorway.

Light streams into my eyes, but it's unsteady. I can see well enough to know that I'm looking at a bald-headed, unshaven man staring out at us.

For a moment his eyes are clouded, but then they sharpen. "Vandals," he says, like his thoughts just skipped back in time to the moment he first saw me on the tower. His eyes go from sharp to heated then, and a flicker of a smile passes over his lips so briefly I almost think I imagined it. But it was there, because now he raises his free hand, and I realize that flicker was a smile of anticipation. Anticipation of the pain he plans to cause us.

He must think he has all the time in the world. Maybe this isn't the same man I hit with Projectura after all. Or maybe, I think, he doesn't quite believe what happened on the tower. Why would he? Even if he hasn't guessed we're racers, he can see we aren't Enchanteds. He'd never guess we might have magic of our own.

He doesn't even react to my own raised arms. I think he barely sees us. All he can see is how pleased he is with himself.

My eyes close. The match ignites and is huffed out quick as lightning, quicker than I can think. I just get my eyes open in time to see him drop to his knees.

Darius scrambles up and pushes past me. He looks back

at me though, wide-eyed and openmouthed, and I know he never saw me use Projectura on the tower. Even the guard, on all fours now braced against the pain, seems less surprised than Darius.

As soon as Darius is beside the guard the flow of energy stops, but I'm not sure if I stopped it or if it stopped on its own. What I don't know about Projectura is everything.

I climb slowly to my feet, never taking my eyes off the guard's face, keeping my arms half raised, just in case. But I don't need to. He may not understand what happened, but he believes it. And he's not going to bait me again.

A feeling rises in my chest, like wings opening.

Darius bends and rifles through the guard's pockets, smiling when he finds a set of keys. "The sandcrawler," he says. He runs by me, but I hear him slow to a stop when I don't follow.

"I'll be right there," I say, not looking away from the guard.

"Don't be long." I hear Darius's steps recede as he sprints away.

But I linger, staring down at the Enchanted guard on the ground, an unrepressed smirk on my lips. His emotions are a swirl of anger and shame, but that's not what keeps me here. What keeps me here is a faint fragrance that tinges the air between us. A warm scent like bread toasting.

Respect.

It lasts only a moment, and then the warmth is gone. His mouth works, ready to spit an accusation, but before he can say a word, I turn.

I hear the engine of the sandcrawler growl to life, but still, I walk. I refuse to run.

EIGHTEEN

As soon as we are away in the sandcrawler, I shrug my bag off my shoulders and clutch it to my chest. It's already daybreak, and the inside of the sandcrawler has the smell of a heater that's been out of use for a long time. The guards must have no reason to drive at night.

"Why did I have to take it too far?" I ask aloud, as much to myself as to Darius. "I couldn't just turn my back and run away. I had to stare him down. Make sure he knew he'd been beaten by an Outsider."

"If I were you," he says, "I'd be a lot less upset and a lot more pleased with myself."

I want to snap back at him that he knows an awful lot about the way I should feel, but instead I say, "Those guards could comm the Enchanted Authority and tell them about the attack on the tower. They could tell them about me . . . that I have magic I shouldn't have."

"What if they do tell?" he asks. "No one could know that the girl was you."

"Of course they could! They could describe me—"

"Maybe they could. But I don't think they would automatically assume you're a racer. For one, you're clean. For another, they think you were there to sabotage their tower. They're more likely to assume you're a member of the Outsider Liberation Army than a racer."

This is something I hadn't thought of. Maybe he's right. Maybe the Authority won't be looking for me among the racers.

With Darius not looking at me, I take the opportunity to look at him. His face glows in the yellow light that's beginning to fill the windows. The rest of him is covered in a coating of gray dust, but I can tell he's wiped his face. For a moment I think he will say something more—I feel a confession on his lips—but all he says is, "There's the road."

I follow the line of his gaze. He's right. We've made it back to the road that leads to the outpost, and I'm surprised to see more than just a few vehicles—trucks and motorized carriages—streaming toward our next checkpoint. Some are still far back in the distance, but they are coming. My stomach sinks. I wonder how many are carrying other racers.

If Darius doesn't want to hear about my worries, there's

still one other thing I want to talk about. "So what happened to you back on the tower? Did you get a shock when you pulled those wires?"

"If you mean from the electricity, then no."

"Then what was it?"

"A memory came back to me." The sandcrawler slows until it stops. He pivots in his seat to look at me. "It's too terrible to talk about." Darius's shoulders stiffen. "I hope you'll understand. I don't want to talk about it."

I want to ask more questions—I want to know *everything* he remembered—but looking at him in profile, the set of his jaw makes it clear he's not going to tell me anything else. He takes his foot off the brake and returns to steering the sandcrawler toward the road.

Maybe I'm violating his privacy, but as soon as he closes off, I reach out with my senses to read him.

The fragrance of anise wafts around him, dark and pungent like black licorice, and I'm both satisfied and horrified that I was right to be suspicious. It's not quite deception I feel, but he's guarding a secret.

Even as my mind begins to spin with curiosity about the memory Darius finds too terrible to share, I know I can't let concern for him distract me. We'll be separating soon, and even now, we're competitors, *not* partners. I know it, and Darius knows it, too. I shouldn't be surprised he's keeping secrets.

It doesn't matter. I'm going to win the race, and I can ask Darius all the questions I want after that.

When I finally spot the flat gray roofs of the outpost, it's not the other vehicles or the other people—some of whom are clearly racers—that unsettle me most. It's the red and yellow lights that flash atop black trucks with darkly tinted windows, announcing the presence of the Enchanted Authority. At least four Authority trucks are lined up in front of the building I take to be the rail station. The rest of the "outpost"—if you can really call it that—is just a few low wooden buildings. Uniformed Authority officers mill about. They appear to be stopping random people on their way to the trains.

"Don't freak out," Darius warns me.

It's too late. My heart is a horse running flat out at a gallop, and I'm its rider, barely hanging on.

"Let's not get too close in the sandcrawler," I say. "In case they're looking for it."

We park far back from the doors, and as we walk to the station, I notice faces I recognize. The ginger-haired racer who almost stole our bike at the roadhouse. Guess he found some other form of transportation to steal. I also spot two of the racers I fought with Jane, including the boy with the huge arms. Darius says, "Don't worry about the other racers."

"Who says I'm worried?" I say, but I can't keep the edge from my voice. I'd have to be a fool not to be worried.

I take off the dead woman's coat. I was wearing it at the tower, so if the guards reported it, they probably didn't describe Mary's gray dress. I hold tight to the strap of my bag where it loops over my shoulder and keep my head down as we pass two Authority officers standing over what appears to be the body of a dead racer on the path that leads to the building. "Do you remember him?" I ask Darius.

He shakes his head.

"I do. I fought him at the lighthouse. He was one of the racers who jumped you."

Unlike the woman we found sitting up expectantly in the road, this dead man is curled up, lying on his side. I can't help but wonder who is home rooting for him. How will they find out he died? Where will his body be taken?

I'm trailing behind Darius as he heads up the path, looking back over my shoulder at the dead man, so I don't see the person until we collide.

"Look out!" a voice snaps behind me. And then she adds, "You Outsiders are too stupid to watch where you're going."

Since we reached the road and I saw this crowd, pressure has been building inside me. Something about the word *stupid* kicks out the stopper that's holding it in. My head flips up and the words fly out before I even turn around. "I'm sorry," I say, in a tone that says quite the opposite. "I didn't see you. I was too distracted by the dead man on the ground."

I spin around to find a female Authority guard glowering at me.

Real horror rolls out of Darius, but the officer stays calm. "You're a racer, right?" she asks.

"I am." I swallow. *Why did I open my mouth? Could this guard already be looking for me?*

"I could arrest you," she says, "but I won't. I won't let you off that easy. If you're too *stupid* to watch where you're going, if you're too *stupid* to know not to speak to me with that tone, arresting you would be merciful, compared to the kind of death you're destined for."

Her lips twitch into a smirk. Inside, I heave out a sigh of relief. She doesn't recognize me. "Thank you for your courtesy," I say, and for once, I control my mouth.

Darius adds, "Yes, thank you," before grabbing me by the arm and tugging me away.

"Are you out of your mind?"

"I didn't know it was an officer—"

"Even so! You knew it was an Enchanted—"

"I know, *I know,* but it was all too much! The dead racer, the disrespect—"

"Since when can an Outsider afford to be concerned about disrespect? You better find a way to handle it, because you're in a race, and that's all that matters right now." His hazel eyes, for all the softness of their color, are as hard as stone.

"Oh, *right*. I forgot." I hear my voice in my own head and I sound so immature, but I don't know how to sound any different right now. Maybe the officer and Darius are right, and I'm an immature, stupid girl who is destined to die before the end of the race. For a moment I'm sincerely concerned I'm about to cry, which would be so much worse than sounding immature—it would prove I'm immature— so I bob my head in a hasty nod and turn to walk the rest of the way to the station doors.

Darius catches up to me and hooks me by the elbow. "Everyone else is heading in," he says.

He's right, and like him, I'd prefer to stay away from the rest of the herd. So we follow a path that skirts the brick wall of the train station, leading to the tracks in the back—four sets, all running in the same direction—and two one-story, wooden buildings. The walls of one are filled with rows of wide windows. The other is made of low walls hunched under a flat roof.

"Barracks, I'd guess," Darius says.

The sun is fully up now, and the air is already hot. The edges of my hair stick to the damp skin at the back of my neck, and the dead woman's coat feels like it weighs one hundred pounds. Along the tracks, a line of Outsiders swing sledgehammers, pounding huge nails into shiny new rails. They move in unison, almost like a line of dancers. My eyes float over the space behind them until I spot the person

I'm looking for—a man in a wide-brimmed straw hat—the Enchanted taskmaster. He stands not five feet away, watching. His hand twitches at his side, and my own palms tingle, too.

I quickly turn my head away. I don't want to see something terrible and not be able to do anything about it.

"I think we should take a look around inside, after all," Darius says. His eyes are on the taskmaster, who is now watching us.

Walking into the chilly, climate-controlled air inside the station is like diving into a pool. I suddenly realize how thirsty I am. The canteen inside my bag is mostly full, so I take a huge gulp and offer it to Darius. "We should refill it before we leave," I say, trying not to acknowledge the needling worry at the back of my mind that the next clue might send us out over the desert on foot again.

The board announcing arrivals and departures flashes a message across the bottom.

ALL GOVERNMENT TRAINS ARE DELAYED DUE
TO TRACK WORK . . .
NO TRAINS UNTIL TOMORROW . . .

Still, the place is bustling with Outsiders. Even when their clothes conceal their missing embeds, it's their lack of luggage—along with their filthy clothes, sleep-starved eyes, and shoeless feet—that tells me they are racers, just like us. I make a rough count. There are maybe twenty I take for racers. But it doesn't matter, really, if there are twenty, forty, or a thousand. As long as I find the clue first and leave them all behind me.

A sign above the clock seems too obvious. *The Truth You Seek Turns Clockwise.* Darius stands beneath it and stares up, one of a tight group of at least a half dozen other racers, all staring at the clock like they're waiting for the clue to reveal itself.

"Everyone here would have seen it by now," I say. "What else acts like a clock?"

Darius's eyes move to the big glass doors facing the tracks. "The sun?"

"Could be," I say. "Or shadows."

Maybe he thinks I'm on to something, maybe he just wants to get away from two officers who have moved close to us, but Darius nods and follows me out a side door. As we go, I catch a few words of conversation between the officers—*sandcrawler* and *found* and *stolen.*

"If I were the type to despair," Darius starts, "now would be the time to do it—"

"We couldn't drive it any farther, anyway. It would've been too risky—"

"So is crossing the Black Desert on foot."

I can't argue with that. We've already seen two racers

dead from exposure. "Maybe we'll leave here by train?" The next government train might not be until tomorrow, but private trains should still be running. We may be able to hitch a ride, especially since Darius has mackels to offer in exchange.

The air is already so hot, Mary's dress sticks to my body in a way I don't particularly like. I sit in the shade of a low roof that covers the mostly empty train platform, and Darius sits beside me. Even in the shade, even with the breeze, the heat is intolerable. I wish I could bottle some of it and keep it for nightfall.

I pull the canteen from my bag and we each take a drink. Darius pulls the apple from my bag. "I wish I had a knife so we could share it."

"This side's mine," I say, taking a bite. "The other side's yours." We pass the apple back and forth, the juice running down both our chins. I get sticky and lose my manners, licking my hands clean. When we're down to the last few bites, he pushes it back at me when it's his turn.

The heat draws a wall of haze from the ground, tricking my eyes into believing I'm looking at a wide lake, spreading across the sand along the tracks. The air rings with the sound of hammers against the rails, occasionally punctuated by the cry of an Outsider. I'm trying to close my mind to it, to think about the clue, when Darius jumps to his feet.

"There's something out on the sand. I've been watching its shadow shorten."

He stumbles forward, so I get to my feet, brushing my damp hands down the front of Mary's dress. Sweat glues a layer of sand to my palms. I throw my bag over my shoulder and scoop up the wool coat.

The sky is nothing but wide and blue—an ocean above the desert. Darius has noticed the slimmest line on the darkest sand, and I wonder if his eyes are that good or if my eyes are just that bad. As we come closer, an object begins to take shape. A sign. A wooden sign painted gray, with a message hand-lettered in white script:

Shadows form the hands of your clock.
Afternoon shadows point your way.

"Afternoon shadows point east," says Darius, raising an eyebrow at me. I can barely see him, I'm squinting so hard against the sun, and my eyes are tearing up, but I think he's smiling. I don't know why. Happy to find the clue, I guess, but I don't like the idea of walking east into the desert.

But I don't know how to argue against it. So we walk east, toward the tracks, and beyond them, the empty sand.

NINETEEN

We hike so long, I can't even see the outpost behind us anymore. Fear that we'll become disoriented and hopelessly lost in this sea of sand robs my mouth of the little moisture it had. My lips taste like paper. If the shape that's growing in the distance turns out to be something other than another clue, I may not produce tears when I cry.

As we get closer, I sense impatience, but it's not coming from Darius. Someone else is out here. The shape in the distance turns out to be another sign. Like the first one, it's gray with white lettering, but I can't read its message because a man is draped over it, like a wilted climbing vine. The neckline of his shirt covers the bottom of his throat, so it's not immediately clear if he's an Outsider or an Enchanted. "Astrid, at last," he says. "I've been waiting here for you all morning."

Another stranger who knows my name.

I shade my eyes with my hand to look at him, and beside me, Darius does the same. *I got this*, I mouth to Darius. Even in the shadow of his hand, I see his lips flatten into a thin line before he mouths his reply. *Be careful.*

"Could you move?" I ask the Outsider.

He slides his back from the sign. It reads:

I am a signal of a coming change. Though I am beautiful
to the eye, I portend death.
Come to my front door as the dawn breaks. Its color will
tell you where to go next.

I don't know the answer to this riddle. I wonder if Darius does, or even this Outsider, for that matter.

There's nothing remarkable about this young man—probably no older than me and Darius—yet everything about him feels wrong. I immediately try to read him, of course, and what I get doesn't help convince me that I should trust him. His feelings are cryptic, as if maybe he's had practice at confusing someone with Cientia. There's definitely sincerity and truth—I believe he's relieved to see me. But I also feel a secret he's hiding, dark and pungent and scented with fennel, not unlike Darius's secret.

And I feel fear.

"You're afraid."

"I am. I'm afraid of what might happen to you. Authority

guards inside the station are asking questions about a female racer." I think he's expecting a reaction. When he doesn't get one, he continues. "They say that even though this girl is an Outsider, she possesses . . . she *uses* . . . Enchanted magic."

"What makes you think it's me?"

"I *know* it's you. I know that you're Astrid Jael, and I'm here to help you. Because I'm Jayden Jael, your brother."

"My *brother*?" I can't hide the shock in my voice, which makes me angry with myself. "But you're not in the race." He tips his head at me. This is not the response he was expecting. Either that, or he's not sure he heard me. "I thought my brother was in the race."

"Oh." He's heard me now. His expression goes dark. "I didn't know you knew that."

"So what's the truth, then? You're not in the race after all?"

"No," he says, "that's our other brother." He runs the back of his hand above his mouth, wiping away a line of sweat. "It's our younger brother, Marlon, who's in the race. I'm your older brother."

My head swims. I think of Darius and his secret memory. I hadn't wanted to admit how much I envied him that. But how much better is this? To be standing face-to-face with someone who could answer all my questions?

"Slow down," Darius says. I think he's speaking to

Jayden, but I look over to see him staring at me. "Why are you so quick to trust him? You can't know he's who he says he is." He turns on Jayden. I can't help but wonder if he really doubts this is my brother, or if he just hopes it's not. "How old are you?" he asks.

"Nineteen. Two years older than Astrid. Who are *you*?"

"How did you know you could find your sister here?" Darius asks, ignoring the question.

Jayden smiles. Not a friendly smile—an unfriendly, *I know what you're trying to do* smile. "I gave a ride to one of the racers. She was talkative, all worked up about a girl racer she'd seen with magic like an Enchanted. *She can fight just like one*, she said. She also said a few racers had alerted the Authority. So I agreed to drive the girl as far as the next checkpoint, which turned out to be the outpost. Then I figured out the clue and came out here to wait. What took you so long?"

He asks this question directly to me, like he's done with Darius. "We were being watched," I lie. If this is my brother, I don't want him to think I couldn't figure out the clue. "It took discipline, but we waited."

The boy scoffs. "Discipline? Until the day you entered this race, *disciplined* would've been the last word I used to describe you."

This comment is the first thing this stranger has said that shows he may actually know me. Darius's gaze holds mine for an extra moment. This *discipline* quip has helped convince him, too.

Which is a bit insulting, if I'm honest. I tug my gaze away from Darius.

I look the stranger over. His build is slight, like mine. But his hair is almost blond, whereas mine is almost black. And his eyes are much rounder than mine. Still, none of these things mean he *couldn't* be my brother, I suppose.

Yet there's this: Three of us stand here, but only one of us looks out with clear eyes from a smooth, well-fed face. He has a vehicle and the freedom to use it. And yet two of his siblings entered the Race of Oblivion? Something doesn't add up. "Tell me this," I say. "Why did I enter this race?"

"You were angry," he says. His eyes change focus, and I can tell he's really remembering it. Remembering *me*. It makes me ache with jealousy to think that I can be seen by his mind's eye, but not by my own. "Our father met the princess at the Apple Carnival. She gave him a royal order giving him access to the healthcare citizens receive, but he died before he could use it. I guess you were angry enough to grab at citizenship any way you could."

"And our brother? Why would he enter, too?"

"He didn't know you had entered. You hid it from him."

Beside me, Darius is growing restless, shifting his weight and kicking the sand. I don't care. Let him move on, then. Because whoever this is—my brother or not—he wants to help me. I have a million questions, and I intend to ask every single one of them, including if he knows the answer to the riddle on this sign and if he can take me there. But first I have to ask the question that's been eating at me since I first learned I had a brother in the race. "Our brother . . . how is he doing? Is he ahead of me, or behind me?"

He hesitates too long.

"You can tell me. He's ahead, isn't he? By how much?"

"That's not it."

"Then how far behind?" Once more, I can't read him, but if his face is any indication, he doesn't want to answer. "Just tell me."

"Our brother Marlon is neither ahead of you nor behind," he says.

He says something else, but a gust blows his words away, and I have to make him repeat it.

"I said I'm sorry," he calls into the wind, and this time I hear him too well. "But our brother Marlon is already dead."

TWENTY

If I ever wondered why they say *heartbroken* to describe grief, I don't have to wonder anymore. As bad as it hurt to learn my father had died, this is far worse somehow. Even though I can't recall my brother's face, it doesn't seem to matter. I feel as if this stranger has cut a hole in my chest, and the wind is just blowing through me now.

"I'm sorry that I had to tell you," says the stranger. And like before, I can't read him. You'd think he'd be a pool of the darkest, deepest pain, but there is just nothing there. Or at least, nothing he's not masking.

But if he's really my brother, why hide his grief from me?

"That's one of the reasons I have to help you. I can't lose you both," he says.

"Plus, if I win, you win too, right?" I say. "Doesn't the winner's whole family receive citizenship?"

"Well, yes, I guess, but that's not why I'm here. I'd be just as happy to take you home right now, if that's what you said you wanted. All I want is to keep you safe."

"How did he die?" I ask. My voice breaks a bit on the words. In response, I feel a bit of sorrow-tinged sympathy, but it's not coming from the boy who calls himself my brother. It's coming from Darius.

The stranger shakes his head. "Astrid, please. Let's not talk about that now."

"I want to know. How did he die? How do you even know—"

"The girl I drove here told me. She described a boy she'd seen dead on the road. A boy—a young kid—with black hair. A *real* young kid. That's how I know it's him. He was the youngest in the race."

My mind goes back to the roadhouse, to the boy with black hair who mocked me by mimicking my words. He was with the ginger-haired racer, the one we stole the battery from. I can't help but wonder if he would've made it if we hadn't taken that battery. But I keep that to myself. Instead I ask, "Do you know the meaning of this clue?"

"I do," says the stranger. He casts a sideways glance at Darius. "But I don't want to tell you here. Come with me. I can drive you there in my truck."

If anything he's said has made me want to trust this man and go with him, it's these words: *in my truck*. The thought of getting out of this desert and carried all the way to the next clue riding comfortably in a truck is more enticing than even the thought of a shower and a clean bed. But maybe because I want it so badly, I know I can't trust the offer too easily. "How is it you have a truck?" I ask.

"We're from the far north, you and me—farm country. You've been breaking your back bringing in the early harvest, right up until they came for you."

"What crop?"

He hesitates just a moment. "Apples. I deliver them in the truck."

"Wait." It's Darius. He's been listening, and now he has an opinion, but honestly, I wish he would mind his own business and keep his opinions to himself. "Don't trust him. Astrid," he says, and he's emphatic. He's tugging my arm, forcing me to look at him. "I know he's lying to you."

"How?" As much as I don't trust this stranger myself, I certainly don't want Darius's advice on the matter. Darius, who helped me only so he could take advantage of the bike I had. Of course he's going to try to disrupt this opportunity for me. "How could you know?"

"Because the memory I had . . . the secret I'm keeping . . . It's about you." His eyes move away, as if admitting this is somehow embarrassing. The wind stirs the curls that shade his forehead. He draws a deep breath and then turns those hazel eyes back to my face, and I know I have to hear him out. "What I remember contradicts what he's telling you."

Something cools the air. I feel a shadow, like a cloud passing over the sun, though the sky is practically clear. It's coming from Darius. It's regret and it's pain and it's the gloomy chill of whatever he's about to tell me. It's true, whatever it is, and I kind of hate him for it. I want to accept a ride from this stranger so badly it hurts. I want to believe I can trust him. And Darius is ruining all that.

But then, if this Outsider is lying, maybe he's lying about my brother's death, too.

"*You* had a memory," Jayden—or whatever this boy's name might be—says. And though he seems to have limitless skill at concealing his feelings, even a person without Cientia could see he's working himself into a tizzy now. "She's supposed to believe the memory of some hapless racer over the word of her own brother?"

"Where were you the day of the carnival?" Darius asks. "Where were you when the princess greeted her father?"

"I was watching with my family."

"With *your* family? Or with *her* family?"

"With *our* family. It's the same family."

"And when her father died? Where were you then?"

My stomach is a bag of snakes. If I could vomit right now, I think I'd bring up nothing but twisting serpents.

"I was beside him."

Darius holds still so long, I almost hope I imagined everything he just said. Or that he's about to tell me that he's been lying and that my brother is telling the truth. But he doesn't. Instead he says, "You're a liar."

"Astrid—"

"This is what I remembered," Darius says, and I'm at once anxious to hear every word and wishing there were no words to hear. "The day of the Apple Carnival I saw the princess greet your father. He was with a young boy—the boy we saw at the roadhouse."

And so this much they agree on. The boy at the roadhouse—the one I regretted speaking to—was my brother.

"And you ran to your father's side when he collapsed, and you tried to help him. It was just the three of you there with the princess—you, your brother, and your father. That's the truth. I swear it."

"Astrid, listen to me." Now the stranger is growing frantic. Whatever defenses he has against my Cientia, they are failing him. He is awash in the kind of desperation I felt in the woman who tried to throw me from the lighthouse, just before she fell.

But still, I don't feel his grief.

"This person is your competitor," he says, in a tone with more disdain and contempt than an Outsider should be able to muster. "He's going to say whatever he has to, to hold you back. I know where this clue points, and I will take you there right now. I'll take you to the clue after that, and the clue after that, until you've won. All you have to do is come with me now." He pauses, waiting for my response. "Right now, Astrid. We should go now, before any others find this clue."

"Did any racers come out here before us?"

"A few. They went back to the outpost, to wait for a train, I suppose. But you can't go back there, Astrid. The Authority is searching for you. Your only choice is to trust me."

"Not true," says Darius. "I know where this clue points as well. You can come with me. We'll flag the next train—"

"There *are no* trains," growls the stranger. But as if on cue, I hear a whistle, far away, and the screech of wheels on rails. We all turn, as if called by the sound, and look toward the horizon.

But nothing appears.

"You heard that, right? There's a train out there," says Darius. "If we hurry, we can catch it."

Both of them stare at me, waiting for me to choose who to trust. And yet I feel totally alone. Their emotions are like mirrors of each other. In both of them I feel urgency and fear and some hidden secret they are keeping from me.

The truth is, I trust neither one of them.

"Where are we going?" I ask Darius. Sand sticks to my lips. I feel it in my mouth, grinding between my teeth when I talk. "If you know the solution to this clue, tell me now."

Darius looks from me to the stranger and back again. His eyes, rimmed in purple shadows by fatigue, are still bright with attention. "The Village of Falling Leaf. It's on the Northern Rail Extension." I stare back blankly, and he must see my confusion at how he could know this, because he adds, "I saw it on the wall map, beneath the clock inside the station."

I consider this. A falling leaf does, in fact, fit the clue. *Though I am beautiful to the eye, I portend death.* "So what's the front door of a village?" I ask.

"The gate? I'm still working on that part." Darius frowns a bit, and I'm not sure if it's because he can't figure this piece of the clue, or because the hot wind is peppering his face with dust.

The train whistle sounds again, and to my anxious ears, it sounds like a warning. I wish I could tell which of these two boys it's warning me against.

Another noise interrupts the wind, but this one comes from behind us. Voices. We all shade our eyes and stare at a small group of people striding toward us from the direction of the previous sign. As they get closer, I recognize them.

"Mr. and Mrs. Arrogance," Darius says.

He's right, and they're not alone. They have at least three racers with them.

"I'm out of time," says my so-called brother, and my heart speeds up. The choice I couldn't bring myself to make is about to be made for me. "You can still come with me, but it's now or never."

"But if you're in such a hurry," I say, and already this stranger looks different to me. His well-fed face is hardening. His round eyes are narrowing. "How is it you have time to take me to Falling Leaf, and the clue after that, and the clue after that?"

"I would have *made* time, if you hadn't been so ungrateful. You've always been ungrateful, and you always will be. Right up until this race kills you." Again, it feels like he's remembering me. But that doesn't prove he's my brother. The voices of the approaching racers are growing louder. This boy who claims to be my brother scowls at me, and then he shoves a canteen at me. "If you won't accept any other help from me, at least take this."

I hesitate, but Darius, of all people, accepts the canteen on my behalf. "I'll hold that for Astrid," he says. He's already carrying the one I got from Jane, since I'm weighed down by both the bag and the coat.

The stranger hands the canteen to Darius, but he smiles at me. I notice a pool of sweat in the cleft above his upper lip. "Good luck." He picks up his own canteen and starts out across the sand, heading toward the barracks. At least I think that's where the barracks are.

I watch him recede into a veil of blowing sand, noticing something familiar about his walk.

Once he's gone, I say to Darius, "I still feel a secret."

He narrows his eyes in the direction of the approaching

voices. "Everyone has secrets, Astrid," he says.

I haven't heard the train whistle since Darius told me the solution to the riddle, but we need to move before these others reach this sign. "There's enough sand in the air that I think we might not be seen," I say. "But we should run, if we can."

So we run side by side, deeper into the desert. The secret is still there, and I can't help but worry that I've chosen to trust the wrong boy.

The voices of the other racers fade behind us. The black sand radiates heat, making it feel like we're moving through an oven. Our steps slow to a walk. Through the haze, nothing interrupts my view to the horizon. No tracks appear, or even the distant silhouette of a train. High over our heads, clouds hang like white gauze torn into strips to reveal a darkening blue sky. The darker the sky, the heavier the weight I'm carrying in the pit of my stomach.

I know I won't survive another night like last night. We have to find that train. "Could you pass me a drink?" I say.

I draw a deep gulp from the canteen Darius hands me, but it comes right back up.

I drop to my knees, gagging and coughing and choking, spewing liquid all over the ground, a black puddle on black sand. "Not . . . ," I sputter when I finally stop coughing enough to speak, "water."

Darius crouches beside me and runs a hand across my

back. "What's happening?" he starts, but I don't let him finish. I jump to my feet as if his touch burns worse than the poison in the canteen.

"It's not water!" I say, and I notice my voice, loud and high, like it's someone else's voice.

But we are alone, just us two.

"Why did you give me *that* canteen? Why didn't you give me the one I've been drinking from all day?"

"No reason . . ." Darius, still on his knees, stares up at me, wide-eyed. "They're both your canteens. I just handed you whichever—"

"Did you? Here, in the middle of the desert? Where no one would see me die?" My thoughts spin wildly through my head. *There's only one winner.* Darius said so himself. "And that stranger . . . You were so hesitant to trust him. You called him a liar. But when he offered a canteen—*this* canteen—you were the one who took it from him." I pace a circle around Darius, not knowing where to go. "Perhaps he's actually *your* brother. I mean, I took your advice, and here we are, alone, surrounded by sand. Did you figure you would kill me here, before I could become a threat to you?"

Instinct is steering me now, and it turns me inward, to check my Cientia. I sense cold fear and a heavy secret.

"Maybe you remembered seeing me at the Apple Carnival," I say. "Maybe you didn't. Either way, you're still keeping a secret from me." I pause to catch my breath, but not long enough to let him speak. "I was right not to trust the boy who claimed to be my brother, but I shouldn't have trusted you either."

The shrill whistle comes again. As quick as a shift in the wind, my attention swings to the distant dunes ahead of us. There, like a ghost materializing out of fog, a train appears out of the blowing grit, spraying sand up on either side as it parts the desert in two. It's streamlined and metallic and shockingly clean, considering the dirt all around it. The tracks it rides had been buried beneath blowing sand, but the train is like a broom, sweeping the rails clean.

Darius runs toward it, waving his arms wildly to catch the engineer's attention. It works, I guess, because the whir of the wheels slows to a *clack clack clack* as the train comes to a stop.

I should feel relieved. Instead, I feel dread at the thought of boarding this train with a boy I don't trust.

TWENTY-ONE

Darius doesn't slow until he's right up alongside the engine. A wad of mackels ripples in the breeze as he shakes his fist at the tinted windshield. The thick metal door opens, but the engineer comes only a half step through. "Sorry," she calls, looking from Darius to me and back again. "We're not taking on passengers."

"We've got money," Darius calls.

"Doesn't matter."

The door clangs shut, an ominous sound. The whistle blares again, and maybe it's because I'm desperate or maybe it's because I can't think of anything else to do to hold a hulking train in place, but I step onto the tracks.

I balance, one foot on each rail, staring into that tinted glass windshield from just fifty yards away. In that glass, I see the reflection of fast-moving clouds, but I know the engineer is peering back at me.

At least I hope she is.

The wind gusts at my back, but I will not be moved.

There is an agonizingly long wait, during which Darius comes to stand beside me but doesn't speak. The train glows like a silver snake sunning itself, and the sky reflected in its windshield goes from cloud-strewn to bright blue to cloud-strewn again. "I suppose every minute the train stands still is a victory," Darius says finally.

And then the door opens again. A narrow set of steps reaches down to the sand from the door, and the engineer steps aside to let a different young woman descend. Her skin glows where the sunlight touches it. Brown ringlets fall to her shoulders, and her big round eyes are almost innocent. She is beautiful, in that way a storm out on the horizon is beautiful.

There's an air of authority in her walk, like she owns these tracks and I have some nerve standing on them.

"What are you doing this far from the outpost?" she asks. She's small but she looks strong, and she wears heavy boots laced up to her knees that make her seem rooted, like she'd be difficult to knock down. "You'd better turn around before the sun goes down—"

"We're racers," I say. "The next checkpoint is the Village of Falling Leaf. We're looking to secure passage there on a train."

"*Secure passage?*" She sticks out her chin and looks me up

and down, as if somewhere on my body is an explanation of how I got to be so stupid. "You're going to have to turn around," she says. She's awash in protectiveness, but protective of *what*? Could there be something special about this train? "Go back to the outpost. Wait for a train there."

"We're not going to be able to do that," I say.

"Well, then stay out here in the desert and die for all I care," she says, "but you're going to have to get off these tracks."

She's planning her move—I feel it like a slap to my face. In my mind's eye I see her grabbing me by the arm and yanking me off the rails. Before she can raise a hand I'm down on the ground, sand splashing up into my eyes as I kick at those tall boots and shove her legs out from under her. She lands hard on her back, and the sound of the breath knocked from her lungs puts a smile on my lips. I'm sweaty and dirty and now sand coats my arms and legs, but the look on her face is worth the misery. While confusion and realization swirl around us like a dust storm—while this girl figures out that I am not exactly what I first appeared to be—I jump back up onto the tracks.

"Astrid?" The door to the train has opened again and a man steps out, dark hair rippling in the wind. He wears a jacket and trousers that are a bit rumpled, but he's still dressed in a suit, and that tells me he cares about the impression he makes. Like the girl, he's not lacking in swagger.

"Another stranger who knows my name," I say. I think he expected to shock me, but I've gotten used to this by now.

But then he says, "No one told me you were in the race," which catches my attention much more than the simple fact that he recognizes me. Because it means he knew me beforehand, and not from the publicity since the race started.

"You know her?" says the woman, pinning me down with her big round eyes.

"Well enough." He gives his head a small shake. "I really can't believe it. You look so different." He moves in closer. Dark eyes stare out from under thick, arched brows, as if he is confirming that I am the girl he remembers. He nods—not for anyone else, more for himself. "All right then," he says.

I want to fight. I think I always want to fight. But he's done. He simply turns and strides toward the train, and the girl follows. I'm still straddling the tracks when he calls back over his shoulder. "Well," he says. "What are you waiting for?"

I exchange a brief, confused glance with Darius, and then we both shuffle forward after them. The young man is an indecipherable swirl of emotions as he stands at the top of the narrow steps. The wind catches his jacket as he holds the door open for Darius and me to come inside the train.

"Wait, *what*?" The engineer gives our host a questioning look, the kind you'd give someone who just played a very bad card. Everything about her is sharp—a sharp glare shooting out from under sharply cut bangs, cheekbones so sharp you could cut glass with them. "You're inviting them in?"

"Don't mind her," he says to me. And then to her, "This is Astrid."

"Astrid?" I can tell by her tone she's heard my name before.

"Yes, *that* Astrid." Our host grins as the engineer cocks her head at an angle, considering me. Then he turns to Darius. "And you are?"

Darius hesitates, then reluctantly gives his name.

"Astrid and Darius," says our host. "Sorry for the reception. We rarely allow visitors."

"We *never* allow visitors." The engineer's eyes shift between me and our host, and then she shakes her head. "And we never should," she says.

"Relax. I have my reasons."

We are led through the engineer's cabin, with its austere control panels and blinking lights, into a room with cloth-lined walls and thickly padded chairs covered in patterned fabrics of navy blue and bright gold. It's all very regal—the kind of room where a head of state might issue execution orders. Our host gestures to a slender couch. Darius and I exchange a fleeting look before we sit.

"This is a cozy place you've got here," I say, "but we don't have time for casual conversation. We need to get to Falling Leaf."

"We have money," Darius adds, and I'm relieved to hear him say *we*. I may not trust him, but for now I need the negotiating power of the cash he's carrying.

"I might as well tell you right away, so there's no confusion," our host says. He's not very old. Twenty at the most. "We're not heading in the direction of Falling Leaf, and even if we were, I wouldn't take you there. I despise the Race of Oblivion and won't help anyone to win it."

"Oh, *you* despise the race?" I ask. "Easy enough for a rich Enchanted." Alarm rises in Darius. I think he's afraid I'll get us kicked off the train.

"What makes you so sure we're Enchanteds?" our host asks.

"For starters, no embeds—"

"Maybe we're citizen Outsiders."

"With a private train? Stop toying with me," I say. "It's clear you know me, so just tell me who you are and where you know me from."

Our host smirks. "Still bossy, I see," he says.

"Stop that—"

"Stop what?"

"Stop *playing*. Tell me who you are . . . who *I* am. No one will find out you helped us—"

"Trust me, I'm not afraid of the Authority coming after me for helping a couple of racers. If they catch up with me, you two will be the least of my worries."

He gets to his feet and flips his hair from his eyes. Arrogance pours off him. Before I can say anything else, he glances at the two women and cocks his head toward the door. The three of them file out without another word.

Darius tries the doors at both ends of the train car. Both are locked.

"If they're going to hold us here, the least they could do is feed us," Darius says.

I open my bag and pull out the bread I took from the woman Jane killed. It's dry and probably stale, but I break off a piece and hand it to Darius before taking a piece for myself. We both eat without complaint, but I can't sit still. I eat while I pace.

"Where do you figure they went?" Darius asks, looking out the window.

Just then, the train begins to move, but we go only a short distance before we stop again. I join Darius at the window, peering out through a gray film to search for a station. All I see is blowing sand.

A minute or so later, the door opens and our host returns, accompanied by a woman and a man. Neither of them is familiar. The man is maybe mid-twenties, dressed in a sleeveless tunic, and one glance tells me he likes to lift weights. A lot. I can't help but wonder if he's been brought in to discourage me from trying to fight my way out of here.

The woman is older, probably in her forties. Her dark brown hair, tightly pulled back from her face, is sleek and smooth. She has not been outside in the wind, that's for certain.

The woman calls me by my name, but it doesn't sound friendly. It sounds intimidating. "I'm Michaela. Please come with me," she says. "Darius, you can stay here with Joseph."

Joseph must be the name of the muscle. It's not our host, because he leads me and Michaela through the car, unlocking the door and showing us into a wood-paneled passenger compartment filled with rows of empty seats. Then our host goes out without a word.

"So what's this about?" I ask. I can sense curiosity in this woman. Curiosity and protectiveness.

"Please," she says. "Sit."

"I'd rather stand. I'm in a hurry."

"That's quite obvious," the woman says, and I think she's laughing at me.

"I'm in a *race*," I snap. "I don't have time to sit around and chat."

"Humor me," she says, leaning toward me and speaking quietly, like she's my confidante. Her makeup is discreet and perfectly applied. I'm suddenly keenly aware of the patches of oil on my face and the circles of sweat under my arms. "I want to help you, I do. But first I need you to answer some questions for me. I . . . like *you* . . . have Cientia. It's my job to determine if you can be trusted. Joseph is interviewing the other racer. When you pass—assuming you *do* pass—I'll answer your questions."

"You'll help me get to Falling Leaf?"

"If that's still what you want."

"Then let's get started," I say.

She smiles. "So, you have Cientia?" she says, when I finally drop down onto the closest padded bench. "You can feel other people's feelings? Anticipate their intentions?"

I surprise myself. I tell the truth. "Yes," I say.

Her smile broadens, but then she turns her back to me. For a moment I think she's going to leave, but she starts pacing up and down the aisle between the rows of seats, asking questions quickly while she walks.

How do you feel about the Enchanted?

Do you believe all Outsiders should have full citizenship?

Do you believe Outsiders should live separately from the Enchanted?

This last one takes me off guard. "Separately? Like if part of Lanoria could be set apart just for Outsiders?"

"Yes."

"It seems to me like equality and full citizenship alongside the Enchanted would make the most sense." I pause. "But that's a first impression, really."

"How long have you had Cientia?"

"I've no idea."

"And that's because you're a competitor in the Race of Oblivion?"

She stops pacing right in front of me.

"Yes."

"And what do you remember from your life before the race? Anything?"

"Just that my name is Astrid, but I only know that because it was written on the map to the first clue. I don't even know my last name, though today I learned that it might be Jael."

"Jael? Like *Jayden* Jael?"

"What?" The face of the boy who gave me the canteen leaps to my mind, and I can taste the poison in my mouth. Like his, this woman's face is well fed. She's even an Enchanted. I've trusted her with too much. "Why do you ask that? Who is Jayden Jael?"

"Never mind. It's a complicated answer."

"So you get to ask me questions, but I can't ask you any?"

"You can ask questions. Just not that one."

I hesitate a moment. "All right, how's this one. Does your Cientia perceive emotions as scents?"

"What?"

"I . . . Maybe that's a strange question, but I just wondered if that's how it works for everyone. For me, sometimes it's a scent. Sometimes a change in temperature."

I feel her relax a bit . . . a warming. "I can't speak for

everyone, but that's how it works for me, too. Scents. Sometimes a taste in my mouth."

I laugh before I can stifle it. "Taste? That must be *awful*."

"Sometimes." Her comm buzzes. She gives it the briefest of glances. "They're ready for us," she says.

"One quick question more," I blurt, but she's already leading me toward the door. "If someone has one, or even two, of the Three Unities, does that mean they might have all three?"

She slows her steps and looks me hard in the eyes. "Cientia is common, as you know. Projectura and Pontium, not so much. So if you can use *two*"—she holds my gaze, but she doesn't ask the obvious question—"you may very well be able to use all—"

The door opens from the other side. It's our host. "Ready?" he asks.

Michaela smiles and nods, but she cuts off her answer to me. We follow him back to the regally decorated train car where we'd left Darius and Joseph, but only Darius remains.

"Where's Joseph?" Michaela asks.

"He had to go back," says our host. "Hearts and Hands match, he said."

My gaze shifts from one to the other, and then I squint out the window. Where is there to go? What Hearts and Hands match is held in the middle of the Black Desert? "He wanted me to tell you Darius passed *with flying colors*."

"Excellent. So did Astrid," Michaela says. She grins at me, and if she was laughing at me before, she isn't anymore. "Congratulations," she says, and I feel her sincerity. It's strangely charming.

"Does that mean you'll take us to Falling Leaf now?" I ask.

"It means you've qualified for an invitation into the Third Way."

"The Third Way?" Darius says, and his voice tells me he's as surprised as I am. "Is *that* what this is?" He looks around, as if he is just seeing the room around him for the first time.

"This train, you mean? Oh no, my dear. This train is nothing compared to the Third Way. You'll see."

She leads us back into the engineer's compartment, our host right behind us. The floor behind the controls has been pulled up like a trapdoor. Beneath it, a ladder drops down into a hole in the ground.

"No way," I say, as Michaela steps aside as if to let me climb down.

"Just because we've earned your trust, that doesn't mean you've earned ours," says Darius, and I realize that as much as I don't trust *him*, I trust him way more than I trust these two.

"You haven't even told us your name," I say to our host. "I'm not crawling into a hole in the ground just because you tell me to. I need to continue the race." I hear a whine of frustration in my own voice, but I honestly don't care. I'm done with this. "If you won't take me to Falling Leaf, then let me off the train," I say, hoping I don't live to regret this. "I'm not interested in joining the Third Way. I'm interested in winning the Race of Oblivion. And I'm going to win—"

"You are just as delusional as ever, Astrid," snaps our host. "You think having Cientia makes you so *special*. So much better than everyone else. Well, prove it. There's a Hearts and Hands tournament going on right now in the Heart of the Desert. Show me that you can beat one Enchanted at Hearts and Hands—just *one*—and I'll take this train right to Falling Leaf. But you have to win."

I am far from certain I can beat an Enchanted at Hearts and Hands. I'm far from certain I can get through a match without a serious injury that could jeopardize my chances in the race. But I nod. The truth is, I've been feeling ready to fight, and if this is what I have to do to get a train ride to the next checkpoint, then it has to be done.

I shoot a glance at Darius, but he doesn't see it. He's staring at our host, who has just made me an offer I'm sure he envies.

"When's the earliest this match can happen?" I ask. "Because I'm in a hurry to get on my way."

Our nameless host crosses in front of me to the ladder and gestures for me to start climbing. "Now is as good a time as any," he says.

TWENTY-TWO

At the bottom of the ladder, I find myself in a dimly lit hallway. It looks deserted, but I hear voices coming from far away. Once all four of us are down, Michaela leads us toward the source of the sound. The quality of the light changes. The walls brighten. I hear laughter and music and children shouting. Finally, the ceiling comes to an end and we are outside. The passageway opens on a town square. A waterway runs through it—a canal with a path on each side. A footbridge covered in a fresh coat of forest-green paint leads to the far bank, where a narrow street is lined with shops and cafés.

Looking up, I see the open sky.

"It's not what you think," Michaela says. "We've managed to duplicate the outdoors quite convincingly. It's difficult to live underground year-round, so we make it look and feel as much like the world above as possible."

I can't drag my eyes from the false clouds, moving across the false sky. "Unbelievable," I say.

"If we're underground, how can there be a stream like this?" Darius asks.

"A buried aqueduct runs beneath the railroad tracks, carrying water directly from an underground source to the water supply of the King's City. We've tapped into it and we siphon off what we need. It's the source of all the water for this compound."

"This compound?" Darius echoes.

"We call this place the Heart of the Desert. It's a safe haven where Outsiders can escape persecution from the Enchanted Authority. In the Heart of the Desert, an Enchanted has no power over an Outsider. We're a fully integrated society."

I turn in place. The square is bustling, crowded with mothers and toddlers, teenagers hanging out in sidewalk cafés, people walking their dogs. It doesn't seem possible that this is the notorious Third Way.

"But the Third Way was eradicated—"

"Many of us died when our original settlement was attacked by the Authority. But not all of us. Those who survived . . . well, we literally went underground."

Michaela smiles, and I'm reminded of all the questions she grilled me with on the train, all about my attitudes.

These people lost everything once. They would lose everything again if this place were to be discovered by the wrong people.

Our host meets my eye, and I begin to understand the reason I felt so much protectiveness in him and the others on the train.

Michaela leads us off the square down a passageway lined with doors, and the illusion of being outside is broken. "These are living units. Apartments." We turn another corner and the passageway widens and brightens. The walls of this hallway—hardly a hallway, really, it's as wide as a city block—are covered in murals, painted to look like a park. On either side we're flanked by images of shade trees, a garden in full bloom, a playground overrun by children. "We're coming up on the entertainment hub," Michaela says. "The Hearts and Hands tournament is being held at the community gym."

I can hear the sounds of a match in full swing—cheers and shouts and groans. Then more cheers again. The gym can't be far.

"We saw part of a tournament at a roadhouse, just yesterday," I say.

"Hearts and Hands is just as popular here as it is on the surface," says our host from the train. "Maybe more so."

"But only among the Enchanted, right?" I start, knowing I have to get my question out while I have time. "What

I mean is . . . have you ever met an Outsider with magic before? Other than me?"

Michaela purses her lips before she says, "No. I've heard rumors of others, children who weren't inoculated, but as I say, those are rumors—"

"What happened to them?"

"Again . . . it's only rumors. I've heard of the Enchanted Authority learning of such children. . . ."

"And?"

"And taking them away."

There's a doorway up ahead. It's clogged with people watching what's happening inside. Two young boys are trying to see between them, but the grown-ups won't yield an inch.

"Taking them where? What happened to these children?"

"No one knows." Michaela stops walking, and I stop, too. She turns and looks at me, and she wears an expression like she's a doctor who's just told me I'm dying. "But like I said. Those are only rumors."

I think she expects her words to scare me, but I'm no more scared than I've ever been. If anything, I'm more *angry.*

More impatient to fight this match and get on with this race.

We've reached the open door to the gym, and Michaela must have some authority around here, because people slide out of the way to let us pass. The main stage is surrounded by spectators—Outsiders and Enchanteds, men and women, young and old. They are as excited as fleas awaiting a fat dog. "They must be expecting a popular fighter," Michaela whispers to me and Darius. I think of Joseph from the train. I hope I'm not going to be expected to battle him. Our host steps past us and climbs right up onto the stage, and the rowdy crowd calms. All eyes turn to him.

"Welcome! Friends . . . and *visitors*," he says. His gaze alights on my face. I am reminded of one of my earliest assessments of him: that he has too much swagger. "We have a few guests with us today. Racers, in fact." He's a good talker, this nameless man who knows me from before the race. I wish I'd learned more about what he remembers of me before I had to step onto that stage. I wish I knew more of my own strengths and weaknesses. "Ah, friends! Believe me—what an excellent fighter this young Outsider is. But alas, she's in the race. I doubt she will live long enough to continue her fighting career."

The onlookers jostle each other, everyone trying to get a look at me, and I feel like a racehorse being paraded in front of investors. A buzz spreads through the crowd.

"I propose . . ." The crowd quiets. In the sudden silence I can hear my heart beating. A cloud of anticipation billows toward the stage. "That you, young racer, fight a real contender. Someone with skill. At stake . . ." His eyes sweep the faces of the people gathered at his feet.

"Enough drama," I shout over their heads. This is all for the crowd, since I already know what's at stake. "Just spit it out."

His eyes—cold and black—bore into me from beneath his heavy brows. "Patience." He steps toward me. His emotions are dark—I've angered him. He's putting on a show, and he does not like to be upstaged. "I will offer you passage to the next checkpoint aboard my private train, if you can defeat the Heart of the Desert's champion fighter."

The *champion*? We never agreed that I would fight the champion, just one fighter. But looking up at him on the stage—his cunning grin, like he's outsmarted me—I see what he's done. He's found a way to ensure I can't win. Maybe to ensure I don't fight at all.

But I won't have it. I'm not backing down. I said I would fight, and I will. My future in the Race of Oblivion is at stake, and I won't be beaten without even trying. I turn to Michaela. "You'll stop it if it gets too bad, right?" I ask her. "I need to be able to walk out of here. Even if I lose, I'm continuing the race."

The sound of the crowd is a low simmer, just waiting to boil over. Everyone's watching me. Waiting for me to respond. "You don't have to do this, Astrid," Michaela murmurs to me. "You can just stay here. Drop out of the race—"

"I'm not a quitter," I say, though I'm not sure where this comes from. I think of the scabs on my back. The older scars underneath. "I'm strong," I say, and I know this is true. After all, I entered this brutal race. "I'm much stronger than I look." I hand my coat and bag to Darius and climb onto the stage.

The crowd erupts. Everyone has an opinion, it seems, and everyone needs to place a bet. If the fans at the road-house were hungry for a fight, these are just as voracious. The people of the Third Way may be more peaceful, but they clearly still love blood sport.

I swallow. My throat is tight. I'm sure I've made a mistake.

Darius looks up at me but then his eyes change focus, and I am gripped by the sickening realization that he's seeing me as I was in his memory. It feels violating, like he's rifling through my pockets. But then he steps close to the stage. "You've got this!" he calls out loud enough to be heard. "This champion doesn't have a chance."

Then I'm moving, because Michaela is onstage now. She has my arm and she's gently leading me to the center of a painted circle. I'm suddenly acutely aware of my clothing. A short dress and sandals are not the best choice for fighting. "Would I be allowed to fight barefoot?" I ask.

"Of course," Michaela answers.

"You can fight naked if you like," a man's voice says from

the opposite side of the stage. "It won't make a difference to me."

I spin to face this heckler, ready to explode into a speech about respect. But then I realize the voice is that of my opponent, and he wasn't speaking sarcastically.

He was speaking literally.

My gaze goes right to the empty sockets where his eyes should be. Judging by the scars that remain, I'd guess that he was born with eyes and they were taken from him violently. Still, even without vision, he strides toward me as if he is staring right at me, stopping in just the right place.

"Frightened? You should be." He's broad and tall, and I need not wonder about his build—perhaps he doesn't care if I fight naked because he's halfway there himself. From the waist down, he wears only a pair of pants cut off at the thighs. From the waist up, a sleeveless tunic that's so tight I can see the taut muscles of his stomach.

"I'm not frightened," I say. I try to remind myself how strong my Cientia is. *Control your breath*, I tell myself. *Stay calm*. But it doesn't matter.

"Self-doubt and fear. The perfect combination. I can't wait to start this match. It'll be over so fast, I'll have time enough to catch a nap before the next one."

"Self-doubt, fear, and *anger*," I say. "But please *do* underestimate me. It will make my victory all the sweeter."

Laughter explodes from the crowd—they're laughing at

me. *But they don't know what I can do.* I glance at Darius, the one friendly face. He nods. *You can do this,* he mouths. The noise has grown so I can't hear him. I can hardly hear Michaela, and she's standing right beside me.

"At my signal," she shouts into my ear.

"How will the champion know?"

"His name is Orsino, and he'll feel my intention. His Cientia is quite strong."

My heart hammers out of time, but I won't let my body betray me. Kicking off my sandals, I shake out my limbs and reach out with my senses. "Wait," I say to Michaela, and her face lights up. I realize she thinks I'm about to quit. But I just have a question. "Are there any limits on the magic I can use?"

Orsino can't hold back his laugh. "Little Outsider," he says, "feel free to use all the magic in your arsenal."

I nod, Michaela's arms come down, and the match starts.

Time slows. The room shrinks down to the borders of Orsino's emotions. I feel his pride, his sureness in the strength of his gifts. But I don't sense his intention to swing his fist until I am staggering back from the blow to my chin.

I catch my feet beneath me before I fall to the boards, but I'm rattled. Orsino takes advantage of my lack of focus. His foot flies up and lands in my ribs, and I fall hard to the floor.

He must be holding back. If he'd hit me with his full strength, my ribs would have shattered for sure. He's showing me mercy, and I need to make him regret it.

The volume of voices in the room rises, but I use it to my advantage. It's so loud, I let it become a cocoon of sound wrapped around me, blocking out all the details—Orsino's shouted name, sympathetic voices calling for me to save myself, cries to stop the fight because I've already lost.

With all that gone, I feel Orsino. His feet shuffle. Then he bends. A roundhouse kick. It's coming. I prepare. . . . I duck. But not in time.

His flying foot collides with the side of my head. I collapse to my knees. The lights in the room dim.

Looking up, I see that the shadow falling over me is Orsino's, as he bends down and shouts into my face. "Don't get up," he says. "If you want to stay conscious, stay down."

For a moment, I intend to follow his advice. But then I see Darius staring over the edge of the stage. Hear Darius call my name. "Let's go," he shouts. "You can beat him!"

Before Orsino feels my attention shift, I climb to my feet and leap up onto his broad back. My arms wrap around his neck; my legs wrap around his chest. I lock my ankles and pull myself up, until I'm practically on his shoulders. My right hand balls into a fist that I drive like a hammer into the side of his head. Again, and again, and again.

He staggers, but doesn't fall.

Instead, he explodes outward, throwing me off and sending me back to the boards. My head slams hard, and for a moment everything goes black. I hear Darius's voice—my name on his lips—as if I'm hearing him through water. And I hear Orsino, too, shouting for me to stay down.

But I won't stay down. I pull myself onto my hands and knees and stagger to my feet.

Something wet drips from my mouth. My bare hand swipes at my nose as I try to regain my balance. But before I can, Orsino lifts me over his head and slams me to the stage floor.

Something pops as my shoulder connects with the wood. I sit up, half expecting my arm to drop from my body. Pain—not the dull toothache kind but the kind that sears like flame—radiates down my arm as I run my fingers over the dislocated joint.

I crawl on one hand and two knees to the side of the stage. The crowd screams—some shouting their approval, others warning me to stay down, all swirling with a storm of pride pouring from Orsino—pride and a touch of something else.

"Pop it back in," I shout at Darius. I slide forward, rolling onto my back and turning my wrecked shoulder joint toward him. "Pop my shoulder back into place."

"I can't—"

"Do it!"

Darius's hands guide my arm up over my head and the ceiling tiles disappear behind big white spots. A scream flies up from my lungs so terrible, it's a sound that belongs only in nightmares. I squeeze my eyes shut and tears flow down my cheeks, but then the pain eases. The joint is back in place. I get to my feet. People are chanting, but my ears are ringing and I can't make out their words.

With my senses fading, my Cientia sharpens. The thing I feel in Orsino—the thing alongside his pride—it's *shame*. Regret at hurting a young girl. He's off balance. I feel it, and I see my chance.

I leap up, but he knocks me back down. Again I'm on my feet, and again I hit the floor. My vision dims. I shake my head and get up, but just to my knees.

"All the magic in my arsenal!" I call out. "You asked for it!" And I raise my hands, close my eyes, and see the match glow to life. I grunt out a breath, the match goes out, and I hear Orsino groan in pain.

The crowd silences. Orsino is on his knees. But even through the pain of Projectura, he crawls toward me.

I can't hesitate. I don't know how long the pain will last and hold him down. A leaping scissor kick connects the heel of my right foot with the bridge of his nose. Blood sprays. He slides onto his side. Arches his back.

Then lies still.

Michaela returns to the stage. Someone in the crowd calls out. "She cheated! You can't use Projectura in Hearts and Hands!"

My head flips up, my heart racing like a thief's. "But I asked—"

"You heard her ask if there were limits on the magic, did you not?" Michaela shouts. "And his invitation to use *all the magic in her arsenal*?"

The heckler silences as a murmur runs through the crowd, but no one else speaks.

Michaela counts it out—*one, two, three.* Loud slaps reverberate through the room. Then she grabs my arm and raises it above my head.

My shoulder explodes in pain.

I cry out, Michaela drops my arm, and I search the crowd for Darius. My head's so full of fog I can't trust that my victory was real, but I know the look on his face will confirm it.

But I'm wrong. Darius is not looking up at me with approval.

He's dropping to his knees, the crowd parting to give him room. His hands fold over his eyes. The room is too loud to hear him, but it doesn't matter.

I feel his scream in my bones.

TWENTY-THREE

Behind me, Orsino gives off nothing—no shock, no pain, no confusion. He's out cold. But the crowd ripples with sensations—surprise, and then fear—as several people bend down around Darius and try to help, try to simply learn what is wrong, but get nowhere. His body contorts, his eyes press into slits, his voice modulates from a scream to a moan to a scream again.

Cradling my elbow to support my shoulder, I bend down to try to talk to him, but he doesn't respond.

A doctor comes in. The crowd makes room so he can give me an injection in my shoulder, which is quite welcomed, and fit my arm into a sling, which is unwelcomed.

The doctor gives Darius a long look, the kind you would give a horse that's gone lame. "A racer too?" he grunts at me. I nod. "What do you know about memory sickness?"

"That it's terrible," I say flatly.

"That's more than most people know. Most people have never even heard of it. Only former racers, and I don't think too many people who survive the race like to talk about it later. Anyway, when a large dose of Oblivion begins to wear off—a dose the size they give you racers—the forgotten memories usually come back in waves of pain. But I guess you know that now." He struggles to his feet. "I'll send someone in with a stretcher. Not much to be done for him but wait it out, I'm afraid." He glances up at me. "Good luck to you, if you continue."

He leaves. The *click, click, click* of his heels fades away, until the room goes silent.

I'm kneeling beside Darius, holding his face still between my hands, not knowing what else to do, when someone taps me on my good shoulder. I turn to see a man and woman dressed in white smocks, with concern in their eyes and rubber gloves on their hands. They set a stretcher on the floor beside Darius. I lift my head. The room is empty. The crowd is gone.

How long have I been leaning over Darius? How long has the only readable emotion been coming from Michaela, seated behind me on the edge of the stage? Orsino is nowhere to be seen. If he woke up and walked out or was carried away, I have no idea.

I stand by as they load Darius onto the stretcher, and I have to bite my lip to keep from telling them to go easy. But his whole body is like a clenched fist, and I doubt he feels a thing. They carry him a short distance down the hall to the infirmary. I guess it makes sense that it's close to the gym.

"He can't go on. At least not yet," Michaela says when we're alone. "If you're going to continue in the race, you should go now, without him."

I feel a bit of pity for Darius, which only makes me angry at myself. After all, I'm the one who just got the tar kicked out of her. I earned the right to get on that train and be chauffeured to the next checkpoint. And now the decision of when to leave Darius has been made for me, which is a relief, to say the least.

A man walks into the gym—an older man with tattoos decorating the scar where his embed once was. He tells me he's been sent to lead me back to the train.

"Good luck. I think you may have a real chance of winning this race," Michaela says.

"I got what I wanted. I earned my ride to the next checkpoint," I say. But then I wiggle my slinged arm at her. "Hopefully, I didn't pay too high a price."

"You have an injury. So what? You're quite resilient," she says. "I saw you lose to Orsino more than once today. Everyone knew you had lost, except for you." This is a strange sort of praise, but I'll take it.

When we get back to the train, my guide shows me to a paneled sleeper car with all the amenities: a bed under a thick red bedspread, a bureau with a mirror, even a sink with running water. "Is the trip so long that I'll need a bed?"

"I watched that match. I'm sure you could use some rest," he says. I catch sight of my reflection. I could use a scrubbing, too. "And it's long enough. You should be able to get a good nap in, at the very least."

I nod, and he's gone.

I shrug off the sling and stretch my arms over my head. My left shoulder aches, but whatever was in that injection, it's killed the swelling and made the pain tolerable. I throw the sling in the trash.

At the sink I wash my face, comb my hair, and reposition Mary's hair clip. Then I sit on the edge of the bed and wait for the train to move. I try to concentrate on the future—try to make a plan for how I'll search for the next clue once I reach the Village of Falling Leaf—but my mind is too restless to let me sit. I decide to go for a walk around the train, maybe find my host and ask if he's got anything to eat, but when I try the door, it won't open. Either it's stuck, or it's locked from the outside.

"Hello!" I call, slamming my palm against the window in the door. "Can someone come help me? Hello!" I call louder and louder, but nobody appears in the hallway. My voice is hoarse from screaming when the train jerks forward and I'm knocked backward onto the bed.

I can't quite smother the suspicion that I was intention-ally locked in, even though I try to tell myself it was an honest mistake.

I raise the shade that covers the window, and I'm greeted by a view of the moon rising over the sand. If I'm stuck in this room, at least I'll get a chance to learn the terrain, in case I need to come back this way after I find the next clue. I prop myself beside the window and stare out, willing myself to stay alert, but exhaustion weighs heavy on me and I fall asleep instead.

When I wake, the door to my room is standing open. It's still dark out. The train is electric, and the night is eerily silent.

I'm not sure why the door is open now, but I don't hesi-tate to leave my car and look for someone who can tell me when we'll reach Falling Leaf. One, two, three quiet sleeper cars, the shades pulled down over the doors. The fourth car I come to is a dining car. Like the walls of my compartment, these are covered in dark paneling. The car is empty except for one occupant—my host, still wearing his rumpled suit.

He sits bent over a teacup, reading a sheet of paper by a single lamp, and I'm not sure he hears me. While I stand here unnoticed, I feel in him the anticipation of a confron-tation. I wonder if it's because I was locked in.

"I'm hungry," I say, which makes him look up.

"Well, it's the middle of the night. There won't be

breakfast for hours, and by then, you'll be off in Falling Leaf." He walks to the far end of the car and opens the door of a small refrigerator. "Do you like eggs?"

When I shrug, he pulls out a small dish and carries it to the table. Despite the unevenness of the track, he doesn't lurch from side to side, but moves with the fluidity of a snake gliding through grass. That's about how much I trust him, too. He sets the dish down in front of me. It contains three chicken eggs, boiled and peeled.

I sit down, uninvited, and pick up one of the eggs and eat half with one bite. It's delicious, in the way food can only be delicious when you've been hungry for too long. "Who are you?" I say, my mouth still full. Right now, I can't be bothered with manners. "And what do you know about my past?"

"You don't believe in small talk, do you?"

"I don't have time to waste."

"True. We're almost to Falling Leaf station."

Though this information is welcome, it doesn't answer my question, and I point this out.

"You haven't changed, I can tell you that," he says. He turns his eyes toward the window, as if the view of dark fields under intermittent moonlight is preferable to the impatient look on my face. "My name is Jayden Jael. I'm your brother."

I can't hold in the laugh. "*You're* Jayden Jael? Another one?"

His eyes fly back to my face. "I'm sorry? I'm not sure what you mean." Confusion stirs in him, but that's not all. He's insulted by my laughter.

"I already met a boy who said his name was Jayden Jael. He also claimed to be my brother, just before he tried to kill me."

His eyes move from my face to the window and back again.

"You have no embed," I say.

"I cut it out. A long time ago." He tugs down the neckline of his shirt to show me his thin, faded scar. He cocks an eyebrow. Like mine, his eyes are dark—almost black—and his straight black hair reminds me of the boy I was told was my younger brother.

Could this be my older brother?

The sudden reminder that my little brother already died in the race makes my heart hiccup out of rhythm, and all at once I know how I can tell if my host is really who he says he is. "If you really are Jayden, what can you tell me about Marlon?"

He tries to keep his reaction small, but it's obvious I've surprised him with this question. "Marlon?" He stands, picks up the paper he was reading when I came in, and sets it down again. He takes a swallow from his cup and then cradles it in his hands. "I can tell you that I remember him as the sweetest seven-year-old I ever knew. I can tell you that he loves you fiercely, but loves our papa more. I can tell you that he's probably never forgiven me for walking away."

He pauses and crosses to the window so I cannot see his face.

"He has a vocal tic," he says. "He does this thing where he repeats what he hears. Because of it, people underestimate him. You were always trying to stand up for him and tell people he's just fine, which usually made him so embarrassed and angry that he shouted at you, which generally proved your point."

Outside the window, red lights flash. We're passing a crossing. White headlights momentarily light the room. It feels odd, to know that outside this train, people are going on with their normal lives. "So he repeats things?" I ask. "Like what?"

"Like one line of a song he would sing over and over. Or a sound he heard. The most annoying was when someone would ask him a question, and he'd repeat it right back. That used to drive me crazy."

My mind fills with the memory of the boy standing in front of me in the roadhouse, echoing my words. I remember how angry it made me. I don't speak, but my host must notice something in my silence, because he turns around to face me. When he sees the tears in my eyes, he stops, and I know that he is really my brother.

"Why are you crying? What's wrong with Marlon?"

I drop my eyes and shake my head. My throat is so thick I feel I might choke, but I manage two words. "He's dead."

"Stop that. That's not funny."

"You think I'm being funny?"

"I know you have no memories—"

"Not from before the race. But this happened during the race. Marlon entered. He didn't know I had entered, too, and . . ."

"What happened to him?"

"I heard that he died on the road between the roadhouse and the outpost. Exposure, I guess." I remember the words the stranger said. *She described a boy she'd seen dead on the road. A boy with black hair. A real young kid.*

My head spins. I seize on the truth in this story that may prove it's a lie.

"The person who told me this . . . It was the same boy who said he was my brother Jayden. So this could be a lie, too. . . ."

"It could be a lie that he's in the race?"

"No, I know that part is true. I've seen him myself. No, the part that he's dead—"

"Don't get your hopes up. People die in this race, Astrid. It's why I hate it so much. And he's just eleven years old! And he's not strong like you. He's fragile—"

"You just said he was fine—"

"Fine for an eleven-year-old! But even *you* couldn't

261

have survived this race at that age." Without warning, he throws the china cup in his hand against the window, sending shards flying and a wet streak of tea running to the floor. "This race . . . Fools like you keep entering it year after year, seduced by the Enchanteds into believing it's an opportunity. What kind of opportunity leaves a dozen or more Outsiders dead? It's just one more way for them to torture us." He eyes the dish with the other two eggs, and I pick it up and pull it into my lap, to make sure it's not the next thing to hit the windows. "Believe me," he says, "if our little brother entered this race, there's a good chance he's already dead."

He paces away from me to the back of the car, hopefully to calm down, and I take the chance to wipe my tears and stop shaking. I glance at the paper he left on the table. It's not typed, but written out by hand, and something strange runs through me—a shiver of recognition—when I see the handwriting. I put another egg in my mouth—I'm kind of sick to my stomach, but I don't know when I'll have fresh eggs again—and I pick it up to read it. "What is this?" I ask when I've swallowed most of the egg.

He throws a glance in my direction. "What does it look like?"

My eyes move over the words *Outsider Liberation Army* and *Manifesto*. "Wait. Are you in the OLA?"

"You could say that." He finds another cup, fills it from

an electric carafe near the refrigerator where he retrieved the eggs, and hesitates. "I can't remember if you drink tea."

I nod. The roof of my mouth tingles with all the questions I want to blurt out: *How long have we been separated? When was the last time you saw me? What are you doing in the OLA, and how is it you have control of this train?*

But the only questions I should be wasting my time and breath asking are questions that could help me. Questions that would give me an advantage in the race. I raise my chin and ask, "What can you tell me about *me*? About my life before the race?"

"Slow down," he says. He opens a drawer and pulls out a second china cup. The train lists heavily onto its side as we navigate a sharp turn, and hot water splashes onto the floor as he pours from the carafe. "I'm not sure how much I want to tell you. Remember, I strongly disapprove of this race."

"So you'd prefer to watch your sister struggle until she dies?"

"I'd prefer to watch my sister quit this choreographed cruelty they call the Race of Oblivion and join the cause of the Outsider Liberation Army." He places the cup on the table in front of me. The train straightens out of its turn and a bit of water sloshes over the side and wets the white tablecloth. "I'm not just some foot soldier in the ranks of the OLA, Astrid. I'm its leader. This is where you belong, fighting for the rights of Outsiders beside your brother."

"Its *leader*? How old are you? Twenty?"

"I'm nineteen."

I'm having trouble reconciling the fact that this man—this manipulative stranger who forced me to risk my life in a Hearts and Hands match before he would even agree to take me to the next checkpoint—is my brother. I don't like it, but I believe it. This claim of being the leader of the OLA is another matter altogether. A million questions prickle at the back of my throat, but I hold them in and remind myself that my priority is winning the race. "Maybe you want me beside you," I say. "Or maybe you're just trying to sabotage my chance to win. You might be my brother, you might even be part of the OLA. But that doesn't mean you're rooting for me. Maybe you have a bet on someone else. I'd say this train looks more like it belongs to a gambler than to a general in a rebel army."

"Ah, but it's not that kind of army."

Behind me, the door to the train car opens. I spin around, feeling suddenly vulnerable in this dark train in the middle of the night. The girl I fought outside the train walks in with the engineer. Their hands are entwined.

"I couldn't give you any names until I trusted you," says Jayden. "Astrid, this is my engineer, Rafaela, and my second in command, Wendy."

"Sorry, but I couldn't help overhearing," Wendy says.

She pouts at me. "You don't believe we're the OLA? Haven't you ever heard of us?"

"Why are you up in the middle of the night?" I ask her.

"I'm here for your mission, same as you." She lifts the last egg from the dish and takes a small bite. Her words make my eyes shoot to Jayden's face. He's smiling, too, the way you smile when you've got your prey where you want them. My stomach flips like a fish out of water, and I turn back to Wendy.

"What mission?"

"*Wait.* Have you heard of us or not?"

It feels like Wendy's ego is at stake here. A mist of insecurity clings to her, and frankly, the reputation of an underground organization feels like the wrong thing to depend on for personal affirmation. I glance at Jayden again and then at Rafaela, who is ignoring this entire exchange in order to serve herself a cup of tea.

"I have. But . . . I guess I assumed the OLA was run by a weathered old fanatic—"

"Not a weathered *young* fanatic?" Rafaela asks, without looking up from her teacup. Wendy laughs, which only ratchets up my discomfort.

I glance from one face to the next. These three are not what I expected from an underground organization fighting for equality for Outsiders. I'm not sure what I expected instead—bandits with the bottom half of their faces covered, I guess. The OLA is famous for blowing up railroad tracks and bridges, and destroying monuments to Enchanted heroes. And they always leave behind their leaflets—manifestos on the rights of Outsiders.

Jayden is glancing out the window again, pretending he's distracted, so I come to stand beside him. "What mission?" I repeat, keeping my voice low. "I need to continue this race. I don't have time for anything else."

"But you *do* have time. You can't collect the next clue until dawn. There's plenty of time before then."

Wendy and Rafaela take seats at an empty table. Their hands entwined again, Wendy drops her head onto Rafaela's shoulder. They watch me and Jayden as if they're watching a play.

"Enjoying yourselves?" I spit. I'm tired of being stared at like a trained dog. Between the Hearts and Hands match and this, I've had enough.

Wendy's head snaps upright and her eyes widen. Her mouth opens like she's got something to say, but nothing comes out. "You better give us some privacy," Jayden says.

There's a loud, exhaled *humph*, but otherwise, they leave without a word.

"First," Jayden says once the door closes behind them, "you won't be manipulated to do anything you don't choose to do. You won't be forced. If at any time you want to walk away, just say the word."

"That's easy enough. I want—"

"Hear me out!" Jayden scowls at me. He has a shorter fuse than I'd realized. "Let me tell you what I need you to do. Sit down," he says, and I do exactly that, as if some instinct inside me remembers him being my bossy older brother. "Tell me what you know of the Village of Falling Leaf."

"I know that the last clue said to come to this village at dawn. Something about the color of the village door will tell me where to go next."

"Is that all you know? Well, then let me tell you why the Enchanteds want to send racers to the gate of Falling Leaf at dawn. The village is surrounded by an ancient wood, one of the favorite habitats of the sharp-eyed boar. And if you don't know about the sharp-eyed boar, let me tell you this: they're quite fast and they can be vicious, but more importantly, they're nocturnal, these boars—that's why they call them sharp-eyed—and right now they're in season. They're so elusive, they're a celebrated prize for hunters, who gather in the wood outside the gate of Falling Leaf, and just before the sun rises, they will shoot at anything that moves." He pauses, and his eyes fall on my face, and for a moment I think I see compassion in them. "You're afraid."

"Of course I'm afraid." I turn away from him, because it's miserable to think of him reading me like that, even without the aid of Cientia. *Is this what it means to have a sibling? To be an open book?* Well, I don't want my book lying open, not to Jayden or anyone, so I turn my attention to the landscape outside the window. We're moving quickly, trees flying by, but up ahead I see the slope of a hill and, clinging to that slope, the outline of a village wall. "That's it," says Jayden. "That's Falling Leaf. And that's the wood where racers will shortly be shot to death before the sun comes up, if they're not torn to shreds by wild boars first."

"I can't figure you out," I say. "You offered me a ride if I could beat Orsino. You apparently have some sort of mission you want me to do here. Now you talk like only a fool would go out there. Like you're trying to talk me out of it."

"I know you won't be talked out of it. I only want you to see how thoroughly you are being manipulated."

"By the Enchanteds, or by you?"

This question catches him by surprise. I can tell by the way his head snaps in my direction, by the way he tries to impale me with his gaze. "I need a favor here in Falling Leaf," he admits. He folds his arms across his chest and leans against the glass. Something warm rises in him, a yearning to be understood. "One that can only be done at night by someone with strong Cientia. I want you to understand . . . approaching the gate of Falling Leaf would be dangerous for anyone who didn't have Cientia as strong as Orsino. That was the reason I insisted on the match. But let me be clear—I am not trying to manipulate you. If I could have this any way I wanted, you would be the person to run this mission, and then you would turn around and come back to this train, drop out of the race, and join the OLA." He takes a step toward me and leans in, and it takes all my effort not to take a step back. He might know me, but to me he is still a stranger. "You're halfway to safety already, Astrid. You've escaped that awful house. And Papa would understand. We could send him money from time to time. I know he would forgive you."

There is a particular sort of guilt in knowing something important that someone else doesn't know. That's the sensation I get when he mentions our father, and I realize that the truth of his death is like a secret, a painful truth that is not yet true to Jayden. It's the complete opposite of the sensation I get when the words *escaped that awful house* casually drip from Jayden's mouth, as coolly as he might say, *Your hair is dirty* or *Your legs are thin*, or any other obvious truth.

He reads my face. "You don't remember, do you?"

"Remember what?"

Whatever softness had taken hold of him earlier, he shrugs off. The man who reminded me of a snake in the grass returns. "Do this mission, and return to this train instead of continuing in the race, and I promise to tell you about *that awful house*, and everything else about your past that you've forgotten."

TWENTY-FOUR

From the compartment where I slept, I retrieve my coat and my bag—both taken from women who are now dead. I've agreed to do as Jayden asks—to complete this mission, even to return to the train afterward—though the truth is I've yet to decide if I'll do either of those things. I'm tempted, of course. Jayden's words about *that awful house* echo in my head like the words of a riddle, written in a code I cannot crack.

To be honest, I won't know what I'm going to do until I see the color of the village gate at dawn.

Though I expect to find Wendy and Rafaela back in the dining car when I return, I find Jayden alone. He's leaning over a silver tray on the table, his hair curtaining off his eyes, a straw held to his nose. As I come closer, I notice several thin lines of black powder.

"Revelry?"

Jayden snorts a line and shakes his head. "Don't worry about me, little sis. I've got it under control. I do a little bit of Oblivion, and then a little bit of Revelry, Oblivion's perfect antidote. When you've seen the horrors I've seen, you'll use them too."

"You don't think I've seen horrors?"

He looks up, and I flinch when I see that look I saw on Darius, the look that tells me he's remembering me, from a time that I've forgotten. "I know you've seen more than most people. That's for sure," he says.

He bends his head again over the Revelry, and I can see the skin of his back at the base of his neck. For the first time since I realized that this person is really who he claims to be—my brother, but also the leader of the Outsider Liberation Army—I wonder how those two things might be connected. What nightmares did Jayden live through that led him to the OLA, and have I lived through those nightmares, too? I think of the lash marks on my back and wonder if Jayden has them. The sliver of skin above his collar is too narrow to give him away.

While we're alone, Jayden goes over the mission with me. He tells me that I should hike beyond the gate, following the village wall, until I come to a few buildings built of rough-hewn logs. "Falling Leaf is a lumber town, and these buildings are dormitories. One houses Outsider labor— you'll know it because it has no windows. The other, built to be much more comfortable, is a dormitory where the taskmasters live. I need you to enter that building, but *don't get caught*. These taskmasters have already killed five Outsiders in the past week—"

"Killed? Killed *how*?"

Jayden scowls at me. I guess I've asked a stupid question. "With an inhumanly strong dose of Projectura, that's how. These people are torturers, Astrid. Have you heard nothing I've said?"

The potato-like face of the taskmaster at the farm springs to my mind. Could *she* kill someone with Projectura? Could *I*? "No. I mean *yes*, I have. I'm listening."

Jayden hands me a silver briefcase and instructs me to leave it inside, in the center of the building, if possible, on the ground floor. Before I can ask, he adds, "It's a device for transmitting voices. The OLA will use it to record intelligence that can be used to prove what's being done to the Outsider laborers here, to expose these taskmasters as the murderers they are. So hide it well. Under a chair is good, in a place where it looks like they gather."

The train comes to an abrupt halt, and Jayden gets to his feet. "Aren't we going into the station?" I ask. Beyond the glass of the windows, the night is thick and black. The intermittent moonlight, filtered through wisps of silver clouds, reveals nothing but dense forest.

"The station is within the village walls," Jayden says. "It

makes more sense for you to jump down here. The gate isn't far. It's just up from the river. You'll find it." The door at the end of the dining car opens and Rafaela appears.

She steps in front of me and uses something resembling a wrench to open the door to the outside. It swings open, and the three of us stand peering out into the night. I notice a soft breeze, the rhythm of crickets, a low gurgle of running water, and far away, a gunshot.

"Keep your senses tuned for hunters," Jayden says, "and your eyes open for boar. Once you've completed the mission, meet me at the village gate at dawn, and I'll lead you back to the train."

I must look pretty scared, because Rafaela says, *"Hey now,"* in that low, drawn-out way people do when they mean to comfort someone. "I heard how you handled Orsino. You can handle this." I nod and try to smile a bit, to show I appreciate her saying that. When neither of them says anything else, I pull on the coat, shrug my bag onto my good shoulder, and jump down from the safety of the train into the danger of the unknown.

The turf along the tracks is soft, littered with the earliest leaves of the fall. But autumn is still young, and most of the leaves are still green and clinging to the trees, making it hard to see, which I hope works to my advantage. It's cool outside but not cold, here in the more temperate north, and I stride off, letting the slim shafts of moonlight light my way. I see little and I hear even less, but it isn't long before I find a path, which helps quiet my heart and invigorate my hope.

I have at least an hour before dawn. I promise myself that if I find the gate quickly, I'll make my way to the dormitories and consider Jayden's mission. But I also remind myself that I owe nothing to anybody. "Your only obligation is to yourself and to the race," I whisper in an attempt to feel less alone, but then my senses flare, and I wish I had kept quiet.

Someone is ahead of me on the path. Not someone I can see, or even someone I can hear, but someone I can feel. *Anticipation . . . the feeling right before you pull the ribbon from a gift.*

The person on the path is a hunter.

I slow, not sure if my best plan is to stay on the trail or slip into the trees. The latter is more likely to get me confused with a boar and shot, so I slow my steps and stay behind. Sound comes from my left, but before I hear it I feel it—*fear and confusion, and the overwhelming desire to be somewhere else.*

This person is clearly a racer.

I continue on the path, and though I see no one, I feel the emotions of the hunter on my right and then behind me. Either one hunter is circling, or there are more than one. This second option is unnerving, to say the least. I could be walking right into a trap laid for a boar, and I could be shot before they recognize I'm not the prey they were hoping for. So I halt and squat down, and off to my left again I feel the racer.

Then I hear him hurrying, kicking up leaf litter behind him. And then I see him—black hair and thin legs and a back bent over as he runs.

Marlon?

I tell myself it's hard to see. I tell myself the moonlight is tricky and unreliable, and a person with brown hair or red hair or even dirty blond hair might look like Marlon in the dark. But none of that matters. All that matters is that hope has flashed across my mind like a flash of lightning in the dark, and I have to follow him.

I stumble along, guided by the sounds of his racing feet, realizing too late the obvious reason why a person would risk running through this pitch-black wood, with so many obstacles hidden in the underbrush. Behind me, I hear a grunting that's almost human, but not human enough. Something is pursuing me, grunting and snorting and trampling the ground under four feet. I lose track of the sound of the racer in front of me when I turn and find myself face-to-face with the charging boar.

Vaulting off the path, I hurdle over low scrubs and downed branches, until my forehead connects with something hard. It stuns me for a moment, until I realize I've walked right into the thing I need the most—a low tree limb.

I throw a leg over and lift myself off the ground, my feet barely clearing the head of the boar as he tears across the ground. His head collides with the tree with such force, the trunk shudders and I almost lose my grip. Moonlight glows in the boar's upturned eyes as he watches me climb.

Now that I'm high enough to see him clearly, I huff out a sigh of relief. He's huge—maybe six hundred pounds—and even in the dark I can see the long white tusks that jut out from his jaw. He lowers his head and turns in place, but then a loud snap draws his attention up again. The branch I'm crouching on is cracking. Another snap and it sags under me. I reach for the branch above my head, but it's thin and I fear it won't hold me.

But then a series of shots rings out like tiny explosions, *bang bang bang*, followed by shouts, and the boar's broad back disappears into the dark underbrush.

I draw a deep breath, clamp my hands tight around the tree trunk, and start to climb down, searching the ground for the hunter who fired the shots. Something ahead of me on the path gets caught up in a splash of moonlight, the way an actor gets caught up in a spotlight on the stage. It's the dark-haired racer I'd seen earlier, and I realize all at once that he is standing right where I was when I thought I might be walking into a hunter's trap.

Then he disappears again into shadow, rustling through

the underbrush, until his careless rustling is cut off by the sound of a single shot.

He stumbles in and out of the light; he's there . . . and then not there. He's back on the path, stumbling like a drunk, then tumbling into the shadows again.

Before I know it, my feet are on the ground and I'm moving headlong through the darkness, without giving a thought to boars or hunters or guns. All I can think of is the face of the boy in the roadhouse and the way I had felt when the stranger in the desert told me that my brother was dead.

When I reach him, someone is leaning over him—a man with a dark vest and a wool cap and a rifle in his hand—but when he hears me approach he takes off. He's either in a hurry to find an actual boar to shoot, or he's in a hurry to avoid having to answer for what he's done.

As if anyone would care. As if anyone would hold him accountable for the death of a racer. Someone so insignificant. Someone who is not expected to live anyway.

Jayden's words come back to me: *It's just one more way for them to torture us.* Could he be right? Could the Race of Oblivion—this one thing I've put all my hope in—be nothing but a trap?

"Marlon," I mutter as I move closer, taking in his gangly legs and his dark hair, his young body facedown in the dirt. "Marlon, I am so sorry," I say as I lift his head and pull it into my arms. He's bleeding from a chest wound, his tunic wet and sticky in the front and in the back, and he turns his dark eyes to my face as his breath comes in halting, stuttering gasps.

TWENTY-FIVE

Damp hair sticks to his forehead, and I brush it from his eyes, and that's when I see that the racer looking up at me is not the boy from the roadhouse who mimicked me. It's the boy I fought at the lighthouse, the one with the tree-trunk arms. And this boy is too big and too old and too strong to be the boy that Jayden described.

It's not Marlon.

Not Marlon, not Marlon, *not Marlon*. Whether Marlon is alive or dead, at least he is not going to die in my arms before the sun comes up this morning.

But this young man is.

Because there is so much blood. It's on his tunic, on his pants, and on my dress. When I slide a hand out from under him, a warm puddle of it pools in my palm. It's too much. I'm not sure the exact quantity of blood a person can lose and still live, but I know this is too much.

"What's your name?" I ask him. I touch his hand. His skin is cool, and he doesn't grip my hand back.

"Knox," he says. His breath is shallow, his voice so low I can barely hear him over the crickets when he says his name.

But I do hear him. I hear that his name is Knox, and I vow that I will remember it. And if I survive this horrific ordeal, I vow I will find his family, and I will tell them that I was with him when he died, and I will tell them that he was brave.

He's such a young kid. He might be fifteen. Maybe even younger. Soft hairs shade the corners of his upper lip. A mustache that will never grow in.

"This has been a long night," he says, and I press my lips between my teeth when the tears sting the backs of my eyes. Tears cannot help him. They can't help me. They're useless, so I blink them away. "I think I'm going to get some rest," he says.

I don't answer him, because my voice might break and I don't want him to know how grim his situation is. So I gather his arms up and hold him tight, and I nod, and he closes his eyes. I hold him there, maybe one more minute, maybe two.

And then he dies.

Not my Marlon, but somebody's.

I set his head down on the ground as gently as I can,

wishing I could do more for him, but knowing that there are worse places to die than this moonlit wood. I feel bad about it, but I wipe the blood from my hands onto his pants. I know his body will almost certainly become food for this pack of boars, but I try not to think about that. He's dead, and I might be next—that's the bare truth—so I push myself to climb to my feet and start moving again.

The sun is still below the horizon when I reach a road of packed dirt that leads to the broad wooden gate in the wall. Behind the wall, stone buildings climb the shadowy hillside. The steep streets are lit by a few flickering gas lamps, but it's a small village and all the shutters are closed against the night. Nothing and no one stir. On this side of the wall, the gate is illuminated by moonlight, but its color is only a dull brown.

Still, I remind myself that things look quite different in the daylight.

Behind my back, not far within the wood, I can still hear the occasional squeal of a cornered boar and the unmistakable ring of gunfire. My chest feels heavy, as if my heart were soaked in grief. The skin between my fingers is still sticky with Knox's blood, and if I picture his face, I still feel the shiver that ran through me when I realized he wasn't Marlon.

I can't just stand here, listening to gunfire and wondering if another racer has been shot. Thankfully, I have somewhere else to go.

The line of the wall runs perpendicular to the road, and I follow it deeper into the trees until I come to a clearing and the two dormitories built of logs, just like Jayden described them to me. The hillside overlooking them has been clear-cut of trees, and I remember that Jayden called Falling Leaf a lumber town.

As Jayden promised, it's easy to distinguish the dorm for Outsiders, which looks like a windowless prison, from the dorm for the taskmasters, which looks like a lodge.

I climb in through an unlatched window and stand still to wait for the feelings of people nearby. It's as quiet as a tomb once the window shuts out the breeze and the chirping crickets. I wait, but I notice nothing. No icy fear or pungent lies. If people are here, everyone must be asleep, at least on this floor.

As I pass by one door after another, with a sleeping Enchanted taskmaster behind each one, I can't help but think of the five Outsiders Jayden says died here last week. Are the people responsible sleeping just a few feet away? How do they sleep so well, knowing what they've done?

They must have nightmares. I know I would.

In the center of the floor I find a dining room, and it takes a long time for my eyes to adjust, but enough moonlight filters through skylights for me to notice a wide bookshelf covering one wall. I know I need to hurry, but I can't help but let my fingers trail across the spines, stopping when I find a book I think might come in handy. It's too dark for me to thumb through it, but *ATLAS* spelled out in black lettering against a white background gives me hope that it will help me find my way around Lanoria's roads, rivers, and railways.

I slide it into my bag and pull out the silver case Jayden gave me. Though the middle of the room is crowded with cafeteria-style tables and chairs, the corners are more inviting, crowded with padded recliners and cozy couches in clusters near the bookshelves. It's easy for me to find a place to tuck the case, beneath an overstuffed love seat. If people gather in this room to have intimate conversations—to share secrets—this is where they would sit.

I'm almost back to the window when I feel curiosity behind me. I turn and find a small Outsider woman, not quite old enough to be my mother but old enough to be my aunt, just a few feet behind me, holding a dripping mop. Her embed flashes in the dark, and there's a faint scent of bleach about her. "You're quiet," I say.

She only nods, as if to prove how quiet she can be.

"Don't tell anyone I was here, all right?" I turn away, wondering if it's at all possible she won't, and wondering if it even matters if she does, when she speaks.

"Are you Astrid?"

I'm not sure what to say, so I just say, "I am."

"Is this part of the race? Is there a clue inside this dormitory?"

"I thought there was," I say, yearning to get back outside. I shuffle my feet like a nervous child. But this is a good cover story, so I add, "But I was wrong."

"Would you do something for me?" she asks.

"I have to go," I say. "The sun will be coming up soon."

She has an apron tied around her waist, and from its pocket she tugs a piece of paper that's been folded down to fit. She unfolds it and turns it toward me so that I can see that it's an article from a newspaper, with the photograph of me perched on the ledge outside the window of the lighthouse, the same picture I saw on the Enchanted man's comm at the dance hall.

"I read about your papa dying, and how you and your brother had both entered the race," she says. She keeps her eyes on the floor between us, as if I were someone important, which makes me feel embarrassed, because I'm not. "My papa died too, so I feel a little bit of a kinship with you. Sorry for your loss."

"Thank you," I say, "but I have to go—"

"I've been following your progress," she continues. "I knew you would come here—"

"Wait." I need to climb out this window, but this statement rattles me. "You knew I was coming to *this building*?"

"No, I knew you were coming to Falling Leaf. You were seen at the outpost, and everyone says the next clue from there points to our village gate—"

"How does *everyone* know that? The clue was in the desert—"

"It's in the news, on account of you and your brother being known for what happened at the Apple Carnival. I guess a newspaperman saw you at that clue—the one that points to our little village—and he took your picture and wrote a follow-up story on you. I don't have that one though."

Mr. Arrogance . . . I almost can't believe it. But if it's truly common knowledge that the next clue will be revealed at the village gate at dawn, and if the Enchanted Authority is truly looking for a female racer who uses Enchanted magic, I guess when the sun comes up, they'll know right where to find me.

"I gotta go," I say again.

I turn toward the window, feeling somewhat self-conscious about climbing out, but not wanting to risk the door, when she says, "Wait. The favor I wanted to ask you . . ."

I whirl around, the refusal on my lips, when she holds out the newspaper article about me and a pen. "Would you sign this?"

"I . . ."

Maybe it's because I don't want to embarrass her by refusing; maybe it's because I don't want to embarrass myself. Maybe it's because I realize I could die at any minute, and maybe this signature on my picture will be worth something to this woman if I do. Whatever my reasons, I take the paper and pen and scrawl my name. Just my first name. I'm uncomfortable with how happy she is to receive it, and how she insists that I keep the pen. "In case you need it," she says.

I'm out the window before she can say anything else.

The sky is brightening in the east as I head back to the gate. When it's just within sight, I choose a tall pine tree with low branches and climb up to where I can see without being seen. As I feared, there's a cluster of officers of the Enchanted Authority just beside the road, huddled over steaming paper cups. Either they don't expect me or they think it's too early, because one shines a battery light between the trees from time to time, but if anything, the whole group appears disinterested. I don't see anyone else, but I feel them—scattered pinpoints of nerves and anticipation. I'm not sure how many are here, but there are other racers staying out of sight among the trees.

When the sun brushes the undersides of the leaves and reaches out to caress the face of the village gate, the officers finally go quiet. It's just an old wooden gate to a far-flung village, and yet nothing could tear my eyes from it right now.

As we all watch, the face of the gate goes from brown to russet, and then, as the sun sits on the edge of the world like a burning ball, the gate glows a vibrant purple, like a perfectly ripe grape, or the skin of a plum. But not for long. The sun pushes higher, clearing the horizon, and in full light, the face of the gate glows red.

But for that thin moment, just as the sun came up, it was purple.

The officers continue to mill around, surely discontent with this assignment, and before long they crumple their cups in their fists. The one with the battery light gives the trees one more sweep, and for a moment I worry he will actually find me, but he's not really paying attention. Behind him, the other officers have already ducked under the gate, which is being slowly raised and is halfway up.

The last officer turns, but then a sound comes from the trees. A muffled cough. The officer hesitates.

Pivoting, he steps into the trees. Sunlight stretches along the ground, but the foliage around me is still in shadow, until he sweeps his light upward. It skims an inch below my left foot. I hold my breath. The officer steps closer and the light sweeps back, higher this time, when a racer drops to the ground in front of me. The officer turns toward him, and he crouches, wide-eyed, under his light.

It's the ginger-haired racer. I cringe at the sight of him, remembering that Marlon had been with him at the roadhouse. I want to beat all the other racers, but none as much as I want to beat him.

He brushes himself off. The officer watches him but doesn't try to stop him when he turns and heads through the open gate.

Once he's gone, others emerge from under the trees—the small woman with the big boots, a squat man I remember from outside the lighthouse. When these have followed the ginger-haired racer into town, the officer lingers, gives the trees one more sweep with his light, and then heads through the gate.

Once they've all gone, I stay in the tree, but I shrug my bag from my shoulder and page through the atlas. There are many small towns with many strange names, but none of them seem to have anything to do with purple.

Will Jayden be able to help me with this clue? I promised to meet him at dawn outside the village gate, but I can't wait much longer. I climb down to the ground, ready to leave, and find him standing right beneath me, hidden in the shadows.

I startle at the sight of him, and he shakes his head. "I thought you could feel the presence of people."

"I can," I whisper, leading him away from the trees. "But there are still other people here." He glances over my shoulder. "Other racers," I add.

His eyes move over the trees and he draws me closer to

the village wall. "First things first," he murmurs. "Were you able to hide the case?"

"Of course," I say.

He smiles at this, the first truly sincere smile I've seen on him. I've seen him smirk, and I've seen him with a crafted thing that's supposed to be a smile, but this is the first genuine expression of happiness he's shown me.

"And no one saw you?"

I think of the Outsider woman, and the autograph I gave her, and the promise she gave me to keep our meeting a secret. "No one."

"Well, I suppose you're going to want some help with that clue. . . ." He glances sideways at me and then at the gate, and then back in the direction of his train. "I know you've decided not to come with me. Otherwise, why would you be flipping through that atlas?"

I glance down at the incriminating book in my hand. "I have to—"

"Save it!" he snaps. I don't appreciate being scolded, even by my own brother, but then he calms down and adds in a whisper, "It's the Amaranthine Forest."

"What?" Noises come from beyond the gate—the whir of engines and the murmur of voices. The Village of Falling Leaf is waking up. I need to get moving.

"The clue," Jayden breathes into my ear. "Amaranthine is a shade of purple. The clue refers to the Amaranthine

Forest. There's a research station there, where they study native species. The entrance is just north of this village."

"Thank you," I say, probably too softly and without looking at him. I can feel his anger, and frankly, it hurts too much to look him in the eye.

"Keep your guard up. An Enchanted Authority train showed up on the tracks just before dawn. A bunch of racers jumped down when it stopped, obviously stowaways. I guess the word is out that the Authority is following you."

"I guess," I say.

He turns and walks away, but then he stops and calls my name, and I can't help but hurry over to him.

"The closer you get to winning the race, the more anxious the Authority will be to arrest you. Do you know why?"

"I . . ." This is something I hadn't really thought about. "Why does the Enchanted Authority pursue anyone? Because I've broken the law—"

"Trust me, there are plenty of lawbreakers in Lanoria, but you've broken a law that represents the whole of Lanorian order—the law against Outsider magic—and they can't let you get away with that." He smiles at me, and I can tell he thinks he's pretty clever. "But here's their conundrum. . . . If you win, you'll be a citizen. You can't be charged with using Enchanted magic if you have the same rights as the Enchanteds. The closer you come to winning this race, the more the Authority will ratchet up their efforts to arrest you *before* you win—"

"*If* I win—"

"Correct. *If* you win."

He turns and starts to walk away again, but now it's my turn to call his name. "Where will you go after you leave here? I'll look for you once the race is done."

"Why?" he asks. His tone is as rough as new sandpaper. I wish he wouldn't throw so much guilt at me. Walking away is hard enough, but honestly, his guilt is making me want to run. "You'll be a citizen," he calls. "You'll have all the rights of the Enchanted, and you'll fall in step with them, just like your friends, those traitors of the Third Way."

"What?" I understand if he's feeling betrayed by *me*, but why drag the Third Way into this? "Why do you call them traitors? They live in peace. *You* were living among them—"

"Among them, but not as one of them. Their compound is a perfect place to hide, and they have resources the OLA lacks. But the Outsiders who have joined them—how do they live with themselves? How do they look in the mirror? They know their own people are oppressed and slaughtered every day, and yet they mix with their oppressors. Some of them even *sleep* with them." He pauses and spits on the ground. "How could any Outsider aspire to coexist with the butchers of their own people?" he asks, and then waits, as if that's a question I'm supposed to answer.

But I can't. I just stare at him in silence, my own admiration for the people of the Third Way suddenly challenged. Could he be right? "But the Enchanted who live with the Third Way are different—"

"If I told you monsters could be tamed, would you want to live with monsters? Even a tame monster is still a monster."

I don't know how to respond to this, so I say, "So that's it? You won't tell me a thing about who I am?"

"I'll tell you every detail if you don't finish the race—"

"I'm going, Jayden. I have to. I might not remember the girl I was when I entered this race, but I know I can't let that girl down." Then, after giving him a few moments to change his mind and tell me more about my past, I say, "Thanks for your help."

"Thanks for yours, too," he says. And then he walks away.

I need to go. Other racers may be well on their way to the Amaranthine Forest, but I can't move until Jayden completely disappears from my view.

TWENTY-SIX

I allow myself one minute to sweep my eyes over the center page of the atlas—the page that shows a map of the whole continent of Lanoria—and locate the Amaranthine Forest. A logging road connects it to the north gate of Falling Leaf, but a hike through the woods will be more direct, and more discreet.

The trees grow close and thick, and the ground is shaded by a dense canopy. I don't hike long before the foliage is already changing, and I realize the Amaranthine Forest's name is its literal description. Trees with all-green foliage are already in the minority; most of the trees around me now have some purple in their leaves. The farther north I walk, the greater the number of one particular variety, a tree with dark purple leaves that turn blue as the season changes them, so that after a while, I'm tramping across leaf litter that resembles the sea. There are other varieties too, one with shades of raspberry and another with lavender, and every now and then I notice a standard green tree, which by contrast looks shocking and odd.

Eventually I come to a high chain-link fence, but there's an open gate where it crosses the road. Right beyond the gate sits a trio of buildings made of purple wood, and above the gate the words *Native Flora Research Station* are carved into a simple wooden sign. Before stepping out from under cover I search the road, but if the Authority is coming, it isn't here yet. I hurry up to the closest door. Two small signs hang right beside the knob. The first is written by hand on a sheet of paper: *No Racers Inside!* The second, printed on cloth and hung like a banner, says: *To find the truth you seek, you must see the forest through the eyes of a bird.*

Though the first sign makes me want to march right into the building and let everyone inside know how much I resent being treated like an unwelcome indigent, the second sign is certainly a clue. I have to keep moving, so I shrug off the insult.

I'm still standing on the path looking up at the door when it swings toward me and a man walks out. He has a mop of white hair on top of a square head, and he needs a shave. When his eyes fall on me he gives a little grunt, and for a moment, I think he's going to retreat back into the building. But then he shuffles down the three short steps and asks if I'm a racer.

"I am," I say, in a voice that makes it sound as if being a racer is the thing I'm most proud of in life.

"Well, then I might as well tell you that there is a nest in one of the rafters that overhangs the bridge. It's a falcon's nest, but the birds have already left it for the season. Anyway, it might help you with this clue."

I don't quite know how to respond, since the last thing I expected from this gruff Enchanted man was assistance, so it takes me a moment to formulate my reply. But then he pushes past me, grumbling to himself. *The faster you all find the clue—or break your necks trying—the faster you will all be gone and we can get back to our work.* Something like that. I can't catch it all because he's speaking to himself instead of me, while he walks away, no less.

It would be impossible to miss the trestle bridge. Towering above the tops of the trees, it carries train track between two high slopes that border this wide valley. It's one of those examples of engineering that stop your breath. It's so massive it's almost miraculous. As I stand in the shadow of this intricate lattice of wooden beams, my mind goes to the Village of Falling Leaf and the clear-cut forest above the dormitories for the Outsider laborers and the Enchanted taskmasters, and I wonder if that's where all this lumber came from.

Looking up, I spot the nest the white-haired man told me about. It's way up at the top, in the rafters that overhang the tracks, so it won't be easy to get to.

My heart takes flight at the sight of that nest, but as fast as it goes up, it crashes back down. Between me and that nest, two racers are already making the climb through the beams. I half expect one to be Darius, since the first time I saw him he was climbing the lighthouse, making it look easy. He's not one of these two, though, which doesn't necessarily mean he's not ahead of me. As long as he was watching the gate of Falling Leaf at dawn, he could have already been here and gone. But instead of Darius, I notice the ginger-haired racer who seems to always be one step ahead of me, and way ahead of him, almost high enough to climb up onto the track, is a racer with dark hair and gangly limbs.

Something flutters in my chest, a flutter of hope, which infuriates me, but I can't help myself. At least from this distance, it could be Marlon.

I grab a beam at the foot of the trestle and throw myself into the climb. This structure is much easier to scale than the lighthouse, even with an aching shoulder, and I'm able to put distance between me and the ground quickly.

I try to talk to myself, to tell myself not to look down, but I can't help it. I drop my gaze all the way to the ground just as I reach the track, and my heart would probably race if it hadn't just stopped. Stopped cold, along with my lungs, at the sight of the treetops so far below me.

But then I squeeze my eyes shut and turn my face up toward the tracks. When my breath comes back and my heart restarts, I swear I won't look at the ground again until I've retrieved the clue and worked my way back down, and even then, not until I'm just a foot above the grass.

By the time I manage to crest the top and get my shaking legs under me so I'm standing up on the track, both the Racer Who Could Be Marlon and My Ginger Nemesis are way down the line and moving farther away, toward a second nest at the other end of the bridge. It might be another falcon's nest—I can't be sure, because it's too far away and the ginger-haired racer is blocking my view. So I move toward the nest I saw from the ground. It's much closer, with the added advantage of drawing me away from the others, which, way up here, seems like the only safe choice.

Standing on these tracks, so high in the air, is sobering, yet it makes my legs as weak as if I were drunk. I can't help but wonder if the person who designed this year's race is some masochist with a fear of heights, because this is the second clue we've had to climb for. Either that, or they are just looking for an easy way to thin the ranks of the racers, since there is no real railing up here, and it would be easy enough to catch your toe on a board and tumble to the forest floor below. With its carpet of blue leaves blown free by the wind, the ground could almost be water, but I know it wouldn't feel like water if I were to fall.

When I reach the nest, I find a plaque nailed to one of the posts directly beneath it, with the following inscription:

1. Your map
2. The lighthouse
3. The dance hall
4. The roadhouse
5. The outpost
6. The first sign in the desert
7. The second sign in the desert
8. The gate of Falling Leaf
9. The Amaranthine Forest
10. ???

Of the Tenth there are Ten, and they are all green. But the Tenth of the Ten is burning.

I don't know what that means, but I can't get out the atlas here, so I reach into my bag and pull out the pen the cleaning woman at the taskmaster dormitory gave me. With a few quick words—*Ten, all green, Tenth is burning*—I make a note of the clue on the palm of my left hand and get ready to climb down.

When I shrug my bag back onto my good shoulder, I hear something. More importantly I *feel* something. I look up to see the ginger-haired racer stalking toward me, and I understand all at once that he is more interested in getting to me than he is interested in getting to the clue. He was up here ahead of me. Perhaps he's already read it.

Perhaps he's been waiting for me.

"Don't do it," I say. "This is *not* a good place for a fight."

"Oh, but it *is*," he sneers, and I realize that he is willing to risk his own life to try to take mine.

Even if I were guaranteed to beat him, I know a fight here would be a mistake. I could win and still fall. And it's definitely *not* a sure win. We've fought twice, and we've each won once. No matter what he thinks, this bridge is definitely not the place for the tiebreaker. So I follow my instincts, and I turn and run.

The wind hits me hard from behind, but he hits me harder. Before I reach the end of the bridge, his hands come down heavy on my shoulders and he throws me to the tracks.

Rolling onto my back, I stare up at him. His eyes are wild. He even manages a smile. I can feel how pleased he is with himself. "Your satisfaction is premature," I say, and I brace myself, anticipating a punch or a kick, but I'm shocked when I feel nothing but restraint in him.

I get it. . . . I realize what he's thinking, and he's right: *This battle isn't about landing the best blow. It's about keeping your balance.* And that's why, still safe on my back, I bring my feet up and slam them hard against his chest.

He's fast, though, and he catches my ankles, and I see

on his face and I feel in the air how satisfied he is. This is exactly what he was hoping for—a chance to pick me up and throw me to my death. And I know he'll do it, if I can't break free. So as he lunges to my right and tries to drag me toward the edge, I reach left and grab hold of the track. My legs hang over on the right for just a moment, but I don't slide after them. Instead, I pull them back up and swing them toward him, knocking his feet out from under him. With a loud grunt, he falls to the track right in front of me.

Before he can get up, I'm on my feet. The temptation to try to beat him once and for all—to end him, the way he wants to end me—is overridden by my singular need to stay alive. So I squat down and reach between the slats that hold up the tracks, looking for a handhold that will let me drop down before he gets up, but he's too quick.

"Not so fast," he says, and his voice is almost a growl. You'd think he'd be ready to quit, but he's as relentless as a rabid dog. Before I can scramble away from his grasp, he has me by the collar of my coat and is dragging me up to my feet.

"Come on!" he calls. I take a few steps back and give him a hard look. He's in a half crouch, his elbows bent and his fists near his face, and I realize he's not going to stop.

One of us is about to die.

Behind his back, at the other end of the bridge, I can

still see the other racer—the one with dark hair that I hope could be Marlon. He's watching this fight from a safe distance. If I'm about to be killed, I sure hope that's really Marlon. I hope he's still living and could still win this race.

"Come on!" my nemesis calls out again, but I won't give him what he wants. I make him make the first move, and for just the thinnest moment before he does, I sense it—his right foot coming at my waist, sweeping me over the side. I raise my hands and catch his ankle, and then I'm leaning into him hard and shoving him away from me with all the strength I can find.

His eyes light up, his arms shoot out, and the wind at his back pushes all his red hair into his eyes. His feet don't stop pedaling backward until he collides with a post and grabs hold of it.

That's when I notice something directly over his head, just an inch or so above his hair—a bulbous and bumpy globe that appears to be made of purple papier-mâché. A hornet's nest. I realize what it is a moment too late, though, because while I'm still standing, staring up at it, a cloud of hornets pours out of a hole near the bottom, a cloud that moves like a billow of smoke, if a billow of smoke wanted to kill me.

If I'm stung, it might mean nothing more than a bunch of itchy welts, or it might mean much worse if I'm allergic.

Instinctively, I pull my hands up into my sleeves and turn the collar of my coat up to protect my neck, when a loud train whistle pierces the air.

It rips my attention away from the buzzing mass around my head. At first, I tell myself it can't be. But then the whistle comes again, and I know that the ginger-haired racer and the cloud of hornets have some new competition when it comes to who will kill me today.

The hornets are suddenly much less frightening—I'll have to risk their stings—as I force myself to look down and grab hold of one of the beams at my feet. Buzzing fills my ears and something pinches the back of my neck, but I block it out and swing over the side of the bridge, hooking my legs on the scaffolding below. Then I'm hanging upside down, and my ginger-haired nemesis is climbing down across from me. Hornets still buzz around my ears and crawl across my face, but it doesn't even rattle me. Because at this very moment, a train is flying across the track, and the Racer Who Could Be Marlon is still on the bridge.

There is nothing I can do. I'm frozen, waiting, but waiting for what? A scream? Some sound of impact?

When the train is long gone and the trestle finally stops vibrating, I know I need to climb back up.

The ginger-haired racer has almost reached the ground, but I can't worry about him now. My left shoulder throbs, but I ignore it, along with the burning from the hornet stings on the back of my neck. All that matters is getting to the top of the tracks in hopes that somehow the Racer Who Could Be Marlon survived.

Pulling myself back up onto the tracks, I'm overwhelmed by the quiet. How can this be the very place I stood just a moment ago? The hornets are all gone, and only the hot scent of metal on metal is left in the wake of the train.

I cross the bridge, staring down into the scaffolding below me, hoping I will find Marlon hanging from the support beams. But all I find is a solitary thick-soled boot.

I know this boot. It was on the foot of the small woman with the big voice who stomped on Darius's hand and kicked him in the ribs at the foot of the lighthouse. The racer I had seen who I'd hoped was Marlon was never Marlon at all. Relief washes over me, even as I notice blood on the tracks.

There's a flutter in my stomach like it's crawling with hornets, and I glue my eyes to the tracks before I notice anything else. I've got to go. I can't think about the racer who died here. I've got to think about the ginger-haired racer, who's already running across the forest floor ahead of me.

Once I'm on the ground I head downhill, kicking up blue leaves and trying to guess how far the road is, when I hear the quiet hum of idling engines. In the distance I spot the research station, and beyond its gate, two long lines of trucks being loaded with pallets of wood. I run toward them at a full sprint until I notice two Authority guards. I can only guess they've been sent here to look for a female racer who uses Enchanted magic. Beside them another vehicle idles, a black truck with a covered bed. The words *Enchanted Authority* are emblazoned on the side.

I'm still under the cover of the trees when I come to a full stop. Something itches at the back of my mind.

I can't pull my eyes from the two Authority guards, and something about their broad-shouldered profiles brings to mind the sound of voices, cheers and shouts of *Apples!* and *Hail the harvest!* And then in my mind's eye I can see Marlon, not the way he looked at the roadhouse, but the way he looked on a day that could only be a memory from before the race.

I'm having a memory.

As images rise in my mind like a dream I had forgotten, I duck between two parked trucks to stay out of sight of the guards. That's when I see him. A man squatting in the bed of a truck tying down a load of purple logs. He is thin—wasting-away thin—and as jumpy as an exposed nerve. Something about him is familiar to me, too, but not so familiar that I trust him. Still, as I creep closer, staying in the shadows to avoid being noticed by the guards, I feel the craving in him. A raw need that's almost as dark as grief.

My right hand works its way into the opening of my bag until it finds, tucked away in the inside pocket, the baggie of white powder I took from the Enchanted man at Poppee's Dance Hall. I creep toward him until I'm right beside his truck. When he sees me, he nearly jumps out of his skin, but then a flicker of recognition lights in his eyes.

"I'd like to offer you a deal," I say, lifting my hand to show him the baggie in my open palm. "A ride out of here in exchange for this?"

When he hops down out of the truck bed right in front of me, for a moment I remember his name, but then it's gone. "Get in the truck and keep your head down," he says, but before I can move, he snatches the baggie from my hand.

Inside the cab, I'm surrounded by photographs of a round-faced woman with big brown eyes and a baby with a face like a wrinkled old man. Something about the look in the woman's eyes gives me a shock of pain in my head and in my gut all at once.

The driver's door opens and the man climbs in. He smells like clove cigarettes. "Offer accepted," he chirps, and I can tell by the way he springs into the seat that my offer has made his day.

The truck shakes awake beneath us. Then we're moving, and my skin crawls as if the hornets are back, and I notice a terrible sound—the sound that female racer made when she collapsed on the way to the roadhouse—the sound of a dying gull. I'm thinking of the screams of that woman and of Darius in the gym, and wondering if the truck driver beside me is as frightened as I was when I first heard that blood-chilling sound.

I try to look at him, but before I can turn my head every speck of the world explodes as red as blood. I close my eyes, and the red runs down behind my eyelids, washed away by an impenetrable black.

TWENTY-SEVEN

The world goes as soundless as if my head's been shoved underwater. I want to open my eyes and look around, but it feels like hands are over my face, holding them shut. I claw at my face, I try to scream into the silence, but then my mind's eye opens on a memory.

A man is waking me in the middle of the night, a man with authority over me. He pulls me from my bed with a whisper in my ear. "You are needed in the garden." I'm young. I know this by my small feet and my thin legs, and also by the nightgown I'm wearing. I remember it was my favorite because it was the first one I ever had that didn't itch.

There are other beds in the room, but if anyone else is awake, they pretend to be asleep. I reach for the man's hand—I trust him—but he won't take mine. Instead he drags me by my wrist to the rose garden.

When we get there, I see a girl watching for us. She's just a child, like me, maybe twelve years old. Her eyes and face are puffy and red from crying.

"I'm sorry, Astrid," she calls to me from the place next to the flowers where another man holds her back. Memories come to me like objects on a darkened table after a lamp is suddenly switched on. She had wanted to see the moon garden—a patch of silver and white flowers her mother had ordered to be planted that would glow in the moonlight. She had taken a risk and snuck out, but she was caught, and now I will pay with a beating. The man who dragged me from my bed grabs the collar of this nightgown I love so much and tears the back open, forcing me to my knees. *No! Not the whip!* I hear the girl scream, and I know . . . this is the first time I've been truly beaten. These are the first lashes that will break the skin of my back.

It seems you no longer respond to spankings, Princess. You have left us no other choice.

As the whip cracks against my skin, I see blood splatter across the white roses. I hear a girl scream, but I don't know if it's me or the voice of the other girl.

.

.

.

I sit up, the hint of stale smoke mixing with the remembered scents of roses and blood. I press my palms against my ears to block out the screams, but they fade on their own. When I open my eyes, I'm still in the cab of the truck. Green pastures divided by low stone walls roll by, outside the window.

Still here.

The driver says my name from far away. I try to answer him, but I can't find the words. My head throbs. A hot pain burns behind my eyes and I squeeze them shut, but even with them closed, I can't block out a searing white light. My hands cup over my eyes, and yet the light grows brighter.

Then my internal vison takes over again.

I am being led to the whipping post. I know this is where I am going, and I know I'm going to die. I'm already wounded and bleeding—I was whipped the day before—but the princess was caught in a secret correspondence with an Outsider boy, a member of the OLA, and I will pay the price.

The Princess . . . Princess Renya. I am her surrogate.

A boy walks next to me. I see his feet, his fine leather shoes, but I don't have the strength to raise my head. He slaps a whip against his palm, but someone reaches out and takes it.

"Let me be the one to do it," a voice says. A voice I know well. "You can stand back and watch."

"With pleasure," says the first boy, and I don't have to see his face. I recognize his voice as well. It's the man who impersonated my brother and gave me a poisoned canteen.

It's Prince Lars.

I turn my head to see the prince's surrogate—Darius—take the whip and flex the leather between his hands.

On my knees, I am bound to the post. I lean over and gag onto the stone floor. I don't have enough strength to spit the vomit from my mouth. The whip cracks against my back, pain bleaches the black behind my eyes a blinding white, and I slide out of consciousness.

.

.

.

I open my eyes to find myself slumped against the door of a truck that is rolling along a road. I scramble upright, my heart pounding, but then I recognize the driver and the pictures of the woman and baby taped to the dashboard. I remember the Enchanted Authority officers at the gate of the Amaranthine Forest and the baggy of Oblivion I exchanged for a ride.

I'm still here. But now that I know the truth—now that I know that Lars and Darius are friends who have teamed up against me—*here* is not the same place I thought it was.

The image of Darius reaching for the whip plays over and over in my mind. It makes me so woozy, I'm worried I might throw up in this truck, but the driver must be worried about that too, because he hands me a paper bag I'd guess he had food in earlier.

"You're back," the driver says. He glances at me so quickly I barely register the look of relief in his eyes, but I see it. It's there. "That's in case you get sick," he says. "The bag, I mean."

I hold it open in my lap, grateful to have it. "How long was I out?"

"Long enough." Another quick glance. "Was it a memory?"

"Yes. A bad one."

"I'm afraid for racers, that's about the only kind you can expect. After all, you entered the Race of Oblivion for a reason."

I don't want to talk about myself with this man who seems so strangely familiar. It's this familiarity that drew me to him when I first saw him at the forest gate, but that makes me recoil from him now. The last thing I want at this moment is for something to prompt another memory in me.

Although . . . I can't regret this memory. As painful and terrible as it is, I need it. I need to know the truth about Darius. That he's a monster. A monster and a liar. I need to know that I can't trust him any more than I can trust Prince Lars.

"Where are we going?" I ask. I glance down at my palm, but my hands are damp. They were curled into such tight fists, there are dents in them from my nails. The words I'd written there are no more than a smudge.

"The Ephemeral City," he says. I don't know what that means, but I didn't understand the words from the clue either, as far as I remember. I look out the window. The world outside is an endless stretch of green beneath an endless stretch of blue. We could be anywhere.

"Is it still the same day?" I ask, and his response starts with a snort. I'm glad he finds this all so funny.

"You've been out for almost a day," he says. "We're still crossing the pastureland, though. We will be, I guess, all the way to the coast."

"*What* coast?" I ask, and I try to remember the words that I'd written on my palm. Something about green and something about burning, but nothing about a city and nothing about a coast.

"Are you worried I'm kidnapping you?" he asks, and now he outright laughs. I notice how different he looks from when I first spotted him next to this truck. Then he was as jumpy as a cornered cat, but now he reeks of confidence. Literally. A scent like warm vanilla has supplanted the stale odor of burnt clove. I don't like either smell, to be honest, so I turn the crank to bring the window down a crack, and a cool breeze ripples through my hair.

The wind turns my mind toward Darius, and I shiver. "Are you all right?" the man beside me asks, and my heart leaps in my chest. "Hey, calm down," he says. "You're fine.

We got away without anyone seeing you. And the stuff on your hand . . . *ten, green, burning* . . . I hope that's the riddle you had to solve, because the answer is the Ten Viridian Isles, and that's where we're headed—"

"You're taking me *there*? To the place in the clue?"

"Well, yeah." He scratches his head. He's as confounded by me as I am by him, though I can't imagine how that could be. "I was already headed there myself."

"Then why did you say you were taking me to a city?"

"The *Ephemeral* City. So not a city at all."

He's giving me a headache, and nothing is making sense, and I'm not sure if it's a side effect of the memory sickness or a side effect of traveling with a man who's been using Oblivion. He scowls at me in a very deliberate way, like he's trying to stay steady and grounded when his feet can't quite touch the ground. His cheeks even look less sunken, like he's been filled out with a sense of his own power. Like nothing bad could threaten him—or me—at least not right now.

The craving I'd felt in him when I'd found him—the craving that had told me he'd accept the exchange of the baggie for a ride—is almost gone, but not quite. He's like a pot of hot water, just on the edge of boiling. His eyes dart from time to time to the glove box right in front of me, and I suspect if I opened it I'd find whatever's left in that baggie.

Outside, the ground is like a checkerboard of green grass

cut into squares by walls of piled gray stones. Cows huddle in one corner, ponies in another. Before I can get a good look, we've passed them by. From time to time, I spot a cluster of grave markers up on a hill, and it's strange to imagine the people who lived and died way out here. Maybe they're the same people who collected all these stones to build these walls.

The sky is pale blue, draped with clouds that look like tattered cloth.

"I guess you've never been to the Festival of Fire Flowers, then?" he says.

"*Wait*, is that where we're going?" I think again about what he's said. The Ten Viridian Isles. It makes sense. They're the location of the annual festival that celebrates the king. "I know what the festival is," I say. "But I don't remember if I've ever been to it. Are Outsiders allowed?"

"Some," he says, and he gives me a sideways glance.

"So then what's the Ephemeral City?" I ask. "If the clue points to the Ten Viridian Isles, and if we're going to the Festival of Fire Flowers—"

"The Ephemeral City is the home of the Festival of Fire Flowers," he says, a bit exasperated, which I find somewhat insulting. "Every year, on the tenth of the Ten Isles, the city goes up and the festival rages. But it's just for three days and three nights. Like most good things in this world, it's only temporary." He says this quite wistfully, and he glances out his side window, so that I wonder what memory he's working through. I'm thinking maybe I should say something, maybe remind him of the round-faced woman and the baby in the pictures, but then he pulls himself back together and continues. "When the festival ends, the whole of the city is undone and shut away, until the following autumn, when the fire flowers bloom again and the city reappears." He gives me another sideways glance. "I'd think you'd know all that, because of your . . . access to the princess."

He's baiting me. Somehow, he knows who I am and he wants to lead me into a conversation about my connection to the royal family. And though I'd like to find out everything *he* knows about my history, I'm not ready to face the past again just yet, not ready to fall into memory sickness again.

And I don't like being manipulated.

Beyond the windshield, the road rises, a long line of black cutting between green. We have time to talk, so instead of taking the bait and asking what he means, I stubbornly ask instead, "How did you become an Oblivion addict?"

"Ah. So you already know who you are," he says.

"I know I'm her surrogate," I say. "How do *you* know who I am?"

"My answer to both of your questions is the same: I'm indentured to the palace. I know who you are because I've seen you there. And I became addicted to Oblivion because the king is addicted to Oblivion, and he sometimes shares it with me."

I make a small sound in response to this, something like *huh!*, and it doesn't take Cientia for him to know he's shocked me. "So you don't remember that part then? That the king was an addict himself? They say that's what got him killed—"

"Killed?"

"Ah! Something else you don't remember." He smiles bigger than he has before, and his front teeth protrude from under his top lip, giving him the look of a happy rodent. He's clearly pleased to be winning some competition he thinks we're having over which of us knows more about my past—a competition horribly stacked in his favor. He doesn't seem to care. Like every addict, he likes to win. "Yes indeed. Killed for his lust for Oblivion." He checks my reaction again, and then adds, "Not an overdose."

Does my face look like I was concerned the king had overdosed? If he had Cientia, he'd know I'm far more self-interested than that.

But he just keeps right on with his story. "They say it was one of the Asps that did it."

"An Asp? Why—"

"Because they were tired of being his suppliers? Because they were worried about the rule of an Oblivion-addicted king? I don't know. I'm just glad no one turned their suspicions on *me*. But I doubt too many people knew I was bringing it in for him. Or that he was paying me for my troubles with little kickbacks of the drug."

The sky in the distance is darker than it is overhead, and I wonder if the coast is closer than I originally thought. My hands flutter in my lap, suddenly cold, so I slide them under my thighs. I'm not ready to get out of the safety of this truck. "I just don't get why anyone becomes addicted to Oblivion," I say, unable to keep my mouth shut. "How could something that sucks away your memories be a drug people want to abuse?"

"Ah, but not every dose takes something away. A smaller dose gives something to the user. If you use just a bit, you get a tremendous surge of well-being." He stops talking. His gaze fastens onto the horizon, and his hands tighten on the wheel. "Could you hand me that little case by your feet?" he asks.

On the floor of the truck, there's a small metal box the size and shape of a bar of soap. When I pass it to him, he opens it to reveal a half dozen clove cigarettes he clearly rolled himself. He gets one lit, drops the lighter back in his pocket, and tosses the case back onto the floor instead of handing it to me. Then he slides right back into his story.

"But you can take Oblivion an inch too far and you can fall into the hole it puts in your mind. Like what they do to racers. I'm much more careful these days," he says, and now his shoulders relax a little as he exhales a cloud of smoke into the cab. I crank my window down a bit more. He doesn't seem to notice. His gaze has found one of the photos of the round-faced woman taped to the dashboard right beside his right hand. "I have someone who believes in me now."

"So . . . ," I start. At the end of the road ahead of us, I can clearly see the line of the ocean. A suspension bridge pushes out into the blue.

"That's the bridge to the first of the Ten Viridian Isles," he says. "Right at the mouth of the Arrow River. We're almost there."

I swallow, and though I know I should try to stay out of sight, I can't help but move to the edge of my seat to stare out at what's ahead. I don't even know if I've seen them before with my own eyes, yet I know that the Ten Isles are beautiful. I know it the way I know that leaves fall from the trees in the autumn, or that they return as new buds in the spring.

"I'm running out of time," I say. "I want to ask you so many things. I want to know everything you know about me."

He slows the truck. We're already crossing the first bridge, trading the rumble of the road for a soft hum beneath our wheels. I can see the other islands from up here, and they are all surprisingly small, linked together by a series of bridges like this one. And in the distance, I can see what looks like a city of colorful circus tents stretching high into the sky.

"Everything?" he asks, his eyes narrowing. He is glancing more frequently at the glove box now. I wonder if the Oblivion he used is starting to wear off. "I'll tell you what I know, but you may change your mind about wanting to know it all when you hear it." The air outside is scented with salt and a smell I can't quite recognize—it's something green that grows only by the sea. The truck starts climbing the second bridge.

"You know you're Princess Renya's surrogate?"

I nod. My hands are cold again, so I start rubbing them together.

"Well, you two are as thick as thieves. You're like twins from different mamas. I don't know how that's possible, to be up-front about it. We've all seen you bleeding right through your clothes, all for a girl who's too selfish to behave. Yet you treat her like a sister." He throws me a sideways glance, and there's a touch of judgment in his eyes that infuriates me.

"I told you I knew I was her surrogate. What else do you know?"

"Do you know that your brother Jayden is suspected to be the leader of the OLA?"

That glance shoots my way again, so I stare out the window. We're on a high stretch of ground between bridges, and looking out, the Isles are all a mix of green and blue.

There's a pond off to the right, fed by a fast-moving creek. Everywhere else I look I see moss and grass and more moss again.

"I know that about Jayden, yes," I say.

"Well, do you know about *your* connection to the OLA?"

"*My* connection . . . ?" I curse myself for making my shock so obvious, yet again. But I can't worry about that right now, because my mind is racing.

If we were anywhere else, I'd whirl on him and pummel him with a million questions. I'd fire them so fast his head would spin, just to get a feel for how trustworthy this accusation really is. I'd study his face; I'd try to read his intentions.

That's what I would do, if we were anywhere else. But we're here, cresting the bridge that descends to the Ninth Isle, and through the dust and dead bugs on the windshield I get a clear view of the next checkpoint—the Ephemeral City—for the first time. And no matter how I want to scream at him, nothing's going to tear me away from this view.

"That's the Tenth Isle, right there," he says, and there's a little awe in his voice, too. "I'll never get used to how it hits you when it first appears."

The Tenth Isle is not a separate island off in the sea. It's an island in a clear blue lake that covers most of the Ninth Isle, so it's an island within an island. It's home to the first trees I've seen since we reached the Isles, trees that are gloriously tall and still mostly green, dappled here and there with flashes of red and gold foliage, and growing up out of the forest is a towering skyline of huge tents, like a circus as big as a village. Under the bright sun, the canvases glow in every color—sea-foam green, sunset red, sky blue—and they dot the horizon, fluttering in the sea breeze, held up by poles rising higher than I thought tent poles could rise. In the center of it all, an enormous white tent stands, its pointed roof held aloft by at least a dozen poles like a castle with a dozen spires, and atop each point, a pennant of a different color flaps wildly in the wind—orange, violet, teal, and black, some solid, some striped, and some starred.

Behind the palatial white tent rises a giant wheel, turning like a clock, carrying gilded gondolas in a wide arc, at least a hundred feet above the treetops. Atop each gondola, rings of flames like wreaths of flowers ripple and dance and spill down to the ground like flowing garlands of sparks.

"That's the Wheel of Fire," my driver says, and I see he's caught me staring out at it.

"It doesn't seem real," I say. "How is it that the whole city isn't set on fire?"

"Haven't you ever seen fire flowers before?"

I say, "I can't remember." But what I'm thinking is *How could I forget something so strange?*

He says, "Fire flowers aren't flowers at all, and I should stop teasing you—you've probably never seen them before. They're only burned at the festival, where chips of the fire trees we're hauling are lit. Each fragment flares into a bloom, but only their resin burns, and their resin doesn't drip, so the flame stays contained. It's a selfish kind of fire. Like the rest of the magic of Lanoria, wouldn't you say?"

I don't answer him. Instead I ask, "What did you mean when you asked me if I knew about my own connections to the OLA?"

He makes a turn off the road into a vast gravel lot and pulls into a long line of similar trucks. At the front of the line, I can see Outsiders waving flags at drivers, motioning them through a gate in a tall fence. "This is the line to the receiving area. You should get down," he says, tugging a folded blanket from the backseat. "Get down on the floor and I'll cover you."

I do as he says, and I go from a view of the Ephemeral City lit by bright sunshine to complete darkness. It's hot and hard to breathe, but before I can say anything, he keeps talking like nothing's changed.

"Like I said, I know about your brother Jayden, and his connection to the OLA. I probably know more than most about them, because they tried to solicit me in the past. Few people can bring goods into the palace without being searched." He's quiet for a moment, and my nerves spike as I imagine that someone is standing beside the truck window. But then a moment later he continues. "I'm not the only one at the palace who knows about Jayden, and I know there are people at the palace who suspect you might be with the OLA, too. I've always assumed it was true, to be honest. And then I saw you in the King's City, just one day before the bombs went off at the Apple Carnival."

"Bombs?"

"Yes indeed. The OLA hit the carnival this year, and the day before, you were talking with someone I'm certain is a member of the OLA, because he was the very same person who tried to solicit me to join."

He keeps talking, but I can no longer make out what he's saying. My ears are ringing, and I'm bathed in sweat, and I can hear someone calling my name from far away.

His words have thrown me into a memory.

It doesn't come on with memory sickness, at least not yet. Instead it feels more like a blow, like I've been hit hard in the back of my head.

I'm in the King's City, and someone is calling to me from across Queen Rosamond Square. It's a boy, someone I associate with my brother Jayden. Then he's right in front of me, and he's adamant about something, and I hear my own voice repeating, *I will. I will.* I strain to see him, but the memory is already receding. I'm peering through the dark, but I can't see his face.

The truck lurches forward and I'm jolted awake, only I don't think I was ever really asleep.

A voice comes from right beside the driver's window. It's a woman, asking to see a bill of lading for the truck. The driver says something he thinks is funny—there's a laugh in his voice—and a piece of paper rustles as it's pulled from a pocket and unfolded. She asks him if he's got an extra clove cigarette, says she can smell it in the cab.

I hold my breath, and my heart beats as fast as a rabbit's. The back of his hand smacks against my leg as he picks up the cigarette case from the floor right beside me.

She thanks him, and her voice is too loud. I feel like I'm suffocating. My head is swimming. Then the truck rolls forward and I know we're clear. But I still feel like I could be sick all over this blanket.

Not out of fear of being discovered. The truck is still rolling and he's whispering, "We're in. Stay down until I tell you."

I hear him, but my thoughts are still far away. I'm remembering Queen Rosamond Square, and there's a frenzy of activity around me.

It's the day before the Apple Carnival. The day before bombs will go off in a crowd, and I was just speaking to a member of the OLA.

What did I agree to do?

TWENTY-EIGHT

I don't know what time it is, but I know it's late enough that I should be starving, and would be, if I didn't still feel sick enough to vomit. I climb out of the truck cab, my dress sticking to my sweat-soaked back under my coat. My driver seems blissfully unaware of the memory I just had. He hands me my bag, jumps down in front of me, but then scowls.

"You all right?" he asks. I'm crouching down in an effort to stay out of sight, his embed blinking right in front of my eyes. "You look kind of shook-up." He checks over both shoulders and then lowers his voice. "She didn't see you," he whispers.

"I know, I know. It's not that." I stare at the ground. That's all he's going to get from me on that subject. The truth is I don't want to talk about that memory, or anything else that might stir up that same kind of queasiness in me. I can't afford to slow down now.

I shuffle my feet. I guess I'm not good with goodbyes. "Thanks for the ride. . . ." Now I can't help but look up at him, embarrassed. "Did you tell me your name?"

"It's Hollis," he says. "My friends call me Holly. You can call me that, when you make it back to the palace." He reaches into the backseat of the truck and pulls out a cap, and with one quick motion, he pulls it onto my head. "That's what you need, a plain gray cap." He straightens the brim that sits low on my forehead and shades my eyes. "A brilliant disguise," he says, and winks.

I tuck the ends of my hair up under the sides and back. "Thanks," I whisper.

Holly grabs my hand and pulls me into a hug. "I don't know if you are OLA or not," he says into my ear. "Just stay safe. This place will be crawling with Authority guards, so keep your head down and your eyes open."

With that he lets me go, gives my bad shoulder a firm pat that almost buckles my knees, and turns around to climb back into the cab. "I'll see you," he says.

I nod, and the truck starts up, and I turn my back. I hurry around a tent where they're selling burning fire flowers in cheap tin lanterns, and I melt into the crowd. I'm not ten yards away before I'm wishing Holly had never left. He might be a stranger, but he was a stranger who was trying to keep me safe, and that's way better than being alone.

People press in on me from everywhere, and by people I mean Enchanteds, with a few Outsiders here and there, doing the jobs no Enchanted would ever do. A small group hurries toward me, bent under a load of sandbags that are used to brace the tent poles. A few more are carrying fat purple logs to a chipper and feeding them through. On the other end, two Enchanted women in tie-dyed dresses are taking the fragments and setting them on stands, lining them up by height on a table at the front of their tent, and lighting them all on fire, so that they give the appearance of a burning garden. A third woman inside the tent is calling out from behind a table to the festivalgoers streaming by. "Get your fire flower today, and enjoy its flame for all three nights!"

And everywhere I look, there are images of King Marchant. His face ripples on the wind on flags that hang overhead, and he peers out of tents on stacks of souvenir plates and china cups. Along the pathways that wind through the Ephemeral City, lampposts are decorated with large banners displaying his life-size image, so that it feels as if the king himself were staring down at the crowds.

I try to keep my eyes on the ground. I can't risk falling into memory sickness. I know I lived in the palace with the princess and her family, so I must have known the king. If just hearing Holly talk about seeing me with a member of the OLA brought on the return of a painful memory, what might happen if I see a familiar face?

Of course, I know a familiar face isn't always a trigger. The memory of Darius walking me to the whipping post, taking the whip from Lars's hand—that horrible memory proves many things to me, not the least of which is that I can look at a familiar face for days without a hint of memory returning.

But then, I met Darius right after I'd begun the race. That initial dose of Oblivion must be wearing off. I should probably expect more and more memories to return.

I'm startled from my thoughts by someone saying Prince Lars's name right behind my shoulder. I spin around to find two Enchanted Authority guards, both men, standing in the shade of that palatial white tent in the center of the city, beside an open doorway. Their eyes are on the legs of Enchanted women, dressed in brightly colored sundresses, as they pass through the open door carrying large trays of wood chips. "He's not here," one of the guards says. "I heard the prince won't make an appearance at this year's festival at all."

"He'll be on the throne soon enough," says the other. "Next year's festival, it will be his face staring down at us from every pole."

As I pass in front of the open doorway, I keep my head down but I raise my eyes, unable to resist peeking inside. In the center of the floor stands a circular stage, surrounded by rows and rows of empty bleachers. Two smaller stages have been erected in the far corners of the tent, and on each one, a Hearts and Hands bout is under way. A family of Enchanteds passes close by on the path, so close they almost bump into me. Like me, they are not watching where they are going. Instead, they are all looking down at a printed program they share between them. "Qualifying matches all day," says the mother, flipping the program over to the back. "With the championship match to start at midnight."

"Midnight!" squeals one of the children, a girl of about thirteen. "That's when the princess will be lighting the torch. Can we go? Can we go? *Can we go?* Please, please, please, *please!*"

The mother says something in response, but I can't understand, because a loud brass band is heading toward me from the other side of the white tent. They are marching, with a flag twirler in the front spinning two flags—one with King Marchant's image and the other with Prince Lars's—and I flush with heat when my eyes fall on Prince Lars's face. But then the flag twirler passes me by, and I'm surrounded by baton twirlers tossing flaming sticks into the air, and I duck my head and walk quickly until the sound of the music is far behind me.

When I stop, I see that I'm right in front of the Wheel of Fire. To my left, a long line of Enchanteds with a few Outsiders mixed in are shifting their weight from foot to foot as they await their turn on the ride. I suppose even Outsiders can ride if they have the mackels for a ticket. There's a rich sweet smell in the air, and it makes my stomach growl. Opposite the entrance to the ride stands a wide food counter, where vendors are frying up doughnuts and funnel cakes, and my queasiness has receded enough for my hunger to gnaw at me.

But then the unmistakable sound of someone groaning in pain draws my attention to a large crowd of people gathered to my right.

Between the onlookers, I catch a glimpse of a huge gear, like an outsize component of a clock. It's turned by Outsiders chained to long wooden arms that extend from the center of the gear. As they trudge in well-worn circles, the gear turns the giant wheel overhead.

The chained Outsiders are many, strapped in by rows, dirty and bent, and their taskmaster stands above them at the hub of the gear, watching, his hands raised, rubbing his fingers against his thumbs.

While I watch, one of the younger men stumbles, and the taskmaster calls to him to get up. When he stays slumped, the other Outsiders on the wheel keep going, so that his feet drag across the ground. I can see this has happened to others—the caked blood on the tops of their bare feet gives them away. The wheel doesn't slow, but the taskmaster hits the slumping man with Projectura anyway. His body shudders. He doesn't raise his head, but vomit spills from his mouth onto the ground. Then the gear moves, and his bloody feet drag through it.

A group of gathered Enchanteds, who seem to be here for no reason except to enjoy the taskmaster's show, laugh until they are red in the face, falling together and spilling their drinks from their cups. They keep cackling, even as the Outsider gets his feet back under him again.

I notice that I am rubbing my own fingers against my own thumbs, my eyes moving from the taskmaster to the laughing Enchanteds and back again. Someone bumps me from behind, and I turn just enough to see the red stripe running down the pant leg of a King's Knight, so I duck into a rectangular blue tent full of burning incense and portraits of King Marchant made of flower petals.

An anxious Enchanted vendor scurries over to me to show her wares, but then she looks me up and down and turns away. As soon as the King's Knights have passed, I merge back into the crowd, heading the other direction.

I'm trying to move quickly, tamping down my anger and my hunger as I pass more and more tents giving off the scents of cooking food, when a woman with her hair and face hidden by a scarf comes up alongside me and grabs me by the arm. I jump back, but the woman tells me not to be afraid.

"I know who you are and I want to help you," she

whispers, never slowing. She slides something into my hand. When I look down, I see that it's a ripe orange. "Take this, and a word of warning," she says. "The prince is planning to wait for you at the final checkpoint of the race, in case you slip through the hands of all the Authority guards and King's Knights who are searching for you here."

I can't stop myself from lifting the orange to my nose and drinking in its sweet fragrance. "Thank you," I say, and I let my gaze brush across her face for just a moment. Her eyes meet mine, and though the rest of her face is covered, her eyes are eerily familiar. I try to read her, but the crowd is so big and it's churning. I can't trust my Cientia here.

She wraps a scarf like the one on her own head around mine, covering me from cap to shoulders. "Stay hidden," she says. "I can't tell you what the next clue is—I don't know it, and no one will tell me—but I know there's a fleet of trucks parked just beyond the west gate, and I know that at least one has the keys inside." She turns her face when she notices a group of Authority guards heading toward us. "Good luck and stay safe."

She wraps her arms around me and pulls me into a brief hug. I smell jasmine on her. And then she's gone.

I tug the scarf across my face and hurry away, but come to a sudden stop when, like an object floating to the surface of a dark lake, a memory rises up out of the depths of my mind. I think it was the jasmine that gave her away, but I know all at once that the woman with the scarf was Princess Renya. I turn in a circle, looking for the back of her head, but she's gone.

With this scarf covering my face, I'm able to finally lift my head and properly search for the clue. One part of me wants to keep hoping that Marlon is alive and keep looking for him, but I'm not speaking with that part of me right now. I can't. Instead I keep my eyes moving, searching for a plaque or a sign or a banner—anything that might contain a riddle that would point me to the next checkpoint.

Surfaces, not faces. This is my mantra as my gaze works its way through the crowd, but I can't help myself when I see someone I recognize as a racer. Near a stage where dancers are performing a folk dance done with razor-sharp swords, I think I spot the woman with the pretty face and the build of a man, but she's slump-shouldered and she has a black eye, so I can't even be sure it's her. And at the entrance to a ride called the Finish Line, I catch sight of a stumpy man who was with Knox when he jumped me and Jane at the lighthouse. He looks well, like maybe someone's given him help along the way.

Somehow, despite the crushing crowds, I manage to make my way around the entire loop—from the front of the Ephemeral City to the back and then around to the front again. There are a million things to see: stilt walkers and kite flyers and jugglers flipping flaming pins through the air. The brass band passes in front of me again, and then in another corner of the city they come up behind me, making me even more confused, until I realize there are probably more than one. I've spotted lots of blinking one-word signs in flashing lights: *truth* and *want* and *wild* and *mine*. But none of those words, even when they're all put together, amounts to a clue.

Frustrated, I lean against a fence post and peel the orange the princess put in my hand. I don't even take the time to separate the sections, but lift the fruit to my lips and bite into it like an apple. Juice runs down my chin and over my hand, and I don't know if anything ever tasted this good before. I feel something strange, like a memory of the princess, like the feeling I have toward her for having given me this orange is a feeling that I've had before—the feeling of being in her debt—and the memory tells me that this is not a feeling I enjoy. Thoughts of her stir up a discordant mix of affection and resentment, which is troubling as well as distracting. So I shove her face from my mind's eye.

But it doesn't help, because it's immediately replaced by the face of my brother Marlon. I'm looking down at him, and he's standing behind a barricade, holding a man under his elbow.

My breath catches. I see the two of them standing there waiting for the princess, and I know that the parts of me that have been missing since the race began are coming back. That the Oblivion I was given is wearing off, and my buried memories are surfacing faster and stronger.

I know I am remembering Marlon and my father. I am remembering the moment right before my father died.

I look out at the masses of Enchanteds, laughing and smiling and laughing even louder. I know it's not real, but I imagine I hear the groans of the Outsiders moving the gear at the foot of the Wheel of Fire. I lift my head and stare up at that monstrous wheel, and I wish with a sudden flare of rage that fire flowers would all at once lose the magic that contains their flame, and I could watch that towering wheel burn until it crashed to the ground.

This is what I'm thinking when a face weaving through the crowd catches my attention. It's the ginger-haired racer, and he is walking alongside the journalists—Mr. and Mrs. Arrogance—who are clearly enraptured by him. The woman is still carrying her camera and the boy is still carrying his notebook, and they're cajoling and smiling and the camera is clicking away. For a terrifying moment, I fear that maybe he has already found the clue and they are documenting it, but I forget my nemesis as fast as I noticed him when I see, just behind his shoulder, the face of a female member of the King's Knights, a young woman who is staring directly at me. I don't know who she is, but I recognize her face. And I know if she recognizes me she will arrest me, and my race will come to an end.

My heart starts running even before I do, so I let it lead me straight into the crowd, toward the only people who might be able to stop a woman with the look of determination I saw on that King's Knight's face. I run right up to Mr. and Mrs. Arrogance, and I'm both horrified and delighted when they recognize me, even beneath the scarf.

"Astrid!" Mrs. Arrogance squeals, and before I can register the blinding whiteness of her oversize smile, she takes my picture. But just as quickly she lowers the camera, leans toward me, and speaks to me in a conspiratorial tone.

"The Authority is all over this place, searching for you." She looks over both shoulders, as if she is the first person to let me know the danger I'm in. "They want to arrest you for using the Three Unities. If they find you—"

"I'm well aware," I say, and her face somehow deflates at not being the one to give me the news. But I know I will turn that around with the tip I have for her. I point back over her shoulder at the female King's Knight. "She is clearly leading the hunt for me. She could give you a good story, don't you think? The inside scoop on their plans for me after my arrest, maybe?" And just like that Mr. Arrogance, who had a moment ago been intently taking notes while listening to the ginger-haired racer, flips his notebook to a fresh page and steps between me and the advancing Knight, who at this moment is lifting a comm to her lips. I need to move, need to get out of sight, so I take advantage of this brief window when the photographer is between me and the Knight, raising her camera. I hear it *click click click* over my shoulder as I push my way deep into the crowd.

I'm almost to the huge white tent at the base of the Wheel of Fire when someone hooks me by my elbow. I'm dragged into the line of people waiting to ride the wheel, and someone whispers into my ear, "Keep your head down." He leans over me, as everyone else in line turns to watch the female Knight stomping by with purpose, leading a tight cluster of Enchanted Authority guards in the direction she thinks I went.

I should feel relief, knowing that for now I've lost her. I should feel a heavy weight of gratitude toward the person who just helped me give her the slip.

He's looking through the crowd, making sure they are truly gone, and then he says, of all things, "You're safe." And at the sound of that voice—the voice I heard so clearly in my memory—every muscle in my body tightens.

Something hot races through my veins, like my blood's all been drained and replaced with fire, when I finally lift my head and glare into Darius's hazel eyes.

TWENTY-NINE

Darius. The boy I hated to leave behind in the Heart of the Desert. But that's where the person I called *Darius* will always stay.

Because now I've remembered who he really is. Now I know he's actually called Kit. Now I've heard his voice and seen his face in my memories. Now I've felt the whip across my back.

The whip I saw in his hand.

"What's wrong?" he asks. His gaze slides from my eyes to my mouth and back to my eyes again, and he doesn't need Cientia to know I'd like to spit in his face. Questions flare in his eyes and he blinks rapidly, as if he's trying to clear them away. But then something changes. The confusion is swept away and understanding takes its place. His expression hardens. "You had a memory return," he says.

I manage a shallow nod.

"A memory about me?"

"Yes."

He folds his arms across his chest, tucking his hands against his body, as if he's cold. I can't stand the wounded look in his eyes. *He's* wounded?

Heat runs down my arm into my hand, and I slap him hard across the face.

His hand flies up to his cheek and he hunches over, turning away. When he straightens and looks at me again, I can already see the outline of my fingers on his skin. Behind him, the Wheel of Fire is turning—we're next in line to board—and I know that it's in my best interest to get on this ride with him, which only makes me more furious. If I could, I think I'd slap every person currently looking at me, and that's a lot of people.

I never should have slapped him. I shouldn't have called attention to us. But I did, and now I need to get out of here before one of the people staring at us realizes who I am and alerts the Authority.

Right behind Darius's back, the wheel comes to a stop and an Outsider attendant pulls open the gate that separates us from the first gondola. It's just a few feet away. Riders spill out, and the attendant calls to us. "Now boarding! Take your seats!"

I don't want to get into that gondola with Darius, but I need to look for the clue, and nothing will give me a better chance to do that while keeping me away from the King's Knights. Darius motions for me to lead the way, so I do.

The gondola is completely enclosed, like we're inside a windowed globe, and once the door is shut and latched behind us, the wheel moves a fraction of a turn so passengers can climb into the next one. The movement makes the floor rock, and I drop onto one of the seats. And then Darius says exactly what I would expect, and the last thing I want to hear: "I can explain."

"Don't bother," I say. "I really don't want to hear any of it. I know all about you, everything you could tell me, so save your breath."

"Oh, you know *all* about me, do you?" he snaps back. I feel rage rise in him, but then he tamps it back down.

He's enraged? I would find that funny if it weren't so maddening. "I remember all of it," I say. "I know you're the boy I always called Kit, the prince's surrogate. And I know you're conspiring with him to kill me, to eliminate me from the race—"

"Wait—"

"And," I say, ignoring him, "I know that you once took the whip from his hands so you could be the one to use it on me. And I know that the beating you gave me was the worst beating of my life." My mouth goes dry, and I force myself to draw a deep breath. "So don't tell me I'm confused or I've got it wrong. I know who you are."

He's sitting on the bench seat opposite me, but he's looking out at the ground, so I look out through my own window. We're only halfway up, but from here I can see two different brass bands cutting through the crowd, a parade of stilt walkers trailing streamers, and a frightening number of Authority guards.

And scattered throughout the Ephemeral City, flashing words in script and in print. On the ground and on the sides of tents. A few blink above open doorways. *Truth, mine, wild, want.* I've seen those already. To them I add *travel* and *through.* It could be part of the clue, but those six words together can't be all of it.

"Look," Darius starts. He's turned back to face me—I can tell by the sound of his voice—but I refuse to look at him. I have a clue to search for. "It's true that I asked Lars to give me the whip," he says. I keep my eyes glued to the ground below. "But I had a reason. Maybe it's not good enough. Maybe I should have done something different. But I did what I thought was right at the time."

"That's garbage!" I shout, and now I do look at him. And what I see is a boy filled with conflict, and I can't deny that's what I feel in him, too—conflict and regret, as he perches on the edge of his seat, looking at me through narrowed eyes, bracing himself for another slap. "That's *garbage,*" I repeat, but quieter this time, "because you volunteered. You asked if you could be the one—"

"I did," he says, "because I knew I had to do anything to get the whip out of Lars's hand. I knew he would kill you if I didn't." Darius pauses, as if he's trying to measure my reaction. But I don't react. So he keeps going. "The prince is a sadistic demon, Astrid. If you remember anything, you must remember that. He enjoyed causing you pain. And that day—that day I believed he knew he would kill you." He sits so still, I would think he'd hardened to stone if it weren't for the way he keeps clenching and unclenching his jaw. "The day this all happened . . . Do you remember the condition you were in?"

I want to say, *I remember I could barely walk or speak*. I want to say, *I remember the taste of vomit in my mouth*. But all I say is, "Yes, I remember."

"The day before, the princess had been seen meeting a boy in town. An Outsider boy who was suspected to be a member of the OLA. Do you know what that is?"

This question startles me at first, but then I remember Darius has no way of knowing where I've been since I left the Heart of the Desert. He couldn't know who Jayden really is, or about what I did for him in return for the ride to Falling Leaf. I simply nod.

"Her parents were furious and called on the prince to give you lashes in front of the princess—enough to make sure she never saw this boy again. They insisted Lars hold the whip instead of Sir Arnaud because they wanted it to be personal. They wanted the punishment to be as much about family as they felt the princess's betrayal had been.

"Lars brought me along. I think he knew it would hurt me to see you suffer so badly. And it was *bad*. It was *terrible*. When it was over, Sir Arnaud and I cut you down and brought you upstairs to the infirmary.

"But the following day, the queen learned that the princess's connection to the OLA extended beyond this single meeting. Sir Millicent found a stack of . . . I can't think of anything to call them but *love letters* . . . in the princess's room. The king and queen were outraged. Their daughter had saved correspondence that called them tyrants. Letters that advocated resistance."

Darius rubs his palms along the front of his pants. This is the first he's moved since he started talking. Then he turns his face back to the window. The gondola crests the top of the wheel's arc and then dips toward the ground again.

"So the prince dragged you from your bed in the infirmary and brought you to the post again. You were so weak." Darius pauses. Near the ground, a brass band drowns out his words. We swing toward the sky again and the music fades. "He knew that another beating like the first one might take your life. The princess knew it, too. She screamed, and in the midst of the chaos on the way to the whipping post, she begged him to strike her instead. He just laughed.

"*Your punishment is to see her suffer. And if you lose her, then maybe that's the punishment you deserve.* That's what he told her. That's when I knew he expected you to die." Darius gets to his feet. I flinch. He dips his head toward the space on the bench beside me. "Would it be all right if I sat there?" When I don't respond, he adds, "I'd like to look out the window from that side. To see that side of the city."

I don't say anything, but I slide over to make room for him. When he sits, I turn and look out the other way. I notice a ring where people are jousting, with a huge crowd watching from grandstands, and beyond that ring a gate in the wall.

And beyond that gate, a gravel lot full of trucks.

I remember the princess's words: *I know there's a fleet of trucks parked just beyond the west gate, and I know that at least one has the keys inside.*

"In desperation, I offered to be the one to strike you," Darius says, interrupting my thoughts. "Maybe that was the wrong thing to do. Maybe, like the princess, I should have offered to take your place. But I was desperate to get the whip out of his hand. I was searching for something he might agree to. In the end, I think the only reason he agreed to it was because he couldn't pass up the chance to watch me—another Outsider, another surrogate—cause you pain. The prince is all about power and control. Watching me strike you, he knew he had control over both of us."

He stops looking out the window. For a moment he glances at me, and I'm so uncomfortable, I cross to the other seat. The gondola crests the wheel's arc again, and it feels as if my heart goes up into my mouth. "I hated it, but it gave me the chance to protect you."

I flinch at these words. "How could you protect me by hurting me?" My tone is so angry, but I have a right to be angry, and I won't back down. "How could you claim to be protecting me—"

"You only lasted five lashes—I stopped as soon as you slumped and I knew you were out. Renya tried to untie you, so Sir Millicent dragged her from the room. But the prince shouted for more. Five lashes weren't enough to quench his bloodlust. He reached for the whip in my hand, but before he could take it, I raised it above my head, as if I would strike him if he tried.

"Sir Arnaud cut you down and I was tied in your place. I don't know how many lashes Lars gave me that day. He exhausted his anger on me—I know that. I woke the next morning on the floor of my room." He glances up for a brief moment and our eyes meet, but then he drops his gaze back to the floor. "He sent me to work in the palace fields as soon as I could stand."

I don't want to pity Darius. How can I pity him when my burden was the same? But I know more of the story now.

If I believe him. At this point, I'm not sure if I do.

"Why don't I remember the name Darius?" I ask.

"Everyone calls me Kit. My last name is Kittering. Kit for short."

That much seems like the truth, but like everything else he has said, my Cientia picks up neither truth nor lies. What I do feel is fear, but I guess we both have good reasons to be afraid right now.

The gondola sweeps up and over the top again. From this seat—the seat where Darius had been sitting before he moved to sit by me—I can see more of the same words, *truth*, *mine*, *wild*, *want*, *travel*, and *through*, but then, as the wheel is slowing, I notice a new one, *land*, blinking in gold letters on top of a large tent that's as blue and as pale as the sky. Then I notice another, *edge*, in red letters between burning flowers in a garden of flame.

I hadn't expected that some words would be only on one side of the city. It seems obvious now, but I guess because I had seen the same words over and over, three or four times each, I just assumed I'd seen them all.

The wheel slows to a stop. We're just at the tops of the trees, and I see one more additional word—*you*. So now I have *truth*, *mine*, *wild*, *want*, *travel*, and *through*, plus *land*, *edge*, and *you*.

Is that all of it? Is that the whole clue? I glance at Darius as the wheel ratchets down a bit farther toward the ground.

It's almost our turn to get off. "You have the clue, don't you?" I ask. "You've figured it out?"

I know the answer before he nods. I can see it on his face. I can feel the heat of his anticipation.

The Outsider attendant pulls the door open. But I need to get back up to the top and look for whatever words I may have missed to make sense of this clue. "I want to go one more time," I say. "Please."

"Sorry. You'll have to go back to the end of the line. Those are the rules."

Darius is already standing when I look through the open gondola door and see two things that sink my hopes. The first is the ginger-haired racer, practically next in line for the ride.

The second is a group of at least five King's Knights passing through the crowd, searching every face.

I think of the truck with its keys inside, somewhere in the lot outside the west gate. The princess took a risk to tell me about that truck. But if I don't get the clue soon, I'll already be running behind, or worse, arrested and not running at all.

Darius is still hovering at the edge of the crowd, watching the King's Knights. For a moment, I wonder if he is about to turn me in. He easily could.

"Darius," I say. I bite my lip and search the crowd one more time, looking for any other option, but I'm out of ideas. The ginger-haired racer moves up in line. The wheel turns another fraction. The next gondola to take on passengers will be his. "I have a proposition for you," I whisper. "I may not know the clue, but I have transportation. If you're willing to share the clue with me, I'll take you to wherever we need to go."

THIRTY

Darius narrows his eyes and looks at me sideways before he says, "You're sure?"

"Yes," I say, though in truth, the only thing I'm sure of is that this is my only option. "Same deal as before. The vehicle belongs to me. I am the driver and you are the passenger." I take a quick moment to glance around. It's loud and bright, like I can almost see the peals from the trumpets and horns. The sun is sliding down, adding swaths of shadow but also lighting faces here and there like a warm spotlight. More than anything, though, I see too many Authority guards, so I duck my head and add, "It might be better if you lead the way. We're headed to the west gate, behind the jousting ring."

"Got it," he says. "Saw it from the wheel. You ready?"

He waits only long enough to register my nod, and then we're off. Darius's size helps him move through the crowd, and I do everything I have to do to stay with him, including jostling and elbowing anyone who gets in my way. If they turn and glare, I don't see it, because I keep my eyes on the ground between Darius's feet and mine. From time to time, Darius murmurs bits of instruction to me, like *Slow down a bit* or *Don't look left*, until finally he simply says, *We're here*.

I raise my eyes to find myself standing among rows and rows of parked trucks. We made it. Behind my back, I hear a cheer go up from the crowd watching the jousting on the other side of the gate. "No guards?" I ask.

"Not yet," Darius says, and I follow the line of his sight to the other end of the lot, where two guards are posted beside the only driveway that leads out. "Which vehicle is ours?" he asks.

I shrug. "Someone . . . ," I start. I don't want to say that it was Renya. "Told me that a truck out here would have the keys in it." We start testing doors, but there are dozens of trucks here, and time is not on our side. We've made it all the way to the far side of the lot without luck, when I notice a delicately painted insignia on the back of a truck that is particularly new and particularly clean. I recognize the insignia with its two winged deer—it's the crest of Princess Renya.

The doors are unlocked, and just as she promised, the keys are inside, on the floor in front of the passenger seat. Darius climbs in and flips them into my hand. "I held up my side of the deal," I say, trying to speak with the tone Jayden used when he spoke to me, because I found him self-assured and a bit intimidating. "Now it's your turn. What's the clue?"

Darius glances around the truck and then asks if I have a pen. I hand him the one from the dormitory cleaning lady, and he finds a scrap of paper under his seat. He writes:

Truth
Mine
Wild
Want
Travel
Land
You
Edge
Desert
Through
Find

"Those are the eleven words that make up the clue."

"And that's all of them?"

"I found the first nine while walking the grounds. I had those all memorized. Then on the ride I added *through* and *find*. Those were the only two I needed to be in the air to see."

"So what does it mean?" But I don't wait for him to answer. I start moving the words around in my mind, shifting them like the pieces of a puzzle. "I wish my brother Marlon were here," I say. And when I see the questioning look on Darius's face, I add, "He's an ace at puzzles."

The words are barely through my lips when I realize that this is a memory. No memory sickness, no pain in my head, just a plain and simple recollection, like it had been there all along. But the casual way it comes to me can't offset the weight of it. For the first time since I woke on that rock in the ocean, I see the cramped apartment in my mind, with its high, small windows and its meager lamplight.

My throat goes thick and my eyes fill with hot tears. Sitting here in this truck, so far away, I'd do anything to be back in that dreary apartment right now.

"What about . . . ," Darius says, "*Travel through the wild land . . .*"

"The Wilds, maybe?" I pull the atlas from my bag and open it to the map of the continent. "That's a place not far from here."

Darius glances at the map in front of me. "That's a nice thing to have," he says. And then, looking back at the list of words he tries, "*The truth you want to find is mine. Travel through the wild land to the desert edge.*" He leans over my shoulder to frown down at the map, and I'm reminded of the time we huddled in the sandcrawler to try to get warm.

I thought I didn't trust him then. I trust him even less now. "Is there a place called the desert edge?" he asks, and I'm relieved he doesn't move any closer.

"Here's *the Wilds*," I say, pointing. "They do border the desert, if we pass through them, but there's no place marked as *Desert Edge* or *Edge of the Desert*. There's a city on the border between them—*the City of Jackals*—and there's a place marked *Mineral Deposit Reserves*. But if there's one spot called the *Desert Edge*, it's not on this map." I stare at the list of words in his hands again. I can't think of any other way to fit them together, but maybe my brain is too clogged with the thought of the ginger-haired racer finding all the words while he rode the Wheel of Fire. If he also found transportation, he could be on his way already. "Mineral deposits and the City of Jackals. Maybe the checkpoint is between those two?"

"They're both on the edge of the desert," he says. "If we head that way, we'll find it." But his voice gives away his skepticism.

"You're not a very good actor," I say.

He rolls his eyes, which warms me toward him, which only makes me angry at myself. "Well, it's hard to fool someone with Cientia," he says. He slides over to the passenger seat. I'm not sure if he's saying something about my distrust of him, but I can't worry about that now. I'm watching the guards at the exit from this lot. They're bored, staring at their comms, and I have an idea to get them out of our way.

I start the truck, but neither guard flinches. There's so much noise from the festival that it covers the sound of our tires on the gravel as I back out and tuck the truck near the rear of the lot.

Then I lay on the horn.

They both look up as if they were just caught napping on the job. One pockets his comm, the other drops his to the ground, and they both hurry this way, weaving through the crowded rows of trucks. That's when I gun it and swing along the side lane, all the way to the front.

By the time they see us, they're watching us disappear down the road.

It's a familiar road, with its grass and moss and bridges . . . Ninth, Eighth, Seventh Isle . . . until, before long, we're off the Ten Isles all together. The road I covered with Holly stretches through the sea of green pastures in front of us, but there's a turnoff to the south right after we cross the Arrow River, and that's the route I take.

This road is nowhere near as smooth as the ribbon through the pastureland, and before long I'm worried about two things: the rocks that litter the road, sharp enough to puncture a tire, and the fireworks in the distance, which I begin to suspect aren't fireworks at all. "What do you think that is?" I ask, after a particularly loud blast that rumbles like thunder. I slow the truck. Darius gives me a sideways glance.

"Not a storm," he says. Another one goes off, just as loud, with an even brighter flash. "Explosives? The OLA?"

There's a hint of sulfur on the breeze. "Out here?"

"Maybe. They just set off that bomb in Falling Leaf—"

"Falling Leaf?" Of course, I know the OLA was there— I was with them—but I didn't think they were planning a bombing. "How do you know that?"

"I heard people talking—"

"What people? Where?"

Darius gives me an odd look. "On the train I took to the Ten Isles from Falling Leaf."

"I meant," I say, glaring at him, "where did the bomb go off?"

"In some dormitory for Enchanteds."

A snake twists in my gut, and I scowl through the windshield. The road is becoming rockier and narrower the farther we drive into the Wilds. Darius is silent, leaving me lots of room to think about Jayden and the case he had me leave in the taskmaster dormitory. *Could that have been a bomb?*

No. *No.* He told me it was a *listening device.* There's no way that Jayden and the OLA would set explosives in a place where people sleep. They want to *stop* killings.

I'm shaking my head and breathing hard—I'm so angry— yet at the same time, so sure that my anger is misplaced. It can't be true. Jayden could never set off explosives with the intention of killing people, and he would never trick me into doing it for him. I'm sure of that, yet that snake still slides around my insides, making me queasy.

Eventually, we're forced to abandon the truck when the road becomes so narrow it's no more than a path. Then even the path thins and disappears.

You could say this terrain has no paths, or you could say it's nothing but paths, depending on how you look at it. If you're willing to climb, there's really nowhere you can't go, but there are no trails, no well-worn tracks to serve as comforting reminders of the people who came this way before us. Darius and I follow a line of broken rock at the bottom of two shoulders of stone. I try to keep to the highest ground possible, where there's a better view of what's ahead and behind. On either side of the path, crevices hold shadows so wide and deep, they could conceal several people—or who knows what else—standing shoulder to shoulder.

Ahead of us a blast goes off. We exchange a glance and step back, when someone calls out my name.

"Astrid!" the voice calls a second time, and first a gun appears from between two rocks, and then a woman, giving off the heady scent of surprise. It takes me a moment to recognize Wendy, Jayden's lieutenant from the train. She seems much plainer than she did before, standing here in dusty boots, her curls tied back, holding a long gun with chapped hands. "What are you doing here?"

Before I can answer, a blast of gunfire sprays over our heads, and we all drop to the ground. My beating heart jumps into my throat, but then I hear Wendy bark into a comm. A *comm*! It's so strange to see an Outsider with one. But then, Wendy's more of an outlaw than an Outsider, with her self-inflicted scar where her embed once was.

"Don't fire!" she says. "It's Astrid. We're coming back. Hold your fire!" Then she turns back to me and gives me an inappropriately big smile. "Did you come to join us?" She glances at Darius, giving him a little nod. "New recruits?" she asks him.

"We're in the *race*," he says, his tone full of vinegar, like Wendy's question is the stupidest thing he's ever been asked. But he doesn't know Jayden tried to recruit me. Or that I promised to come find the OLA after the race.

We follow her up a slope of broken rocks to a ridge that's concealed by boulders on all sides, and in the center of those boulders, we find a tight knot of soldiers. They crouch in a circle, backs together, and when they see us coming up the hill they first raise . . . and then, after an excruciatingly long moment . . . lower their weapons. They each hold a long firearm like Wendy's, and on the ground in the space between their backs, there are three open sacks overflowing with what appear to be metal balls. At a closer look, I realize they're grenades. Jayden watches us approach, and I can feel uncertainty in him. But it's okay if he doesn't want to trust me. I don't want to trust him either.

"What are you doing in the Wilds?" he asks, his gaze flicking from my face to Darius's and back to mine again.

"You *know* what I'm doing," I say. "What are *you* doing here? Don't you prefer to set off bombs in more crowded places than the Wilds?"

He flinches. I think I catch a whiff of mint, the scent of guilt, but there's a hard wind blowing in off the desert, and before I can be certain it's there, it's gone.

"Funny, that's what we were off to do. We were headed to the Festival of Fire Flowers—thought we'd stir things up a bit—but then we saw the prince's motorcade turn south. Well, there's no point in stirring things up at the festival if the prince isn't going to be there, so here we are." He pats the back of the man who stands beside him, a man who's built like two Jaydens put together. The man smiles. He's missing a tooth in the front, and I feel so much aggression in him, I can't help but wonder if it was knocked out in a fight.

Before I can say another word, an explosion goes off just beyond the boulder to our right. Bits of rock fly through the air like shrapnel, and we all hit the ground at once. I land with Darius's hand on my back and Wendy's shoe in my eye. Without even raising his head, Jayden grabs one of the grenades and, rising a hair higher on one knee, lifts his eyes just long enough to fling it at a distant ridge. It goes off like a much bigger bomb, but before the sound of the blast recedes, it's answered with gunfire that rings across the wall of rock just above our heads.

I flip onto my back and watch the sky brighten as another explosion goes off, this time to our left. How long will we last before their aim improves?

"Jayden, you've got to get out of here! Why would you fire on the prince's entourage?"

"We didn't fire on them. We only returned their fire," he shouts, as another blast rings out.

"They must have known it was you," I say.

Jayden makes a small noise in his throat, like a scoff. "Or they believed it was *you*."

On my back, I turn my face toward him, and if I didn't know him when I came upon him yesterday, I know him now. He smiles at me, a thin sarcastic smile that hardly counts as a smile at all, and I'm thrown back to a time when we were children, and he sat up with me all night once, because I was afraid of a storm. He was so kind to me until the next morning, when he teased me mercilessly. "Aw, come on," he says, as I feel tears welling up behind my eyes. "Don't start crying on me now."

"I'm not," I snarl, and just that quick, my aggravation with him stops the tears before they can spill over.

The blasts have quieted down, and Wendy and the others sit up. Darius glances at me as we both prop ourselves up on one elbow, ready to drop at any moment. There's a look in his eye. . . . Not fear. More like disbelief. He has that look of surprise a person gets when they realize they've been duped into joining something they want no part of, and now it's too late. "Why is the OLA traveling with guns?" Darius asks. "I thought your goal was to disrupt, not murder—"

"Only a fool would enter the Wilds unarmed," Wendy says, as she crawls on her belly to a spot where she can see between the boulders toward the prince's position. "They're overflowing with monsters."

"Too bad your memories are missing," Jayden calls over his shoulder to me, as he takes up a spot at Wendy's side. The sky is turning the dark blue of evening, and the clouds are whipping by overhead, like birds hurrying back to their nests. "I used to tell you so many stories about Lanoria's monsters. About buzzards in the Black Desert that will peck your eyes out before you're fully dead. Killer boars in the forests. Man-eating lizards that will stalk you through the Wilds."

I don't tell him that I do remember, that it's all coming back to me now. All I say is, "So you brought guns to use against monsters, but you're using them on people instead."

Another loud blast rings out, somewhere in the space between the prince's position and ours, and we all fall flat on our backs again. After just a moment, Jayden flips back onto his stomach and peers through the boulders, aiming between them, ready to shoot. "Ah. But it turns out, little sis, that people can be far more monstrous than actual monsters."

I squeeze my eyes shut, thinking of the dormitory in Falling Leaf, wondering if the people there awoke to an explosion like the one I can hear to our left, far too close to our left. I wonder if the cleaning lady who gave me the pen survived. Maybe nobody died at all. Maybe they all did. I want to ask Jayden about the listening device I put there for him—if that was the bomb—but I don't dare. I'm too afraid of what the truth might be.

"Jayden," I say, "I need to get around Lars and his men so I can continue the race. I need to reach the edge of the desert."

Now he sits up, as if his horror at my request outweighs his need to keep his head from being blown off. "What makes you think I would help you? I told you on the train. . . . The Race of Oblivion is nothing but a tool of oppression in the hands of the Enchanted. I've no idea why you would want to aid them in their tyranny, but I will not help—"

There are few things that could stop my brother midrant. I doubt even explosions at close range would stop him from making his point. But something disturbs the air, something more alarming than even an explosion to my blast-numbed brother's eyes. The sky shimmers like it's melting, and then a sound—a distant hum like wheels on rails—grows louder, deeper, until it's a sound all its own, a buzz of energy I feel in my chest and on my skin. The warm sunlight cools, as if the coming shades of evening were suddenly crashing down.

I remember the princess, all the bridges I've seen her make, but the form that takes shape beside Jayden isn't the princess. It's a black-haired boy, crouching on his knees. He's dirty and barefoot and shivering, and he holds his arms out wide.

It's *Marlon*!

It's my little brother, Marlon, looking almost exactly as he looked when I spoke to him in the roadhouse. The light grows again—evening brightens to noon—until all at once he sees us, as if we are all right there beside him. I swing my head around, looking for Renya. I've no doubt that this is her magic.

But there's no one but Marlon, his arms raised, his fingers stretched—and I realize with a jolt that this is not Renya's magic at all.

It's Marlon's magic.

"Pontium," Jayden breathes. "Astrid, look, it's Marlon. It's *Marlon*!" He reaches out to touch him, but of course he can't. "Marlon, are you all right? Where are you? Are you all right?"

"Astrid, I need you," whispers Marlon, and I can barely hear him. He rocks from side to side, and what I'd thought was shivering I now realize is movement. "I'm in a truck.

Someone grabbed me at the festival—two King's Knights—
and now I'm in the back of a moving truck—"

"Where are you? Where are they taking you?" I try to
keep my voice down, but I want to scream. I can hear loud
music—a jig being played on a fiddle and drum—and I realize it's coming from Marlon's side of the bridge. "Where's
that music coming from?"

"They're playing it over their comms," Marlon says. "I
can't see outside the truck. I don't know where they're taking me. I don't know. *I don't know*," he says, and now the
tears are coming, and I am struck by the fear that I'll never
see Marlon again. "I need you to win, Astrid," he says. His
arms are still held wide, but they quake like his muscles are
fatigued. "I know you're in the race—I saw your picture. I
talked to the photographer who took it, too, at the festival,
right before the Authority grabbed me. I'm scared," he says.
And for a moment, his arms sag and the air between us
shudders. But then he straightens, his face a tight grimace.
"I need you to win so we can both be citizens. Then they'll
have to let me go."

I'm so close to the image of Marlon, if he were really
here, my breath would ruffle his hair, but then Jayden's
pushing in between us. "Marlon, it's me, your brother,"
he says. Marlon's eyes go wide. "I promise to make sure
she gets to the edge of the desert, Marlon," Jayden says,
and the words break in his throat. "I'll make sure she

makes it to the next clue."

Then Marlon asks something strange. He asks if we know how to find the mine.

"Mine? What mine?"

"In the clue. *To find the truth you want, travel through the wild land to the mine at the edge of the desert.*" Then he adds, "*The finish line.*"

A *mine*? I shrug my bag from my back and pull out the atlas to look at the map again. And it's right there. *The Mineral Deposit Reserves.* That's where a mine would be. We think we're so smart, Darius and I, but we had the clue figured out wrong.

No one's as good at puzzles as Marlon.

"In the Mineral Reserves," I say, and then I ask, "What's the part about the finish line?"

"The ride at the festival—the Finish Line—its sign flashed like all the other words in the clue. I think the mine might be the end of the race." His voice is nearly drowned out. The whistle is back, then the roar. He won't be able to hear me much longer, but I blurt out one more question. "How are you able to use this magic?"

"How are you able to use this magic," he repeats. But then he adds, "I've always had magic, just like you—"

"What? But Marlon—"

"And just like you, I've kept it hidden." The bridge collapses like a coil, and there I am, on my knees, with my brother Jayden on his knees in front of me, his eyes and nose red and damp. A blast goes off behind us, but we're both still far away, in the back of that truck with Marlon. Jayden presses the heels of his hands against his eyes, and when he looks at me again, he's still far from composed.

Then he's scrambling, stuffing supplies in my bag, handing me a full canteen, and telling me he's sending me off with Wendy. "She's our best scout. She can get you around the prince's line." He pauses and swipes his nose with the back of his wrist. "We'll keep them busy, keep them distracted, to give you the best chance," he says.

I try to sneak a glance at Darius, but he's looking right at me. "What?" I say.

"Our deal was if I gave you the clue, you'd get me there."

"You didn't give me the right clue. Marlon—"

"I got you this far." I want to argue, but the truth is, there's not even a vehicle involved anymore. There's just the knowledge that the mine is the next checkpoint—the finish line—and Wendy is leading the way. I don't know how I would stop him from following us, short of Jayden threatening to shoot him if he tried.

I consider this—all I'd have to do is say the word—but if I do leave him here, I could be condemning him to death. Of course, he could die just as easily coming with us, but at least it would have been his own choice. "I can't stop you from following us," I say.

Rafaela volunteers to come along, too, and when she does, Wendy crawls up beside her and kisses her. "If we're gonna die, we're dying together," Rafaela says, and my chest goes hollow. I hope someday someone loves me enough to risk their life to be by my side.

"Astrid!" Jayden calls from behind me when we've already hiked down from the ridge. I squint back up at him, but he's running down to meet me. When he catches up, he draws me into an embrace. He smells like gunpowder. "Be careful, little sis," he says into my hair. "Now that I have you again, I don't want to lose you."

"You be careful, too," I say. When he lets me go, I force a smile. "See you soon."

He gives me a sad smile, a brief nod, and then he turns and hikes away. Just like when we parted at Falling Leaf, I can't leave until he disappears.

It's a hard hike, so no one talks; we all save our breath for the effort. But when we're finally on a level straightaway, the echo of the blasts moving farther behind us, Rafaela decides to break the silence. "Congratulations on the bomb you set in Falling Leaf," she says.

"What?" I say, but before she can respond, something lands between Rafaela and Darius. It explodes, kicking up a cloud of dirt so thick, it's impossible to see.

THIRTY-ONE

Before I can see again, I know someone's hurt. No one screams like that unless they're in horrible pain. But when the wind blows the dust clear, I realize the person screaming isn't the person who's hurt.

It's the person who loves the person who's hurt.

Rafaela is flat on her back, and Wendy is hunched over her leg, so I can't see the wound until I move closer in. "It's all right, it's all right," Wendy murmurs, pulling herself together, but it's only for Rafaela's sake. I still feel her raging fear.

Rafaela gives her a hard look and says, quite calmly, "Tell me the truth."

Wendy slides over so Darius and I can see Rafaela's wound. Her foot and ankle are covered in blood. I don't want to touch her more than necessary, but I work her shoe and sock from her foot, open the canteen, and let running water reveal the extent of the damage.

There are three long gashes—two shallow, one deep—and to be honest, they all look pretty gruesome. "Can anybody back with Jayden fix her up?" I ask Wendy, after she finishes describing the injury to Rafaela and promising her everything will be all right. "Do you have a medic?"

"Carlos can fix it," Rafaela grunts. "You just gotta get me back there."

Darius has already fashioned the ruined sock into a bandage—it's bloody, but at least it's not covered in dirt like everything else—and she grunts but doesn't scream when he helps her to her feet. Wendy looks stricken, her eyes darting from Rafaela's bloody foot to the rocky slope ahead of us.

I nearly say, *You have to take her back*, but I hesitate. Instead I say, "What options are we looking at? How will I get to the mine if you take her back?" I'm about to suggest that Darius should return with Rafaela so Wendy can continue with me, but before I speak, Wendy says, "Keep going downhill." Though I sense her guilt for leaving us, I also know she isn't wavering. I won't be able to persuade her to go a step farther without Rafaela. "The mine you're looking for . . . The entrance will be marked by a flashing green light. You'll need to cross a stretch of sand before you reach it. So it's downhill all the way. Uphill leads to rocks; downhill leads to sand." Another explosion goes off somewhere in the direction we came from. Rafaela shifts her weight onto her injured foot and winces. She shoves her gun into my hands.

"Take it," she says when I try to pull away. "I won't be able to use it. And Wendy's got one."

I sling the strap over my shoulder. It's not too heavy, but I still worry it might slow me down.

Another blast goes off, this one closer than the last. "No time for long goodbyes," Wendy says. "Just one word of advice. When you come to a cave that leads underground, go through it. You can stay aboveground, but that path will slow you down. The cave gets dark, but it's a shortcut. Good luck." And then she's helping Rafaela take her first step, and then her second, and there's nothing for me and Darius to do but walk away.

I'm wondering how long I should wait before I make a break for the mine, when a gunshot rings out from right behind us. We both duck instinctively, and I swing my head to look back over my shoulder. On the ridge to our left, I spot a female Enchanted Authority guard, her sleeves rolled up to her elbows, raising a long gun in our direction. "Sniper!" I shout to Darius, as another shot rings out. The echo fills my head. I look back again, lifting the gun in my hands, but the guard is gone. Then Darius grabs me by the arm and starts running.

He pulls me along as he runs up and over jagged boulders

and down precariously high ledges, and I'm reminded of the climbing skills he displayed at the lighthouse—skills I don't share. He runs and climbs much faster than I do, and though I try to keep up, I stumble now and then and he nearly drags me. I'm shocked he hasn't let go of my hand. He'd make much faster progress without me. Maybe it's because I have the gun.

When my feet get caught up beneath me and I finally stumble and drop his hand, Darius goes a few steps before he stops and turns back, his feet skittering on loose stones. He's running toward me, shouting for me to give him the gun, when another shot goes off not far behind me. I roll onto my back and raise the gun, and as soon as I spot the guard, looming over us on a high rock ledge, I fire.

I miss—I'm not sure I've ever fired a gun before—and she fires again. Darius lets out a guttural grunt. I manage to get off another shot, the sniper scrambles out of view, and I turn to see Darius, his left hand clutching his right shoulder.

"We need to run," I say.

"No kidding," he says, then groans as he straightens. I want to tell him to save his smart answers, but my knees are bleeding from my fall, and they wobble a bit as I get back onto my feet. "Do you think you can keep up?" he asks.

My only answer is to run right past him.

A vulture is circling overhead, but otherwise, everything is still. The only sound is our breathing and the crunch of the rocks under our feet. I want to look back for the sniper, but I know that would only slow me down. So I run on, down a gravel incline that leads to the base of a large rock that fills the path like an outsize boulder. I'm imagining trying to climb it—my palms are lacerated and sticky with blood—when I notice, farther down and to the right, the dark mouth of a cave.

"This must be the shortcut," Darius says from directly behind me.

I swallow. I'm not anxious to head into a dark underground passage, but Darius scrambles down, and I'm not about to let him take a shortcut without me.

The entrance is under a low-hanging rock ledge, and we both have to stoop. I notice Darius's shoulder. Blood runs down both the front and back of his tunic. I almost ask if he's all right, but I don't want another smart answer, so I keep the question to myself.

Light reaches only a few yards into the cave. Then we're in complete darkness. "Wait," I say, stepping back into the light. "Jayden gave me supplies. I'm not sure what . . ." I dig through my bag, my heart racing, until my hand falls on something just the right shape, and I pull out a battery light.

It throws a paltry yellow glow only a few feet in front of us, but it's enough to get me to shuffle a few steps into the cave. That's as far as we've gone when the air around us stirs with movement. Something flies past our ducked heads. I turn to watch as a hundred bats take flight and pour out of the cave and into the light.

When the cave goes quiet, I shiver. But I take a step, and then another. The cave won't be a shortcut if I don't move as fast as I would move aboveground. I swing the light from side to side, and the cave breathes out a gust of cool air. Darius asks, "Can I take your hand?"

"I'm all right," I say. The truth is, holding his hand might help me stay calm, but I want to win this race on my own terms. I don't need a man to lead me.

"I didn't mean . . . I'm glad you're all right, but I'm not so good. I can hardly see, and the dark is not my favorite place."

My foot comes down in a puddle. I shine the light at the walls. They're wet. Water drips down and trickles along the floor of the tunnel. The air reeks of mold and bat droppings. I reach out and let Darius take my hand.

We shuffle like this, following the trickle of water, and the cave is so silent, I almost think I can hear Darius's heartbeat. My Cientia felt rivalry in him before—a hunger to win—but in this cave, I feel only his fear. The light is fading, the circle narrowing. I hope the battery holds until we reach the exit.

"Do you hear that?" Darius asks me. And I do.

"Wind."

We pass a shallow pond where the water pools. We're

climbing now, the trickle running toward us as the floor slants uphill. The air in the cave is still damp, but every so often, a dry breeze blasts across my face. Then I notice we don't need the battery light anymore. We're almost out.

The light grows, but it never becomes bright. Meanwhile, the wind grows louder. We're at the end of the cave and the Wilds are behind us. In front is nothing but sand, stirred into the air by a windstorm.

We push forward into the wind, and Darius startles me when he cries out. I have to turn back to look at him. His shoulder has become a bloody mess, and he's fallen slightly behind, but he stumbles forward and grabs my arm and points into the distance, and I see what he sees—a pulsing green light. "Could be the entrance we're looking for," he says, and for the first time in a long time, when I feel a twinge of hope, I don't force it away.

Walking into the wind is exhausting, like swimming against a current. Every muscle aches as I shuffle forward. The wind is moving so much sand it's changing the terrain, piling it up in places like drifts. "Can you still see the green light?" I call over the gale. I have to squint against the pelting sand, but I can see well enough to know Darius shakes his head. My Cientia has felt nothing but fear in him since the cave. His tunic is stained through with blood that has soaked down from his shoulder. "You look terrible," I call to him.

"It's nothing," he says back. "Just grazed me."

I roll my eyes, though I know he can't see me. One high black dune looms in the distance. I point to it, and Darius nods, but he doesn't answer—there's no point in trying to speak. That last brief exchange left sand sticking to my teeth and tongue.

At last, when we reach the towering dune, it acts as a windbreak but also a shield, and the constant pelting finally abates. I chance a look over my shoulder, but I see no one. So I let myself drop onto the ground for just a minute. Just long enough to take a drink from the canteen.

Darius drops down beside me.

Sitting here with our backs tucked up against this dune, ripples of black sand roll up and over our legs, like waves on the ocean when the tide is coming in. As I watch, wave after wave grows and breaks, piling up and weighing us down. I search the desert all around us for the sniper or other racers, but all I see is a thick cloud of airborne black sand.

I jiggle my legs to work them free, but more sand blows in so fast, all at once my legs are buried again. A shadow falls across us, and I raise my face in time to see a sand wave growing so tall and so high, I have to duck my head. I cower against Darius, and the sand smacks into the side of me, filling up my ear and burying my arm.

I try again to kick my legs free, but I can't. And even as I try to free myself, more sand rains down. I turn my face into the wind. Another massive wave is building, cresting and coming straight for us. It slams into me, covering my chest and both arms up to my collarbone. If I had hope of getting free, that last wave smacked the hope right out of me. I wriggle my legs and swing my shoulders, but I only sink farther down.

It's as if the desert and I are battling at Hearts and Hands, but somehow I missed the starting signal, and now I'm half beaten already. Panic-stricken, I turn toward Darius. He is all but gone, consumed by the sand up to his chin.

"Can you move? Can you twist yourself free?" I call over the roar of the wind.

He shakes his head. "It hurts too much," he says. At least that's what I think he says. His words are garbled by the sand covering his mouth. "It's hot and heavy against my shoulder, like it's grinding right into me."

Blood rushes in my ears, a droning as loud as the bellowing wind. I writhe in place, struggling to free my hands. Nothing. The sand is so heavy, it crushes my chest, making it hard to breathe. Another wave of sand crashes over us, and Darius coughs. "One more wave like that one," he calls out, "and I think I might drown in it."

"Hold your breath! Tip your face back and draw a deep breath and hold it!"

With Darius holding his breath, I thrash like a wild animal under the sand. The weight holding me down shifts slightly, my left side rises, and I pull my left arm free. I shriek with joy, but it's a joy short-lived. Under my legs the sand shifts again, and my whole body slides lower, maybe six inches, maybe a foot. Sand stings my lips, crowds through them when I gasp, and fills my mouth. My nostrils clog when I try to draw in a breath. Spitting and coughing, I struggle to raise myself, but I sink back down.

When I finally stop struggling, the sand is over my chin.

But I have one free hand, and I can dig. I scoop sand out from around Darius's mouth and nose, and then I start digging my right arm free. It's slow going—for every two inches I gain, the sand takes one back—but finally, both arms are free.

My hands are bleeding, my fingernails tearing from their beds, but I don't let that slow me. I dig. I squirm and writhe. My skin is as raw as skin burned by fire, but little by little, I manage to free myself from the clutches of the sand.

I want so badly to just lie here and catch my breath, but I don't dare. I need to get to my feet to stop the sand from pinning me down.

I turn in place. The storm is slowing—not much but enough. In the distance, I spot the green light.

The sight of the light sets my heart racing, but I won't leave until I've freed Darius. I can't leave him here to be swallowed up by the Black Desert, but I can't waste time either. So I dig, barking orders at him not to move—not to try to help me—because every time he struggles he sinks farther down. He finally holds still and I work, my hands bleeding into the sand, but the storm is over. The waves of sand have stopped coming now. Darius is out and sitting on the sand in half the time it took me to free myself.

I pull the canteen Jayden gave me from my bag and pour water over Darius's shoulder, until the sand is mostly cleared from the wound. "More than a graze," I tell Darius, "but it's nothing compared to Rafaela's injuries. You'll survive."

Though he still gives off nothing but fear, he smirks. I think he says *thanks*, but his voice is just a rasp. Then he points at the green light in the distance, and I nod.

Without another word, I start moving, eventually working my legs into a run. It's not easy—my knees ache and my injured shoulder throbs—but I do the best I can. I outrun Darius, at least. When I realize that I can't hear his footsteps, I turn around and see that he has fallen far behind. So far behind, I wonder if he's even running.

I shouldn't wait for him. I need to go. I can beat him—I'm sure of it—but other racers could be gaining. I watch Darius stagger forward, but then he bends at the waist, coughing and gagging. He coughs so hard and so long, it brings back a memory of my father.

I shrug my canteen from my shoulder and hand it to him when he catches up. He takes a deep drink, but coughs it back out onto the ground. His chest is heaving. "I can't run," he says. "I'll be able to soon, but not until I catch my breath."

I could leave him the water, I think, *but I should take the gun.* "It's a race," I say. "I'm going."

"I'll be right behind you," he says. He makes a face at me: half grimace, half smile. "And when I catch up to you, I won't hesitate to pass you."

"You're on," I say. And then I drop the canteen, pick up the gun, and run.

THIRTY-TWO

I run as hard as I can, the blinking green light coming in and out of view as the terrain becomes hilly again. The sand is behind me—I've crossed the finger of desert that reaches into the Wilds, and it's nothing but gravel and boulders from me to the mine. At times I'm forced to climb, at others to descend. None of it is easy on my aching legs and I'm tempted to stop and rest, but that intermittent flash of green keeps me moving forward.

I wish I didn't, but now and then I can't help but look back. Not just for Darius, but to see if any other racers might be coming up behind me. As I scramble to the top of one rise, I look back and see Darius falling farther back. And behind him, still out on the sands, a shape is moving fast.

Another racer is closing in.

I scramble down a shallow hill littered with jagged rocks. The wind is still blowing hard, and the sun is setting, and no matter how much ground I cover, the green light never seems to get any closer. I climb another shelf of rock, and when I look back, the racer who was behind Darius is now between him and me. He is running fast—much faster than I am—and from here the last rays of twilight illuminate the top of his head, and I can easily see who it is.

It's the ginger-haired racer, my nemesis, the one who tried to throw me from the railroad tracks at the Amaranthine Forest.

The one who will overtake me if I don't find a way to get out of here fast.

I scramble down the other side of the ledge, and, thankfully, the ground levels out and I'm able to pick up speed. At last, I'm gaining on the green light, growing close enough now that I can make out the dark, open mouth of the mine. I'm running like a piston, like a cog in a machine, thinking of nothing but the relief I will feel when I get there, when the toes of my right foot catch on a rock and I tumble hard to the ground.

My bad shoulder throbs, and though my coat and bag both pad my landing, my head smacks the ground hard. For a moment my vision goes black, and then it fills with stars. I blink it all away and the evening light returns, but still, I'm slow to get up.

I'm brushing my scraped and bloody palms down the front of my legs when I first hear the footsteps behind me.

I spin around and look back, but I know who it is before I see him. The ginger-haired racer has almost caught me, and I wonder how he could be so fresh. Perhaps he avoided the sandstorm, or maybe he's just so excited about the prospect of overtaking me. It doesn't matter, I tell myself, as I take off running again. But my legs are wobbly, and his footsteps grow louder behind me. Eventually, I hear him right behind my shoulder, and his shadow falls over me just before he slams me to the ground.

Cientia can't help me in a fight if I'm pinned down by a knee jammed into my pelvis. I squirm, trying to throw him off, but with his weight on me, all I can do is flail. His fist comes down hard against my cheekbone and I cry out, which makes him so happy he bends his face close to mine. "This is where I beat you," he hisses. "This is where you lose the race."

His voice startles me with its familiarity, and all at once I stop trying to shove him away and just stare into his face. *His suddenly familiar face.* Since I remembered Renya, so many memories have been surging back. Not painfully like they did at first, when they came on with a wave of memory sickness, but more like pictures on a screen that's suddenly come into focus. Or, like now, the past comes back as images spinning in my brain like a wheel, until all at once the wheel stops, and one image sharpens, grows clearer, until I recognize who the ginger-haired racer is.

"It's you," I say, and his face flinches. He's as muddled by the sight of me as I am by the sight of him.

From up close, I can see that his lashes and eyebrows are the same copper red as his hair, framing eyes of a scalding emerald green. "Astrid . . . ," he says to himself. Then to me, "You're *that* Astrid. . . ." His fists relax, and his weight shifts, as if he's trying to take me in.

His confusion is like a door in a wall, and I grab this chance to kick it in. His eyes go wide, but that's the only reaction he manages before I throw him off me and struggle to my feet.

By the time he gets back up, I'm ready, reaching out with my Cientia, waiting for his intended move. But all I feel in him is a churn of emotions: resentment, frustration . . . even hatred.

"We met in Queen Rosamond Square, a day before the Apple Carnival," I say. The memory comes back to me on an endless loop, a few seconds of my life repeating over and over: this ginger-haired racer scowling because I just told him no. "You asked me to help the OLA," I say.

"I asked you to help your *brother*. To help the cause of all Outsiders, but you were too selfish—"

"I told you I couldn't." I remember now. . . . I not only suspected that Jayden was with the OLA . . . I knew he was. This racer had approached me and told me as much. He'd asked me to help them.

I refused, but not for the reason he thinks. Ever since I'd figured out that Jayden was in the OLA, I'd wanted to help, too. But right before this racer approached me, Renya had finally convinced her father to give Papa the royal order so he could get medical treatment. Once that happened, I couldn't take the risk of being caught working for the OLA. My father's royal order could have been rescinded at any time. I had to stay on the royals' good side. My father's life depended on it.

"I remember all of it now," my opponent says. And that's when I feel it. His intention shifts. This time, when his fist flies at my face, I'm ready for it. I block his punch with my forearm. Still, he's strong—a lot stronger than me—and I reel back from the force of the blow. My arm aches from the impact.

His foot flies at me next, but I dodge out of the way, and while he's still off balance, I use whatever strength I have left in me to jump into a kick that puts him on the ground. A memory comes to me just then, a memory of training with the princess. I remember the first time I knocked her down as we practiced, and how satisfying it was.

But this racer is a better fighter than the princess. His reactions are quicker, and as he's falling from my kick, he knocks my legs out from under me and takes me down with him. I land hard on my shoulder, and it throbs so bad it makes me forget my forearm. I'm aching and I'm dirty and I just want to stay down, but I can't give up now. I climb back up and get ready, and when he rises up on his knees I plant my foot in his ribs. He hits the ground again, and when he lifts his head, dirt cakes to a bloody gash on his chin.

Still, I'm bleeding too. His blood doesn't mean I'm winning.

"I hated you when you refused to help us," he grunts. He manages to stagger back to his feet, but he's unsteady. "You joined the race in spite of your brother. In spite of how much he adored you and wanted you to join the OLA—his sister with *magic*. Magic, like the hated Enchanteds. And yet he's always raved about you. Always bragged. *She's special*, he would say."

He throws a punch, and I'm shocked when I block it. His story has me so off balance. But I sharpen my Cientia and try to tune him out.

"She's loyal to the royals, I told him. Loyal to them, even when they haven't been loyal to her!" He's wrong, of course, but I don't owe him an explanation. "More loyal than even Renya," he adds. He takes a hard swing at my jaw. I duck, but he connects with the top of my head.

I'm trying to concentrate, to shut down my mind except for my Cientia, but all I can think is *He just called her Renya. . . .* He didn't say *Princess Renya* or even *the princess*. He called her by her first name.

Could this be the boy Renya was seen with? The boy who wrote her those letters?

There are clouds in his eyes. He's awash in the same burnt-hair-scented astonishment as me, and I can only imagine he's fitting the past together the same as I am. Like trying to grab puzzle pieces out of a tornado.

"When I heard you'd joined this race," he says, grunting with the effort of another swing, which I block, "I knew I couldn't let you win it—some spoiled, Enchanteds-loving girl who turns away her own brother when he asks for help. A girl who promises to give a message to the princess, but never does."

For a moment, I'm distracted by this last part—*What message did I promise to give to Renya?*—but then he realizes I'm distracted, and he sees an opportunity. His foot sweeps up and kicks me hard in the ribs, and I fold and crumple to the ground. He kicks me again, this time in the head, and my ears ring like I'm inside a bell. But I still hear his words: "I chose not to tell Jayden you'd entered in the race, because unlike him, I realized the race could be an opportunity. A chance to gain citizenship and use it to help the OLA," he says, his foot landing in my ribs once more. "All while keeping you from the victory. I vowed I would beat you," he seethes, with one final kick for good measure. "And now I have."

I'm facedown in the dirt, but I feel him take the gun from the place where it fell, pinned underneath my left arm. I wonder if he'll shoot me. I suppose he will.

But if he considers it, he decides against it. I must appear too beaten to pose a threat. Or maybe he just can't bring himself to kill Jayden's sister. His footsteps head in the direction of the mine before they fade away.

It takes all my strength to lift my head, but I do. Maybe it's because I can't accept the loss. Maybe it's because it hurts just as much to lie here on this jagged and uneven ground as it does to get up. Or maybe it's because the thought of Darius coming along and finding me like this is more painful than the throbbing in my ribs or the aching in my shoulder. I use all this to motivate me, to drive me to lift my head just high enough to watch the ginger-haired racer leave, and as I do, I notice that he's limping.

He's injured. He didn't come through that fight as well as he'd like me to believe.

I watch him as he slows, from a brisk run to a staggering run, until he's hardly running at all. And my heart beats in my chest like a bird desperate to break out of her cage. Because I realize that what I do in the next few moments could decide my entire race. Getting up now will be one of the hardest things I've ever done, but if I do it, I might still have a chance to overtake him.

He's at the top of a long, gentle incline. He's had it easy

for a while, but now he's got to start scrambling up and over boulders again. But as hard as the path in front of him is, the mouth of the mine is terribly close.

I will myself up. I force my legs to move again. He doesn't know I'm following, and that gives me an edge. In his mind, I'm back in the dirt. In his mind, he can afford to take his time and be careful.

My legs throb. Blood runs down my right shin from my knee. Everything hurts. But I've suffered before. Suffered when there was nothing to be had for it except simple survival. But there's more at stake today than surviving until tomorrow. I will change my tomorrows with what I do today. With what I do *right now*.

My pace quickens. Every part of me aches, every cell of my body whispers *quit*, but I refuse to listen. My will is stronger than that. I push myself, and I gain on the ginger-haired racer. I've crossed the gentle incline and reached the place where I need to climb again, when my foot sends a rock tumbling and my nemesis looks back.

I keep climbing, but then he raises the gun in my direction.

For the space of a heartbeat I freeze, but then I defend myself the only way I can think of. I stand my ground, raise my hands, and close my eyes.

The match lights behind my eyelids.

A gunshot rings out.

I huff out a breath, the match goes out, and I hear the ginger-haired racer cry out in pain.

I open my eyes, and my legs buckle. Blood pours from a wound just below my right knee.

On the rocky slope above me, the ginger-haired racer drops to the ground and rolls back downhill, falling over a rock ledge like a rag doll. He doesn't stir after that. I wonder if he's out cold, but I don't have time to check. I need to move.

Maybe a hundred yards away, the entrance to the mine looms, and it's such a welcome sight I almost cry, even though it's all uphill from here. I try to pull myself up, but my shoulder is aching and my right leg won't hold my weight. My head swims and I collapse to the ground, not an inch closer than I was before I tried.

It doesn't matter. If I have to, I'll crawl to the mine from here.

I pull myself forward, my gaze latched onto the dark recess of the cave's mouth, when two armed men emerge from out of its shadows.

Two King's Knights.

I'm strangely relieved that I'm too hurt to stand. If I weren't so beat up, I'd have been standing and they would have seen me, but instead, I'm so dirty and broken, I blend right in with the rocks.

Lucky me.

They tip their heads, listening. Nothing sounds like a gunshot. Maybe they heard the other racer shoot at me. Their eyes sweep the landscape, but they look out, toward the horizon. Neither of them seems to suspect that anyone could be close by.

I stay down, hidden somewhat by a low ledge of rock, and a third man emerges from the entrance to the mine. There, his dark blond hair shining, his clothes as perfect as if he had never walked a single step through the Black Desert or the Wilds, stands Prince Lars.

These circumstances allow me only one option: to stay low, to wait for them to relax, to wait for them to turn and head back into the mine. The evening light has retreated, and stars are beginning to fill the sky. When at last they all go back inside and I'm sure they can't see me, I crawl forward. Rocks dig into my palms and knees. Gravel sticks to my bloody skin. Eventually, I find the gun where the ginger-haired racer dropped it.

I rise up on my one good knee, plant the gun, and let out a low, painful groan as I drag myself up. One sliding step, then another, using the gun as my walking stick, I hobble toward the mine. One-fourth of the distance. One-half. Three-quarters, and my right knee won't hold me anymore. If it were just pain, I'd push through it—I've got lots of experience on my side—but the leg is shaking and I know it's played out.

I said I would crawl, and I will.

The blood on my hands slicks the ground. The point of each rock makes itself known. But I won't give up.

A memory forms in my aching head, as bright and as illuminating as a sunrise. I'm in my family's apartment standing at the sink, and my father and brothers are at the table behind me. Marlon is there, and Jayden too, and Papa, dishing out his best advice to get me through a storm that has just started.

Courage gets a few to the summit, my father is saying, *but fear convinces most to choose the mud. Don't* you *choose the mud, Astrid,* he continues. *You are far too strong for that.*

My throat goes thick. I drag a bloody hand across my nose. *I'm at the summit, Papa,* I whisper to myself now. *No more mud for me.*

I swing my head around for just a moment, throwing one more look back at where I've been, and I spot another racer.

Darius.

He's not far away, and he's gaining, running much faster than I can crawl. I turn back toward the mine and dig down for all the strength I can find.

Darius is too far back for me to hear his steps, but they ring in my ears just the same. I imagine I hear them growing louder and louder, driving me forward, until I reach the threshold of the mine. Beyond the opening, a small group of Authority guards slouch against the close walls, since they have no chairs. The only furniture is a single tall stool that I imagine the lowest ranking officer had to carry, and on it sits the prince.

No one is watching the entrance. One officer is telling a story about a woman he met in the City of Jackals, and I'm glad I can catch only bits and pieces. The other guards laugh, even the women, but then one says, "Oh, shut up." The prince, a distance away flanked by the two Knights, looks at his comm while the Knights study theirs. They are bored, and they are distracted. No one notices me at all until I drag myself through the mouth of the mine and crawl right into their midst.

Lars's eyes go wide and he turns to the Knights, but it's too late and they know it.

Because I've been seen by others, and a small commotion is starting. Several very stiff and official-looking men and women, wearing long black robes and impatient expressions, see me and start prancing around like startled chickens. A voice calls out, "A racer!" A flash goes off as someone snaps my picture, and I can see by the look in Lars's eyes that he, like the Knights, knows it's too late. I turn my eyes from his, focusing instead on the effort it takes to pull my legs behind me, until I collapse at the feet of the robed man who was the first to call out when I appeared.

A man I remember.

His skin is as pale and as knobby as driftwood. This is the man I met after the explosion at the Apple Carnival, the one who registered me for the race.

There's another small commotion starting—someone else is crossing the threshold—and I turn to see Darius, staggering past the beams that mark the entrance. He stays on his feet for just a moment, his chest heaving. I don't know if I've ever seen a person more covered in blood. He sways, and then he drops into a heap right beside me.

But the driftwood man doesn't acknowledge him. His eyes are on me alone. He reaches down with both hands and pulls me, painfully, to my feet. My knee aches like I'm being stabbed, blood drips from my shredded hands, and my head pounds like a drum. Still, I hear every word he says.

"Congratulations," he shouts, as if he intends all of Lanoria to hear. "The Crown of Oblivion is yours!"

THIRTY-THREE

My body rocks so wildly, it wakes me. I try to sit up, but shooting pains in my knee and a sharp ache in my shoulder keep me on my back. I'm in some sort of truck, lying across the rear seat.

"Where am I?" I ask the back of the driver's head. But it's the man beside him—a man so small and still I hadn't noticed him there—who turns and looks back at me. It's the driftwood man. He smiles, and I know some people have smiles like the sun, but he has a smile like the moon, mysterious and canny. He flicks his gaze over me, landing on my bandaged knee. I have no memory of it being bandaged. I have no memory of getting into this truck. "You're awake," says the driftwood man. "How're you feeling?"

"Like I don't know where I am or where I'm being taken."

"Ah, well, that's good. Not too much pain then?"

"Plenty. Where am I?"

"We're in a sandcrawler. Well, a specially modified sand-crawler. It's quite impressive, actually—fitted to cross the terrain of the Wilds. We're almost to the train."

I scowl at him. My head is swimming and he's talking too fast. "Train?"

"You're going back to the King's City aboard one of the royal family's private trains. You won the Crown of Oblivion! Don't you remember? They gave you something for the pain and then you went out like a light, poor thing. But you *won*. Aren't you glad you entered?"

This is a strange question. After all I've gone through to win, you'd think the answer would be an immediate yes. But then, the things that I'd hoped to obtain by winning the race seem as far from my grasp as they ever were. I'd hoped to bring my family together, but the tiny apartment we called home is still lost to me, Jayden is a stranger, and for all I know, he's dead. And my brother Marlon—the person who means the most to me in the world—is less safe now than he was before the race.

So I'm a citizen, but without my family, what good is citizenship to me?

When we arrive at the train, I'm lifted onto a stretcher by Authority guards and taken directly to a private compartment. It's the picture of luxury—silks of blue and green decorate the bed and the windows. "This is the princess's compartment," I say. "I remember it."

"Well, your memories are back then," says one of the guards as I'm delivered to the bed. "The princess will be happy to hear it. She gave express instructions for you to use this compartment." I was already dizzy, and the speed with which I've gone from being hunted by the Authority to being attended to by these guards isn't helping me get my footing. These same two men might have arrested me if they'd recognized me at the Festival of Fire Flowers.

I won't let my filthy hands touch the pristine bedding. I feel like an earthworm. I probably look like one, too.

The officers leave, and with difficulty I slide my feet to the floor and make my way to the sink, holding the edge of the bed, then the desk, then the basin for support. What I see in the mirror would probably frighten me if I hadn't just seen blood-covered Darius in the mine. I was more shocked by my reflection back at the roadhouse, in Mary's bathroom, even though there are many more layers of dirt and blood on me now. My hair is matted like a bird's nest, and my face is gaunt and hollow. But more than all that, the things that stand out to me the most are the signs of fatigue—the purple circles under my eyes that make me look like I lost a fight.

Then again, I guess I did. I think of the ginger-haired racer, lying still where he dropped from that rock ledge, and I wonder if he's alive.

The hot water in the sink helps pull me back to the present. It feels so good, I wash my face, my throat, my hands, and my arms. There's no shampoo that I can see, so I wash my hair with hand soap. When I'm through, the towel I use to wipe up the sink comes away black.

I'm ruminating over what to do next—now that I've won citizenship for my whole family, I need to get answers about Marlon and news about Jayden—when there's a knock at my door. Before I can answer, it's opened from the outside, and three people stand in the doorway. One is Prince Lars. At first, the other two are strangers to me, but then my memory slides things into place and I make sense of their faces. It's like I'm looking at one of those puzzles where you have to try to see both the profile of an old woman and the profile of a young girl. These two, dressed in the uniform of the King's Knights, transform in an instant from strangers to people I know. One is Sir Arnaud, and the other is his daughter, Sir Millicent.

"Astrid," says Sir Millicent, and her face pinches into something that might be called a smile. "My congratulations to you. You are looking quite well, considering." This is what my father sometimes called a backhanded compliment, which is another unexpected memory. I think she assumes I will smile, but I keep my face neutral. She hasn't given me any reason to smile yet. "We've come to request that you join us in the dining car."

The train sways, and all four of us have to grab hold of the walls to keep our balance. My knee buckles, but I stay upright. I wish I had clean clothes to change into, but I suppose I should be happy that at least my face and hands are clean. I swallow, reminding myself that I've already been declared the winner, so it would be difficult if not impossible for Lars to poison me or throw me from this train without having to answer a lot of questions, especially with these two Knights present. So I nod, and my eyes move from Millicent's face to Arnaud's face to Lars's, but when they land on Lars's blue eyes and his angry smile, a memory rushes back that I had forgotten was ever there.

I'm in a white room, and there's music and fire and a man looking down at me as I lie on a cot. In his hand he holds a bloody knife, and King Marchant lies crumpled on the floor at his feet.

Like a gust of wind, the memory of the king's murder comes rushing back to me, and it's as if the wind blows the clouds from my mind. The man in my memory—the man hovering over me and whispering that I will be dead before I can remember what I have just seen—is Prince Lars.

And there's something about the way his gaze is pressing heavily upon my face that tells me that he knows that I remember, too.

I'm wearing only one sandal—I lost its mate outside the mine—so I kick off the other one and follow them out. With my bare feet and dirty clothes, I feel like a helpless urchin rather than the winner of a prestigious race, and I'm sure that's not by accident. If there were ever any danger that I might forget my powerlessness, Lars has made sure that I won't forget it today.

But none of that matters. I might look and feel powerless, but I'm not. I won the race, and I won the rights and privileges it guarantees. Citizenship for me and for Marlon, and even for Jayden.

And my victory means even more than that. It means I've won the right to never again be made to feel powerless.

I don't know what I was expecting to find in the dining car, but I wasn't expecting to find the queen. It's been some time since I last saw Queen Mariana—she's been ill for months—but she must've made a complete recovery while I was in the race, because she's looking quite well. She is an older version of Renya, dressed in navy blue—she loves blue—with her long auburn hair loose, and she is seated at the head of a dining table. Other than a clean white tablecloth, the table is bare. Prince Lars enters the room first, and he takes a seat beside his mother. Sir Arnaud and Sir Millicent enter behind the prince, Sir Arnaud bowing and Sir Millicent folding into a deep curtsy, and I suppress a shudder when I realize how much pain it will cause me to fold into a curtsy myself. But there are some things that must be done no matter the pain, and paying respect to the queen is one of them, so I reach out a hand to brace myself against the back of a chair and execute as close to a full curtsy as I can manage. I lose my balance and end up clinging to the back of the chair, but I stay upright, and the room fills with a mist of embarrassment on my behalf until the queen gestures to the other seats at the table. "Please, sit."

I hesitate, but her eyes insist, so I do as she says.

"Astrid, let me get right to the point. First, my congratulations. However, I must immediately make it known to you that an objection has been raised to your victory in the race. The objection is based on the accusation that you cheated through the illegal use of the Three Unities. This objection has been raised by my son, Prince Lars, who has asked me to nullify your victory and name the second-place finisher, Darius Kittering, the victor in your place."

I try not to react. But the queen has strong Cientia, and I'm sure she knows the horror I feel.

"Essentially, this meeting between you and me is a tribunal. My late husband created the Race of Oblivion as a means for worthy Outsiders to earn citizenship, and until my son is crowned king in his place, it will be up to me to make decisions concerning this race. The Race of Oblivion meant a great deal to my husband, and it is my intention to maintain the validity and integrity of this contest in his memory. Do you understand?"

So this is it. This is how Prince Lars will steal back all the rights I have won for me and my brothers. How he will clear the way to prosecute and punish me—or worse—before I'm able to expose him as the murderer of the king. I feel his eyes on me when I say, "I understand, Your Highness."

"Lars, you have witnesses? Bring in the first to testify."

Sir Millicent stands and walks to the door, and my heart stops and my breath leaves me in a rush when I see the photographer, the one Darius called *Mrs. Arrogance*, enter the room behind her. She's barely recognizable. Her hair, which was so perfectly styled, is now a disheveled mess, and her crisp clothing is filthy. But worst of all are the purple bruises that stand out on her face—one over her left eye, one on her right cheek. "What happened?" I say before I can stop myself.

"I fell," she says, her voice barely above a whisper, and I know this is nothing but a lie. Someone hurt this self-assured, beautiful, assertive young woman, in an effort to convince her to testify against me. And she's an Enchanted! Whether it's intended to or not, the sight of her both breaks my heart and fills me with dread, because it makes it quite clear how far Prince Lars is willing to go to strip me of the Crown of Oblivion.

"What is your name, my dear? And what is your testimony?" asks the queen, though she's not even looking. Her comm lies faceup on the table in front of her, and her eyes are on the screen. Maybe the queen can't look into the face of someone she knows was injured by her own son.

"It's Candace, Your Highness," Mrs. Arrogance says, or at least I think she does. Her voice is barely audible. "And I came here to testify that I observed . . ." Her voice trails off. There's a tremble in her lower lip.

"Go on," growls Lars.

I'd like to read the emotions in this room, but everything is overwhelmed by Mrs. Arrogance's fear.

"I just want to say, I never witnessed it myself, but as a journalist, I asked many people about Astrid." Her eyes move to my face, and I think I see a flicker of an apology, but then it's gone. I can't blame her. Who knows how Lars might punish her for even an apologetic glance in my direction. "And many people I spoke with . . . racers especially . . . shared stories of Astrid fighting like an Enchanted. That is to say, as if she had Cientia."

Candace's testimony is accepted, and she is dismissed, but the queen asks Sir Arnaud to escort her to the doctor. "Shame on you," she says to Lars as they leave. "She's one of our own." She shakes her head and clucks her tongue, the way she did when Lars was a little boy.

The prince presents two additional witnesses. One is the man from the guardhouse, the first person I ever used Projectura against. The second is the racer with the pretty face and the build of a man, the one who was with Marlon at the roadhouse, and who I noticed had a black eye at the festival. Her eye is looking better today. She tells them how she saw me fight several racers at the lighthouse and win easily, and how there was no doubt in her mind I had done it with the help of magic.

When both of these witnesses have been dismissed, Lars stands and puts his hands on the table, leaning close to his mother's ear. "That is all I have, Mother, but is that not more than enough? What more could you need to hear?"

The queen doesn't meet her son's eye, despite the proximity of his face to hers. Instead, her gaze falls upon my face, and a flicker of fear runs through me. Something in the look she gives me tells me she knows all my secrets. "I'd like to speak with Astrid alone," she says.

As the others leave the room, Lars grunting his disapproval under his breath, the queen gestures to the chair at her immediate right, the place her own son just occupied. "Please, come closer."

I do as she says, of course, but my feet feel as if they have grown into the floorboards, and my body is heavy as I drop into the chair. Taking this seat feels as dangerous as placing my own neck into the guillotine.

"Did you know," she asks me, her words dripping from her lips like syrup, "that your mother was a friend to me, very much like you are a friend to my daughter Renya." I look up and meet her unrelenting gaze, and I know that this woman is as sure that I can use Enchanted magic as I am.

"I am aware that my mother was indentured to you," I say, and this is the truth. I know almost nothing about my mother's relationship to the queen before her death.

"Things happened back in those days when we both were young and newly in love and starting our lives," the queen says, and I wonder why she should speak to me in this way. I try to imagine this woman and my mother as close as Renya and I are, but I can't picture it. Then again, I can no longer picture my mother at all, and it makes me jealous and angry to know that the queen has memories of her when I don't.

If it's true they were close, something bad must have happened. Otherwise, how could the queen have brought the children of her dead friend into the palace, to suffer in place of her own children? How genuine could their friendship have been if she were able to do that?

The queen is leaning forward on her elbows, closing the space between us as if she wishes to take me into her confidence. My heartbeat grows faster, and my breathing slows, and I feel as if I've gotten myself into terrible danger. An alarm is sounding in the back of my mind, telling me I should evacuate, but there's nowhere to go.

"Things happened, both good and bad, when we were young and our children were young . . . things I can almost forget, but never fully can." Perhaps the queen taught her son how to mask his emotions, because my Cientia gets nothing from her at all. It's like my magic isn't real after all. "We shared secrets," she continues. "Secrets that have grown, bloomed into bigger secrets. Some of those secrets have to do with you."

I swallow. "What kind of secrets about me?" I ask.

"I think you know," she says, and I do. She means that she knows the secret of how I am able to use Enchanted magic. The secret I have yearned to know all my life. I wait, my heart dragging me forward like a wild stallion, pulling me closer and closer to the truth I know the queen is able to reveal.

But then she waves a hand at the door. "Let the others back in, won't you?" she says, and she has already turned her eyes back to her comm.

Lars bursts through the door as soon as I've pulled it open, which I expected, but I hadn't expected Darius to follow right behind him. He's bathed and he's dressed in clean clothing, and he leans on a crutch. The prince storms straight across the room to his mother's side, but Darius lingers near the doorway.

"I wanted to win," he says, in a voice so low only I can hear, "but I didn't want to win like this." He's like a wintergreen candy—I notice the mint of guilt and the sweetness of honesty. For once, I trust he's telling me the truth.

Sir Arnaud and Sir Millicent stride in, with a casualness that tells me they expect no surprises. No one is holding out hope that I will be spared. Not even me.

The queen stands, and though she is not tall, her presence is enormous. Her hair is a bit redder than Renya's, her eyes a bit darker, and her lips scarlet. Everything about her reminds me of a fire flower . . . a flame that is self-contained.

"Well?" Lars says.

"My son," the queen says. "You are so much like your father." She runs a hand down the front of her navy blue gown, and I feel a flicker in the atmosphere. Something changes. And then she says, "Astrid has used some unorthodox methods to win the Crown of Oblivion," she says. "But . . ." She hesitates. I heave a sigh. Lars takes a step back. "None of her actions warrants stripping her of the prize she has won." Lars drops his fist onto the table. Not hard, but the sound fills the room. "However . . . ," she adds.

In the quiet of the queen's pause, the rhythm of the wheels against the rails sounds like a heartbeat. Beyond the window, the moon casts a pale light over the darkened pastureland. Headlights stand out against the gloom. A truck is traveling on the ribbon of road beside the tracks. I think of Holly, the things he told me about the king. About his addiction, and how he secretly shared Oblivion with him.

I realize all at once that I have lived most of my life with Renya and her family, and yet what do I really know of them? They are an enigma, a secret hidden from everyone around them. Maybe even from themselves.

"To compensate the second-place racer," the queen says, and her eyes sweep across the room to land on Darius for just a moment before they fall heavily on Lars's face again, "the two of them will *share* the Crown of Oblivion."

THIRTY-FOUR

S hare the crown?

My eyes find Darius's face. He's already watching me. *To share means to divide, doesn't it? What part of the prize will I have to give up so that he may have it?*

"Share *how*?" the prince asks. The train banks into a turn and the room tilts. My palms press down on the top of the table to hold me steady as I wait for the queen's reply. I feel as if I stand on a knife's edge—on one side is citizenship and on the other arrest—and the queen's answer to Lars's question will determine which way I fall.

"I mean that Darius will receive the full benefits of the victory, without any benefits being taken away from Astrid. They will share it—"

"So they *both* win?" Lars looks from his mother to Darius and back again, and I see all at once that she has just called Lars's bluff. By giving the crown to Darius without taking it from me, the queen has given Lars what he asked for while protecting me at the same time.

I should be happy, but instead I feel like a charity case, which makes me angry since I earned the crown and shouldn't need charity to keep it. But then again, here is one more chance for the royals to show me how powerless I am. For the queen to make a quick and casual decision as to whether Darius or I deserves the Crown of Oblivion, after all we went through to compete for it—after people *died* competing for it!—makes it feel like little more than a carnival prize. Something the queen can easily divide between her two squabbling children.

Surrogates, indeed.

But I don't care. I can't afford to care. Because at least for now, Lars can't hurt me. I'll be a citizen, and Marlon will be, too.

My eyes meet Darius's, and I read in him a churning mix of opposing emotions. He's like a drowning man pulled from the sea by his sworn enemy. Surely Lars has rescued him, but we both know he did it less to help Darius and more to hurt me. And yet I feel in Darius a shock of relief, and despite the hurt in our history, I'm happy for it.

"Feel free to go, if you'd like," the queen says, flicking the back of her hand in my direction. I'm being dismissed, in no uncertain terms. But before I go, I have to ask about Marlon. "Your Highness," I say, "my brother Marlon was also in the race." I hesitate. I don't dare tell her about the Pontium bridge Marlon made and reveal that he—like me—can use the magic of the Three Unities. "I know he was at the Festival of Fire Flowers," I say, being careful to share only what I could have been told by others. "He made it that far. I've heard that he was seen being taken away by two King's Knights." The queen's eyebrows rise. I think I've surprised her. "He'll be a citizen now—along with me—so I hope, whatever has happened to him, he will be brought back home as quickly as possible."

"Of course," says the queen. I hope she means it. I can't read her, and she's looking down at her comm.

"Is the princess on the train?" I ask. "May I see her?"

"The princess was sent ahead to the palace," answers Sir Arnaud. "She traveled on an earlier train."

Back in Princess Renya's compartment, I lie awake in the dark, too anxious and too lonely to sleep. Before my memories returned, I didn't miss Renya at all. You can't really miss a person you don't remember. But now almost all my memories are back, I think, especially my memories of the princess. Since I saw her at the Festival of Fire Flowers, since she wrapped the scarf around my head and whispered a warning into my ear, I haven't been able to forget her. I think of the orange she pressed into my hand, something so small but so precious to a racer, and I hold on to the thought of this gift as I imagine asking her to help me find Marlon.

He bridged to me—he's reachable by Pontium. I wish he'd bridge to me again, but I won't let his silence scare me. It could simply mean he's being watched. But once I have help from Renya—someone who doesn't need to fear the King's Knights—I know we will find him, and she will order them to bring him home.

The sun is up by the time we reach the junction at Falling Leaf, and an Outsider brings a breakfast tray to my door. I stay in my room all morning, and another tray is delivered at lunchtime. By the time I've eaten half of it, the train is slowing to a stop at the outpost.

I'm not sure if someone will come for me, but I don't wait to find out. I take my coat and my bag—not that I'll need them, but it would feel sad to leave my only two possessions behind—and I find my way out and climb down to the platform. The queen and the prince are at the center of a swarm of Outsider servants several cars away, but I don't see Darius. Maybe he's still on the train. I'm thinking about going back to look when an Authority guard calls out my name and tells me he's assigned to drive me back to the palace. He leads me to a motorized carriage that gleams under the hot desert sun, its pristine appearance absurd against the dirt and sand of the outpost. "Who else will be riding with us?" I ask.

"No one, miss. This carriage is reserved for the winner of the Crown of Oblivion."

"But there are two winners—"

"And two carriages. Prince Lars's order," he says. "You are each to have your own private vehicle."

I try to smile, but all I feel is irritation. Lars is trying to make me feel isolated and alone, and I'm furious that it's working.

On the long drive back, we pass the place on the road where Darius and I nearly froze to death, and the place we found the racer who actually did. We pass the roadhouse, the Village of Hedge, the lighthouse, and then Camp Hope, where home used to be. I get only a glimpse of the maze of gray, low-slung buildings before the carriage turns through an opening in the city wall.

When we finally come to a stop inside the palace gate, someone pulls the door open from the outside. It's Renya, and despite the fact that I'm still barefoot and filthy and so stiff and aching I can hardly move, the first words out of her mouth are "You look wonderful!" She pulls me to my feet and into a hug. My knee throbs and my head spins, but I don't say a word. I just drink in the relief that pours out of Renya and envelops us both like mist.

Once we're inside, she leads me up the central staircase to her bedroom. The steps are difficult, but the princess lets me lean on her, and I don't ask her to slow. I don't know where Lars is or if he's even back yet, and I want to get out of sight and into a place I feel safe before he gets the chance to confront me again.

The door is hardly closed behind us when Renya whirls on me. "You should sit," she says. "I have a lot to tell you." And I feel it in her . . . something she's both excited and anxious about. So excited and so anxious, it makes me scared.

"I have something important to talk to you about, too," I say, thinking of Marlon, "but you go first."

The room is almost exactly as I remember it, with one exception. There is a second bed. Renya must notice my eyes on it, because she says, "They said you could return to the dormitory downstairs, but I insisted you stay with me. At least until you can find a more permanent place to live." She bites her bottom lip. "I hope you don't mind, but I had your things brought up." She opens a drawer in one of the two carved-wood dressers, and inside I see all my personal clothing—socks, underclothes, a few dresses, tunics, and one skirt—all folded and put away neatly. "And here," she says, gesturing. On her vanity, I find my most precious possession—a framed photograph of my parents on their wedding day. It's been given a place of honor in front of the mirror, beside Renya's hairbrush and my comb.

I pick up the photograph and look at it closely. My parents were only a little older than I am now when this was taken, but they look so healthy and well compared to my haggard reflection in Renya's mirror. My mother holds a chaotic bouquet of random flowers dominated by lilacs, their stems tied to a small green book. My father's hair is cut short and a bit uneven, but the look on his face makes it clear he does not care.

This would have been taken while my mother was indentured to Renya's mother, the time when they were close and shared secrets . . . at least, according to the queen.

"Sit down on your bed," Renya says. Her face is serious. "I have a lot to share with you. I need to tell you quickly, because soon Gretchen will be coming in to help us dress for the ball."

The ball. Of course. Every year, the race ends with a celebratory ball, where the winner receives the Crown of Oblivion. Gretchen is the princess's maid. The thought of a maid helping me dress is disconcerting enough. The thought of facing a crowd, smiling as if I'm happy while Marlon is still missing and the horrors of the race are so fresh in my mind, fills me with dread.

But maybe Marlon can be found *before* the ball. Holding on to that hope, I do as Renya asks, and I sit.

"First things first." Renya keeps her voice so low she has to stand just a foot in front of me to be heard. "I assume you know that your brother Marlon was a contestant in the race." I nod but my heart stutters out of rhythm, for fear of what she might say next. Fortunately, she doesn't make me wait. "His name is not on any of the lists of the known dead," she says, but we both know the official lists of the dead are incomplete. Some people are never found. They just fail to return from the race, and their loved ones are left to wonder if they ran away or died.

"This is the very thing I wanted to talk about," I say. "I saw Marlon." I stop short of sharing with her that I saw him because he used Pontium. I only say, "At the Festival of Fire Flowers, two King's Knights threw him into a truck, but I don't know where they took him."

Renya looks stricken, as if she knows what her brother is capable of as well as I do. Maybe she does. "If you'd like, I'll try to bridge to him."

There's nothing in this world she could offer me that would be a greater gift than this. I nod and whisper, "If you could," but she's already holding her hands above her shoulders. The light in the room is already changing.

Everything dims, and I wait, holding my breath, anxious to see Marlon's face. I hear the familiar sound—the buzz of energy filling up the room. But then the light flickers and brightens again. The buzz dies down to a hum and goes out. Renya's arms sag. Her hair floats in the air, full of static. She shakes her head.

"What happened?" I ask.

"He's out there," she breathes, and I realize she's winded. "I felt him, but I just couldn't get to him." She drops onto the bed beside me and she takes my hand. She's freezing. "He's out there. He's alive. I felt his energy and I could almost see his face. But then he slipped out of my reach."

She takes a deep breath and lets it out. "He's too far away. Or maybe underground. Somewhere that Pontium energy can't reach."

"But he's alive?"

"He's alive," she says. "So we'll get him back. I don't know what orders those King's Knights are following, but he's alive, and we'll get him back."

The air in the room chills. Renya sounds so sure, but she can't hide her fear from my Cientia. Fear enough to send a shiver down my own spine.

But then Renya is back on her feet, pacing. "There's more," she says. "I know this is a lot to take in all at once, but there's something else I learned while you were gone. Something I can't keep from you a moment longer."

She crosses to her dresser, digs down to the bottom of one of the drawers, and lifts out something small and green. She holds it out to me. It's a small book with a worn cover, the same small green book my mother holds in the photograph taken on her wedding day.

"How did you get this?" But before she can answer I snatch it from her hands and open it. It's filled with pages of looping handwriting. My mother's name is written on the inside cover, beneath the words *Diary of.* There's also an inscription in my father's handwriting. *To my beautiful wife on our wedding day. May you fill this book with many happy memories of our lives together.* "How did you get this?"

I say again, and as happy as I am to have it, I'm furious that Renya had it first. That she might have read it, might know my mother's secrets. I remember the queen's words from the train . . . *We shared secrets. Some of those secrets have to do with you.* It feels like everyone's been given access to my mother's secrets except me.

"When my father died, I found this among his things," Renya says, and I can tell by the way she says it, she knows how terrible that sounds.

"Your *father?*" I say. "That makes no sense—"

"It does, though. . . ." Renya keeps her eyes on her hands. She's rubbing at her palm with her thumb, as if she has an itch that's driving her mad. "Because there is quite a bit in there about him." I feel as if the air has been knocked from my lungs. The little book had fallen open in my hands, but I clap it shut. "Wait," she says. "It's not what you think . . . not exactly. It was all one-sided. *Completely* one-sided. You can read it yourself. Your mother writes how my father claimed to be in love with her, but she felt nothing like that for him."

Now it's my turn to pace. I let the book fall open again, find a page marked with a red ribbon.

"The page that's marked . . . I thought you should read that page. It explains a mystery you've long wondered about."

The page Renya has marked bears a date just a few days

after I was born. My eyes skim the page, catching on the words *he sent the queen's own midwife* and *no inoculation against magic.* "He asked what he could do to show his love for me," I read aloud, "so I asked him not to deny magic to my child."

I close the book again and stare down at it in my hands. It feels like a living artifact, a ghost sent to tell my mother's story.

To tell my story.

"But I'm . . . I'm my father's daughter?"

"I didn't read all of it, of course," Renya says, "but I read enough to know that my father's feelings for your mother were unrequited. So yes, most certainly you are your father's daughter."

I walk to the window. Renya's room overlooks the boxwood maze and the rose gardens. "I always assumed it would turn out that I wasn't inoculated, but I could never have guessed that *this* would be the reason why," I say. And then, before I can really work through the impulse, I find myself blurting out things I promised myself I wouldn't mention, because they relate to the one incident in our past we never discuss. But Renya told me a difficult truth, and I feel like I owe her the truth, too.

"I met the boy—*your* boy—the one from the OLA," I say. "The one you were seen with in town. The one who wrote you those letters."

"The one who . . . ?" She stops, and her eyes widen with realization, and she says, "You thought they were the same boy? That the boy I was seen with—"

"Yes, the boy from the OLA—"

"The boy I was seen with," she says, measuring her words, "and the boy who wrote me the letters . . . You're correct that they both had connections to the OLA, but they were *not* the same boy."

"So the boy I met in the race . . . ?"

"The boy I met with in town was a headstrong boy with red hair. A boy with something to prove—"

"That's him," I say.

"I remember his name was Aengus. I didn't know he had entered the race."

"But he's not the boy . . . the boy who wrote you . . ." The words *love letters* are on my lips, but I leave them there.

"Not the same boy," she says.

Someone knocks at the door. "Excuse me, Your Highness." An Outsider woman pokes her head in, and I recognize her as Gretchen, Renya's maid. "You both need to start dressing for the ball."

Renya scowls at me. "You can't dress until you wash," she says, and I'm a bit insulted by her tone. But then, this is the friend I remember, after all. You don't have to choose your words carefully when you're the princess. Renya offers her own bathroom for me to shower and tells me to come over to her dressing room to pick out a gown as soon as I'm ready. She embraces me before she leaves, and her fingers trace across the scars on my back. "I can't wait to help you choose a dress," she says. "I have so many pretty ones that will cover your scars."

I give her a weak smile. I know she means well, but I can't help but resent her desire to cover them up and forget them, as if they were never there. Whether they are visible or not, I can never forget.

And who will bear her punishments now? Will the back of another Outsider girl become scarred, now that I will be a citizen? The thought of it turns my stomach.

Once Renya leaves, I intend to be quick, but I first return to the open drawer where Renya pulled out my mother's diary. I need to stash it away again, for safekeeping. Reaching under her nightgowns, my hands find folded papers wrapped in a ribbon. My heart gallops toward a cliff when I pull them out and my eyes fall onto what could only be the letters we were just talking about.

I'm not sure how she managed to keep them, how it is her father didn't throw them into the fire right in front of her eyes. How the queen didn't shred them and feed them to the palace goats. But these *must* be them—their weathered folds prove these letters have been opened and read many times over. Maybe Sir Millicent didn't find all of them. Maybe these were hidden separately. It doesn't really matter. All that matters is that here they are, wrapped in a red ribbon in my shaking hand.

I know that I shouldn't read them, and I know just as well that I will.

After all, didn't she read my mother's diary? If she can know my secrets, can't I know hers?

I slide out the first letter, the one that appears to be the most worn.

It feels so light for something that holds so much weight. Weight enough to bend the courses of our lives. To Renya, it was a romance with a boy, but it was also a flirtation with rebellion. With ideas that could bring down her own family's reign.

And what was it to me?

Proof that my life was just a pawn to the royals. Proof that I could trust no one. Not Renya, not Lars, not even my fellow surrogate Kit could be trusted not to hurt me.

Kit . . . *Darius.* I think of him as he was on the Wheel of Fire, sitting so still, telling me his side of the story as the world flew by outside the window. How he struck me to protect me from the bloodthirsty prince. My head goes light, like I'm still on that wheel.

I unfold the letter.

Dearest R, it starts. For a moment I feel horribly guilty, but my eyes still float down the page. The words *beauty* and *fire* and *longing* jump out, and I decide I've made a mistake.

I can't read this letter. I thought it was something I was entitled to, I thought it would make me feel even somehow, but it only makes me feel dirty. My shaky fingers refold the letter and slide it back under the ribbon.

But the letter has been turned so the back page is up, and my gaze lands on the signature at the bottom of the sheet. *Yours, D.K.*

That's when I realize I've seen this handwriting once before.

Truth

Mine

Want

You

A list of words to a clue, written on a dirty scrap of paper found on the floor of a stolen truck. My eyes return to the bottom of the page. My ears start to ring and my eyes cloud, but I can still read the initials scrawled there.

D.K.

Darius Kittering.

Renya's secret romance was with Darius.

THIRTY-FIVE

My hands are shaking when someone knocks on the door that connects this room to the dressing room. I turn, and Renya is standing in the open doorway. Her face loses its color when her gaze falls on the letters, still in my upturned palms.

Gretchen pushes in behind Renya, and she scowls at me. "Haven't you made any progress at all?"

Renya crosses to me, and with an accusatory glare—*she's* accusing *me?*—she takes the bundle of letters from me and replaces them in the open drawer. Gretchen sweeps into the bathroom, and I hear the water running in the shower.

"*Darius?*" I murmur, while we have the room to ourselves. "Why didn't you ever tell me?"

"*Tell you?* Do you think I should be giving out the names of everyone I might know to be involved with the OLA?"

The OLA . . . The idea that Darius is involved with the

OLA shocks me almost as much as the fact that he's *involved* with Renya. I fall back onto the bed Renya had brought in for me. This absurd bed that's practically as plush as Renya's, with half a dozen pillows scattered across the top. I grab one of those pillows and pull it to my chest, trying to process all this.

Gretchen is back, talking fast, but I don't catch a single word. She snatches the pillow from my hands and shoves a bathrobe in its place. She's pulling me to my feet and dragging me to the bathroom.

"Get washed!" Gretchen orders as she shoves me forward and closes the door between us. "Shower up and meet the princess and me in the dressing room. I have quite a few stunning dresses for you to try!"

I rest my back against the inside of the bathroom door. I thought I knew what it meant to be unmoored and disoriented. I experienced it when all my self-knowledge was stripped away. Now I've been given more knowledge than I ever had, and I'm just as unmoored and disoriented as I was when I had none.

I shower so quickly, the hot water does little to clear my mind. My hands are still shaking when I wrap myself in the bathrobe Gretchen gave me—soft and white and embroidered with Renya's name—and slide my feet into matching slippers. I feel drunk on all the truths I've learned in just the last hour. When I woke up in the race I was hollow and empty, and now I'm full to overflowing, but to be honest, I don't feel any safer.

So I remind myself that when I woke in the race, I pushed forward, and that's what I have to do now. I entered the race for one purpose: to secure safety and independence for me and for Marlon, and until I get those things, I need to keep going.

Until I get those things, I'm still in the race.

When I exit the bathroom I find Renya waiting for me, alone, wrapped in an identical robe.

"I have some explaining to do," she says, "and I want to do it quickly, before Gretchen comes back. I don't need the whole staff gossiping about what might be going on between you and me. We need to carry on as if everything is normal."

"Normal?" I say. I sit down on the extra bed—*my* bed— and try to focus. The light in the room is golden, and outside, birds are singing in the gardens. I draw a deep breath and let it out. "I don't even know what that is anymore."

Renya walks away from me, but she stops in front of the vanity, so I can see her face still, reflected in the gilded mirror hung above it. Her brow creases. She draws in a deep breath and turns to face me again. "I want no more secrets between us. I want to tell you everything, but I need to know I can trust you—"

"Why would you ever doubt you can trust me—"

"Because you wouldn't commit to what I had committed to. What Kit had committed to. I know Aengus tried to recruit you, I know he told you your brother Jayden wanted your help, and I know you said no. But I had said yes. And Kit had said yes. Those letters—"

The door to the dressing room opens. "Ladies!" Gretchen calls to us, and we both move dutifully toward her. I feel queasy, the words *what I had committed to* spinning in my mind. The floor beneath my feet feels unsteady, and I'm glad that, once we're in the dressing room, Gretchen doesn't stop me from sitting on the edge of a padded chair. "I want you to start with these," she says to Renya, handing her two gowns—one blue, one green. "And you, Astrid, the Queen of Oblivion," she says, running her hands over a long rack of gowns in the center of the room. I've never heard the title *Queen of Oblivion* before. I can't tell if it's a real thing or just something Gretchen's coined to tease me. "Let me know how you feel about these three." Now I'm back on my feet, letting Gretchen drape the dresses over my arm. "Oh!" shouts Gretchen, and I leap back. "I left the ivory one I want you to try in the wardrobe. I'll just run and fetch it. Start trying the others," she says, and she's out the door again.

On cue, Renya launches back into her story. "The romance between me and Kit—that ended before it started. It ended the night you almost died paying the price for something so foolish." She doesn't look at me but paces, and I catch her reflection in one of the huge mirrors that line the wall, and then the next, and then the next. Her eyes are wide, her cheeks flushed. "But though we both put that part of it aside, neither Kit nor I could put aside our commitment to the cause. We both kept in touch with Jayden. We both continued to do what we could for the OLA. And now . . ."

She sits on the arm of the chair I just got up from. My head is swimming as I try to keep up with every word that she says. I'm relieved she's stopped pacing because I can't handle the movement. The air in this room feels close. "Why didn't I feel this secret in you, all this time?" I ask.

"The letters, the boy, the OLA . . . the things that led to that beating . . . They're the only things we never discuss, you and I," she says. She takes my hands. Mine are icy, but hers are hot. "I never had to keep it from you. You never even went near it."

I realize this is true.

It wasn't until the race, until I forgot all that I thought I knew, that I began to see the world of Lanoria through open eyes. Until then, I didn't understand the OLA at all.

"I placed a bomb for Jayden during the race," I say. "But I didn't know it was a bomb. I . . . I wanted to help, but I didn't want to hurt anyone."

The door flies open and Gretchen storms in, carrying an

ivory gown on a hanger. "This is the perfect dress for you, Astrid," she says. Her eyes go wide as she looks from me to Renya and then back again. "Ladies, we need progress! You can catch up on gossip later."

I take the dress from her hands. "Yes. Sorry," I say, and she steps back out.

"Now Kit and I are working to help Jayden find Marlon," Renya says as soon as the door is closed, barely missing a beat. "I know what Marlon means to you, Astrid. But don't worry. Wherever Lars has taken him, we'll find him, and we'll bring him back."

She gets to her feet and stands in front of me, chewing her bottom lip again, watching my face intently with wide eyes. She's waiting, and I think worrying, about my reaction.

"You're helping *Jayden* find Marlon? You and Darius?"

She nods. "That's one of the reasons I went ahead of all of you, on an earlier train—"

"You're in touch with my brother Jayden—"

"Yes—"

"And have been—"

"Yes."

What sort of reaction could ever fit a revelation like this one? This makes the fact of her father's love for my mother seem quaint. This is so much more. This is deception and subterfuge and *rebellion*. This is believing in the value of a cause so completely that you become willing to turn on your own people.

Your own family.

I guess Renya had her reasons for keeping her secrets from me.

Until now.

She's given me a gift, by trusting me with her secrets, but she doesn't yet know how great a gift it is. She doesn't know I'm keeping a terrible secret of my own, one I feel I can trust her with now.

"I want to help find Marlon, too," I say, and immediately she releases her bottom lip. But I have to raise my hand to warn her I have more to say. "We have to find Marlon, because I know what Lars is capable of."

Her smile flattens. Her brows knit into a frown. "I think we all do. He's all about oppression. Like our father before him—"

"No, that's not what I mean. I mean, I know what your brother is capable of because I know what your brother has done." Renya presses her lips flat. "I was in the room when your father was murdered, Renya. I'd just been given the Oblivion." Now Renya takes a half step back. "And it wasn't an Asp who killed your father. It was your brother, the prince."

Renya's eyes widen and her mouth falls open, but then her hands go to her face. When she drops her hands again her eyes are wild, but while I watch her, she takes it all in with long, slow breaths, until a few moments later, the only word for the look in her eyes would be *resigned*. I'd thought she might tell me I was wrong or at least that I was confused—that the Oblivion I'd been given had deceived me. But she purses her lips once, nods, and says, "Does he know that you know?"

"I think so."

"Does anyone else know?"

I shake my head.

She nods again. She's scared—I can feel it—but she's trying not to let it show. "This will require some sort of action, of course, but first we need to find Marlon." She wrings her hands once, but then she says, "Thank you for telling me the truth."

"No more secrets between us?" I ask.

"No more secrets." She takes a step toward me and I think she might embrace me, but there's a knock on the outer door and Gretchen barges in, this time with another Outsider maid—a frightened-looking older woman—in tow. Gretchen has been Renya's maid since she was weaned, so she can get away with bossing the princess around. I feel sorry for this other woman, who certainly doesn't want to anger a member of the royal family.

Gretchen clears her throat. I can't help but wonder if this is what it feels like to have a mother. "The two of us are not leaving until you are both dressed and ready for this ball."

With Gretchen and the other woman helping, the process of dressing becomes a whirlwind, and before long I'm standing in the middle of the room in an ivory silk gown with a high back that fits like it was made for me. After the shower I wrapped my knee in a clean brace, and now I slide a pair of soft leather flats onto my feet. I should be able to stay upright, even if I can't dance. Renya is dressed in a gown of emerald green, which fits her so well, it makes her look like the carefree princess she's so good at pretending to be.

The princess even I believed her to be, until today.

When we arrive at the palace ballroom, nothing feels real. An Outsider footman with a ruddy face and the most ornate coat I've ever seen gives me a short nod before opening the door and holding it so Renya and I can enter, side by side.

We walk into a room festooned with flowers, all of them white. The ceilings are high and the lamps are low, and spotlights illuminate elaborate arrangements of white blooms and silver foliage. Above the center of the dance floor, an enormous hanging basket holds cascading blooms—white roses, daisies, magnolias, even white tulips and daffodils—all twisted into vines that tumble like streamers over our heads. Dozens of tiny white lights twinkle among the blooms.

"I should have told you—I tried to stop them, but it was too late. The theme tonight is *In the Moon Garden.*"

My stomach pinches at the words, but I try to ignore it. Could it have been intentional? Could this be a move by Lars to keep me feeling insecure? Well, I won't let him succeed. "White flowers," I say, forcing a smile at Renya until it no longer feels forced. "I guess I chose the right dress, then."

It looks as if every citizen of the city is here, the room is so crowded. A tiny panic tickles the back of my mind, but I tamp it down and force myself to take deep, even breaths. Strangers clasp my hands and congratulate me. I smile and nod, not knowing what else to do. The music is loud, and the conversation even louder. I catch myself scanning the crowd for Darius's face—so much has changed since I last saw him—when Lars emerges, cutting a path through a mass of dancing bodies. He is dressed in a very crisp black suit. Across his shoulders he wears a red cape, reminiscent of the King's Knights.

"Sister," he says, greeting Renya. "Astrid." He bows as I curtsy, and before I can speak he is extending his hand. "Will you honor me with a dance?"

Though every cell of me flinches away from him, I place my hand in his.

"I requested a slow-tempo waltz. I thought it would be easier on your injured knee."

We reach the dance floor. My ears are ringing with music and panic, as I try to understand why the prince wants to dance with me in the first place. Maybe it's traditional for one of the royal family to dance with the winner of the Crown of Oblivion. Is it traditional for him to leer at them, too? After all the pain Lars has caused me, when his hand touches my waist, I shiver.

My leg throbs. I bite my bottom lip to keep the grunts and groans inside, because I'm not sure how well it would go over in front of all these people if I stopped in the middle of a dance with the prince. I can keep going. I certainly have endured worse pain than this. I'm grateful that Renya took so many dance lessons. She taught me most of what she learned, so I could dance the part of her partner when she practiced. Occasionally, we even switched, and she would lead.

After the song ends, having not caught even a glimpse of Darius, I find myself in a quiet corner of the mezzanine with Lars. I'm not sure how we got here—he whisked me up the stairs before the music ended, as if it were all part of the dance. He has not taken his hand from the small of my back. "Astrid, can I tell you a secret?"

My eyes slide to him. I'm thrown by his choice of words, though I try to appear relaxed. I doubt I succeed. Lars is standing closer to me than he's ever stood. As usual, I can't read his emotions.

Can he read mine right now? I wonder. I'm sure that he can. Even a person without magic would be able to tell I'm afraid.

I keep my eyes from his eyes. Instead, my gaze moves to his mouth. I notice his parted lips. His tongue runs along the back of his teeth, like he's hungry.

"Do you remember the day Renya and I had to attend the ballet on behalf of our parents?" he asks, his voice a whisper. "Our father was called away on some official duties, and our mother was too sick to leave her bed."

The ceiling up here on the mezzanine is low, and the air is still and stifling. Beads of sweat tickle the back of my neck before sliding down my spine. "Last year," I say. "It was when the trees were flowering—"

"You were so sick from the pollen." I let my eyes move to his. I don't know where he's going with this story, but I want to get out of here. I wonder if Renya has noticed us missing. "You wore a pink dress that belonged to Renya, because the theater objected to Outsiders attending. They said Renya and I were too old to need surrogates along—"

"To be fair, I'd tend to agree."

Lars lets a small laugh escape. "I was eighteen. Perhaps that's too old to be accompanied by a surrogate. And Renya was sixteen. But you know that Renya doesn't want to go anywhere without you, and our parents weren't there to stop her. But you were miserable. You sneezed through the whole first act. If you weren't in the royal box, I think the other patrons would have picked you up and tossed you out." His eyes sweep over me, from my face down to the hem of my borrowed gown. "You look lovely in this. It suits you."

Something reaches me from Lars. An emotion slips past his defenses, and my Cientia picks up a longing in him.

"Why are you telling me this?"

"Because it was one of the first times I realized how much I want to protect you. I felt so defensive of you that evening. I could perceive the anger in those Enchanted snobs all around us, and it infuriated me. That was one of the first times I realized that I . . . that I had feelings for you."

The fear that started when I first found myself tucked away in a corner with Lars spikes at this confession from him. It's not a confession, though. It can be nothing but a lie. I remember that evening. The other patrons at the ballet had shown contempt for me, but Lars had felt the same way. I remember his anger—not at the other Enchanted, but at his sister for insisting I come along.

I can't help but challenge him, even if I'm putting myself in danger. "*Feelings* for me? I have to say, I'm surprised. I remember that evening so differently—"

"Oblivion," he says, as if this one word erases his blatant lie. "Haven't you been told? When memories return after Oblivion steals them, they're often distorted or inaccurate.

You may think you remember things from your past, but you may very well have the details wrong."

"So . . . ," I stammer, my mind racing. This can't be true. If it were true, Renya would have told me. This can only be another trick by Lars to deceive and manipulate me. "You say that was the first time you realized your feelings?"

"If I'm completely truthful," he says, dropping his eyes as if he's embarrassed, "the first time I realized I had feelings for you was when Kit asked me to let him take the whip." One of his hands rises to my throat. A fingertip traces over the scar where my embed once was. "I was so relieved to be able to put it in someone else's hand. I just couldn't stand to strike you anymore."

The touch of his hand on my throat sends a shiver of loathing through me. I wonder if he feels it, and I honestly don't care if he does. He is a liar, and I know it. He can try to mislead me with his own version of that day. It won't work.

"But let's not dwell on that tonight," he says, finally withdrawing his hand. "After all, you will be a citizen now. You will never find yourself under the whip again."

"I'm looking forward to that," I say. My eyes meet his, and in my glare, I hope my message is clear. *You have lost your power over me. I won the Crown of Oblivion, and everyone knows it. I will be a citizen and you will never be able to threaten me again.*

Lars returns my stare. His eyes are fearsome, like the eyes of a snake about to strike.

And then he does.

"And your brother. He's still missing, isn't he? That must be terrible for you. I've already put the best people to work on the search, investigating this rumor you heard that he'd been snatched away by King's Knights. I won't rest until he's found."

And there it is. The leverage he still has over me.

His smile broadens. "It would be my pleasure to see to it that your brother came home to you, safe and sound. Of course, even with the best people searching, there can be no guarantees he'll be found alive. Bad things sometimes happen to people who enter the Race of Oblivion. You know that. But I promise you this. . . ." He reaches for my right hand and brings it to his lips. I shudder, and this time I know he feels it. His hand tightens around mine. "I promise I will personally oversee the search. I will do that for you, as a friend. As long as you are my friend, Astrid, I will be yours, and you will never have to worry about your brother."

THIRTY-SIX

Here is his threat, disguised as a promise. Because of course, by promising to help my brother as long as we are friends, he's made it abundantly clear that he can *hurt* my brother if we are *not* friends.

Voices filter up from the stairs. People are coming this way. Lars releases my hand, and though I try not to jerk it away, as soon as I am free of his grasp, I can't help but recoil.

I feel like a fish freed from the hook, but still not back in the water.

"We should go back," I say to Lars. "Your guests are going to notice you're gone."

"Me? *You* are the guest of honor. I would think it's more likely they would notice your absence."

When we return to the party, Lars's hand still hovering on the small of my back like a gun stuck in my ribs, I finally spot Darius. He's across the room, watching me. Lars whispers into my ear, "I think we should dance. As the guest of honor, you should be seen." I feel Darius's stare as Lars leads me out to the dance floor. I feel it, but I don't see it, because I can't look at Darius's face as he watches me dance with Lars.

The song is slow, but it doesn't matter. Even slow steps are painful steps. The weight of Darius's stare burdens me even more, and I'm forced to tell Lars I have to sit down.

"You're hurting," he says.

"A little."

"Let me find the doctor—"

"I just need rest—"

"Nonsense. You need something for the pain. I saw the doctor come in with her husband. Let me ask one of the staff to find her."

Something for the pain amounts to something Lars could dose me with. I'm the one person who knows he killed his father. He has plenty of motive to eliminate me. But before I can waste another breath objecting, Renya comes rushing up like a gust of wind. "Astrid, let me help you. We'll just step into the ladies' lounge and take a peek under that knee brace. You look a bit winded." Maybe it's because it will free him up to look for the doctor, maybe it's because Renya never takes no for an answer, but Lars gives in.

"Fine," Lars says, but even though his words say he's relenting, his posture says he's not. As he folds his arms across his chest, he elbows a couple dancing nearby. He doesn't notice. "But let me know how it looks. If we need to get the doctor . . ."

The rest of Lars's words are swallowed up by the sound of the crowd as Renya leads me away. "Kit was looking for you," she whispers as we cross the threshold into the outer room of the ladies' lounge. The room is filled with over-stuffed couches and love seats—the perfect place to rest and prop my leg up—but it's crowded. Renya gives my knee a quick look. A few women wince at the blood that's oozed out from under my brace, which is embarrassing, but a few others fill up with pity, which is worse. "It's fine. A little blood but nothing terrible. I think you're just tired," Renya says, before whispering into my ear, "Let's go. I'll deflect my brother while you find Kit."

It doesn't take long to find him. As soon as we are through the door and into the hall, Darius intercepts us. And though I'd seen his face from across the room, up close I notice how he has been transformed for the ball. Not so much changed as . . . *revealed*.

He is dressed in a black suit of soft silk, almost as fine as the prince's, with an ivory cape draped over his shoulders. His hair has been trimmed on the sides and in the back, but long tendrils of curls still frame his face. When his eyes meet mine—those hazel eyes I've come to know—I lose my breath.

I curse myself for it. For wanting to accept everything he told me in the Wheel of Fire about the day he hurt me. For wanting to try to forgive. Because now the fact that he held the whip is all the more complicated.

Now I know he is the boy who wrote the letters that started it all.

"Kit," Renya says, "we were just coming to look for you." She turns to me and adds, "I'll go let my brother know you won't be needing the doctor." Then she floats away.

"The doctor?"

"It's nothing," I say. "I overdid it, I guess."

"Right. So listen," he says, and he looks a bit stricken, like he did when he had to admit to me that he had come to find me because I had the bike. "I know you saw the letters. Renya told me she told you the truth. . . ." He pauses to collect himself, dropping his gaze to his hands. "The truth about us."

"About you both being involved with the OLA?" I say. "She told me. I can't say I'm not rattled. I . . . So did you know Jayden when we met him? When we boarded the train?"

"I didn't. I'd never met him before. None of them.

Aengus was my only contact—he was in the race. The boy with the red hair." I nod. "He recruited me. Me, and then Renya," he says.

"I thought you were the one who recruited Renya. I thought the letters . . ."

"Astrid, those letters . . ." He crosses his arms, defensive. He wipes a hand over his face. "Those letters were written by a boy who was young and naive. A boy who was passionate about a forbidden girl, about a forbidden cause. We both made mistakes, Renya and I, but it was you who paid for those mistakes. I'll never forgive myself for that. I don't know if she will, either. We hardly spoke to each other after that. The whole silly romance was over—"

"But . . ." I hate to say this, but I have to. "You were forced apart. So you must still have feelings—"

"It was a *flirtation*," Darius says, cutting me off. His tone is so adamant, it seals my lips. "It ended as quickly as it began. It's behind us. I have no feelings for her anymore, and I know she has none for me."

There's a sweetness in the air. The scent of perfume, and of flowers, but also of truth. Of course, I know much of what Darius is telling me is verifiable. The rest of it will require trust. "How do you know she has no feelings for you?"

"She's told me. In fact, she's admitted to having fallen in love with someone else."

Someone else? I can't stop myself from blurting, "Who?"

He only shrugs. And the fact he doesn't know makes it easier for me to accept his claim of being over her, too. "I'm sorry for treating you so badly. For never befriending you," he says. His brow creases and his eyes go dark. "I've always felt like I should steer clear of you. The royals exploit the bond between you and Renya, so I avoided any bonds at all. Especially with you, after what happened in the whipping room that day. I'm afraid that will be with us forever, like a ghost."

He pauses, maybe hoping I will jump in and say he's wrong, but I can't. The truth is, I'm afraid he could be right.

"Even today, even believing you and I had formed a bond in the race, I've been afraid of what would happen now that we're back in the place where we were never friends. The place where you hated the sight of me."

I allow a small smirk to turn up the corners of my lips. "I did hate the sight of you. That's quite true."

He takes the smallest step toward me, but it changes things. A moment before, we were two people standing together talking, but now he's so close, when he sighs, I feel his breath on my cheek. A ringlet obscures one of his eyes, and I don't stop myself when impulse tells me to push it back into place.

"But those letters you wrote," I say. I hate to talk about them now, with him standing so close, but I have to ask.

"Did you think you loved Renya when you wrote them?"

"I did," he says. And I shift my weight away from him. I'm glad he's being honest. "But I could no longer remember her while I was in the race. And while I was outside the control of my memories—all my complex memories that controlled how I treated so many people—I developed feelings for someone else. And in comparison to those feelings, my past feelings for the princess, my past feelings for *anyone*, are nothing but vapor."

That rebellious curl falls loose across his forehead again. I let my fingertips brush across his brow, and touching him feels so right. My heart races as my fingers trace across his cheekbone, his jaw. . . . I draw in a deep breath as if I'm standing at the edge of a cliff, about to step off. And then I do. I give into the urge to thread my arms around his neck. My breath catches in my throat, as if I'm actually falling.

But I can't fall, because Darius's hands grip my waist and pull me against him. A gasp escapes my lips just before he leans in and covers them with his own.

Darius's kiss is tentative, but if he's questioning, I kiss him back with an urgency meant to silence all his doubts. His arms tighten around me, and when he finally lifts his head, his lips brush down my throat, coming to rest on the curve at the inside of my shoulder.

We are not far off the main hall, and the music and voices seem to be growing louder and louder the longer we stay here. My eyes move to the center of the room, and I pull back. "People are approaching," I say, and Darius steps back, too. My leg quivers a bit when I shift my weight onto it again.

"Are you all right?" he asks.

"I should sit," I say, but he's already leading me to a chair. An Outsider passes by with a tray filled with crystal goblets. Darius takes two and puts one in my hand—something dark red and sweet and completely unfamiliar. Darius drinks his quickly and, remembering the corn vodka, I do the same. He laughs when he sees my drained glass.

"Well, I guess you were thirsty." He takes my glass and then something shifts in him. His playfulness dissolves. Willfulness, dark and heavy, fills the space between us. "I don't want to push you, but . . . there's somewhere I want to go, and I want you to come with me."

"Where?"

"Downstairs. To the room with the whipping post—"

"In the middle of this ball?" I ask, getting to my feet.

"I need to confront it," he says. He glances around, as if he's worried we might be overheard. "There's a shadow over all my memories—the shadow of that post. I need to confront it to be able to overcome it—"

A couple dressed in matching silks dyed the color of wine approach us, their hands extended. Hasty introductions are made—they are Duke and Duchess of Something-or-Other, and they are so honored to meet us. Both gush about our great accomplishment in winning the Crown of Oblivion, and as they lavish Darius and me with compliments, the duke lifts the back of my hand to his lips. His paper-white cheeks appear almost transparent beside my sun-darkened skin. His wife's perfume stings my throat. As soon as they step away, Darius turns his gaze back to me. "I'll go alone," he says. His eyes are as cold as stone.

I know there's no changing his mind.

"No," I say. "I'll go." I think my words surprise me more than Darius, but I hate the idea of him leaving me here even more than the idea of going with him to that horrible room. "But I don't understand this at all."

Getting to the doorway of the ballroom is the easy part. But just as we reach it, I see Lars moving through the crowd, his head turning from side to side. Could he be searching for us? His eyes land on Renya, and he takes off toward her. "We need to hurry," I say.

When we make it to the second cellar, goose bumps spring up on my arms. The air is damp and chilly compared to the warm stuffiness of the ballroom. I rub my hands over my arms, and Darius takes off his cape and drapes it over me.

Our feet move along the corridor floor soundlessly. This might be the first time I have ever approached this room without the echo of heavy boots ringing in my ears. Still, my pulse pounds in my temples. I fear this room, the way I might fear a lion's den. Does that mean I fear the post, as if it were a lion, waiting to devour me? The closer we draw to the darkened doorway, the greater my understanding of Darius's need to come here.

He was right. We need to face it. To take away its power to threaten us.

A quiet click of the light switch brings the room into view, and it's surprising how something so small can loom so large. The floor can't be bigger than ten square feet, the walls bleached clean of even a trace of blood. The post itself is nothing more than a block of wood. How can something so benign command so much fear?

Not through any strength of its own.

Yet if you lined up all the memories that have awoken in me, from the strongest to the faintest, the memories of this room would be at the head of the line. Before memories of teaching my brother Marlon how to read. Before memories of long motorbike rides through the countryside with Renya. Before almost every happy moment I can recall. I wish Darius's plan of confronting this place could change that, but I don't think it can.

It can't change the past, and the past haunts me. It haunts us both.

"It hurts just to look at it," Darius says. "Like the pain has somehow become a living thing that swims within my veins. When I look at that post, I feel it clawing at me from the inside."

I don't know what to say, so I reach for his hand. The comfort his touch gives lasts only a moment, though. We both jump when we hear footsteps echo from the other end of the hall.

Stepping in out of the doorway, Darius and I both stand with our backs pressed against the wall. The cold seeps through the fabric of the cape Darius wrapped around me, chilling my scarred skin. I shiver. But then Renya steps through the door, carrying an ax.

"How did you know?" I ask. "Why would you ever look for us here?"

"It just makes sense," she says. "I wanted to come down here, too, but on my way, I stopped at the toolshed." She holds out the ax and I take it from her. It's so heavy, I almost drop it.

"But—"

"Don't ask questions," she says. The panic that rises in me whenever Renya takes a risk—the panic that she will be caught and I'll end up in this room—abates when I realize what she intends for me to do. "Go ahead," she says. "Take the first swing."

My gaze meets Darius's. His eyes are aglow. "Do it," he says. "Let's put it to death."

The ax might be heavy, but the thought of killing the

whipping post gives me strength. The first blow wedges right down the middle. When I pull the ax free, the wood splinters and breaks. The second blow breaks a chunk free. It flies off and lands at my feet. Though the post is clean on the outside, the inside of the wood is stained red. Tracks mark the places where my blood and Darius's have seeped down into the cracks and fissures, leaving bits of us behind.

I hand the ax to Darius. His first blow lands hard at the base, removing a wedge. His second blow almost knocks it down.

He puts the ax in my hands again. "You get to end it."

I lift the ax, prepared to land the killing blow, and I wonder if I've ever felt so powerful. Even when I beat Renya for the first time at Hearts and Hands, even when I knocked down that guard with Projectura. All the magic in the world can't add up to the strength I feel right now, raising this ax to ruin the whipping post for good.

But before I can bring it down, someone takes it from my hand.

I spin to find Lars behind me. "One of the staff said they saw the princess heading to the stairs with an ax," he says.

Renya clears her throat.

"Congratulations to both of you," Lars says, gesturing to the post. As usual, my Cientia uncovers nothing of Lars's mood—I didn't even feel him coming. His lips attempt a smile, but his eyes show anger. "You are clearly the victors in this battle."

For all intents and purposes, the post is destroyed. It's certainly beyond use. Fragments of wood litter the floor. The remaining stump is splintered and mutilated. But it still stands. The final blow would have knocked it over, but it still stands.

"I hate to interrupt, but the queen is waiting. It's time for the two of you to be crowned."

My eyes dart to Renya's. For some reason, I hadn't imagined the Crown of Oblivion to be an actual thing. "I thought it was simply a title."

"Oh no," says Lars. "We will have a proper coronation."

And though he may be skilled at cloaking his feelings from my Cientia, I feel his smugness. I hear the snicker in his voice. His amusement at the idea that Darius and I should be crowned.

I snatch the ax from his hand, and I slam it into the side of the post. It topples to the floor. "Fine," I say, shoving the ax back into Lars's hands. "I'm ready."

THIRTY-SEVEN

Upstairs, at the door to the ballroom, we find Sir Arnaud. "Where have you been?" he asks in an angry whisper, but he doesn't wait for any of us to reply. He simply raises a hand, and the orchestra quiets. A hush falls over the crowd inside. The guests have been waiting for this moment. The dancers on the dance floor part, as the dance music is replaced by a processional. Renya and Lars lead us across the room to a wide dais that had earlier been covered in flowers and candelabras. Now it holds a sort of altar, and behind the altar, dressed in a gown of the brightest blue, the queen.

Perhaps Prince Lars finds this coronation amusing, but it would seem he is the only one. The evening has gone from frivolous to solemn, and nowhere is that more clear than in the expression of the queen.

Her eyes meet mine as I climb the three short steps to stand right in front of her. I think of the secret in my mother's diary—that I was never vaccinated against magic because the king was in love with my mother. I think of the queen's words to me on the train—*we shared secrets.* Is that one of the secrets they shared?

Could that explain why she invited Jayden and me—the children of her friend—to become surrogates to her own children after my mother's death?

"Please kneel," she says, and Darius and I drop down onto a narrow pillow that's been placed on the floor in front of the altar. My injured knee aches at the effort, but I swallow the pain down.

"Astrid Jael," the queen says, "I place on your head the Crown of Oblivion, and bestow upon you all the rights and privileges with which it is endowed." Something is placed on my head, but it's much lighter than I was expecting. I can't help but think of the flower crowns Renya used to make for me when we were children. This crown is heavier, but not by much.

"Darius Kittering," the queen says, before repeating the oath she swore over me. When the crown is on his head, she tells us to rise.

Straightening, I steal a glance at Darius and see that the crown he wears is cut from polished mirror. In the reflection, I see myself, a mirror crown upon my own head. The band is a smooth surface, but above the band a chain of interlocking circles forms a ring, each circle inlaid with tiny pieces of reflective glass, bouncing light in every direction.

"I present to you," says Queen Mariana, "this year's King and Queen of Oblivion."

The assembled guests break into applause, and Renya comes up to congratulate us. Lars follows her, first shaking Darius's hand, and then clasping his hands around mine. He drops my left but holds on to my right, so that he and I are facing the crowd, hand in hand.

Something in his grip is like a claim. He may only be holding my hand, but I feel like he's holding me down.

But he drops my hand when the first explosion goes off.

It doesn't sound close—maybe outside the palace wall—but the floor beneath us vibrates and the guests around us scream. The dance floor is packed with a few hundred people standing shoulder to shoulder, all pressing forward in order to see, and above us, on three balconies that overlook the center of the hall, hundreds more crowd behind railings. A second explosion goes off, this one from a different place outside, and the room in front of me erupts with movement as people push toward the various exits. But there are many exits, and no one seems to know which way is safest, and for some reason, the orchestra begins to play.

They take up a traditional piece of music, with drums and tin whistle and fiddle, and I realize this is a sort of recessional. It's a piece of music meant to close out the coronation and signal the crowd that it's time to celebrate, but the music serves only to add to the confusion.

Some people stop where they are and look around, and I can see that they are wondering if the explosions might have been some sort of stagecraft . . . a part of some elaborate show, along with the music and the cascading flowers and lights. One more way to celebrate Darius and me. Another blast, this one much closer, seems to go off right behind the wall at my back, and the palace shakes on its foundation. Dust rains down on our heads from the ceiling above.

The music meanders to a stop: first the drums drop out and then the flutes and the strings, and everyone seems to hold their breath, but then commotion returns. People run in every direction. Watching, I can't help but worry that the onlookers at the railings above will fall, or that the people on the dance floor will be trampled, when a voice booms through the hall.

"Ladies and gentlemen!" I recognize the voice of Sir Arnaud, who has taken hold of a small microphone that had been mounted on the altar. "Stay where you are. Do not panic. The King's Knights are assessing the risk, and then we will conduct an orderly evacuation. Until then, no one is to leave."

These instructions are met with even more shrieks, which are cut off by Sir Arnaud barking even more instructions into the microphone. "No one is to leave!" he repeats. "Stay where you are, or the doors will be locked."

If threats like this are his way of silencing the crowd and getting their attention, it's working at the moment. But then a door opens and a King's Knight rushes in—it's Sir Millicent—and the crowd parts to let her make a straight path right to where the prince stands beside me. She hands him a folded note.

"This was delivered to the guards at the front gate, Your Highness," she says, her voice low to avoid being picked up by the microphone only feet away. "It's from the OLA, and it lists their demands. Well, their one demand."

Lars opens it and I can easily see the name of my brother Marlon. That's all I'm able to make sense of on the handwritten note before the prince crumples it and throws it down.

Another blast rings out, and the floor beneath us moves like a ship on rough seas. Plaster breaks away from the ceiling and cascades down as a long, jagged crack runs up the wall. A section of railing on the second balcony breaks away and tumbles to the floor below. The crowd devolves into chaos again, as people push the doors open and run for their lives.

"Stay where you are!" Now it's Prince Lars on the mic, and people shriek, but they freeze at the command of their prince. "There is no safety in a stampede! Guards, secure those doors!" In a frenzy of activity, Authority guards do just that.

Through a tall glass window, I notice a blaze. The south

wing of the palace is burning. Flames are reaching into the evening sky.

I step forward and grab the microphone.

"May I have your attention," I say. My stomach twists like snakes tying themselves into knots. "The forces attacking the palace are demanding the release of a boy who was captured by the King's Knights during the Race of Oblivion. As soon as the prince releases this innocent boy, we'll all be safe."

A rumble of voices ripples through the crowd, and another explosion rocks the foundation under our feet. I nearly fall from the dais, but Renya catches me. I'm still wobbly when the prince snatches the microphone from my hand and backs away from me, an expression of disbelief on his face. But he recovers quickly and barks into the mic, "Arrest this woman, for conspiring with the Outsider rebels!"

A few guards advance, but the princess pulls me to her with one arm and throws the other up, her hand held palm out.

All eyes move to the prince.

"Ladies and gentlemen," he says, turning in place and staring out at the dust-covered crowd, "I have no knowledge of this boy. I can't release a prisoner I don't have." Then he steps to Sir Arnaud's side and says simply, "Take Astrid Jael into custody now."

Sir Arnaud moves toward me, and I bring up my fists,

ready to fight. Arnaud flinches and his hand hovers over the sword at his hip, but before he can draw it, two things happen at once.

An explosion goes off so close, the back wall of the ballroom cracks and pieces fall heavily to the floor. And at the same moment, the light in the room begins to change.

The twinkle lights seem to flash on and off rapidly, but then I realize it's not the twinkle lights at all. The ambient light is dimming and brightening, over and over, as a hum begins to build, as if the string section has begun to play. I spin around to face Renya, expecting to find her with her feet planted and arms upraised, transmitting the energy that's roaring in my ears. It's grown so loud that the mass of guests on the dance floor are cupping their hands over their ears, but I see that Renya is standing as she was. This is someone else's Pontium magic, and just as I realize what this means, a light glows in the middle of the room. Maybe guests are shrieking again—it's too loud to hear—but they clear a space where the light gathers and then thins.

The flames outside the window ripple higher, and now they're almost all the light we have as the Pontium hum quiets and the light dims. Then all of us—all the guests on the floor and those on the balconies above, and the orchestra and the King's Knights and all of us on the dais—we all find ourselves peering into a dark, low-ceilinged dungeon, and behind a wall of bars, my brother Marlon is down on his knees.

The room seems to teeter and rock from the dizzying effects of Pontium. I hear an explosion, dust rains down both in the ballroom and in Marlon's cell, and I realize with a shock where Marlon is.

He kneels on a stone floor, but even on his knees, his arms are held wide. This is *his* Pontium magic. I think of how Renya couldn't reach him, and I know now it's because he's far underground, in the fourth cellar—the dungeon level—of the palace. Renya's Pontium couldn't reach that far, but Marlon was able to build the bridge.

"Astrid!" he screams. He's panicking. I can see it in his face and hear it in his voice. "Explosions keep going off, one after the other, and they keep getting closer!"

"Hang on!" I call back. "I know where you are. I'm coming for you!"

Other than the hum of the Pontium energy, the room is nearly silent. There is a collectively held breath, as stark realization floods my Cientia. All eyes are on Lars. But then another blast sends debris falling on our heads, Marlon calls out my name, and the crowd moves like a wave. Everyone breaks into a run.

The room fills with dust as the walls crumble around us.

THIRTY-EIGHT

I need to get out of this room, to get to the stairs that lead down to the lower levels, to get to Marlon before this whole building comes down. The back wall is wide-open to the gardens, and fire is racing across the hedge. While I watch, the draperies that line the windows of the ballroom ignite. It won't be long before I won't be able to escape.

I turn in place, looking for Renya and Darius, but the room is so full of smoke, I can't see. Defying Lars, some Authority guards and King's Knights are guiding guests to the exits. Sir Arnaud holds the queen under her arm and is calling out for Sir Millicent, but she doesn't reply. I turn toward the stairs, but Lars blocks my way.

His fists are up, and I realize he doesn't intend to run out of here. He intends to prevent me from getting to my brother in the dungeons.

"Why worry about me now?" I call to him over the

shouts of the crowd. "Why not save yourself while you can?"

"You think you've turned my people against me!" he calls back, and although he usually can mask his emotions from me, I can feel his desperation all too clearly. "But you're wrong. I will win them back when you and your brother are dead."

This is one fight where I can't wait for my opponent to throw the first punch. Instead, I try to do what Lars is usually so good at. I try to block my intentions, try to fool him by planning a lunge forward, right up until the moment I lean back and kick high at his face, my foot flying up from beneath yards of ivory silk. But his Cientia is primed and he blocks me easily. He throws a kick of his own at my ribs before I can get myself set, planting his foot squarely in my side. I fold in half, crumpling to my knees.

He kicks me again and I'm flat on the tiles.

My breath is gone. My ears ring with Lars's laughter. The cool floor feels good against my cheek.

But I can't stay down. I *won't* stay down.

A column stands a few feet away, and I crawl to it and use it to pull myself to my feet. I see Marlon's face in my mind, hear the fear in his voice, and I let go of the column and turn to Lars.

I should be unable to stand. I should be unable to fight. But I've had lots of practice at persevering.

When I bring my fists up, I see the prince falter—not a loss of balance but a loss of concentration—and I see my way in. I gather my skirt and I spin into a flying kick, a move that can do so much damage if I land it well, and this time, I do. My heel connects hard with his jaw. I feel it give, feel him shudder beneath my foot, and then he's tumbling backward. I land on my bad knee, and I buckle, wincing. But I can't hesitate now. I stagger to Lars, pin him beneath me, and slam my fist into his temple. After the second blow, I realize he's no longer flinching. He's out. I want to jump up and run right for the door, but getting to the dungeons won't help if I have no way to open Marlon's cell. I reach into one of Lars's jacket pockets and then the other. Nothing. My heart is pounding so hard I feel it in my throat, but then I reach into his pants pocket and find a set of keys.

Outside the ballroom, the palace is in chaos. The roof is on fire. Wind churns the flames. A burning beam shatters overhead and falls just behind me. People scatter, some trying to escape for themselves, some trying to rescue others. A few appear to be trying to put out the flames. I turn around just once more to look for Renya or Darius, but I don't see them and I have no more time to look.

I sprint for the stairs down to the lower levels.

The stairwell is littered with debris, and more is coming down. Explosions roll, one after the other, like waves crashing to the sand.

Maybe this assault started as a means to save Marlon, but it has escalated far beyond that. Tonight, the OLA has declared war upon the monarchy. How can there be anything less, now that they've brought the palace down?

I reach the first cellar, the infirmary, where I was dosed with Oblivion before the race.

The second cellar, where I suffered under the whip, but where Darius and I overcame it tonight.

The third cellar: cold storage. Wine for the king.

The fourth cellar, a place I've never been. The dungeons, where the enemies of the crown are rumored to be left to die. I don't know if that's true, and I may never know, because the fourth cellar is a nearly pitch-dark labyrinth of stone walls and metal bars. It's so dark, the remains of hundreds of prisoners could be stacked behind these bars and I wouldn't be able to see them.

After the din upstairs, my ears ring with the silence. But then someone coughs—a cough I recognize—and I know I'm in the right place. "Marlon!" I call, and from out of the dark at the end of the passageway comes a reply.

"Astrid!"

Without any light, I make slow progress, taking careful steps toward the sound of his voice. "Is anyone else down here?" I ask.

"I don't think so," Marlon answers, but that doesn't help me much. I'd like to know if I'm walking into a trap. But

I feel only one person, a person full of fear mingled with hope, and my stomach flips at the thought that Marlon's put his hopes in me.

A rumble comes from above—either another blast or part of the building collapsing—but it's muffled all the way down here. Still, Marlon gasps in response, and I realize I'm just a few feet away from him now.

"Marlon, keep talking so I can find you," I say.

"Keep talking so I can find you," he repeats. I take a few shuffling steps. "Keep talking so I can find you," he says again, and he's right in front of me now. I reach for him, but my hands smack against a wall of bars.

Blindly, I work the keys in my hand, counting them. Four keys in all. I have four chances for one to fit.

"Do you know where the lock is?" I ask, running my hands over the bars.

"They had a battery light when they brought me here. I saw the lock just for a moment before they walked out." I feel his hands pass over mine as he searches. "It's here."

"Did you see them?" I ask, once I've found the lock. "Was the prince with them?"

I try the first key. It doesn't fit. "I don't think so," Marlon says.

I'd hoped for a yes. Not just because I hate Lars, but because I'd hoped the right keys were in his pocket.

I try the second key. It seems to fit, but it doesn't turn.

But even if Lars wasn't here, he might be holding the key. He might even have his own. He likes to feel like he's in control.

I try the third key. Not a fit.

I try the fourth and final key. It's thick and oddly shaped, and it doesn't even slide partway into the keyhole.

I've tried each of the keys, and none of them works.

There's another rumble, and the ground shakes beneath my feet. My heart races. Dust falls on my head from the blackness above me. If these lower levels start folding in on themselves, we'll never get out of here.

I work the keys through my fingers again. This can't be the end. After all we've gone through, all we've overcome, this dungeon can't be our grave.

I run my fingers over each key again, until I think I've found the second key—the one that fit but wouldn't turn. After one false try, I slide it into the lock, but it still won't turn. I rattle the door, slide the key in and out again, jiggle it in the lock.

And it turns.

"Marlon! It's open," I say, as the door swings toward me. I can't see him, but I feel his arms go around me, just the briefest of hugs.

Going back through the dark is easier. There's a hint of light coming from the stairwell, so we make our way toward it. We climb, and as we rise through the corkscrew, the world around us grows louder and smokier, until we reach the ground, where we're surrounded by flame and moonlight.

What's left of the palace is empty, except for two people. Prince Lars, waiting for us. And Sir Millicent, trying to drag him away.

"I told you they would come," he says to her when he sees me and Marlon. "She took my keys. And now I'm going to take them back."

"You don't want to fight me again, Lars. I knocked you out before and I'll knock you out again."

"I was never *out*," he says over the roar of the flame that's running up the walls. "I felt you go for those keys in my pants. It was quite enjoyable," he sneers. Even now, even with the palace in ruins, he still mocks me.

"Lars!" calls Millicent. She's got him by the hand, trying to drag him, but his eyes are latched onto mine. "We need to get out of here now!"

I bend to Marlon's ear. "Run," I whisper.

It takes him a moment to process what I've said, but then he takes off for an opening in a collapsed wall where moonlight streams in. Now I can face Lars alone. But he surprises me. He leaves me and chases down Marlon. He drops on him and forces him to the floor at the foot of one of the few columns still standing, only a few feet short of freedom.

The column may still be standing, but the ceiling it was

holding aloft is all but gone. And maybe it's from the force of the impact just beside it, or maybe it would have happened anyway, but at the moment Lars and Marlon fall, the column does, too.

By the time Millicent and I reach them, they are slick with blood, though I can't tell which of them it's coming from. Maybe both. Without even talking about what needs to be done, I wrap my arms around one end of the column and Millicent wraps hers around the other, and we lift.

Marlon rolls out from beneath it. He moves quickly— maybe the blood isn't his.

Lars doesn't stir.

Millicent and I set the column down beside them, but she can't wake Lars. Marlon tries to get to his feet, but he winces and goes down. "Don't try. I'll carry you," I say.

Standing over him, I look down into Lars's moonlit face. Millicent shakes him but gets no response. I bend lower, touching his throat, his wrist.

Nothing.

"Leave him," I say to Millicent. "He's dead."

"No!" she wails. I'm startled. I never imagined she had feelings for the prince. But I don't have time to argue with her. She's made her own choice. I throw Marlon over my shoulder and hurry to get clear before what's left of the palace comes down.

I run until I reach the palace wall. The hedges are burning

and flames shoot from the palace roof, but out here, the air is cool on my face. So cool, I shiver. I lay Marlon down on the grass and sag against him. He's looking around at the commotion, and I feel his fear again. "Where are we?"

"We're safe. That's where we are," I say. "We're safe."

"We're safe," he echoes.

In the distance, backlit against the flames, I see the silhouettes of people still swarming around the palace. Some are huddling on the lawn, some are standing. Some are running back and forth, and I can tell, those are the people looking for loved ones.

I don't know where Darius and Renya are, and the thought of them lying somewhere injured and in need of my help makes it hard to stay where I am. I need to look for them, to let them know I made it out and so did Marlon, and to make sure they did, too. But I can't leave Marlon here alone. Not yet. As soon as he's a little stronger, as soon as he's breathing normally instead of panting, I'll go look for them.

I drink in the sight of his face, so happy to have him back. The one who was brave enough to enter the race. The one who solved the riddle of the final clue for me, and whose Pontium bridge convinced Jayden to help me make it through the Wilds.

Because of him I entered the race, and because of him I won.

"Marlon," I say, but he doesn't answer me. He just lies nestled against me, like he did when he was little. "I'm sorry I entered the race without telling you," I say. "If I had told you, all of this could've been avoided because you never would've entered the race yourself."

"It's all right. I know why you didn't . . ." He trails off. His eyes flutter and then he grimaces in pain. Slumping forward, his chin falls to his chest.

Something is wrong with Marlon.

I run my hand over the back of his head, and it comes away bathed in blood. "Marlon?" I say, but again, he doesn't answer.

I need a medic. I need a medic *now.*

But looking out into the tumult as the palace burns, I don't know how I would find one, even if I were willing to move Marlon, which I'm not.

I need to find the princess. If anyone can bring a medic to Marlon, it's her.

I leave Marlon curled on the grass and stand, bolt upright, following my instincts. . . . The only thing I can trust in this moment. If it doesn't work, I'll have to find another way, but somehow, I think it will work. I have such strong Cientia, I've learned to use Projectura, and my own brother has Pontium. Isn't it possible that I have it, too?

I raise my hands, plant my feet firmly on the ground, and try to summon the magic in my veins. I've heard that

Pontium is fueled by a spark that binds people connected by love. Do Renya and I have that connection? Do Darius and I? I can only try, to dig deep into my cells for that spark.

I hold my hands a few feet apart, let my eyes fall closed, and breathe deep, sending my breath up my arms to my open palms. Nothing. I breathe in and out, imagining my blood burning along my veins, carrying energy to my fingertips.

Still nothing. I'm failing.

But when I try to drop my hands, my arms stay rigid. A weak pulse spirals out from the center of my chest, like ripples moving away from a stone dropped into a lake. My hands hum like plucked wires, carrying a signal along an invisible line. The darkness around me thickens, but then a spark lights in the space between my palms. The spark grows, brightens, reaches around me like a glowing lasso until it engulfs a space beyond the place where I stand.

In front of me, a boy appears. It's Darius. He looks up from the place where he lies on the ground. A woman is bent over him, tying a bandage onto his arm. Renya hovers over them both.

"Astrid," Darius says. "Can you see us? Where are you?"

"I'm at the edge of the south lawn, beside the palace wall. It's Marlon! I need a medic—"

Before I can say another word, the bridge collapses all at once, and I'm jolted against the wall. I fall back so hard, I stumble to the ground beside Marlon.

"Hang on," I whisper to him.

To my surprise, his eyes flutter open. "Stay with me," he says.

"I'll stay with you. Of course I will." I look up. People are already sprinting toward us. A medic carrying a stretcher. Behind her, several others. Even in silhouette, I can see that one is Darius and one is Renya. "Here comes help," I say. "The princess is bringing help for you."

Marlon turns his head and stares across the dark lawn. His eyes fix on the approaching knot of people. The skirt of Renya's tattered gown ripples around her ankles as she runs.

Marlon watches as they all come closer. "Stay with me," he says again. He's shivering, so I draw him up against me, until his hair is tucked under my chin.

"I won't leave you," I say. "I won the Crown of Oblivion. We're both citizens now. We're safe. No one will hurt either of us again."

"No one will hurt either of us again," he repeats, and when I hear my own words, I realize how big a promise I've made. So be it. No matter what I must do, no matter what sacrifices I must make, I will keep that promise.

The medic reaches us, then bends down and holds a battery light to check the place where blood oozes from a gash on the back of Marlon's head. "It's gonna need stitches, all right," she says, in an accent that reminds me of Jane's in the race. I tighten my grip on Marlon. "I'll just put on a temporary bandage to hold him during transport," she says. My arms encircle Marlon, keeping him warm and still, while this medic—this *Enchanted* medic—wraps his head in gauze. "When we get him to the hospital, they may run more tests, just to be sure there's nothing else he needs."

The hospital. The Citizens Hospital. Where my brother will get the best care. Because we're citizens now.

I look up to see both the princess and Darius standing over me. Both of them scowl, their faces dark with concern, and the princess drops down to sit beside me. "Lars is missing," she whispers into my ear. "They're searching the debris. They think he may have been killed as the roof collapsed."

I nod. I know the prince is dead, but I keep this to myself. I don't want to talk about Lars. If things had gone differently, I could've been the one lying back there in the rubble, or even Marlon. No. I won't talk about Lars. Starting now, I'm shrugging off the dark shadow he's cast over my life.

Someone squats down across from me, beside the medic. It's Darius. "The last time I saw you, you were wearing a crown," he says, with a sad smile.

"I lost it," I say.

"Me too," he answers.

But it doesn't matter. Because now the medic is taking Marlon from my arms, and Darius is helping to place him on the stretcher. Marlon reaches for me, and I ask the medic if I can accompany him to the hospital.

"Of course," she says. "You should be checked out, too."

My eyes meet Darius's. Beyond his shoulder, the palace is a mass of flame and shadow. "It may still be found in the rubble, but even without that mirrored trinket, you still have the crown," he whispers. "No one can ever take it from you."

He slides an arm around me, supporting me as I get to my feet. He stays right beside me, his warm hand wrapped around my cold one, as we follow the medics across the grass.

One last time, I glance at the palace. *You've escaped that awful house.* That's what Jayden had said, and now it's really true.

I think of my crown, shattered and filthy in the wreckage. It breaks my heart a bit. I fought so hard to win it.

Still, I know that what Darius says is true. The Crown of Oblivion, and everything it stands for, can never be taken from me.

I know the crown is mine.

ACKNOWLEDGMENTS

Writing a book is sometimes like creating a painting—you start out with a blank canvas and add to it until it's complete. Writing *Crown of Oblivion* was more like creating a sculpture—I started out with a big misshapen block and had to cut away to uncover the book inside. It wasn't easy, and there were times I thought I had chiseled the book free, only to find that there was still a better book buried inside.

Thank you to my editor, Alexandra Cooper, who has an incredible talent for seeing the true book buried under all the rough stone. You have such a powerful instinct for uncovering the essence of the story and leading me to it. If you ever doubt the truth of that praise, just pull out the first draft of this book and you'll have all the proof you need! I am so grateful to have had the benefit of your talents on this book.

Josh Adams, I am also grateful for everything you have

done that has led me here. Before we met, I never thought I'd be writing the acknowledgments for my first published book, let alone my third. Your guidance and advice have been priceless, and I am so proud and thankful that you are my agent.

To the team at HarperCollins: thank you, Rosemary Brosnan, Alyssa Miele, Jessica Berg, Joel Tippie, Shannon Cox, and Kadeen Griffiths. Thank you to Tracey Adams at Adams Literary. I also want to thank artist Jason Chan for capturing Astrid so vividly in the cover illustration.

I have a lot of writer friends to thank! Amie Kaufman, thank you for your friendship and guidance. Thank you, Meghan Rogers, for all the encouragement and support you bring to our lunch dates! Jodi Meadows, Luke Taylor, Stephanie Garber, and Sarah J. Maas, thank you for all the positive energy, wise words, and commiseration. You all have helped me so much.

To my early readers, Kat Zhang and Jennifer Kelly, thank you for taking the time to read critically and help me see what was working and what was not. Your input really made a difference. Thank you also to Deborah Hawkins and the other readers who read for sensitivity and authenticity. Your advice helped make this a better book.

I want to thank all the contributors to PublishingCrawl. com as well as the readers of that wonderful blog. Your encouragement means so much to me. Thank you to all the other book bloggers who support me and my writing, especially Bonnie Wagner, Kelly Nagy, Amanda Webb, Irene Justice, Mishma Nixon, and Sabrina Simmonds. Sarah Kershaw, thank you for your design and marketing help. Thanks also to the teachers, conference coordinators, booksellers, and librarians who have helped readers discover my books, especially Sara Huff at the William Jeanes Memorial Library.

Thank you to all my friends who remind me that I can reach my goals, especially my church family. To the amazing high school Sunday school class, you guys are the best! You have no idea how much you all inspire me.

I have a wonderful family, and this book would have fallen apart without their love and support. Thank you to my sister Lori, who has been there to make the other parts of my life easier so I could get my writing done. Thank you to my father. Your love has always lifted me up. To my son, Dylan, thanks for your encouragement, for being an example of hard work and persistence, and for making me laugh. To Mia Bergstrom, thank you for bringing so much girl power to our family. And I can't forget my fur babies, Nashville and Jeepster.

To my husband, Gary, thanks for getting me through another manuscript. You are my heart, and you bring joy to every day of my life. For all the laughter, all the encouragement, all the reminders of the things worth remembering, thank you.

Thank you, God, for so many miracles and blessings, especially for all the people listed here.

And to the readers who cared enough to read to the last word of these acknowledgements, you are the reason writers write. Thank you so much!